Midwife of Normandy

A novel

Carole Penfield

Sycamore Lane Press

Midwife of Normandy is a work of historical fiction. Any references to herbal remedies and/or midwifery techniques are not meant to be considered as a substitute for professional advice. They are not to be considered as viable treatments.

Apart from the well-known actual people, events, and locales that figure in the narrative, all names, characters, places and incidents are the products of the author's imagination or are used fictitiously. Any resemblance to current events or locales, or to living persons, is entirely coincidental.

Sycamore Lane Press

P.O Box 5088

Lake Montezuma, Arizona 86342

Front page design by Victoria Cooper

Formatting done by CalebsBookFormatting.Homestead.com

ISBN-13: 978-0692790663
ISBN-10: 0692790667

Dedication

For Perry, my dearest love, heart and soulmate

And for my fellow "Janeites"—the words of Miss Austen's unforgettable novels and letters flew through my brain as if her spirit had been sitting next to me, whispering inspiration into my ear, encouraging me to incorporate some of her famous lines into this work. I hope you find as much satisfaction in searching them out as I had fitting them in (with a few minor adjustments).

To the woman, he said, I will greatly increase thy travail and thy pregnancy; with pain thou shalt bear children…

Genesis 3:16

Through the years, our female ancestors have developed the perfect combination of ingredients in this particular distillation. You see, Clare, it lessens the pain of childbirth and erases any memories of those pains. It is a magic elixir.

Midwife of Normandy, 1670

Aboard the Celia

1685

As chill morning winds filled the sails and the Alabaster Coast glowed in the early-morning light, I was sorely tempted to toss my journal overboard. Perhaps Lucina anticipated that my handwritten record would outlive me for many years when she stood next to me at the ship rail and grabbed my arm just as I was about to fling the leather-bound volume into the deep water.

My precious daughter is wise beyond her five years. Lucina has a rare gift for foreseeing the future.

Journal of Clare Dupres, 30 octobre 1685

LOOKING ABOUT THE sparse, dark cabin with its single bunk, wooden stool, and tiny table, Clare tried not to compare it to her luxurious bedchamber at Maison Dupres, lost to her forever. The sailor's orders to relinquish his cramped sleeping quarters to her family had apparently come directly from her brother, a partner in Smithfield-Barton Enterprises, owners of this English shipping vessel. He would be waiting to greet them at the dock in London.

The cargo space was loaded with cases of exquisite floral-patterned silk, designed by Dupres & Sons exclusively for the English royal court. For that reason, the partners had been able to procure precious paperwork, purportedly granting the Dupres family safe passage to England. Even so, when Delphine had hugged her dear sister goodbye at the dock, she'd insisted Clare wear a heavily veiled bonnet to conceal her telltale auburn hair and cautioned her to remain within the safety of the cabin until the ship sailed.

Sitting by the poor light from the flickering candle, Clare opened her journal to a blank page. The sea was calm, but her mind was in turmoil. Cap'n Silas, captain of the *Celia*, said they would be traveling for several days, making several stops along the way. She resolved to pass the time recording the trials of the past ten days. Painful as the task would be, she knew it was necessary to preserve in writing the unspeakable events for the sake of her daughter. *When Lucina reaches the proper age, I will permit her to read my journal so that she might understand why we left France as we did. Surely putting these events down in words will ease my troubled mind…*

What on earth was she thinking? Clare would never forget what had happened, no matter how many scores of words she might write. All hope had vanished. Her hand hovered over the quill pen perched in a pewter inkpot, and her heart ached for her loss. As she dipped the pen in the ink and held the tip over a fresh page, two black blobs dripped on the paper like two dark shadows. She tried to rub them out, but the stains were permanent. Like bad memories, they could not be erased.

Two days ago, when the long-awaited travel documents had been placed in her hands, her hopes had risen. For a few moments, standing in Delphine's parlor, she had fantasized that she and her husband could be happy again. There *would* be another home for them at their destination. Perhaps not as grand as Maison Dupres, but they would be free from religious persecution and she would be able to resume her midwifery profession. No longer would the tyranny of King Louis affect her life—Protestants were welcomed in England, according to her brother's letters.

Eyes closed, Clare had envisioned her husband sitting in a beautiful new English garden, sipping refreshing ale, while Lucina and Jean-Pierre frolicked around the lawn chasing butterflies. They all waved to her as she set off in her carriage to another birthing. But hope had gradually faded and reality had hit hard this morning. *How foolish I was to dream things could ever be the same for us.*

Through the thin walls, Clare heard the noise of the lines being pulled and felt the motion of the vessel slowly drifting from the dock. Standing on tiptoe on the bunk, Lucina peered through the porthole.

"Maman," she begged, "please let's climb on deck to wave goodbye to Tante Delphine. And just look, a big crowd has gathered on the shore."

Clare was not alarmed by the mention of a crowd. As a child growing up in this seaport village of Dieppe, she had often stood among throngs of local residents on this same pebbly beach to watch ships depart, never expecting that one day she would be a fugitive fleeing France forever.

Clare preferred not to go on deck—at least not until the vessel was farther from the pier, in deeper waters. But Lucina's childish excitement at what was to her a new adventure persuaded Clare to overcome her own reluctance and set aside her misgivings. She held Lucina firmly by the hand and allowed her daughter to lead her to a spot along the rail. Soon a group of unexpected passengers surrounded them.

When Clare and Lucina first boarded, they had not realized that other Huguenot refugees were huddled in the hold, hidden among the boxes of Dupres textiles. During the night, these brave men, women and children had been hauled aboard inside barrels and crates, fearful of being captured by the soldiers who patrolled the French coast.

Standing at the rail, Clare and Lucina turned in amazement as the refugees emerged from the cargo space like a flock of blackbirds. Falling to their knees on the wooden deck, they began to sing psalms of gratitude to God for their deliverance from the terrors of King Louis XIV.

Suddenly their peaceful faces turned dark and their voices stopped. Something was terribly wrong. Swinging around, Clare saw what was unfolding on shore and the blood drained from her face. "Dear God," she cried out. "No. This can't be happening!"

PART I

CLARE'S JOURNAL

Chapter 1

Clare's Surprise Gift

1668

ON THE MORNING of her fourteenth birthday, Clare awoke with the strange feeling her humdrum life was about to change. Lying in her dark alcove bed, separated from the kitchen by an old blanket that had been strung across a pole to provide a bit of privacy, she tried to remember the details of her recurring nightmare. Something about a deserted mansion, a child's voice crying out… but like most dreams, it quickly faded, replaced by the comforting sounds of Maman's voice. "Time to get up, sleepy girl."

Clare pulled aside the blanket. As her eyes gradually adjusted to the dimly lit room, she searched for a sign. Something just *had* to be different today—after all, it was her special day and this afternoon there was to be a family celebration in her honor at Uncle Dupres's home. The door to Papa's study was open and Clare could hear him rustling about with his books, as usual. The door to the bedchamber where she used to sleep next to her parents in a small truckle bed also stood ajar. Maman was standing close by, stirring something bubbly in the iron kettle hanging above the kitchen hearth fire.

The worn oak table on the packed-dirt floor of their cottage was set for breakfast—three wooden bowls for the family's customary porridge, three spoons, and three mismatched cups for tea. All in their ordinary places. Clare sighed as she swung her legs off the straw tick onto the worn braided rag rug and scanned the room. Everything was so boringly familiar.

Then her eyes suddenly alighted on the sight of a package sitting on the table, wrapped in brown paper and tied with a red satin ribbon. *It must be a gift for me! Could this be the sign?* Brimming with anticipation, she quickly pulled a petticoat over her shift and pulled her arms through an old linen smock, thinking about the fancy new gown she would wear this afternoon. Hopping out of bed, she almost forgot to fold her quilt, until Maman sent a warning glance in her direction.

Their simple breakfast was ready. Papa came out of his study and they sat at the table, bowing their heads and holding hands in prayer. Clare knew she should be concentrating on his words, but she fidgeted on the bench and her eyes kept drifting toward the beckoning parcel. Maman ladled a large helping of porridge into each bowl and Papa began to eat, urging his daughter to do the same. Clare watched him glance at the package with a surprised expression, but he said nothing about it.

Will this meal never end? Clare toyed with her spoon. *Papa will surely chastise me if I don't finish every bite—remind me to be grateful for the roof over our heads and simple food to fill our bellies. A blessing for the family of an impoverished Protestant minister living in France under the rule of a Papist king who despises us.*

But the wrapped package diverted Clare's attention from Papa's prayers. She felt certain it contained the key to her future. *If only I could remember the details of that dream last night. Why does it haunt me so?*

At last the meal was ended, the dishes dried and replaced in orderly fashion on the shelf. Maman handed Clare the package, kissed her on the forehead, and wished her a blessed birthday. Carefully untying the ribbon, the young girl gasped at the contents—a beautiful embossed-leather journal. Papa raised his eyebrows and sucked in his breath. He asked Maman how she had been able to save enough money to afford such an expensive present on his meager earnings.

Clare knew Papa preferred to ignore the fact that Maman earned a little on her own as a midwife, although not much. Most of her patients were poor wives of farmers and fishermen, butchers and tradesmen.

Eagerly leafing through the crisp new pages and inhaling the delicious scent of the calfskin binding, Clare skipped to the window, seeking a closer look at her new treasure. As she pushed aside the weathered curtains, early-morning sunshine poured through the open casement. A salty sea breeze carried in the scent of the pink geraniums growing in the window box, mingled with the acerbic smells of the curative herbs growing in Maman's physic garden.

"My daughter needs a sturdy journal to keep birthing records," Maman explained to Papa. "I have decided the time has come for her to begin her apprenticeship as a midwife."

Clare couldn't believe her ears. "Truly, Maman? Are you really going to start taking me to birthings with you?" For countless generations, the women in Maman's family had taught their daughters the skills and knowledge necessary for attending women during confinements. Clare had anxiously been awaiting her turn, and now it was about to begin! She also knew she would be expected to bear a daughter of her own one day to carry on the ancestral heritage, which meant she had to wed. For now, though, she would concentrate on learning to become the finest midwife in all Normandy.

"Go with me? Certainly not yet, Clare. We will begin your lessons at home with books and diagrams. I will train you in the skills of combining herbs to assist women in travail. You are still too young and immature to attend confinements with me. Midwifery is not a game—if something goes wrong or the child is born deformed, the midwife gets the blame. However, if you study hard and pay careful attention to my teachings, I'm confident you will soon be ready to attend actual birthings."

Papa groaned. Clare knew he disapproved of his wife working outside the home. He often complained that she should stay home and devote her efforts to caring for her family, to preparing his only daughter for marriage, not a career. Follow the example of the other goodwives from their church.

But Maman said she was proud of her vocation. When Papa told her being prideful was a sin, she would reach for the French Protestant Bible and read him the passages about God looking upon midwives with favor. As minister of the local Huguenot church, Papa could not argue with the scriptures.

"Well," said Papa, "if my daughter is to keep a journal, it would be well for her to copy some inspirational verses from the Psalms onto those expensive pages."

"I think our Clare has a mind of her own. I feel certain she will fill it with words of her own choosing," responded Maman.

"Let's hope she can show proper humility in her writings," he said.

Chapter 2

The Girl Who Wanted It All

Two days ago, I received this beautiful journal as a sign that my life is headed in an exciting new direction. My intent is that this shall become a keepsake for me and my children, to preserve a lifetime of memorable events and adventures that I just feel in my blood are my destiny.

Journal of Clare Dupres, 3 octobre 1668

MAMAN WAS CALLED out to a birthing and Papa was preparing to leave for a meeting with his church consistory. "Are you sure you're not afraid to stay home alone?" he asked, looking at his daughter with uncertainty. "I could walk you over to Uncle's house to stay with cousin Delphine."

"Oh, Papa," Clare said. "Stop worrying about me. I'm old enough to stay home by myself. Writing in my journal will keep me busy." Nonetheless, Clare knew that he *would* worry. She was an only child.

For a long time, Clare had wondered why she had no sisters or brothers until one evening she'd overheard a discussion between Uncle and her parents. Papa had insisted his prayers had led to the miracle of her birth after twenty barren years of marriage. Uncle had laughed at Papa's divine theory. "More likely the unusually harsh winter of 1654 forced your wife to stay home with you in your cozy featherbed for a few uninterrupted months. The deep snow and icy roads in Dieppe interfered with her foolish routine of galloping about the nearby villages, birthing other peoples' babies at all hours."

"Foolish routine, all right," Papa had said, nodding. "At least we agree on that."

Maman had blushed and berated Uncle. "Mind your own business, Jean Dupres, and I'll tend to mine." Her voice had been filled with amusement, not anger—Clare knew Maman was terribly fond of her husband's widowed brother. "Whatever the reason for Clare's late appearance, I am relieved to finally have a daughter to carry on my ancestral heritage."

When Papa left the cottage for his meeting, he warned Clare to keep the door bolted. They lived on Rue de l'Église, close by the Catholic cathedral. Papa was somewhat wary of Papists, although Maman insisted the townsfolk were friendly enough and especially grateful for her presence at their travails.

"I promise not to let any strangers inside." Clare waved goodbye to him and set her writing materials on the small table by the window. She pulled her journal from its hiding place, a niche behind a loose brick inside her alcove bed. She thought it best to keep it safe from prying eyes, especially since Papa's students came to the cottage for tutoring.

The morning hours passed quickly, as she thought how best to begin her life story. *Since Uncle Dupres and my cousins graciously entertained me on my birthday, I'll start writing about them.*

~~~

Papa's eldest brother, Uncle Dupres, was a rich merchant who designed, sold and exported fine fabrics. Growing demand for French silks among the English and French elite had increased his wealth considerably, leading him to become a prominent member of the rising gentry class of Normandy.

As the eldest son, Uncle had inherited the family business as well as the half-timbered building on the main road, across from the port, which served as his home and shop. A freshly painted sign on the ground-floor window displayed the company name: Dupres & Sons, Purveyors of Fine Fabrics. The sign was embellished with brightly colored poppies, daisies and roses painted by Jacques, who had recently completed his apprenticeship with his father. Already Jacques's talent for designing unique flowered silk patterns was blooming, and his reputation along with it.

The upstairs apartments, where Uncle lived with his three children, reflected his wealth. Heavy velvet draperies hung in front of the
~~~

parlor windows, tied back to reveal a commanding view of the sea. Luxurious tapestries adorned the plaster walls. Massive mahogany bedsteads were draped with silk in six bedchambers, some of which were never occupied. Turkish carpets lay on the gleaming oak floors, instead of braided rag rugs.

Of course Uncle had a bevy of servants, whereas Clare's family had only one girl-of-all-work to do the cleaning and laundry.

From a childless great-aunt, Uncle Dupres had also inherited an abandoned gothic stone dwelling in the countryside near Rouen, which intrigued Clare—although she had never been there, she visualized Maison Dupres in her daydreams. Situated on the River Seine, the place had been partially destroyed by fire years earlier. Uncle said he could have chosen to renovate it as his country home, but preferred to reside with his three children in Dieppe, close to the port and to Papa, his only brother.

On the afternoon of Clare's birthday, Uncle had greeted them as they came upstairs. "Delphine," he bellowed. "Come see your cousin in her beautiful new gown." Delphine came rushing from the kitchen, wiping her hands on her apron. Clare twirled around in front of them as they murmured admiration at the billowing low-necked gown with lace-trimmed sleeves. Uncle explained he had given Delphine the fabric because of a slight imperfection in the weave. He couldn't include it in the shipment to Versailles because every inch of fabric for the bed hangings at King Louis's impressive new palace had to be flawless.

"Oh, Clare," Delphine exclaimed, "you look *très élégante*. The robe fits you perfectly. I'm glad I sewed those pin tucks in the stomacher—the blemish in the fabric is hardly noticeable."

"I am thrilled to have such a wonderful gown, but why didn't you use this beautiful burgundy silk to sew yourself a new dress? Nobody sews a fine seam as well as you, Delphine."

"What need has a spinster like me for such finery?" said Delphine. "When Father gave me the fabric, I thought immediately how well it would look with your auburn hair, Clare."

"Spinster?" Maman interjected. "Delphine, you are only twenty-four. Surely there is still time for you to find a husband." But Delphine always claimed it was her Christian duty to stay at home, overseeing the servants, running Uncle's household, and caring for her birth family. She had been busy raising her two younger brothers since their mother had died ten years earlier, when Jacques was six and Pierre only four (same as Clare). "I am content with my life as it is," she always insisted, but Clare suspected otherwise. Delphine had once told her in confidence about a handsome lad who died at sea—afterwards, she could never face the pain of loving and losing again. A faraway look on her face had briefly shadowed sadness at the memory, but her normally sunny disposition had quickly returned.

From Clare's earliest years, she had spent many happy hours at Uncle's home. Delphine was like an older sister to Clare, often herding her three young charges to picnics at the pebbly beach across the road. Pierre and Clare would hold hands and totter together to the shoreline, screaming at the coldness of the seawater on their toes. Clare remembered how Delphine had scolded them for drenching the hems of their long dresses.

"Look how nicely Jacques behaves," she had said. "He sits quietly next to me on the blanket with his sketchbook, while you two ragamuffins run wild." But Clare had sensed Delphine was hiding a smile.

On rainy days, Delphine had sung popular ballads to the three children. Clare remembered one particular tune about a jilted maiden who jumped to her death from a high window. In her lilting voice, Delphine had warbled the refrain:

Take heed, all ye maidens, be wary, be wary.
He promised to marry ye, yet he did tarry.
Be wary, young maidens, take care.

"I don't like that ballad," Jacques cried. "Hearing about dead people gives me night scares."

Pierre had laughed at his brother. "Nothing frightens me."

"You must learn not to be so sensitive, *mon petit*," Delphine said. "It's only an old ballad. I like the tune, don't you?" She had taken Jacques by his hands and tried to dance with him, but his serious body stiffened. As Jacques frowned, Pierre grabbed Clare's hands and they skipped around the kitchen, giggling and singing *be war-ee, take car-ee.*

In Clare's childish imagination, she envisioned the young maiden of the ballad inside deserted Maison Dupres, her spirit wandering through the dusty rooms, searching for the gentleman who jilted her. Uncle checked on the deserted *maison* from time to time, when passing it on his business trips to Paris. Clare always wanted to hear about those visits—he told her the condition was deteriorating.

"Do you ever see ghosts there, Uncle?" she'd once asked. He'd just pinched her cheek and laughed. "Where *do* you come up with such ideas, Clare? Ghosts indeed!"

Everyone was beginning to wonder when the birthday feast they had been promised would be ready. The mantel clock struck four. Stomachs were rumbling. Finally Delphine announced, "The food is ready," and they all trooped into the dining room. They sat around Uncle's mahogany table, chatting about the weather and the upcoming fair and enjoying the food, when suddenly Pierre surprised them by announcing his plan to join the French Navy.

Jacques looked up from his plate at his brother. "You're too young."

"Begging your pardon. That's easy for you to say. You don't need to seek a profession to support yourself."

Jacques shrugged. "Can't help it that I was born first. Eldest son gets all. That's the way things are." Clare knew that was why Uncle had inherited the Dupres fortune and why Papa had had to seek his living in the church.

"Boys!" Uncle scolded. Sometimes he forgot that they were no longer little children. "The French Navy is no place for you, Pierre. You will study law at the college in Rouen."

"I'd rather be a naval officer in a jaunty uniform. Why can't I join?"

"King Louis does not think kindly on those of our religious persuasion. Protestants are never chosen to be officers in the French Navy. You would end up swabbing decks."

"I don't understand. We are all Christians. Just because we don't accept the authority of the Pope or worship idols of the Virgin—"

"That is enough!" said Uncle, slamming his hand on the table. It was obvious Uncle Dupres did not wish to discuss this subject with Pierre over dinner. "Tomorrow, instead of wasting time with your sailor friends at the pier, you will stay in and study your history lessons." An uncomfortable silence ensued.

Finally Maman changed the subject. "Delphine, thank you for cooking Clare's favorite chicken dish. It was delicious." Papa agreed and suggested she give his daughter the recipe to copy into her new journal.

"New journal?" exclaimed Delphine, looking at her cousin. "How excited you must be to have a place to record your secret thoughts. Our little Clare is a dreamer—she won't want to fill her diary with recipes."

Cousin Delphine can almost read my mind. I dearly love her for understanding me so well. When the women stood to clear the table, the servants being away on their half day off, Delphine said, "Clare is excused from helping because it is her special day."

Maman said, "Very well, but just this once. You spoil her enough as it is. Giving her grand notions."

The birthday girl wandered into the study, where Papa and Uncle had gone to smoke their long clay pipes by the fire. Pierre was sitting at a table in the corner, shuffling cards aimlessly. Across the table, Jacques was drawing in his sketchbook as usual. Comfortably settling on the window seat, Clare pulled a volume of Shakespeare from the shelf, turning to *Love's Labour Lost.* She claimed it was her favorite. But this afternoon, she was distracted by the fireside conversation.

"I heard unsettling rumors when I traveled to Paris on business last week," said Uncle. "The King is busy overseeing the construction of the new palace. He is setting up his own silk factory at Versailles, to avoid doing business with Huguenot weavers and manufacturers. Soon I will be losing the French royal trade."

"Ah, but you still have your export business," said Papa.

"True… however, many of my suppliers, the artisans who work from my silk patterns, are beginning to flee France. And that's not all the bad news—"

Papa shook his head and held up his hands. He apparently did not want to hear any more. The two men sat in silence for a while.

"What other bad news?" In the heat of conversation, the men forgot Clare was sitting close by.

"Nothing for a pretty young girl like you to worry about," Uncle said, rising from his armchair and patting her on the head.

"But I wish to know."

"Clare Dupres! Mind your manners. This is not a matter for women," scolded Papa. "Go help Delphine and your mother in the kitchen."

I hate being treated differently from Jacques and Pierre. They're never told to help in the kitchen. As she replaced the book on the shelf, she heard

Papa whisper to Uncle, "My daughter is strong-willed, just like her mother. I don't know what will become of her."

"Never too early to start arranging a good marriage for her," Uncle responded. Clare wanted to burst into their male conversation—tell them she would pick her own husband when she was ready. But she didn't want to anger Papa, who frowned at her impudence, so she bit her tongue in frustration.

Pierre put down his cards and gazed out the window. He suggested taking Clare for a short walk, and Papa reluctantly agreed. Uncle checked the time on his gold pocket watch. "Be back in one hour, and stay away from the pier."

They walked to the beach, holding hands as they had when they were toddlers, with a light bouncing step. Pierre reached down and picked up a seashell—offered it to her as if it were a precious jewel. Like a bolt of lightning piercing her heart, Clare realized that she loved Pierre, and not just as a cousin.

~~~

Clare was startled by the sound of Papa's boots crunching up the front path. Reluctantly blotting the final words, she quickly put her journal away, amazed that she had already filled two whole pages. *Maman will probably scold me for wasting paper, but I can't help myself—the words spill from my pen like rushing water.*

She made Papa tea and toast. Soon his students would be arriving. Lately, he had been tutoring Pierre in Hebrew and Greek, hoping the lad would follow him in the church. Papa could not be more wrong, thought Clare. She could tell Pierre was not interested in becoming a clergyman. A boisterous, strapping youth, he was more interested in learning about sailing ships from the English seamen who frequented the port, which was mostly how he had learned to speak their tongue.

Clare had begged Pierre to teach her some phrases. Thinking she was too dull to learn on her own, Pierre lent Clare some of his English books. He was surprised at her quick ability to speak and understand that strange, harsh-sounding language.

In addition to classical languages, Papa tutored his male students in French history and mathematics. Clare thought it unfair that girls were not educated beyond learning letters and numbers, but Clare had the benefit of Papa's teaching for a simple reason—their cottage
~~~

was so small that she could hear his lectures in his study from where she stood in the kitchen doing chores.

Clare became well versed in French history, more so than Pierre, who was frequently rapped on the knuckles for lack of attention to Papa's lectures. While she scrubbed the table with sand, she learned about the civil wars of religion between the Catholic kings and her Huguenot ancestors. As she peeled carrots, she listened to Papa lecture about the Edict of Nantes, which had ended the bloody carnage by granting Huguenots freedom of religion.

This afternoon, when she was cutting potatoes for supper, she overheard a boy named Georges raise troubling questions—was the Huguenots' right to worship now endangered by the new king? By his act of dissolving Parliament, was Louis XIV planning to revoke the Edict of Nantes? Force all his French subjects to convert to Popery? These questions made Clare uneasy. She stopped chopping and listened to Papa's response.

"Your concerns are unwarranted, Georges. The Edict of Nantes has protected us for more than seventy years. Now, *messieurs*, our history lesson is done for today. Don't forget to study your Latin for tomorrow."

Clare pondered Papa's assurances to Georges as she dumped the potatoes into the boiling kettle. She wanted to ask Papa more about it, but then he might start closing the door to his study if he knew she was listening, so she remained quiet. As the students left Papa's study, Pierre hesitated for a minute and gave Clare a broad grin. "Hope you're writing flattering words about me in that journal of yours."

"And what makes you think I'd be writing anything about you?" she said, blushing.

Pierre winked, grabbed the strap holding his books together and strutted out, calling to the other boys to wait up for him. And at that moment, dreamy-eyed Clare's thoughts shifted to Pierre. She forgot about King Louis and French history and just about everything else, including the stew, which was starting to stick in the kettle.

The next morning Clare was pulling turnips from the garden, counting them *en anglais*. "One, two, three…" These would be chopped and added to their never-ending bottomless stew. "Six, seven, eight…" Each day, she would add more vegetables from the garden and sometimes a bit of dried pork, along with fresh water from their well. *How I wish we could afford servants to do these endless, boring chores to free up my time to write in my journal. Someday I will have a horde of servants at my bidding.*

"Ten, eleven, twelve, thirteen—"

"You're wasting your time learning to speak English," said Papa, stepping out into the garden plot.

"I was just practicing."

"Oho. I suppose you would like to run off with one of those handsome English sailors at the dock," he said.

"Stop teasing me, Papa, I'll never leave France. Why would I ever want to go? I already have my whole life planned to perfection. I am determined to marry the man I love, have two children, live in a fine maison and become a wealthy midwife."

"Oh, the impossible dreams of an innocent young girl on the brink of womanhood," chuckled Papa. "I think I'll start calling you *la jeune fille qui veut tout*, the girl who wants it all."

"Why shouldn't I have it all? I can and I will. Just wait and see."

"Life doesn't always turn out the way you wish, my dear one."

Clare should have heeded his words, but thoughts of Maman's birthing lessons and her awakening passion for Pierre filled her mind and heart to overflowing. *My future will be as rosy as the posies Jacques painted on the business sign.*

Chapter 3

Chickens Are Not Enough

CLARE HAD DECIDED early on not to waste the valuable pages of her journal to copy biblical verses. Maman had given her daughter permission to write what she felt was important, although she *had* hinted that nothing was more important than the birthing lessons—so Clare wouldn't forget them when the time came to pass on the knowledge to the next generation of females.

Sighing, Clare drew a few small hearts and penciled in "Clare & Pierre" or practiced writing her future name: "Madame Pierre Dupres" in flourishes. But what she *didn't* write about was her clandestine meetings with her handsome cousin. Although her parents promised not to read her private journal, she was wise enough to realize how angry they would be if they knew. So when she happened to "run into" Pierre on her errands to the fishmonger's or the chandler's shop, and they ducked into a dark alley for a few minutes alone, she did not record their secret hugs and kisses in her journal. No need to tempt fate.

"Dear me," she said aloud one day, flipping back over the few pages she had written, mostly during the first few days after receiving the journal. Maman was busy stitching an unusual lumpy something-or-other and listening to Clare's complaints. "After describing our family, our cottage, Uncle Dupres's family, his business, his homes—there is little else I can think of writing in here, Maman. Nothing much has changed in my humdrum life."

To be honest, Clare *had* written a few lines about the onset of her flowers and her budding breasts. She had briefly recorded her dream of visiting the mysterious Maison Dupres, where she was certain a ghost roamed the halls, but was convinced such a visit would never occur. And she had described the detailed plan for her future perfect life, in French and also in English.

"Almost two years have passed since I received this journal and still I wait for exciting adventures to begin."

"You are but fifteen," said Maman. "Perhaps it is unwise to crave adventure. Once you begin attending birthings with me, you will find many interesting things to write."

"And when will that be? You have been giving me lessons at home for almost two years. Why can't I start going now?"

"In my opinion, you are not yet ready. I realize how bright you are, but you are still careless. Your attention wanders from my charts and diagrams. You appear to be dreaming when I take you into the shed behind the cottage and try to teach you about herbs. And you recollect what happened when I first showed you the herb book, do you not?" said Maman, shaking her head.

Clare remembered that day well. Maman had pulled out a bulky book, about the size of their Bible, from the bottom of her birthing bag. At first, Clare groaned, thinking it was a book containing lengthy descriptions of herbs and their healing properties. Like *Culpeper's Herbal,* only longer. But to her surprise, except in its outward appearance, this was unlike any book Clare had ever seen—there were no pages inside! Instead, a finely worked miniature mahogany cabinet had been carefully concealed in the hollowed-out volume. Tiny drawers opened with tarnished brass knobs, each drawer containing a different dried herb. There was even a slot for a small glass-stopper bottle filled with residue of an ominous green fluid.

"This herb book was built by my great-grandfather, a master craftsman, to his wife's specifications. It has been passed down from mother to daughter and someday it will become yours, Clare."

Clare thought this was much more interesting than Maman's endless sketches and diagrams. She read and translated the Latin words written on yellowed labels fronting the drawers. *Papaver somniferum*, opium poppy. *Datura stramonium*, thorn apple. *Atropa bella*, belladonna. But Clare recoiled in horror when she read the next label—*Hyoscyamus niger*. "Henbane," Clare had said in amazement.

"That was the poison I read about in Uncle's volume of *Hamlet*—the poison poured in his father's ear."

Burning with natural curiosity, Clare leaned forward to smell the dried herbs in the drawers. Wrinkling up her nose, she became giddy and the room began whirling about. Maman had pulled her back before she fell over.

"Be careful, Clare! Never put your nose so close. Some of the dried herbs in here can cause hallucinations. You see why I don't yet take you to birthings."

"Hallucinations? Maman, why would a midwife carry such dangerous substances?"

"You will learn in time, my daughter," she said. "Mixed in proper proportions with other ingredients, including laudanum, these herbs can safely aid women in confinement."

Pointing to the greenish residue in the small jar, she added, "Through the years, our female ancestors have developed the perfect combination of ingredients in this particular distillation. You see, Clare, it lessens the pain of childbirth and erases any memories of those pains. It is a magic elixir."

Clare mulled over the implication of what Maman had said. *Magic elixir.* It sounded intriguing. "I will write down the formula in my journal," Clare said, heading toward the loose brick over her sleeping alcove.

"No, no!" Maman exclaimed, grabbing her arm. "The magic elixir is a closely guarded and valuable family secret. It must never be committed to writing. You will learn to memorize the formula by repeating it time and again until it is embedded in your memory. And when you marry and have a daughter of your own, you will teach it to her in the same manner."

"What would happen if someone should write down the formula?" Clare asked, wondering why Maman was so insistent.

"It is said that on the day that happens, the elixir will lose its mystical powers."

"I think I understand," Clare said, although she really didn't. Day after day, Maman drilled her on the formula for the magic elixir until she was certain Clare had committed it to memory.

A few weeks later, Maman had finished sewing her lumpy project. It was a dummy replica of a womb, made from an old linen sheet and stuffed with feathers. The open end, or "cervix," was tied with a shoelace and could be stretched open or pulled tightly closed. A small cloth doll was tucked inside the opening, head down, its belly attached with a length of twine to a liver-shaped "placenta." This object Maman had fashioned from scraps of the old burgundy birthday gown Clare had outgrown—the rest of the rich fabric had been refashioned into a stylish petticoat for her growing daughter.

"How clever of you, Maman, to make this model. Now I can practice pulling out a baby."

"Midwives don't pull them out—nature does that. But sometimes babies get stuck in the womb because they try to come out feetfirst. What do we call that, Clare?"

"Breech birth."

"Ah, so you have been paying *some* attention to my lessons. That pleases me. Once you learn about the contents of my birthing bag, I believe you will be ready to start attending real births." And so the lessons had continued.

The large carpetbag Maman carried to birthings was enormous. In addition to her polished silver knife, folded sheets, towels, a measuring spoon, and the unique herb book, it contained a small jar of goose grease. As a young child, Clare had always imagined the bag was large enough to hold a small infant. Maman had laughed and said she was being absurd—the purpose was to carry supplies, not to steal away a child. Still, the thought of kidnapping a baby and hiding it in the carpet bag was intriguing. Clare wondered if any other midwife had considered the possibility.

"Do you remember what I taught you about goose grease?" Maman asked as she laid out the ingredients of her bag to show to Clare.

"That you smear it on the cervix when it dilates. Here, let me practice on the dummy womb," said Clare, sticking her finger into the greasy substance. But Maman pulled it away. "Do you wish to ruin the cloth? I'm far too busy to make another prototype," she scolded. "There you go again, rushing into things without considering the consequences. Wash your hands carefully, as you would before a birthing, and put the jar back into my bag."

"Sorry, Maman. Truly I am trying to learn patience. Just like I embroidered on my sampler—'Patience is a Virtue.'" Papa had suggested that.

"I don't mean to scold. I'm proud of your progress, daughter, and feel confident you will be a successful midwife."

As Clare replaced the jar on top of the folded sheets, she saw several lengths of pink ribbon inside. "What are these for?"

"Well, that is a lesson for another day."

Just when Clare was beginning to give up hope that she would ever go to a real birthing, word came that a new patient, Farmer Roget's wife, was in travail. "Would you like to come along as my assistant, Clare?"

Clare shivered in anticipation. *Finally!*

The Rogets lived within a fifteen-minute walk from the Dupres' cottage. By the time Clare and her mother arrived, the patient was surrounded by neighbor female gossips, there to distract her from the pains of her travail. They would keep her company until the birth was complete. Clare noticed their sighs of relief at Maman's arrival, as they had been sitting up with the laboring woman all night.

Maman introduced Clare as her assistant, which made her feel proud as a peacock. She helped unfold the sheets and set out the pink ribbons. They both scrubbed their hands in hot water with the farmer's lye soap, ignoring questioning looks from the gossips.

"Madame Roget," Maman said to the perspiring woman who lay on a bed of straw. "Would you like to try a dose of my special elixir?"

"Why else do you think I sent for you?" the mother-to-be huffed testily. "If you're as good as the butcher's wife told me, well…oooooh—the pains, they come so close. I feel as if my body is splitting in half." She clutched her distended belly.

"Breathe," Clare said, trying to be helpful. "Think about floating on the sea."

Maman watched with approval as her new assistant shook the bottle and carefully measured one spoonful of the green elixir, being careful not to spill any. Madame Roget swallowed the bitter fluid with a grimace.

What followed alarmed Clare, despite her mother's preparatory lectures—Clare had been dreaming about Pierre, instead of listening. The laboring mother's face did not relax as Clare had expected. Instead, it became red and contorted. Madame Roget began to scream and thrash about, cursing like the sailors who hung about the harbor.

Shrieking, she vowed she would never again let her husband or any damn man into her bed.

Clare stood gaping, empty spoon in hand, as Maman slipped a clean sheet between the laboring woman and the straw tick.

"Hand me the ribbons, Clare," Maman said, unperturbed by the woman's ravings. "Help me tie her wrists and ankles to the bed-posts." Seeing Clare's horrified look, Maman assured her that Madame Roget would have no memory of her harangue or of being tied up and reminded her daughter that the elixir induced a dreamlike state, a twilight sleep. The gossips, however, were not reassured. They looked uneasily at each other, wondering if their friend was being murdered. It was a look Clare would see again many times in the future.

For the next twenty minutes, she paid careful attention as her mother guided the tiny baby through the birth canal. Fortunately this child was coming down headfirst. Clare watched Maman catch the slippery infant in her skilled hands. When she held the baby upside down and slapped its tiny buttocks, a lusty cry emerged. She placed the squalling infant on Madame Roget's belly and reached for her knife.

After cutting and tying off the cord, Maman handed Clare the infant girl and instructed her to clean and swaddle the babe. Clare had practiced swaddling the rag doll inside the dummy model womb. But a slippery, wiggly baby was far different. *Goodness, I almost dropped her.*

Several of the unmarried gossips got up to leave, thinking the birthing was complete, but Clare knew there were two more important steps. First, gently massage the mother's belly to expel the afterbirth. Then look it over carefully, to ensure complete removal.

"Why do we inspect it, Clare?" questioned Maman.

"To decrease the risk of childbed fever. Sometimes it doesn't come out as it should."

"Good girl. You remembered. So many untrained midwives fail to take this precaution," Maman said, shaking her head sadly. "Childbirth presents a grave risk to women in travail—many women die from improper care." Standing side by side, the midwife and her assistant inspected the discarded placenta; satisfied, they stuffed it into the birthing bag to take home and bury in their herb garden.

Madame Roget gradually awakened from her dreamlike sleep. To the amazement of everyone except Maman, the farmer's wife had no recollection of the pain or her cusswords. Only the slightest pink marks on her wrists and ankles, which she was too sleepy to notice, reflected her struggles.

Clare would never forget witnessing the effects of the magic elixir for the first time. Farmer Roget had thanked them kindly, saying, "It hath pleased God now to restore my wife from the peril of childbirth." Almost as an afterthought, he handed Maman two chickens in payment for her services.

As the two walked home, Clare asked Maman, "Are two chickens adequate compensation for your efforts? Considering the benefits his wife received from the elixir?"

"He paid me what they could afford." Maman shrugged. "Besides, these gifts are worth more than coins. Once you spend coins, they are gone forever. Chickens will continue to provide us with eggs."

Chickens! After what Clare had just witnessed, she began to understand the true value of the magic elixir and grew excited. Normandy was home to nobles and aristocrats, even wealthy merchants like Uncle Dupres, who could afford to reward her generously. She would become the only *sage femme* to offer a pain-free birthing experience for their wives, and why not their many mistresses too? Clare knew rich men kept mistresses. She even suspected Uncle Dupres "visited" a widow he politely referred to as his "lady friend" on business trips.

At that moment, Clare saw her future as clearly as if she had looked into a crystal ball. "Maman, one day when I became a full-fledged midwife, I shall limit my birthing services to elite women who can reward me properly. No wives of poor farmers—or fishermen whose beds undoubtedly reek of herring."

Maman was appalled. "Such thoughts are terrible, Clare. The elixir was developed for all women in need, not merely the wealthy. Your attitude is decidedly unchristian."

But Clare didn't care. That evening, recording details of the Roget birthing in her journal, she reflected on her idealistic plan to acquire her coveted fortune and concluded: *Chickens are not enough for me.*

Chapter 4

Picnic on the Pebbly Beach

ALTHOUGH CLARE NEEDED to continue with her birthing lessons, Maman allowed her the next day off to visit Delphine, telling Clare she had done fairly well at the Roget birthing. On her way out the door, Maman handed her an empty bucket and told her to collect pebbles from the shore. A storm last week had washed away a spot on their front walk, and Maman wanted to repair it. Clare swung the empty pail as she walked down the road.

Delphine was humming in her kitchen, packing a hamper. "Such a fine day," she said. "Father is in Paris on business and Jacques plans to go to the beach to sketch the ships in the harbor. He closed the shop early. Can you join us? I made plenty of hard-boiled eggs and bread, and a jar of fresh apple cider to quench our thirst on this balmy day. Can you manage carrying the blanket along with your bucket?"

Clare looked around. "Where is Pierre? I need his help gathering pebbles for Maman."

"Probably hanging around at the pier," said Jacques, examining her face.

Why does Jacques always seem to be studying my expression? He never has much to say to me.

"Let's go," said Delphine, and the three of them headed toward their usual picnic spot, close to the shore.

Jacques helped Clare spread the blanket. The sky was blue-gray, cloudless with just a hint of sparkle. The gentle waves lapped on the shore, leaving patterns of lace, which quickly dispersed. It was a glorious, summer day. The finest, purest sea breeze on the coast—acknowledged to be so—and deep water ten yards from the shore—no mud, weeds, or slimy rocks. So Delphine rhapsodized on the virtues of Dieppe port, their own little piece of paradise on the Normandy coast. A place that belonged to artists as well as seamen.

It dawned on Clare that Jacques was not sketching ships. It was her face he was drawing. *This isn't the first time he has captured my image on paper. I cannot imagine why he wastes his time in such pursuits. I consider my figure to be light and pleasing and my hair a rich hue, but otherwise my appearance is unremarkable.* Clare's eyes scanned the shoreline, searching for Pierre.

~~~

"I smell food," said Pierre, bounding toward them. He lifted Delphine in his muscular arms and swung her around. "I'm starved."

"Put me down this instant or I won't give you anything to eat." She was laughing at him.

I wish Pierre would swing me in his arms like that, Clare thought, envious.

While they savored the food, Pierre told them he had been conversing with the English captain of the merchant ship *Celia*, anchored offshore. He had been asking whether Pierre knew of any artists in town who would take his likeness. Nothing special—just a small sketch to bring home as a gift to his fiancée in London.

Pierre had explained his brother was an artist, but only sketched flowers and his cousin Clare, the loveliest flower of them all.

An expression of irritation arose on Jacques's face. On the other hand, maybe it was embarrassment. "That's not true, brother. I sketch many things. Why make up such tales?"

"Tales? Do you not agree that Clare is the loveliest flower in Dieppe?"

Then it was Clare's turn to blush. "Stop saying such things about me." She turned and began to fill Maman's bucket with smooth, round pebbles.

Pierre called to the man who was walking in their direction, and introduced Cap'n Silas to the family. Delphine held out a cup of apple cider, which he accepted with a hearty nod. "Thank ye, ma'am. *C'est délicieux.*"
~~~

She smiled at the man and he gave her a broad grin in return. Clare thought it a pity that Cap'n Silas was already engaged to another woman. She hadn't given up hope of Delphine finding a husband.

Jacques offered to make a quick sketch for him. "Most grateful, I'm sure. Mighty grateful for this favor." Cap'n Silas posed, standing with his back to the sea, strong arms crossed against his chest. He was a very hale, healthy, well-looking man, a little weather-beaten to be sure, but not much. Jacques reached for his bit of charcoal and started splashing broad, deft strokes on the paper.

That fateful day, Clare never expected to see Cap'n Silas again. But one never knows when strangers might have occasion to cross paths again—when a small favor given might reap a greater favor in return.

Delphine sat stock-still, busy watching her talented brother create a lifelike image of the sea captain. Pierre pulled Clare to a standing position. "Come with me," he whispered in her ear.

They climbed the alabaster cliff to the highest point from the pebbly beach. Out of breath, they stopped at Dieppe's deserted castle. Once a protective fortress against invaders, this rambling medieval complex of ramparts, turrets and towers now stood empty. The view from their vantage point was spectacular in all directions: the sea to the north, the town of Dieppe to the south.

Peering down at Rue de l'Église, Clare spotted Maman bending over her herb garden. *She probably thinks I am busy collecting her pebbles on the beach.* Pierre and Clare ducked behind the wall when Maman stood, wiped her brow, and stared up at the castle for a moment. Then they took a deep breath when she turned back to her plants.

"Phew. That was a close call," giggled Clare. "Fortunately, she is too busy to see us alone up here."

They knew they were shirking their chores, but neither cared. A sudden breeze whipped Clare's cap off and sent it sailing into the sea, like a white seagull. Pierre just laughed. He pulled out her hairpins and flung them into the moat. Ran his fingers through her long auburn locks, as the wind wound her hair around her head. Clare grabbed his neck and pecked him on the cheek as they stood in the shadows.

Still breathing heavily from the climb and the excitement of their escape, they walked to the edge of the cliff, hallooed and waved at Jacques and Delphine. Jacques craned his neck back from his sketchbook. He probably guessed what Pierre and his cousin had done, purposely leaving him behind when he was busy doing Pierre's friend a favor.

Jacques's frown was tinged with anger, but the seagulls swallowed his shouts, his pursed lips a silent warning to them.

"Jacques is worried that we might fall off the edge," Clare said.

"No, Clare, that is not the reason he is scowling. He is envious."

She had always suspected Jacques was jealous of his younger brother. But she was sixteen and madly in love with Pierre.

"We better climb down before we get in trouble," she said.

"Not before you give me another kiss, a real one this time," he said, enfolding Clare in his arms.

Had anyone seen them together on the cliff, her reputation would have been ruined. They were no longer innocent children, but since she planned to marry Pierre, Clare cared not what people thought. If only he would propose.

Delphine's old ballad filled her head. *Be wary, be wary, take car-ee.*

Chapter 5

The Bent Carriage Wheel

Maman says I am making good progress as her assistant. Over the past two years, I have helped her birth three sets of twins and four breech babies. Last week, she finally allowed me to birth a baby completely on my own, as she stood by and supervised.

Papa is still determined to have me marry. To please him, I have begun to sew kerchiefs for my trousseau. He hopes I will marry cousin Jacques, always praising his elder nephew as steady, industrious and pious. He boasts that Jacques memorized all the psalms. Why should I care? Jacques lacks animation—too quiet for my taste. Shoulders bent over from so much sketching. So unlike his lively, handsome brother.

"What about Pierre?" I ask Papa. He frowns and says, "That boy is full of pride and self-conceit. He always carries forth an expectation of applause." Papa does not appreciate Pierre's ambition. One of these days, I will tell Papa I plan to marry Pierre.

Journal of Clare Dupres, 6 avril 1674

THE WINTER SNOW turned to rain this week. When Clare came in from the shed after grinding dried herbs, she was surprised to see Uncle Dupres sitting at the kitchen table. He had decided to stop by for a cup of tea. She picked up her stitchery and sat listening to Uncle's account of his latest business trip.

Maman handed him a piece of her freshly baked bread and asked, "How was your journey, Jean?"

Clare hoped he had stopped at Maison Dupres along the way—she could never get enough of hearing about the old mansion. This time he hadn't stopped there, but Clare's initial disappointment quickly faded when he began to relate an exciting adventure he had enjoyed along the way back from Paris.

"The roads were terribly rutted from the melting snow," Uncle said. "I was driving my cart behind a large black carriage, when suddenly their back wheel flew off and the door popped open."

"Goodness, I hope nobody was hurt."

"The carriage was listing to the side. I climbed down and went to offer assistance. First, I helped a fine-looking gentleman climb out. Then he reached in and lifted his wife out. She must have been about your age, Clare, maybe a year or two older. An exceedingly handsome young thing, wrapped in a fur-trimmed cloak. They were obviously members of the aristocracy, so I bowed to them."

"What made you think that?" Clare asked.

"Their carriage had a gold coat of arms emblazoned on the door. Two footmen in scarlet livery were clinging onto the back and the driver's box was draped in velvet."

"Oh, how very grand," she declared.

Uncle continued his story. The gentleman had put his arm protectively around the lady's shoulders and asked Uncle to help the other passenger shouting from inside the carriage, tipping precariously from his weight. "Holy Mother of God," the trapped passenger kept screaming. "Help me." It wasn't until Uncle pulled him out that he realized the hysterical man was dressed in priestly vestments.

He had asked Uncle to retrieve his black hat, which had fallen out the window into the mud. As Uncle handed it to him, he had said, "Kind sir, I will include you in my prayers to the Blessed Virgin for saving my family." Confused, Uncle blurted out, "Your family? But … you are a priest."

"Oh, you misunderstand. I am Père Benedict and those are my cousins—his Honor, Le Marquis de Montjardin, and his wife, the Honorable Lady Louise," he said, pointing to the couple standing across the road.

"Ah, then they must be from Chateau Montjardin in Rouen," said Uncle.

"You know of it?" said the priest, somewhat surprised.

"But of course. I am Monsieur Jean Dupres, purveyor of fine fabrics to the gentry and aristocracy, as you will observe from the painted sign on the side of my cart. The housekeeper at Chateau Montjardin recently ordered a bolt of velvet from my shop, which I delivered in person."

"Hmm, a merchant," sniffed the priest, looking Uncle up and down. During his condescending appraisal of Uncle's appearance and the cart brightly painted with flowers, Père Benedict muttered that it looked to him like a gypsy caravan. Suddenly his attention was diverted by the sound of the tenuously teetering Montjardin carriage toppling over. He twisted around, causing his muddy hat to fall off again.

"I suppose you are accustomed to fixing bent carriage wheels," the priest said. "You appear to be a common laborer." Uncle took affront at his insult and refused to retrieve the muddy hat again. Rankled, he stood arms crossed, staring at the priest.

Just then, the Marquis stepped over, handed Uncle his card and bowed to him. "At least *he* recognized me as a gentleman," said Uncle to Maman. "A step below his own class but certainly not of lowly peasantry rank."

"Of course not," Maman said as she refilled his teacup. Uncle continued his tale. The Marquis apologized for his cousin's misunderstanding and expressed his gratitude for Uncle's assistance. However, he seemed exceedingly distracted about his wife. Kept asking her if she was having any pains.

Uncle heard her barely audible whisper—"No, but I am extremely anxious to return home to the chateau." He noticed Lady Louise, cradling her rounded belly in both hands.

Maman interrupted Uncle's story. "Goodness. The Marquise was obviously breeding. She should not have been riding in a carriage if she was that far along. What if her child had been born on the road?"

"They were returning from a visit to his parents at St. Germain, a celebration at the palace. His father is one of hundreds of courtiers to King Louis. The Marquis said he could not refuse the royal invitation to join the party, so they were forced to extend their stay."

"Hmph," said Maman. "I still think it was unwise for a woman in her advanced condition to be so far from home."

"Well, from what I hear in Paris," said Uncle, "our glorious King has become quite the tyrant and demands complete fealty from his courtiers. They fawn all over him." He began regaling Maman with details of royal gossip. How Louis kept a stable of mistresses and sometimes grabbed the nearest female in the corridors of the palace for his personal pleasure. How he was spending millions of *louis d'or* to furnish the new palace at Versailles, with its spectacular hall of mirrors. How the gardens with flowing fountains were taking shape.

Uncle often described these rumors at great length on his return from business travels. But he had a tendency to become sidetracked. For now, Clare was more interested in hearing about the adventure of the misfortunate aristocrats on the road.

"Uncle," she interrupted, "what became of the Marquis's carriage?"

"My, you are an impatient young lady, aren't you?" He requested yet another refill of Maman's tea and, after slurping it from the saucer, continued relating his tale. A spoke on the wheel was badly bent. The footmen told their master that the wheel *could* be remounted, but the carriage ride would be wobbly and there was no guarantee it would not fall off again. There were no other travelers on the road. Rouen was slightly out of Uncle's way home, but he could not leave these noble strangers stranded, so he offered them a ride in his delivery cart.

Having no other choice, the Marquis lifted his wife onto the seat next to Uncle and squeezed in next to her. There was no room for the priest. To Father Benedict's apparent consternation, he was left behind with the footmen.

Uncle started to laugh. "You should have seen the expression on the man's face as we drove off." Before he launched into a detailed description of the priest's demeanor, Clare tried to guide the conversation back to the noble passengers, wanting to hear every detail.

"How did you find the ride to the chateau? Did you converse with the Marquis or his wife?"

Uncle reached for another slice of bread and spread a thick layer of raspberry jam to the edges. His nature was such that he enjoyed eating sweets and took great pride in his expansive stomach, a sign of his growing wealth.

"At first the situation was awkward, to say the least. But the Marquis was very genteel and did not complain about riding in my cart. To break the silence, I jabbered about my family. You know how I like to boast about my children. Bragged about my son

Jacques's artistic talent, Pierre's application to the law college in Rouen, and Delphine's delicious cuisine—"

"Did you tell him about *me*, Uncle?" Clare asked, exasperated.

"Oh, I *may* have mentioned your name, Clare." Uncle always enjoyed teasing her.

She tugged on Uncle's sleeve and begged to hear more about the Marquise. "Ah yes," he said, wiping the crumbs from his face. "Lady Louise was fairly pale and silent during the trip, occasionally sighing. She perked up when I told her about you, Clare. She said she hoped to meet you someday. Perhaps she was just trying to be polite."

"Oh." A prick of disappointment.

"But she did reach into her reticule and retrieve one of her calling cards. It's in my pocket. Would you like to have it?"

"Would I? Oh, yes, Uncle. I would be so pleased to have it, to tuck in my journal." He held the card tightly in his fingers, teasing Clare while she eagerly pulled at it. Finally he opened his palm and surrendered the treasure to her.

"How very unlucky to have a broken carriage wheel," clucked Maman. But Clare examined the elegant card in her hand and thought it the luckiest thing that could have happened.

Uncle stood up and stretched, preparing to return home. But Clare wanted to hear more. "You said Lady Louise perked up when you told her about me. Did you tell her I was learning to be a midwife?"

"I believe I told Lady Louise that my favorite niece shows great skill in birthing babies. Not that you will need to use those skills once you marry and move to Rouen."

Marry and move to Rouen? Clare's sewing needle hovered midair and she held her breath, wondering if this was another of his jokes.

"Clare," he said with a twinkle in his eyes, "if you continue sitting there without finishing your trousseau, you won't be prepared for your nuptials. I suspect you will be receiving a proposal of marriage from my son any day now."

Clare's heart began to beat faster. She felt heat stinging her cheeks and tried not to show her excitement. *So, my plans are materializing at last. Pierre is finally going to propose.* She fancied jumping up and dancing around the room with joy.

Of course she could not exhibit such unseemly behavior. Her mind raced with plans. *My darling Pierre and I will move to Rouen, find cozy lodgings, and live on my earnings while he studies law. An acquaintance with a noblewoman in Rouen like Lady Louise will be just the thing to enhance my professional reputation and success as a midwife. Then Pierre and I will be able to purchase Maison Dupres from Uncle!*

Clare smiled to herself and began stitching in earnest. She must finish the trousseau quickly.

Chapter 6

The Proposal

RELENTLESS RAIN POURED for the next seven days on end. It was so damp that the girl-of-all-work was forced to peg the wet laundry indoors on ropes strung across the kitchen. The white linen sheets reminded Clare of ghosts, causing her to shiver. She sat close to the fire in her dressing gown, shoulders wrapped in a shawl, working tirelessly on finishing her trousseau—lace-edged shifts and petticoats, kerchiefs, caps. She was edgy with impatience for Pierre's proposal.

Maman peered out the rain-streaked window and said, "Jacques is coming up the path to the cottage. He's carrying something under his cloak, probably to keep it dry." She hurried Clare into the bedchamber, telling her she must dress properly for their guest.

"Guest? It's only cousin Jacques," Clare said. "He has probably come over to sing psalms with Papa."

Maman was insistent. She pushed Clare into the room, closed the door, and laced her into stays and a clean muslin gown. Then she pinned up her loose curls under a fresh linen coif, shaking her head as Clare's auburn locks refused to stay in place in the damp weather.

"Why are you acting so strangely, Maman? What is going on?"

"Hush. A young woman should always look her best. Now turn around." Clare complied. "Yes, you look well enough," said Maman with a sigh.

Clare ambled out of the room to resume her stitchery and saw Papa sitting in the corner with Jacques. Her short, wiry cousin clutched a flat parcel wrapped in brown paper to his chest.

"Ah, here she is," grinned Papa. "Jacques has brought you a gift, my dear."

A gift? Today is not my birthday.

Maman was madly gesturing to Papa to join her in the bedchamber. He finally understood that she wanted Jacques and Clare to be left alone. Clare walked over and sat at the edge of Papa's seat. "*Bonjour*, cousin," she said with a nervous sense of dread. She was certain her parents were peeking through the cracks in the door, but all those ghostly white wet sheets obscured them from view.

Jacques cleared his throat. "I brought you a gift, Clare." He handed her the parcel and she carefully untied the cord, feeling the shape of a frame. Unfolded, the wrapper revealed a small portrait Jacques had painted of Clare sitting in a meadow, surrounded by yellow buttercups. In tiny script at the bottom, he had written, "*And cuckow-buds of yellow hue do paint the meadows with delight.*"

"Why, what a fine likeness. Thank you, Jacques." She studied the picture, puzzled by this unexpected gift, and ran her finger around the smooth wooden frame.

"The quote comes from *Love's Labour Lost.* I remember you once said it was your favorite Shakespeare play."

"Did I?"

Suddenly, Jacques reached for Clare's hand and knelt in front of her.

"Marry me, Clare. I want you for my wife."

Clare was shocked and confused. This was not the brother from whom she had joyously anticipated a proposal. Choosing her words carefully, she said, "Jacques, I am very sensible of the honor of your proposal, but I don't believe we are suited for marriage. I care for you as a cousin, but could not make you happy as your wife."

For a few minutes, Jacques was stunned by Clare's response to his proposal. He rose from his knees, dropped her hands. Then he waved away her words with his right hand. "I understand that it is usual with young ladies to reject the addresses of the man whom they secretly mean to accept, when he first applies for their favor. I am therefore by no means discouraged by what you have just said, and shall hope to lead you to the altar before long." With that, he turned and left the cottage.

Clare stood by the window and watched him rush away in the drenching rain. *That was the longest speech I have ever heard Jacques utter.*

Wherever did he come up with such pompous words? He probably copied them from a book and memorized them, as he has with psalms.

Soon her parents came out of the bedroom. Clare could tell they had heard the entire conversation. Maman looked thoughtful, but Papa—well, he was livid.

"You turned him down? How could you do such a thing? You are throwing away the chance for a good life as the wife of a wealthy merchant," he said. "Need I remind you that Jacques is to inherit the entire Dupres fortune? His father has leased a new building in Rouen to expand the business. Jacques is already planning to move there."

"But I cannot love Jacques. He is dull."

"Love? What does love have to do with it? In marriage, husband and wife are one person and that person is the husband. I know you are strong-willed, but you must learn to be modest, submissive and docile as a wife and then a certain fondness may develop."

"I love Pierre and intend to marry him."

Clare's father pounded his fist on the table. "You foolish, childish dreamer! Pierre has no money, no prospects. If the rumors I hear are true, he will not become a lawyer. He has nothing but his vain good looks and fancy talk."

She wanted to stop Papa and hear about these rumors, but he continued his diatribe. "Look around at this cottage. Do you want to live with dirt floors forever? Jacques can give you a better life than I have been able to provide my wife and child. A fine house to furnish, a carriage, money—"

"I don't care about money. If I can't marry Pierre, I will remain a spinster like Delphine," Clare said defiantly. "I will earn my own money as a midwife."

"You cannot support yourself on dreams and a few chickens. Besides, even assuming Pierre *could* study law, has he proposed marriage to you?"

"We have talked of it," Clare said defensively. *To be truthful, Pierre and I have enjoyed our secret trysts and kisses, but it is always me that brings up the idea of marriage. At such times, Pierre changes the subject.*

"As I thought," said Papa, reading her thoughts. "Pierre is no fool, Clare. He understands the reality of his life. He will never marry you."

Maman tried to placate her husband. "Clare is only nineteen. Many young women wait until their midtwenties to marry. Jacques did not accept her refusal. You heard what he said. He will ask her again in time."

"A man like Jacques will not wait forever for our pigheaded daughter to change her mind. There are as many eager young women who would jump at such a chance as there are fish leaping in the sea."

Chapter 7

Broken Dreams

Papa has been in a silent rage for weeks He barely speaks to me, except to tell me the butcher's daughter has been paying particular attention to Jacques lately, praising him on his fine singing in church. I feel badly that I have disappointed him, but why does a man always imagine a woman to be ready for anyone who asks her?

Journal of Clare Dupres, 6 mai 1674

MAMAN AWOKE ONE morning with a stomachache. When a message came that Madame Roget's second lying-in had begun, she told Clare to go by herself—she was confident her daughter was ready to birth babies without her supervision.

Clare was elated that she had finally completed her apprenticeship. But she was also relieved at the opportunity to escape Papa's glowering mood that prevailed like a dark cloud in the cottage.

"Sorry, Papa. I have to leave now," she said as she grabbed her birthing bag and rushed out the door. He just gazed at her without a word.

Clare ran into Pierre on her way to the Roget farm. He was headed toward the post to see if his college acceptance letter had arrived. She desperately needed to speak with him in private and asked him to accompany her on Saturday to the woods, to pick wild mushrooms. He agreed to meet her at their secret beech tree —the one where he had carved their initials inside a heart with his knife.

~~~
~~~

When Clare arrived at the Roget farm, the gossips were already in the confinement chamber chattering away. She listened as she set out her birthing tools.

"Got a letter from my man, off fightin' in the war with the Dutch."

"The war is costly—I hear construction has stopped at Versailles."

"Bread is very dear these days." They all nodded in agreement—times were hard, especially for the poor. Madame Roget was puffing, her face red from her travail.

Clare recognized the little Roget daughter, running around in her short petticoats. Hard to believe she was almost four years old. Seeing her evoked memories of the first birthing Clare had attended with Maman, bringing that little girl into the world and watching the strange miracle of the magic elixir at work.

Confident now in her ability to handle any birthing situation, she administered the elixir, and five hours later, a healthy boy was born. Farmer Roget was delighted to have a son—all fathers want boys—and he rewarded Clare with a skinned rabbit and a goose.

She would give the hare to Delphine, to make *ragoût de lapin.* As for the goose, Clare held it by the neck and wondered if it would lay a golden egg—like the fairy tale Delphine used to tell her. She had not been to Uncle's house since Jacques's proposal. The situation was awkward.

When will I begin to attract patients who can afford to reward me properly? I have become especially impatient for this to become a reality, now that I am under pressure from Papa to accept Jacques's proposal.

Maman had not pressured Clare. She told her daughter to establish herself as the trusted local sage femme so she could retire. Still, Clare knew she worried about her fertility. From time to time she reminded Clare of her obligation to bear a daughter.

~~~

On Saturday, Pierre met Clare at the beech tree and they sneaked deeper into the woods, careful as always not to be seen alone together. He sat on a stump and whittled a twig, as Clare gathered mushrooms, carefully avoiding the poisonous species. Pierre seemed distracted. Wood shavings flew in all directions.

"Pierre," she blurted out. "Do you love me?" He put down his work, scooped her off the ground and planted kisses on her neck.
~~~

"You silly goose. Of course I love you."

"Then let's elope."

Pierre put her down and looked into her eyes. Placed his hands on her shoulders and held her at arm's length. She waited for his answer. A wind whistled through the branches and a slight drizzle began to filter through the leaves.

Finally he said, "My darling Clare. You are a beautiful, talented young lady, but we cannot marry for a simple reason—you have no money and neither do I."

"But you *shall* have money when you become a lawyer. And during your studies, I will support us with my midwifery earnings."

She knelt next to his tree trunk seat. He was looking at his feet, holding his hands on the sides of his head. Her fun-loving cousin appeared so serious.

"You must understand," he said, "I would never allow a wife of mine to work outside the home."

"But why not? I could still care for your needs, bear you children. We could have it all. With our combined earnings, our life together would be blissfully comfortable."

Before Clare could say another word, Pierre placed his hand over her mouth. "Listen to me, Clare. I cannot read for the law. I received a rejection letter from the college in Rouen."

"Rejection letter? I don't understand. I thought they were impressed with your knowledge of classical languages and mathematics."

His voice turned angry. He lifted his knife and stabbed it into the ground. "It's not my lack of qualifications. Things have changed," he said bitterly. "King Louis has issued a new edict prohibiting Huguenots from the study of law."

Clare felt dizzy. "What? That cannot be true. Why would he do such a thing?"

"Because he can. He calls himself the Sun King. Believes all Frenchmen should be Catholic. Don't you see? It's another restriction intended to pressure Huguenots to convert. My father would completely disown me if I became a Papist."

"Oh, Pierre," she said in despair. "What is to become of you?" *And of my carefully planned life?*

"My brother offered me a position in the family business as a shipping clerk. Oh, he would love bossing me around, lording it over me," After a moment, he added, "Of course I turned him down."

She understood. Pierre was too proud to accept a subordinate position to his brother. He gave her a halfhearted shrug. "I have no choice, Clare. I must leave France to seek my fortune."

Suddenly Clare sensed the world she knew breaking like a glass bottle dropped on a brick floor, shattering into a million shards. She clutched her throat, stifling a wail. "Noooo," she moaned, trying to think of an alternative, anything that would not pull them apart.

For once, though, she was completely at a loss for ideas—Clare Dupres, mistress of planning the perfect life, was dumbfounded. She held tightly to Pierre's hands as if she could keep him in the woods with her forever. They sat quietly, listening to the raindrops splatter on the wild grass.

Pierre finally broke the silence. "Remember Cap'n Silas? The man on the beach? He came to the shop last week to see Jacques. I happened by to say hello, as they were deep in conversation."

"And?"

"To my surprise, he offered me a job on his ship. I was flabbergasted, thought about it for a day, and then decided life on the high seas would be better than a lowly position under the thumb of my brother. You know, as a boy I always dreamed of being a sailor, voyaging to exotic ports."

"But you've never been at sea, other than on a fishing skiff."

"I've studied navigation from books and learned about sailing ships from talking to sailors in port."

"I can't bear it. Take me with you," Clare pleaded, tears running down her cheeks.

Pierre kissed her fingers and pulled away. "*C'est impossible.* I know my brother has proposed to you. Marry Jacques. He will treat you well."

"I don't love Jacques. I only care for you," she sobbed.

He removed the kerchief from his neck and gently wiped her eyes. "We are victims of circumstances beyond our control. There is nothing to be done. Once you are married to Jacques, we will become sister and brother. I shall always have fond memories of our times together. Wish me luck, Clare."

Suddenly she was alarmed. "Are you leaving soon?"

"In two days' time… when the ship leaves. Delphine is packing my trunk as we speak."

"But hasn't King Louis forbidden his subjects to leave France without written permission from the authorities? Threatened to confiscate their goods if caught?"

Pierre let out a bitter laugh. "Ha. What goods have I? Nothing but a small interest in our family house. I'll just slip away. I'm a nobody in France—no inheritance, no money."

Clare knew he was right, but that did not lessen her pain or her acute sense of loss. All she could think of was how she hated King Louis for ruining her happiness. Little did Clare know at that moment that worse was yet to come.

"Shall I come to the pier to see you off?"

"No," said Pierre. "Climb the cliff to the deserted Dieppe castle Monday morning and wave goodbye to me from there. I wish to remember you standing in our favorite spot, with your hair blowing in the wind. I shall blow a farewell kiss to you from the deck of the *Celia*."

~~~

The next morning in church, Papa preached a special blessing for the sailors who would soon be departing from Dieppe, invoking the power of God to keep them safe. He prayed for calm waters. Clare sat stone-faced, remaining silent during singing of the psalms, although she could hear Jacques's loud, clear voice rising above the others. He turned and smiled at her. She felt uneasy and deliberately lowered her eyes, avoiding his gaze. Had Jacques done something to cause this calamity?

Clare saw Delphine standing outside the church, talking to friends. "Clare, we are having a few people over to say goodbye to Pierre this afternoon. Please join our fête."

But Clare said she felt unwell and apologized. She did not feel like celebrating. As she left the churchyard, she noticed the butcher's daughter flirting with Jacques.
~~~

Chapter 8
Betrothal

I have neglected my journal this past six-month because word of the magic elixir has spread among the local elite—I have been busy as a bee with birthings, finally receiving valuable rewards for my services. I keep the coins in a pouch, hidden behind the loose brick. Soon, I will need a larger pouch. Maman still disapproves of my "unchristian attitude." One thing is certain—we don't go hungry with all her chickens scratching in the yard! An abundance of eggs means omelettes on Sundays, instead of porridge for breakfast.

Journal of Clare Dupres, 2 octobre 1674

FOR WEEKS AFTER Pierre left, when she wasn't at work, Clare would climb the cliff, looking out to sea for his return. Although she knew he intended to seek his fortune at sea, she harbored the hope that he would become homesick. Miss her. Find a way to come back. She was aware that Jacques watched her from the shop window, but she did not care.

Jacques patiently allowed Clare time to come to grips with the fact that Pierre would not return. Gradually, he began visiting the cottage again, bringing her small gifts. An orange. A bit of chocolate. A bright ribbon for her hair.

He invited her to attend the harvest fair with him, and for the first time in months she smiled at him. Together, they devoured sticky candied apples and danced to the lively country music. Although Jacques declined to participate in the greased pig contest, he did swing a large hammer so hard that it rang the gong—his strength surprised her. A week later, Jacques gently began prodding Clare to accept his marriage proposal.

He was now in the process of setting up the new shop in Rouen, which kept him away from Dieppe for a few days at a time. When he returned, he would describe the thriving city atmosphere or show her sketches of people hurrying about. Clare knew that once the shop was completed, Jacques would be moving there. *If* she married him, she would have to give up her thriving midwifery practice in Dieppe. But Clare had still not made up her mind to accept his proposal. Despite his gentle attentions to her, he never said he loved her. And part of her still lamented the loss of Pierre.

In mid-November, Jacques said there was a delay in finishing the interior of the store—the counters he had ordered would not be available until January. He began taking Clare on long walks in the snowy woods. She averted her eyes from the beech tree with the carved heart. Once again, Jacques asked her for an answer and she finally promised to give him her decision on Christmas.

A week before Christmas, as Clare walked home from shopping, she noticed the *Celia* in port. She ran breathlessly to the pier, but Pierre wasn't aboard. Cap'n Silas greeted her cordially as he headed toward Uncle's shop, bearing packages and letters. It wasn't Clare's business to ask, but she hoped he was not the bearer of bad news—perhaps Pierre had drowned at sea. She felt drained and went home to the cottage filled with dread.

This will be our first family Christmas without Pierre—so very sad. Surely Cap'n Silas has brought news of him. I expect the letters will be read aloud at Delphine's holiday dinner.

~~~

"Joyeux Noël," declared Delphine. She kissed their cheeks, all frosty from snow. "Come warm up by the fire. Something to drink? Before we sit down for dinner, I have news to share." Clare shivered, but not because she was cold.

They handed their wraps to the servant and admired the greenery decorating the parlor. There was even a sprig of mistletoe hanging in the doorway. Ever the frank midwife, Maman pointed to it and told Delphine to save some–mistletoe was helpful for menstrual cramps.
~~~

Looking out the window, Clare noticed the *Celia* was gone from the port. *What did I expect—of course, Cap'n Silas must have returned to London for the holidays.*

Delphine was wearing a new, delicately carved ivory brooch, which she said was an unexpected gift that Cap'n Silas had carried back from Africa. It was greatly admired by all, unlike anything Clare had ever seen. But she was more interested in the news he had brought.

Poor Pierre had failed miserably as a sailor—suffered severe *mal de mer*. He'd spent his days and nights in his hammock, green about the gills. When the ship had returned to England, Pierre had sworn he would never step foot off land again.

"Ah well," said Papa philosophically, "none of us expect to be in smooth waters all of our days."

"What has he been doing in England all these months?" asked Maman.

"Luckily," said Delphine, "Cap'n Silas persuaded the Smithfield-Barton partners to give Pierre a desk job in London, keeping records of account. Apparently they are pleased to have a worker who speaks fluent French and English at their dockside office."

Delphine read Pierre's letters aloud. They were mostly about London and his exciting new acquaintances, parties he attended. Clare's face dropped, hurt that he had not mentioned her name once. She looked over at Jacques, who appeared uncomfortable with the discussion about Pierre. He was shifting in his chair, looking at Clare, then looking away.

"What do you think of that?" said Maman. "Pierre working as a shipping clerk for the owners of that boat with a lady's name. *Clarissa*? *Cornelia*? I never understand why they use female names for their vessels. It's not as if women work on them."

"It's called the *Celia*," said Jacques quietly. "Named for Celia Smithfield, sister of the owner, Samuel Smithfield."

"Ha! So much for Pierre's disdain of clerking positions," said Uncle. "He turned down Jacques's generous offer and now he is doing the same job in a foreign country. Spending Christmas alone. That boy of mine never had much sense."

"He's not spending Christmas alone," said Jacques, looking at Clare for a reaction. But she was still trying to absorb the fact that Pierre would never return to Normandy. How could he, if he would never set foot on another ship? It didn't dawn on her yet that Jacques seemed to have a great deal of information about his brother's situation that he wasn't eager to share.

"Dinner's ready," announced Delphine.

~~~

It is such a happiness when good people get together—and they always do. After stuffing themselves with roast goose, boiled potatoes, and a multitude of sweets for dessert, the guests split up. Papa and Uncle went into the study. Clare began to sip tea with Maman and Delphine when Jacques came up behind her and pulled her out of her chair. "Come with me," he said, gently but firmly.

He guided her toward the empty parlor. As they passed under the mistletoe, he pulled her to his chest and kissed her softly on her lips. "You promised me an answer, Clare." He ran his fingers through her long hair. She didn't resist, still feeling warmth from the dinner wine. "You are the loveliest flower in all France. I know you will be a wonderful mother to my children." He kissed her again, this time more urgently. A faint shiver of desire ran down her spine.

Perhaps Jacques does care for me a little, although he never says he loves me. Why are those words so important to me? I try not to compare his gentle kisses to Pierre's hot-blooded kisses. Pierre is lost to me. I realize now that there are few options for a young woman with no dowry. Maybe marrying Jacques won't be so bad. But after what Pierre said about never allowing a wife of his to work outside the home… I have to ask…

"You know being a midwife is important to me, Jacques. I don't want to give up my career. You won't stop me, will you?"

"Can you really do that and be a proper wife and mother too?" Doubt crept into his voice, onto his expression.

"I *know* that I can. Promise me, Jacques."

He just stood silently and stared up at the mistletoe. Clare heard his heavy breathing, felt his lust for her as he pressed his body against her. She construed his silence as acquiescence.

"Very well, Jacques. I will marry you."

"Do you mean that? Oh, I am the luckiest man in all of France. Let's make the announcement now." With that, he left her to fetch the rest of the family. Clare heard them hooting with delight as they came rushing toward her with congratulations. She hoped she wouldn't live to regret her decision.
~~~

Chapter 9

Excursion to Rouen

My parents are absolutely thrilled about my betrothal. Jacques was disappointed that we couldn't marry right after the first of the year. I told him to be patient—it's the bride's prerogative to set her wedding date. Besides, I had already promised three of my most prominent patients to assist at their confinements in March.

I did not let these anxious ladies down, especially the Baroness M__, who gave birth to small but healthy twin boys last week. Oh, how my rewards pouch has expanded! But now that my midwifery practice has quieted a bit, I can no longer delay. It is time to plan my wedding. Difficult to believe it's been almost a year since Jacques first proposed.

Journal of Clare Dupres, 5 avril 1675

DELPHINE HAD BEEN helping Clare finish her trousseau, as the busy young midwife never seemed to have much time to sew. When Clare dropped by for tea one day, Delphine was busy tatting lace edging for the silk pillowcases. Clare was surprised to see Jacques sitting nearby at the escritoire writing a letter. *He must have returned from Rouen yesterday.*

When he heard Clare enter the parlor, he hastily folded the paper and slipped it under a pile of ledgers. At first she was perplexed…it was almost as if he were hiding something from her. Clare reminded herself not to let her imagination run away—it was probably a business letter to his new store manager.

"Well, here is our Clare. Come in, dearie," said Delphine. "I was just asking Jacques to take me to Rouen to see the new shop. But wait…I have an idea! Brother, why don't we invite Clare to join us for a few days?"

Jacques beamed at the suggestion and offered to hire an open carriage for the journey so they could enjoy the fine spring weather. "I am anxious for you both to see it, especially you, Clare. Although the upstairs rooms are still under construction, the business is up and running. I'll book two rooms at a nearby inn—you girls can go shopping while I attend to some business."

"Oh, please say you will come with us, Clare?" begged Delphine. "You deserve a break from your hard work. I hardly see you anymore."

"Let me talk to Maman," said Clare.

~~~

At first, Clare was reluctant to leave Dieppe. Papa had been unwell. He seemed so frail as his age advanced. Yet, he continued to carry out his ministerial duties, including a funeral the previous week during a particularly nasty rainstorm.

"Go," urged Maman. "It is nothing but a trifling spring head cold. I'll stay here with him."

Clare *was* curious to see her future marital abode, even if it was to be rooms above a store. But what she truly longed to see was the crumbling gothic estate she had always shown such curiosity about. Returning with her answer the next day, she asked Jacques whether they could spend a few hours visiting Maison Dupres.

"Why are you so interested in that rickety old place?" he said.

"I think old haunted houses are romantic. Please, Jacques. May we go see it?"

"I suppose so, if it pleases you. Your happiness means the world to me." He came to her chair, leaned over and whispered words in her ear. The hairs on Clare's skin stood on end and she blushed like a scarlet poppy. *Soon, very soon, I will announce the wedding date.*

~~~

The small party left Dieppe early Friday morning to assure arrival before dark. Clare prickled with excitement as she waved goodbye to Maman.

Stopping for a noon meal at a coaching inn provided a chance to stretch their legs, freshen up, and obtain fresh horses. During the afternoon, Delphine chattered nonstop. Unbothered by the bumpy road, Clare silently admired the interesting landscape as they drove through unfamiliar villages and orchards.

The scent of apple blossoms was heady. Occasionally their carriage came to a standstill as farmers drove herds of sheep across the road. The verdure of Normandy, seen under a sun that was bright without being oppressive, filled her heart with promise. Feeling Jacques's dark silent eyes on her, she smiled sweetly at her soon-to-be husband.

He pointed down a side avenue toward an old convent. Said it was home to the Sisters of Sorrow. Her eyes fell on a cassocked priest clambering along the dirt road on a tired mule. *Why does Jacques think I would be interested in a cloistered cluster of buildings inhabited by Papist nuns?* Clare shrugged, more interested in seeing beautiful homes set back from the road. Residences of the elite. Yet—an unexpected frisson chilled her. Something about the sight of that priest unnerved her.

Shaking off her momentary disquiet, she inquired whether they would be passing Maison Dupres. "No," Jacques said, "it is on the other side of Rouen, along the south road toward Paris."

When they reached the northern outskirts of Rouen, he pointed to an arched gate fronting an enormous chateau. The sight took her breath away. "*Quel beau château,*" she exclaimed. "Does it resemble Maison Dupres?"

Jacques laughed. "Hardly. This is Chateau Montjardin, home of the Marquis."

"The name Montjardin sounds vaguely familiar. Where have I heard it?" murmured Clare.

"Lady Louise, wife of the Marquis de Montjardin, is a customer of my shop," said Jacques. "Just last month she came by to inspect my new shipment of floral silk."

"Really," said Delphine. "I'm impressed, brother, that you are already attracting upper-class clientele in Rouen."

"The Marquise is redecorating the nursery in the chateau. Her young daughter, a girl of about three, and a nursemaid accompanied her. The child insisted she wanted pink silk with roses. When her mother told her she was not old enough for silk bedhangings, she began crying and stamping her feet. The embarrassed nursemaid swooped her up and rushed her out to the carriage."

"Reminds me of you, Clare, when you were that age," said Delphine. "You cried when you couldn't have your way. I suppose we all spoiled you. But you were utterly charming even during your tantrums." Jacques nodded in agreement.

"Wait. I remember the name now," Clare exclaimed. "A few years ago, Uncle Dupres helped the Marquis when his carriage wheel fell off. His wife gave Uncle her calling card. I still have it tucked in my journal."

"Why did you keep it?" asked Delphine.

"Uncle apparently told Lady Louise about me. She said she looked forward to meeting me one day. Can we stop by the chateau for a visit?"

Jacques looked horrified at her suggestion. "One simply does not 'stop by' the home of aristocrats without a prior invitation. We may be wealthy and genteel, but remember, we are below their station in society."

Clare gazed wistfully at the rolling lawns, the small lake, and the portico fronting the great doors. A premonition crept over her—someday she would be welcomed into this grand castle. Clare sat back and savored the fresh country breezes and warm sun. She was glad she had decided to come on this weekend jaunt with Delphine and Jacques.

Reaching their destination at dusk, Delphine and Clare were mesmerized by the views in Rouen—so different from Dieppe. The arching clock tower hanging across the cobblestone street. The massive *cathédrale de Rouen* reaching toward heaven. Carriages and waggons everywhere, and people hurrying on foot. The stench of ordure assaulted their noses. They agreed to meet beneath the clock tower on Rue du Gros-Horloge the following day for breakfast, and then visit Jacques's shop. That night at the inn, Clare shared a bed with Delphine while Jacques slept in a room one floor below. Tucked under the blankets, Clare's mind turned to Pierre. *But for King Louis, he would have been studying law in this bustling metropolis.* Clare casually asked Delphine if she had received any recent letters from Pierre.

"No, he is a wicked correspondent. I write to him every week, giving him the news from Dieppe, but I get no letters in return. It is most vexing."

"Then he knows Jacques and I are betrothed?"

"Yes, I suppose he does. I'm certain I wrote about it in my letters. Have you set a date for the wedding? Jacques is becoming impatient."

"Not yet. But shortly, I think."

Clare tossed and turned on the lumpy bed, trying to get comfortable. *How strange to think that soon I will be sharing a bed with Jacques.* Once again, she thought about Pierre, tried to imagine what he thought upon hearing the news of her engagement. Did it sadden him in the least?

"Delphine, I am puzzled to this day why Cap'n Silas was so quick to hire an inexperienced French landlubber as crewmember on the *Celia.* And then to arrange Pierre's promotion to an office clerk position in London after he…um… failed as a sailor. It doesn't make sense."

"Go to sleep, Clare. This is not the time to be thinking about Pierre."

"You are holding something back, Delphine. It's fine to tell me. I'm over Pierre, and engaged to marry Jacques. I'm only curious."

Delphine hesitated for a few moments. "I don't know for certain, but I suspect Jacques paid Cap'n Silas to hire Pierre and take him away from France. When I confronted him about it, Jacques told me Cap'n Silas was simply grateful for that portrait and hired Pierre as a personal favor. I'm not sure I believe that."

Although the candle sputtered, Clare could still see the troubled expression on Delphine's face as she continued. "Jacques has been jealous of Pierre since they were boys. He envied his younger brother sneaking off with you, leaving him behind."

Clare jolted upright in bed, "So Jacques bribed Cap'n Silas in order to break off my attachment to Pierre? How could he do such a thing!"

"Don't blame Jacques, Clare. He is a caring man. When Pierre got the rejection letter from the college, Jacques tried to find a way to help him. He remembered Pierre's dreams of travel, his friendly relationships with the English sailors."

"Still, he could have helped Pierre financially so he wouldn't have had to leave France. Shared his wealth."

"That's not the way things happen, Clare. You know as well as I, the eldest son gets all. Pierre was destitute, except for a part interest in our home. Jacques bought him out, paid him far more than his share was worth. He did not want Pierre to go into the world without some coins in his pocket. Jacques is not heartless—he just wanted you for himself."

"Jacques doesn't love me. He has never said he does. I am just a possession he stole from his brother." Clare felt bile rising in her throat.

"The word *love* is not in Jacques's vocabulary, Clare. He is different from Pierre. Timid. Shy with women. But I know he cares for you. I see it in his eyes when he looks at you—in his many sketches of your face."

However, Clare felt angry and hurt. Betrayed. Sold to the highest bidder like hogs in the market. She made up her mind. *When we return to Dieppe, I will break off the engagement. Although I am stranded here for the next few days, I am determined not to marry treacherous Jacques. What he has done is unforgivable.*

Clare did not confide her decision to Delphine, but her inner agitation was obviously apparent from the expression on her face.

Delphine became alarmed. "Clare! It was foolish of me to share my silly assumption with you. I have no proof that Jacques paid Cap'n Silas, and…well, I'm sorry I said anything. Please, forget the whole matter and promise you won't tell Jacques."

"Fine," said Clare tersely. Delphine drifted off to sleep, but Clare got very little rest that night.

Chapter 10

The Shop

THE NEXT MORNING Clare's stomach felt uneasy when they approached the shop. Prominently hanging above the glass window was the familiar sign: "Dupres & Sons, Purveyors of Fine Fabrics." The sight of the flower-bedecked wording irritated her.

"Good morning, Clare. I trust you slept well," said Jacques.

"Why is the word *sons* still part of your business name?" she demanded.

Jacques stared at her expression—obviously her attitude had changed overnight. She was sullen and unresponsive to his anticipation of showing off his business premises. Delphine shrugged.

"Are you unwell, Clare?" he asked with concern. "Yesterday you seemed somewhat more cheerful."

"I am perfectly fine. Let's go inside." Clare brushed past him into the shop.

Jacques introduced them to his store manager, Monsieur Leclerc, who bowed and followed instructions to give the two ladies the full tour, as Jacques retreated to the back. The efficient manager pointed out the utilitarian oak shelves lined with bolts of gray muslin and serge, bins filled with pins and needles, boxes of buttons. A wooden counter sat in the center of the room, large enough for unfolding bolts of cloth and with a scissors hanging from a cord. A few customers in plain dress were milling about, looking for inexpensive goods.

Somehow, Clare could not imagine the aristocratic Lady Louise shopping here. The only flower in sight was on the sign. *So dull, so wretchedly dull! Just another plain dusty shop, tedious like its owner*, she thought with disdain.

Monsieur Leclerc stopped for a few minutes to help a customer. When he finished, he apologized for the interruption. "Follow me, please. Monsieur Dupres has something he is anxious to show you himself." He led the way through a wide doorway, separating the store from the back room with heavy brown velvet drapes. *Probably a dusty storeroom back there.*

What a surprise greeted them! Delphine gasped. Jacques was standing there, waiting to see their reaction. It was like stepping into another world—a fairy tale land. Flowered silk covered the walls. A large Turkish carpet was centered on the polished oak floor. The room was elegantly furnished with low tea tables surrounded by cushioned chairs. The scent of lavender permeated the air, masking the odors which crept in from the street. Candles gleamed in crystal chandeliers.

This, the manager explained proudly, was Monsieur Dupres's own original idea. A private boutique reserved for customers of "the quality," who could afford the very finest. In this room, elegant women sipped complimentary champagne as they viewed the private collection consisting of the most exclusive silks, satins and velvets. Here was a mercantile salon that catered to aristocrats and wealthy gentry, by appointment only.

Clare was speechless. This innovative store serving customers of all means, with its demarcation of class status, would mark Jacques Dupres as a highly original merchant and would in time undoubtedly increase his wealth.

Suddenly she was anxious to see the upstairs rooms. They were still under renovation, but she insisted. They climbed the stairs and before them stood a blank canvas, filled with busy carpenters. Jacques put his arm possessively around his fiancée's shoulder, led her around piles of sawdust from one empty room to another: parlor, kitchen, bedchamber. On the top floor, a large undivided space designated by Jacques as future nursery. All rather dark spaces, Clare noted, shaded from the sun by the buildings crowded across the narrow street.

"I trust," said Jacques with a most satisfied smile, "that it will very speedily be furnished; it waits only for a lady's taste. It is your prerogative, Clare, to decorate these rooms to your liking. Choose wall colors, furniture, window coverings, mantel ornaments. Spare no expense."

The rooms were tiny boxes. The apartment lacked an outdoor garden. Casement windows opened to the street below, with distasteful noises and odors invading the space. Certainly no refreshing sea breezes here.

Is this confined space to be my home? Clare walked over to the window and looked down. The store sign obscured her vision, and once again that sense of irritation pervaded her head. *Dupres & Sons. Jacques already plans to fill that empty nursery upstairs with sons, courtesy of my body.*

But then her mind returned to the elegant salon below. Was that not the very place to meet the women with whom she wished to become acquainted? The wives (and mistresses) of the aristocrats, her future midwifery patients who shopped here? She could almost imagine herself sitting in the salon, sipping champagne with Lady Louise and her *enceinte* friends.

A tempting vision, but I am resolved to cancel my betrothal when we return to Dieppe. I am still riffled by Jacques's deceit. To think, I am stranded here for several more days before we can leave. How will I manage?

"Jacques, I need a few moments alone. Please. I'll be down shortly."

Jacques looked confused. He had thought Clare would be bubbling with enthusiasm over the new lodgings. "Take your time," he said, removing his arm from her stiffened body.

He found his sister talking to the carpenters. "Delphine, I believe Clare is overwhelmed. I think it would be best if you took her back to the inn. Instead of dining with us this evening, we can arrange for a tray to be sent to her room."

Delphine agreed; Clare was obviously just tired.

The next day, they attended church in Rouen. Clare remained cool but polite. But when Jacques announced that on Monday he would drive them out to see Maison Dupres, anticipation of the excursion lightened her mood. She politely thanked Jacques for showing her around Rouen and allowed him to kiss her on the cheek. She would make the best of a bad situation and try to enjoy the rest of this little holiday with as much courtesy and good temper as she could muster.

Chapter 11

Maison Dupres

EARLY MONDAY MORNING, the promised journey to the deserted mansion commenced. As they drove along, Clare watched for the first appearance of Maison Dupres with some perturbation, and when at length they turned into the courtyard, her spirits were in a high flutter. Her mind was too full for conversation, but she saw and admired every remarkable spot and point of view. It was a large, handsome, albeit neglected stone building, standing well on rising ground and backed by a ridge of high woody hills beyond the river. She was delighted.

Jacques produced a rusty key, which gave them entry to the front hall. Delphine looked around at the gloomy room and ran her finger along the window ledge, managing to raise a cloud of dust.

"Not very promising, is it?" she coughed. "The house is situated too close to the road."

Clare was not put off by the dust or proximity to the road, which had likely been a narrow horse path when this mansion was built. "Look, Delphine. The floors are made of marble, in a handsome black-and-white pattern. With proper cleaning and polishing, the original luster will return. And just look at the splendid carved balusters on the winding staircase." Despite the neglect of years, the rooms were lofty and she could see promise of great elegance if they were restored to their former grandeur.

Jacques trailed behind silently as they passed the study and entered the dining salon—a well-proportioned room, handsomely fitted out with wooden shutters. Folding back the shutters and rubbing a clear spot on the dirty casements with her kerchief, Clare gazed with delight at the whole scene, the river, the budding trees scattered on its banks. From every window there were similar beauties to be seen.

When they entered the kitchen, a smatter of mice scurried out of the larder. Delphine stifled a scream, but Clare saw only potential—bright copper pots hanging above the hearth, a scrubbed oak worktable, plus a few other improvements and it would become quite serviceable.

They ascended the grand staircase to the next level, where a large bedchamber with a marble hearth bore tall windows overlooking the front courtyard. From a smaller adjoining chamber, presumably the lady's boudoir, they viewed a *parterre* garden choked with weeds and a few mossy Greek statues. Clare's heart gladdened, visions of lavender spilling over the stone borders.

On the top floor was a moderate-sized nursery under the eaves. Surprisingly, there was only one other room, next to the nursery—a bleak windowless room containing a narrow rusty bedstead. She presumed it was sleeping quarters for the nursery maid. *I wonder why there is no window?*

Returning down the servants' narrow stairs, avoiding a few broken risers, they discovered an oak-paneled room across from the master bedchamber. Sunshine poured in through the casements. "Perhaps you inherited your artistic talent from your great-aunt. This looks like it might have been an art studio," Clare told Jacques. A few steps further down the hall, they inspected two small guest bedchambers with creaking floorboards and torn faded drapes.

"No wonder my ancestors abandoned this house and the adjoining lands," said Jacques. "Seen enough yet?"

"Adjoining lands?" Clare asked, perplexed because the gardens as seen from the windows had not appeared extensive.

"Did you not notice the sheep we passed along the road? They are raised by our tenant farmers. My family owns the land and they pay my father quarterly rents."

She pondered this information as they exited through the kitchen door. *I have underestimated the fortune Jacques is to inherit. Why, he is to be a member of the landed gentry, as well as a wealthy Rouen merchant.*

Clare caught up to Delphine, who was inspecting the outbuildings: dairy, laundry, barn, storerooms, and large stable. On the floor above the stable, they looked into a few low-ceilinged rooms.

"These must have been the servant quarters," remarked Delphine, covering her nose with her kerchief. "That broom standing in the corner is covered with mould. Let's join Jacques in the garden."

Jacques stood at the edge of the overgrown garden, his head tipped to one side. It looked to Clare as if he were trying to picture the raised beds of Maison Dupres long ago, filled with colorful flowers. Weeds covered remnants of stone rubble. *Didn't Uncle once say part of the house had burned down years ago? If I lived here, I could clear away the weeds and build a heated conservatory on that spot. Cultivate herbs year-round. And I suppose flowers too.*

Clare examined the back wall of the maison from the bottom floor to the roof. Mismatched bricks filled a space on the top floor, behind a balcony. Probably once a window.

"Delphine," she said, "do you remember that old ballad you used to sing to us when we were little? About the maiden who jumped out the window? *Be wary, take car-ee*—the ballad that frightened Jacques."

"Why do you ask?"

"Oh… no reason."

When the time arrived to return to Rue du Gros-Horloge, they climbed into the carriage. Turning out through the iron gates, Clare took one last lingering look over her shoulder at Maison Dupres receding from sight. *Of this place*, she thought, *I might have been mistress. Instead of viewing the rooms as a stranger, I might have rejoiced in them as my own.* Clare began to feel something like regret, but stubbornly reminded herself not to back down from her resolve to break off her engagement.

~~~

Tuesday morning brought the gloom of rain. Nonetheless, Delphine was determined to purchase one of those fashionable flat straw bonnets to decorate with silk flowers, feathers and bows. After their successful expedition to the milliner, they decided to save their visit to the bootmaker's shop for the next day. Instead, they stopped for tea. Delphine chattered away but Clare barely listened. She was still ruminating about Maison Dupres. *Was that where the maiden in the ballad lived?*
~~~

Returning to Jacques's shop, Delphine asked the clerk to show her some buttons. He pulled out a case. Clare was fascinated by a selection of unusually thick ones, with cloisonné covers—"smuggler buttons," so named because they opened to reveal spaces where one could hide gemstones. "A novelty item. Smugglers don't shop at Dupres & Sons," the clerk assured her.

Delphine was more interested in flat wooden buttons. Clare wandered over to the window, wondering when the rain would end. "Mademoiselle Dupres," said the manager, coming out from the salon with a large package wrapped in brown paper. At first, Clare thought he was talking to Delphine, but he walked toward her. "Monsieur Jacques asked me to give this to you with his compliments."

She dreaded opening it—could feel the slipperiness of satin inside and knew it was fabric for her wedding gown. She wished they could cut this journey short so she could tell Jacques the betrothal was off. She wanted to tell him as soon as possible, but knew the trip together to Dieppe would be extremely uncomfortable. *Act calm, like you do when your patients are having difficult travails*, she told herself. *In two days you'll be home and it will all be over.* Clare smiled and thanked the manager for the parcel.

As the clock tower chimed five times and the store was about to close, a messenger rushed up to the door with an urgent missive for Jacques. It was from Uncle Dupres, urging immediate return to Dieppe. Papa's health had taken a turn for the worse.

Chapter 12

Vows and Promises

CLARE WAS FRANTIC to return home at once, but Jacques insisted it was unsafe to journey at night. Heavy clouds obscured the crescent moon, and highwaymen lurked in the wooded areas waiting to rob travelers. She fretted all night. Delphine tried to reassure her, but Clare blamed herself for coming on this trip when she knew Papa was unwell.

They departed Rouen early the next morning, this time in a closed carriage. The rain beat down on the roof in time to the rapid beats of her heart. The ride home seemed interminably long.

Clare folded her hands, trying to pray. Jacques sat across from her, reading psalms aloud from the open Bible in his lap. Although she knew he had memorized them, he seemed to derive comfort from seeing the words in print. Occasionally he gave her a sympathetic glance or patted her knee, which she found oddly comforting. Delphine was unusually quiet.

~~~

Maman sat next to the bed with a bowl of cool water sponging Papa's brow. She looked exhausted. Delphine lifted the basin from her hands, taking over. Papa was sleeping—a raspy, breathy sleep.

Clare and Maman moved into the kitchen and sat down at the kitchen table. Clare poured some tea for Maman.

"The neighbors have been so kind, bringing me food and offering sympathy. Yesterday afternoon, a group of parishioners from our
~~~

church stood outside the cottage in the rain for an hour, chanting prayers for their beloved minister."

"Maman, you need to rest—"

"It's his lungs, I heard them rattle two days ago. He was too ill to attend church. He's never missed a Sunday in his life."

"Did you send for a physician?" Clare asked, immediately regretting her foolish words.

"Whatever for?" Maman stared at her daughter in disbelief. "So they can bleed him? Cover him with leeches? Don't you know by now, Clare, after all I've taught you, that physicians cause more harm than good?"

"Of course, Maman. I'm sorry. Your herbal potions are the best possible remedy. Papa will soon rally."

Maman shook her head and stared down at the tea leaves like a fortune-teller. "He is old and tired, barely hanging on to life. Do you know what Papa said yesterday? It was not death he feared—but the prospect he wouldn't live long enough to see you marry Jacques. Oh Clare dear, he will have no peace until you do."

Clare sipped her tea and pondered her decision to break off the engagement. What would become of them if Papa died? He had no pension and little in savings. Their cottage belonged to the church—they couldn't stay there.

Delphine came out of the bedroom. "Clare," she said, "he is awake and asks to speak with you… alone."

Then she added, "He is very weak."

~~~

It all happened so fast. Like a whirlwind, they furiously planned the wedding for the first Monday in May. Jacques rushed back to Rouen to make sure the lodgings above the shop would be ready in time for their return. He agreed to paint the walls yellow, to brighten the rooms. With Maman's consent, he took the portrait of Clare in the meadow among "cuckow-buds of yellow hue" for their marital bower.

Before leaving, he had asked Clare what she wanted for her bride gift. A band of gold set with sapphires? A pearl necklace? He would give her anything her heart desired.

"There is only one gift my heart desires, which will make me truly content. A promise that we will renovate Maison Dupres as our future home."
~~~

This took him by surprise. He paused for a moment in his thoughtful, quiet manner. Finally, he said, "Very well, my dearest. I want above all things to make you happy. You shall have the maison."

Despite her misgivings about Jacques's treachery with Cap'n Silas, Clare felt that he had a generous heart and a kind, caring disposition. He would be an understanding husband. He kissed her and told her not to worry—he would be back to Dieppe in plenty of time for the ceremony. Clare had no doubt that he would.

Delphine and Clare hurriedly stitched the flowing satin wedding gown. Jacques had chosen the color of the fabric to match her blue-gray eyes. Delphine said it looked too plain for a bride, so she added fashionable gold ribbon bows to the sleeves and the billowy skirt.

The night before the wedding, Maman kissed Clare and wished her happiness. She had decided if Papa did not survive, she would move in with Uncle and Delphine. At least until Clare was ready for services as her midwife.

Clare said she hoped it would not be for a few years. "I have to become accustomed to marriage and establish a clientele among the *enceinte* aristocrats of Rouen."

"Don't wait too long," said Maman. Clare could tell she was talking about starting a family, not looking for prospective patients.

~~~

The morning arrived, and the couple exchanged vows "to love, honor and obey…'til death do us part." Tears of joy ran down Jacques's face. Bells rang out and friends stood at the church door, throwing rice and calling out congratulations. A small wedding breakfast was prepared by Delphine.

Papa hung on to life by a thread. His wish to see Clare married to Jacques was fulfilled, although he was too weak to officiate and had to be carried to a seat in Uncle's pew at church. Later that afternoon, returned to the featherbed in the cottage where Clare had been conceived, Papa took his last breath. He was at peace.

Because they were in mourning, Jacques and Clare did not have to suffer the customary ritual of the bedding ceremony, where noisy celebrations included tucking newlyweds into bed and locking the bedchamber door. Impatient as any normal bridegroom would be, Jacques respected Clare's wishes to remain in the cottage with Maman for a few days, to sit watch over Papa's body and to finish
~~~

packing up the cottage. All in all, their wedding day had been one of mingled joy and sadness.

In accordance with Papa's final wishes, Clare wore her wedding gown to his burial, shocking the other black-clad mourners. She heard their whispered disapproval behind her back. Maman told her to ignore the rumormongers, especially those who questioned why Clare had been in such a hurry to wed. "You owe no apologies for inappropriate grieving attire. After all, you were honoring Papa's final wishes."

And Clare certainly wasn't with child. Standing next to her new husband at the gravesite, she watched tears of sadness streaming down his cheeks as the pine box was lowered into the ground. *So different from the tears he shed when we exchanged our marital vows. I guess I never realized how deeply emotional Jacques is.*

Clare supposed she would always wonder what had made her change her mind about breaking off the engagement. Was it the vow she had made to her dying father to marry Jacques so she could support her aging mother? Was it Jacques's promise to let her renovate Maison Dupres as their future home?

Or was it the shocking blow she had received when Uncle Dupres related the latest news from Pierre—his foolish son had gone and married an English lady named Celia Smithfield, who was already large with his child!

Chapter 13

Newlyweds

So now I am a married woman—Madame Jacques Dupres, currently residing above the shop on Rue du Gros-Horloge, the street of the large clock in the heart of Rouen. Farewell to childhood and romantic fantasies. Dieppe is no longer my home.

Journal of Clare Dupres, 15 juin 1675

THEY HAD SPENT their first night together as husband and wife at a nondescript inn a few miles outside Dieppe. Jacques had been very gentle with Clare during their coupling. It was over in less than five minutes. Being a midwife, she knew what to expect and the experience was not as terrible as some said. Nor did she expect any grand passion from her husband, although he was prone to tears.

Clare assumed in time she would accustom herself to such a nightly routine. *At least it was not during my peak monthly fertility cycle. Henceforth, I shall use vinegar-soaked sponges and douches at appropriate times of month to prevent conception until I am ready to have children. Of course I won't share my intention with Jacques. No need to tell him that I am obstructing the laws of nature.*

Jacques told her he was most anxious for a son, now that Celia had borne a boy for Pierre. Should Clare fail to match that feat, the entirc Dupres fortune would be entailed on Pierre's son. Clare decided she would definitely bear a son for Jacques, but only when she was ready to begin breeding.

Madame Leclerc, wife of the shop manager, had prepared their apartments in time for their arrival. The formerly dark, empty rooms were now furnished, and a few of Jacques's floral sketches had been framed and adorned the sunny yellow-painted walls. The same floral designs were repeated on the bed hangings. Mirrors in the parlor reflected the light of the candles. With a cheery fire burning in the hearth, the familiar portrait above the mantel, candles in the wall sconces, and the smell of hearty stew in the heavy iron kettle hanging over the fire, it was quite a welcoming change from the cold, dark, empty rooms she remembered from April.

Among the items of furniture Jacques had purchased for her was a dressing table with a deep locking drawer on the bottom left. She was relieved to have a place to lock up her journal and especially the pouch with the reward coins, since there were no loose bricks to use as hiding places. It was also a convenient spot for her secret sponges and vinegars.

Still, there was the odoriferous stench from the street seeping through the windows with which to contend. In addition, would she ever get used to the chiming of that giant outdoor clock every hour, day and night? So close to the bedchamber it made her teeth rattle.

Clare looked forward to overseeing the renovation of Maison Dupres. It was one of her highest priorities, and she even offered to use some of the birthing rewards in her pouch to assist with the expensive refurbishment. Jacques was insulted and soundly refused to consider her "ill-gotten gains."

She took umbrage at his choice of words. *Why, it is like saying I stole these treasures, or worse yet, received them in exchange for services as a prostitute.* But she bit her tongue, learning to hold back her strong opinions. Instead, she thanked him for allowing her to keep the contents of the pouch for a rainy day, which satisfied his male pride. *I guess I am beginning to think like a proper wife. Still, I intend for the contents of that pouch to increase as I establish my professional reputation among the local women of quality in Rouen.*

~~~

When Clare had uttered her final, tearful farewell to the little cottage of her childhood, Maman had handed her a packet of herb seeds to carry to Rouen in her birthing bag. With no garden, and no sunny window box, Clare knew not where she should plant them. She would save them for Maison Dupres.
~~~

Settled in above the shop in Rouen, Clare soon became accustomed to the routine of married life. Madame Leclerc proved helpful in hiring a few servants to come in daily. Unlike her family's previous reliance on one girl-of-all-work, Jacques generously insisted that his wife take on a cook, a parlor maid, and a scullery maid to handle all cleaning, serving and meal preparation. But she declined to hire a lady's maid. "The parlor maid has ample time to help me into my stays," she said. "There is little enough for her to do in such a small apartment. As for my hair, I suppose it won't show under my caps."

Jacques had calling cards printed for her. He told her she must return calls to the many neighbors who made the first *mariée visite* to their parlor in the afternoons.

"Bride visit?" she asked.

"Not to wait upon a bride is very remiss," he said. "If the neighbors are unavailable to receive you when you arrive at their homes, you are to leave your card with the servants."

What a waste of time, Clare thought, but thanked him for the cards and advice. She much preferred to sit in the elegant salon behind his shop, searching for prospective patients. As ladies sipped champagne with their aristocratic friends, admiring and selecting fabrics, she carefully observed their bellies for telltale signs of breeding.

One day an idea came to mind. She suggested to Jacques that she could hand out those (useless) calling cards to his elite customers in need of a midwife. He was scandalized—threatened to ban her entirely from the salon if she ever ventured to act in such way. Clare soon realized she would have to find another, more discreet way to circulate notice of her services.

As newlyweds, Jacques and Clare received a few invitations to dine during the first summer. Mostly from his suppliers, the weavers who translated his floral designs into woven cloth. But their middling wives were not the type of clientele she hoped to attract. Besides, her stifling city lodgings lacked a garden for chickens.

Jacques insisted she have breakfast in bed every morning. He habitually rose early, and sometimes his nightly urges returned in the mornings before the tray of coffee and rolls.

This is quite one of the evils of matrimony. Sometimes I feel like a slave to his manly desires. He must think if he can find a way to keep me in bed forever, I will give up thoughts of my vocation and begin producing sons.

But Clare was not one to sit around like a china doll and be petted like a lap dog. One morning, she awoke before Jacques and soon was rustling around upstairs on the empty top floor. Walking around the dusty space, frowning, trying to decide how to turn the space into two temporary guest rooms to accommodate Uncle, Maman and Delphine when they visited. This space was smaller than the tiny cottage in Dieppe, and the stairwell leading up so narrow she was uncertain Uncle would fit through.

Jacques was disappointed that she was not planning to turn the upstairs into a nursery. She assured him that there was plenty of time before they would have need of one.

"Clare…" he began.

"You agreed this was temporary, Jacques. I wish to begin restoring Maison Dupres. We must have a proper home, a place in the country where our children may breathe fresh, clean air and have a garden to play in. In the meantime, it is important to have room for our guests."

"I suppose so," he said uneasily, but she could tell by his face that he hoped a child would come before restoration of the dilapidated maison. "I just thought…"

She stopped him, putting her hands around his waist. "Please let me begin renovation of Maison Dupres soon."

"It could take years," he said. "Perhaps we should look around for a different house in the country to let, one that would be ready to move into."

But he had promised Clare Maison Dupres, and she obstinately refused to consider any alternative.

Chapter 14

An Unlikely Friendship

Jacques is still dragging his feet about proceeding with the restoration of Maison Dupres. He is always so slow and deliberate about making decisions. I am losing patience.

Journal of Clare Dupres, 20 août 1675

PEERING OUT THEIR parlor window one stifling morning, Clare saw a parked carriage with the Montjardin coat of arms on the door. She practically tripped over her petticoats running down the stairs. Gasping for breath, she slowed down and stood at the entry to the salon. This was the chance she had been hoping for.

As she slipped into the room, she observed three fashionably dressed ladies sipping champagne and felt certain one must be Lady Louise—but which one?

Two of the women were obviously beyond childbearing age and did not match Uncle's description of the lady he had rescued from the broken carriage. Clare remembered him saying Lady Louise was about her age and uncommonly handsome.

Judging from appearances, the younger one facing away from her had to be the Marquise. She was slender and petite, with flaxen hair piled stylishly on her head, dressed in an elegant gown, a pretty shade of pink with a violet floral overskirt interwoven with silver thread. Clare recognized it as the latest style from Paris, from the fashion plates Jacques displayed on the salon walls. Lady Louise's kidskin gloves were neatly folded on her lap as she took small tastes of her bubbly drink.

Clare hesitated, knowing it would be inappropriate to walk over and introduce herself and that Jacques would be irritated. The two elder ladies basically ignored her. She stood nervously for a few moments, pretending to examine some swatches of material, while overhearing bits of the ladies' conversation.

"What an extraordinary shop. I never expected to find one so fine in Rouen," exclaimed Madame Brouille in a booming voice. "And this salon—why, it is as exclusive as any in Paris."

"It came highly recommended by Countess de La Tournelle," said her companion in blue. "The manager of this establishment keeps careful records of her fabric choices. When she dresses for a soiree, she has no apprehension of finding another guest dressed in the same silk design."

"The same design—*quelle horreur*!" Madame Brouille motioned with her gloved finger to Monsieur Leclerc for refills. He glided over to the table with a fresh bottle, champagne fizzing out the top, and poured more of the complimentary beverage into their empty glasses. Only the Marquise politely thanked him. The others hardly took notice.

"Speaking of parties, dear Louise, is the Marquis still planning to host the annual harvest ball at the chateau?" asked Madame Brouille.

Clare held her breath as the young lady answered in a gentle, lilting, almost musical voice. "*Mais certainement.* Our celebration is timed for the first full moon, you understand. For the comfort and safety of guests who travel the dark, hazardous roads of Rouen."

Clare's stomach lurched. *I would give anything for an invitation to that ball, a party where all the aristocrats of Normandy would certainly be in attendance. Such an opportunity to meet elite women in need of my midwifery services would rarely come my way.*

Holding two swatches of flowered silk in her hand, Clare slipped across the carpet and approached them. The two elder ladies frowned, doubtless shocked by her impudence. *Jacques would be furious if he knew my intentions. Luckily he is away today.*

Curtsying to them, Clare said, "Excuse me for interrupting, ladies. I was wondering if I could solicit your opinion as to which of these two patterns best suits my complexion. My husband designs such exquisite fabrics that I find it difficult to make a selection."

Lady Louise turned and contemplated her face. Suddenly, she smiled with a nod of recognition. "Can it be? You must be the new wife of Monsieur Jacques. Last time I was here to place an order, he told me he was soon to marry his cousin. I am so happy to meet you at last, Madame Dupres."

"Please, call me Clare," she insisted. "I am not yet used to being called Madame."

Lady Louise introduced Clare to her companions. "Monsieur Jacques's father once saved my life, shortly before Hélène was born. It was quite a frightful experience, having the wheel fly off our carriage on the journey from the royal palace. He was extremely kind to us. Drove us home in his cart and talked nonstop of his children and his niece Clare, the midwife."

"You gave him your card," Clare responded. "I saved it, hoping to meet you one day. And here you are, in my new home. Of course, our apartments above the shop are temporary lodgings," she added, pointing upward. "We soon plan to renovate Maison Dupres as our permanent home." *Jacques is going to kill me.*

"Renovate that mysterious old place on the Paris road?" noted Madame Brouille, wrinkling up her nose. "That would be quite an impossible feat. It was abandoned years ago. Some tragic scandal or other, involving a gentleman's son and a nursery maid. Oh no, you most certainly don't want to renovate."

"My eldest son passes Maison Dupres when he comes up to visit," said the lady in blue. "He is surprised the dreadful eyesore with the bricked-in-window still stands. We discussed it once, agreed the landowner should tear it down and build a neoclassic-style villa on the property."

"I beg to disagree," said Lady Louise. "I think the idea of restoring an old house is enchanting, especially if you're lucky enough to have a talented husband like Monsieur Jacques, who can design light, airy fabrics to be used in the décor. Sometimes Chateau Montjardin feels so dark and dreary indoors. All of my husband's ancestors, frowning down from gilded frames on the walls. Not to mention the ancient coat of armor in the grand salon. But I dare not change anything below the nursery floor. Someday, *if* I have a son," she sighed, "he will inherit the chateau in the same centuries-old condition."

"You mustn't give up hope for a son, dear," said Madame Brouille, patting her young friend on the arm. "You're still young."

"Yes, of course." She took another sip of champagne, but her sweet smile had faded. Clare feared she would leave the salon before she could arrange to meet her alone, converse privately without her two opinionated companions interfering with Clare's plan.

Taking a deep breath, she said, "Lady Louise, would you care to accompany me out to Maison Dupres one day soon, to give me some ideas for the renovation?" Clare was literally quaking in her shoes–she could not believe she had just invited this aristocrat to spend a day with her. *I want to impress her, to assure her we are not just simple merchants but belong to the rank of landed gentry. Perhaps then, she will invite Jacques and me to her harvest ball.*

"What a marvelous idea!" Lady Louise's face brightened, and she bubbled with enthusiasm at Clare's invitation. Reaching into her reticule, she pulled out a tiny gold notepad and studied her schedule. "Would next Monday be too soon for you?"

Clare pinched her finger to be sure she wasn't dreaming. She liked Lady Louise immensely. Of course she wanted an invitation to the Montjardin ball, an entrée into Rouen society. But it was more than that. Clare missed Delphine and longed for the companionship of a female friend with whom she could share secrets, gossip, and confidences.

"Monday would be perfect!" she exclaimed.

Thus began Clare Dupres's close friendship with Lady Louise, Marquise de Montjardin—one that would ultimately save both of their lives in unexpected ways.

As Clare climbed upstairs, she realized she had to convince Jacques to begin the renovation without further delay. It would be easy enough to pretend to be enceinte, but that wouldn't be fair. No, she did not wish to begin their marriage with a terrible lie like that. Besides, Maman would be at her door as soon as Jacques spread the joyful news, and she would see right through Clare's deception.

Instead, Clare began to use her feminine wiles to fascinate and please her man, entice his embraces with enthusiasm while pretending modesty. He soon fell for her charms and gave in to her dramatic tears and pleas. Before long the renovation of the crumbling mansion was underway.

Chapter 15

Maman's Deception

Despite the differences in our religion and social status, my friendship with Lady Louise has flourished. As Louise helped me select wall coverings and fabrics for Maison Dupres, we became true confidants. On one occasion, we even traveled together in her coach to Paris so that I could order a few pieces of new furniture. Last fall, when the restoration was completed, Jacques and I moved into our elegant maison.

Jacques and I began attending the glittering Montjardin harvest balls. Now my reputation among the elite of Rouen is well established and my pouch of rewards is practically exploding! My husband's growing business keeps him away from home for long periods. He showers me with gifts of jewelry when he returns, happiest when I am not off at birthings. During our intimate times, I am careful to use my secret sponges, and so far, they—or luck—have prevented conception. Perhaps I am being selfish, but I'm not ready to start breeding just yet. For now, I'm content to enjoy my career and beautiful new home.

Journal of Clare Dupres, 10 mai 1678

MAMAN TRAVELED FROM Dieppe for a long visit, ostensibly to see the heated conservatory Clare had designed where plants would thrive year-round—exotic flowers for Jacques's designs and herbs for Clare's midwifery potions. She suspected Maman had other motives in mind for her extended stay.

When Maman arrived, she appeared unusually frail, having difficulty managing the stairs of the newly renovated maison and easily winded from exertion. At times Clare tended to forget her advanced age and worried that she might lose her soon, but Maman denied any infirmity. She said it was her will to stay alive until Clare gave birth to the necessary female child.

Upstairs, she peeked into the master bedchamber and boudoir before Clare led her to the guest room on the east side, the chamber with the best view of the evening sky.

"I must say, Clare, this house looks much homier than when I first saw it." Pulling aside the bed-curtains, she perched on the edge of the quilt-covered guest bed. "The renovations must have been quite costly, but I suppose you can afford the best, what with your unchristian attitude about limiting your patients to those of wealth."

"Let's not begin your visit with a quarrel, Maman."

She reached for Clare's hands and pulled her daughter close, looking her over from head to foot, fingering the strand of pearls around her neck with a frown of disappointment.

"It's not what you think, Maman. This necklace was a gift from Jacques for our third wedding anniversary, not a birthing reward."

"That's not why I'm displeased. Your belly is not expanding."

Involuntarily, Clare's hands covered her flat abdomen and she blushed. Tried to look away.

"Clare, is your husband inattentive to you in bed? Why are you not yet with child?"

"There's plenty of time for that," she answered defensively. "Jacques is away so often....my midwifery in such demand...the renovations..."

"Excuses! You don't fool me one bit. You're as ripe as a plum. I know what you are up to."

Quickly changing the subject, Clare suggested she take some nourishment and rest from her exhausting journey. "I'll have Marie bring up a tray for you. She is our new cook, daughter of a Huguenot farmer from Torcy-le-Grand. She makes an amazing omelette."

"I taught you how to cook omelettes when you were a girl. Wouldn't think you needed to hire a cook."

"I haven't forgotten how to cook, but Jacques and I sometimes host dinner parties. And when Louise comes, she raves about the food and threatens to steal Marie from me."

"Louise? So now you are on a first-name basis with the Marquise of Montjardin?"

"Don't look at me like that. Of course, I always use her title in the presence of others. But she is my best friend, Maman."

"Does Lady Louise consider you *her* best friend?"

Clare hesitated for a moment. "Well, I think she does. We often visit. But I suppose she has many friends."

"As I thought. Be careful, daughter. She is a Papist, is she not?"

"Oh, that doesn't matter, although her cousin, Father Benedict, tries to convince me to convert when I see him at her chateau. Still, I would trust Louise with my life. I wish you could know her like I do, Maman."

That evening, Jacques welcomed Maman warmly and asked for news of Dieppe. She gladly obliged. Told him how empty Delphine's house felt since Uncle passed last fall, buried in the graveyard next to Papa. All those empty rooms—Delphine was thinking of turning it into a boarding house. The Huguenot church in Dieppe was always filled to the walls on Sundays. She liked the new minister, although he was not as inspirational as her late husband.

Clare's ears perked up when Maman related news of Pierre and Celia. Their little boy was sickly, and Celia had not yet conceived a second child.

"Jacques," Maman suddenly asked, "when is your next business trip to Paris?"

"This coming Monday. Unfortunately, I must be gone for four days."

"You must take your wife with you."

Clare was startled by her suggestion. *Go away with Jacques? Out of the question.* Clare started to object, but Maman gave her one of those knowing looks, like when she caught Clare disobeying her as a child.

Jacques chimed in, "What a splendid idea. My wife does look tired, doesn't she? All those long hours with her…umm, patients. It's not as if we needed money."

"Maman just arrived—"

But her mother waved away the objections. "I'm planning a long visit. What do four days matter?" she insisted. "Yes, you will go with your husband. A married couple needs time to be alone, undisturbed," she said, sipping her wine.

Jacques looked happier than Clare had seen in a long time, and she quickly realized she had no choice.

"Then it's settled. Clare shall accompany you to Paris. I'll help her pack."

Clare wondered why Maman was so eager to get rid of her, so soon after her arrival. *What is she up to?*

~~~

Six weeks after returning from Paris I find it difficult to keep food in my stomach. Maman smiles and hands me a stale biscuit to nibble on. She reminds me that morning sickness usually abates in three months.

By the time I realized Maman had purposely removed the sponges and vinegar from my trunk, Jacques and I were in bed at the Paris hotel. Too late for a quick trip to the nearest apothecary. Jacques is overjoyed that a child is on the way.

Journal of Clare Dupres, 10 juillet 1678

~~~

The morning sickness is gone, my belly is expanding, and at Jacques's insistence I have stopped attending confinements. I spend my days at home sewing little gowns and caps, writing letters, and recording events in this journal. Sad news from England—Pierre's little son died of typhus. But in her latest letter, Celia said she prayed for my coming child to be healthy and strong. Although I have never met Celia, I feel close through our correspondence. I hope she begins breeding again.

I suppose I forgive Maman for hiding my sponges. I hate to admit it, but she was right. My fertility might have diminished had I waited much longer. I will give birth to this child and hopefully another, soon after. Only then will I return to my fulfilling midwifery practice.

Journal of Clare Dupres, 8 octobre 1678

~~~

Jacques made a surprise announcement—he decided to let Monsieur Leclerc run the day-to-day business at the shop in Rouen and live with his family in the upstairs apartments. From now on, Jacques would work from home, sketching new floral silk patterns based on the bright flowers thriving in the heated conservatory. He told Clare there seemed to be an insatiable demand for French silk in England. According to Pierre's letters, King Charles and his courtiers lived a lavish lifestyle. Clare knew the English king and his brother James, Duke of York, had been exiled in France during their youth. No wonder they had developed a taste for fine silk.
~~~

Even Jacques begrudgingly admitted they owed much to Pierre for bringing Dupres & Sons such a lucrative royal account.

~~~

Maman is here for the holidays and plans to stay to birth my child. She says I have no need for mistletoe now that I am breeding. My time of confinement grows near. How wondrous to feel the life within me grow.

Journal of Clare Dupres, 15 décembre 1678

~~~

Praise God for our healthy son! We baptized him Jean-Pierre Dumont Dupres. Maman was surprised I turned down the magic elixir for the birth. I said I needed to experience the pain of travail at least once, to understand why the secret formula was so important. After eighteen hours of birth pains, I regretted my decision. Next time, I will gladly submit to it.

Journal of Clare Dupres, 3 février 1679

~~~

Maman insisted on a wet nurse for Jean-Pierre, although Clare's breasts ached to nurse him. "Suckling a child is known to delay another pregnancy," Maman said, reminding Clare that her fertility was waning and she hadn't produced the necessary female child to carry on the ancestral tradition. So Clare reluctantly kept the wet nurse until Jean-Pierre was weaned, but after each feeding, she cuddled him in her arms so he would know she was his mother. Clare luxuriated in bed for thirty days, telling herself this was not so bad after all. Soon she returned to Jacques's bed.

"No sponges," warned Maman.

~~~

My son has passed his first birthday in good health. It is difficult for me to describe how I feel, watching him grow. Already he teethes on his small wooden toys and toddles about the nursery. Jacques painted the nursery walls a soft cream and plans to paint little red-and-blue-uniformed toy soldiers marching around the walls.

Journal of Clare Dupres, 30 mars 1680

They were sipping coffee when Maman advised Jacques to paint dolls on the opposite wall from the toy soldiers. "This one will be a girl," she told him. Jacques sputtered and almost choked on his drink.

"Maman," Clare scolded. "It's too early to be sure."

Maman raised her eyebrow. "Why should he not be told of the impending birth in October? Is he not the father?"

She knows full well I have not left Maison Dupres since my little son was born, and that I returned to Jacques's bed months ago. After all, she sleeps in our house and must feel the floorboards tremble each time we couple. And Jacques rarely travels these days, thought Clare.

"Is this true, Clare?" he asked in bewilderment.

"Is what true? That there is another child on the way, or that you are the father?"

"So," he said proudly, "Jean-Pierre is to have a little brother. I hope you won't mind missing the harvest ball this year."

"You know I will, *mais c'est la vie.*" She shrugged.

"A little *sister,*" insisted Maman. "I can tell by Clare's belly shape, it will be a girl. At least she doesn't suffer from the morning malaise this time."

"So true. I've never felt better. I'm blooming like the flowers in the hothouse."

"Well, a girl to make you two happy would be fine. There will be more sons later. I couldn't be more thrilled with the news." Jacques hugged Clare, then grabbed his sketch pad and went out to the garden, humming his favorite psalm.

Some days he preferred to design wildflowers, rather than the carefully cultivated hothouse flowers. He was especially inspired by an invasive weed with a spindly yellow blossom—the bulbous buttercup. Despite Clare's instructions to their gardener to keep them away from her herb beds, they managed to sneak in. Such ugly weeds, she thought, especially after Maman had told her how they were used by beggars to temporarily disfigure their appearance. The very same buttercups on the portrait Jacques had painted when he first proposed. Who would have guessed?

Occasionally, Jacques drove into Rouen to visit Monsieur Leclerc and to review the business records. Being isolated at home, fondly dandling her little boy on her knee, Clare was blissfully ignorant of the growing political unrest in France. The construction of Versailles was nearly complete. Unbeknownst to her at the time, the King's advisors were apparently plotting to increase the pressure on Huguenots to convert. If Jacques heard these rumors from Monsieur Leclerc, he did not share them with her—either because he wanted to protect his breeding wife or because he did not believe them to be true. Even if she had known what was going on at the time, could she ever have imagined how it would affect her own little family?

~~~

As the time grows near for my second confinement, Maman helps me interview prospective nursemaids. Lifting my chubby little boy is becoming difficult for me, although I love sitting in the rocker, holding him against my rounded belly. Anyway I will need a reliable nursemaid when I return to my birthing practice, which I plan to do when this new baby turns two.

I made it clear to Maman that I would not hire a wet nurse this time. Although I agreed to have the elixir during my travail, I plan to suckle this new child myself. Maman concurs, so long as I promise her a granddaughter. And to give her naming rights, too. I laugh and offer her a chicken instead, but she is serious about choosing the name.

Journal of Clare Dupres, 8 août 1680

~~~

Madame Leclerc knew many families in Rouen and sent two ladies whom she thought would be suitable nursemaids. The candidate who shone in Clare's mind was a childless widow of forty, Claudette Lamont. Her references were excellent and she was very attentive to baby Jean-Pierre, who sat quietly sucking his thumb on Clare's lap. She had excellent experience, having worked for several merchant families. Living in would suit her, as there was a Catholic church within walking distance where she could attend Sunday afternoon Mass.

Maman advised Clare to choose the other candidate, a sharp-nosed, disagreeable woman who had four grown children. Her attitude, she told them during the interview, was to use the rod when necessary to put the fear of God in children.

"I will have Claudette," Clare told Maman. "Why would I hire the nasty one, who would beat my poor innocent child for sucking his thumb?"

"You were too busy being pleased by the widow Lamont's adulation of the child on your lap to listen closely to what she said."

"What? That she wants me to hire her twelve-year-old niece Giselle as a housemaid? Why should that matter—we have need of another servant for this growing family of ours. To clean the grates, polish, dust and clean up after Marie in the kitchen."

"Do what you want, Clare. You've always been stubborn. But I have a bad feeling about that niece. Claudette told us Giselle's prostitute mother abandoned her when she was ten, left her to roam the streets and beg. Her father is unknown. Mark my words, you're courting trouble, having that young girl in your home."

"Oh, Maman, you worry too much. I must have Madame Claudette and that's that." She stomped out of the room in a childish fit.

Clare would live to regret that decision.

Chapter 16

Birth of the Moon Goddess

I am delighted with Claudette—how carefully she watches after my son. Childless herself, Claudette took in her ten-year-old niece when she discovered her sister had run off with a gipsy. Giselle is a strange, skinny child who stares at me when she comes to light the morning fires in our bedchamber. She seems polite enough to me, but Marie says the girl puts on airs—doesn't like being a housemaid, having to sleep in a room above the stable. I told Marie to warn Giselle to hold her tongue, but I fear if we dismiss her, Claudette will leave.

Maman has decided my second child will be birthed in her bedchamber, claiming it is warmer in there when the afternoon sun pours through the windows. But I know the real reason—this room has the best view of the evening sky, especially when the full moon ascends. Maman always professes to be a Christian, but she still has a few pagan beliefs.

Journal of Clare Dupres, 7 octobre 1680

CLARE'S PAINS BEGAN after breakfast. Feeling helpless, she sat on Maman's bed, watching her mix the elixir, as her belly expanded and contracted like stormy ocean waves furiously beating against the alabaster cliffs in Dieppe. The elixir tasted worse than it smelled, but she swallowed it in one gulp. Nothing happened at first, then slowly, slowly…slowly… she began to drift…

~~~

I feel strangely empty. Where am I? This is not my bed. I am lying outdoors, under a tree, listening to a balmy breeze rustle through the
~~~

budding green leaves. Maman is kneeling next to me, shaking me. I hear her voice, whispering, "Clare, wake up."

"What are you doing here, Maman?" She helps me sit up and brushes dried twigs off my shoulders.

"Doing here? I came to find you. Did you trip over a tree stump, dear? I don't see any bruises on your head, but your hair is a mess."

"My head feels foggy. I need to rest."

"No time for that now." She pulls me to my feet. "We must get ready for the *fête*. Your father and I wish to talk to you before we go, prepare you for the unhappy news."

News? What is Maman talking about? I look down at my hands. They appear so young. My gold wedding band is missing. And where has this gray apron come from? It looks like something I threw away years ago, when it ripped. I creep over to a stream. Gleaming moonlight filters through the branches, shedding sufficient light to see my reflection. I am shocked at the strange, youthful face staring back at me.

"Stop dawdling, Clare," chides Maman. "We must get back to the cottage so you have time to dress properly. Your yellow silk gown, I think."

Suddenly I am transported to the cottage bedroom in Dieppe. The pink geraniums are blooming in the window box. Papa is fingering the soft gown Maman has laid out on the bed. I drift toward him.

"Clare, dear," he says, turning in my direction. "King Louis has issued a new edict—Huguenots may no longer study law in France. I'm afraid Pierre has no choice. He sails for England on the *Celia* tomorrow."

"Tomorrow? What day is this?" I ask in confusion. "What year? I thought you were dead, Papa."

"Dead? Do I look that bad to you?"

"Clare took a nasty fall in the woods," Maman explains. "It seems to have affected her mind."

Papa looks concerned and brushes his hand across my brow. "It's May, 1674, dearest. Are you too unwell to attend the *bon voyage fête*?"

Maman offers to send a note to Delphine, excusing us from coming.

"No!" I cry. "I mean, if Pierre is truly leaving France, I won't have a chance to see him, ever again." I begin to wail, tears streaming down my ice-cold cheeks. "How can I marry Pierre if he goes to England?"

"Marry Pierre? Out of the question," says Papa. "He is young, penniless and irresponsible. Perhaps he will make something of himself as a sailor. Marry the older brother. Jacques is a good, steady boy and will inherit the Dupres fortune."

"But, Papa, I love Pierre."

"Someday you will understand. Love has nothing to do with it."

"Nooooo…"

"Be sensible, Clare, you know you must marry and have a daughter," says Maman, her voice fading as I run to my curtained alcove next to the hearth, throw myself down on the comforter and weep until there are no tears left in my eyes. But I can still hear her voice echoing, "A daughter, a daughter…"

~~~

Maman pulled aside the window curtain and said, "I was beginning to think you would never wake, Clare. It's a daughter! Congratulations, darling, you have borne a healthy, baby girl."

Gradually Clare opened her eyes and felt the spongy flatness of her belly. Maman handed her the most beautiful infant she had ever seen, already cleaned and swaddled. As Clare hugged the babe to her breast, she looked around in a daze. *Why, I am back in Maman's bedchamber, at Maison Dupres. What an odd sensation.*

"I had the strangest dream," she said. "It seemed so real."

Maman reminded her that the elixir puts women into a twilight sleep, sometimes bringing back painful memories. "You cried out and tears rolled down your face. Were you feeling physical pain from the birth itself?"

"No. The elixir *is* truly magic," she whispered.

Maman gently took the tiny girl from Clare's arms and held her up to the bright moonbeam shining through the window. "My granddaughter took her first breath when the full moon crested in the sky. Her intelligent eyes opened wide as she searched for signs of Lucina, the moon goddess. I'm certain she saw her."

Clare must have been very groggy, but could swear she saw the baby nod in assent. She rubbed her eyes and tried to shake the sleepiness from them.

"You have fulfilled your ancestral destiny, Clare. I am very proud of you."
~~~

"How can I ever thank you, Maman?"

"You have already thanked me by promising me naming rights."

In her haze, Clare couldn't remember. "Jacques said if it was a girl we should call her Delphine."

"No, not for this special child. We shall name her Lucina. Like the Roman moon goddess who protects women in childbirth. I predict that one day, our little Lucina will become a famous midwife with the power to see the future."

Clare reached out her arms. "Time will tell. But for now, hand my daughter Lucina back to me so I can suckle her."

PART II

GATHERING STORM CLOUDS

Chapter 17

The Brazen Wench

Maman stayed on with us at Maison Dupres and lived just long enough to see Lucina take her first steps. Sadly, she weakened and died shortly thereafter. I miss Maman more than I can say, but feel her spirit watching over me.

Jacques and I are truly blessed with two healthy children, while Pierre and Celia still have an empty nursery. Jacques wants more sons, but I am done with breeding. Now that Lucina is two, the time has come to resume midwifery. Needless to say, Jacques is peeved.

Lady Louise is enceinte again. Her third daughter was born two years ago—same day as Lucina arrived, so I was unavailable to assist her. However, this time I have promised my dear friend I will be available when her time comes. She is desperate for a son.

Journal of Clare Dupres, 30 octobre 1682

SHORTLY BEFORE SUNRISE, a knock sounded at the front entrance to Maison Dupres. Marie was kneading dough in the kitchen. "Giselle," she called to the serving girl lying on a pallet close to the hearth, "go see who's a-knockin' at the door."

"I din't hear no knockin'."

"Are you deaf, girl? That banging on the brass knocker's louder than a cannon booming. Now get up and see who is making such a racket."

"I should've stayed in my room above the stable last night, even if it are freezin' out there," whined Giselle, pulling her thin blanket up around her ears.

Marie walked over and tugged at the blanket. The girl resisted, holding on with both hands. "Leave me be," she moaned.

"Get up and stop your complaining. It's a wonder Mistress keeps you on here, what with that attitude of yours. Now get up off your lazy you-know-what and go answer the door, like you been taught. And be quick about it."

Giselle reluctantly stood up. Grabbing the candle from Marie, the lanky, unkempt servant stumbled into the entry hall to unbolt the heavy centuries-old oak door. A large glossy black carriage with a gold-embossed coat of arms stood at the foot of the stone steps.

A liveried messenger held a folded note in his white-gloved hand. "This is for Madame Dupres. It is extremely urgent," he said. Giselle noticed he clung to the note.

He looks like he don't trust me to give it to Mistress. Jes' 'cause I ain't dressed all fancy-like. Maybe I should tell him to climb them inside steps to her room and give it to her hisself. "Wait here," she said, yanking the folded note from his hand and closing the door in his face.

Giselle turned the note over in her hands. She recognized the familiar red wax seal. Resisting the temptation to set the note on the silver salver, where her mistress would find it later, Giselle clomped up the grand staircase and burst into the master bedchamber.

Clare was already sitting up in bed, rubbing sleep from her eyes. She frowned at Giselle. "How many times have I warned you not to enter our private sleeping room without knocking?"

Saying nothing, Giselle simply thrust the thick parchment letter into her mistress's outstretched hand and started to head back to her pallet.

"*Attends*! You may not leave until I dismiss you. Hold that candle closer so I can read this."

Giselle stood shivering as Madame unfolded the note. She noticed that Madame's husband looked mighty unhappy. *He don't like her goin' off to them birthin's, that's fer sure. Man like him gets lonely without a woman in his bed. Bet anythin' they'll be havin' another row this mornin'.*

Clare refolded the note. "It's from Lady Louise, Jacques. Her lying-in has begun. Giselle, you will help me dress." She cast aside the quilt, wrapped a shawl around her shoulders and climbed down from the curtained bed onto the flowered carpet. Her bare feet carried her past the tall shuttered windows toward her boudoir, lit only by the glowing embers in the hearth and the candle carried by Giselle, reluctantly trailing behind her.

"Come back to bed, Clare," Jacques urged in a husky voice.

"No. I promised to assist Louise at her lying-in."

Here they go again, thought Giselle.

"Why must we always be disturbed in the middle of the night? Can't it wait till morning?" Jacques grumbled.

"Babes neither know nor care about clocks. They come at their own time."

"My dear, I wish you would give up this midwife nonsense. You have two young children of your own who need their mother at home. And I need you to warm my bed."

Giselle snickered. She knew what Master *really* wanted.

"Oh, Jacques," Clare said in an exasperated voice. "Now is not the time to have this conversation again. I must dress and hurry to the chateau. Claudette will tend to the children. They'll be fine."

Giselle followed her mistress into the boudoir, brazenly glancing backward over her shoulder toward Master. She laced her into a corset, fastened her black woolen gown, and wound her long auburn plait into a loose circle behind her head. Pinning the hair in place, Giselle purposely pricked Madame's scalp several times.

"Ouch! Be more careful, will you? Oh, never mind. I shall finish dressing myself." Clare reached for her lace-trimmed coif. Giselle knew Mistress would never go out with her head uncovered, no matter how urgent the situation.

The girl stepped aside, crossing her arms across her bony chest. Shivering in her thin shift, she eyed with envy the heavy cloak Madame pulled from the armoire. *I'll have fine clothes of my own someday—think I'll jes' sneak upstairs later when Mistress is away and try on her new yellow silk gown. The one she wore to that fancy ball last week.*

Since coming into service at Maison Dupres three years ago, when she was twelve, Giselle had been trying on Madame's many gowns and promising herself that if the jewel casket was ever left unlocked, she would try on the pearls too. She closed her sleepy eyes and pictured herself sashaying down the curved stairway in the billowy yellow-flowered dress.

"Why are you still standing there? Dreaming again, I suppose," snapped Clare. "Did you perchance leave the messenger standing out in the cold?"

"*Oui*," she answered in an insolent tone.

"Go down at once and tell him he need not wait for me. You should know my ways by now—I always travel to birthings in my own carriage."

"*Oui, madame*." Giselle made a halfhearted curtsy and walked slowly downstairs. She longed to return to her warm bed, but knew she would get in trouble if she failed to bolt the door after Mistress left.

The messenger from Chateau Montjardin stood patiently outside. Giselle studied his appearance for a moment. *Mighty good-lookin' fellow in that handsome red livery. Proberly even better lookin' if'n he takes it off.* Giselle flashed a smile at him, but he merely looked at her with questioning eyes.

Finally, she said, "Mistress says you kin leave."

"Leave? I was specifically instructed to fetch *this* midwife. The Marquise was adamant—she insisted I was to bring Madame Dupres back in the carriage."

Giselle shrugged. "Mistress likes to travel in her own carriage, tho' it's not half as handsome…as yers." She stood by the open door and watched him climb onto the high box of his empty carriage. As he drove off into the rising sun, the chill morning air crept around her bare ankles.

Madame's driver, Girard, was hitching two horses to her more modest carriage. He wore the bright green livery bearing the Dupres family crest on his broad-chested jacket. Giselle watched him light two lanterns to hang from hooks on the carriage. *Guess he knows Mistress's fussy-mussy ways, all right.*

Giselle recalled the first time she had seen the inside of that carriage. Girard had been washing the glass windows, and the doors were propped open. Unlike the Montjardins' stately vehicle, Madame's had no springs. Nonetheless, it was far more luxurious than anything Giselle had ever ridden in. The walls were lined with pleated silk, the cushions were covered in soft blue velvet, and the windows were fitted with pale blue shades which could be pulled down for privacy.

"Why, it's like a moth's cocoon!" Giselle had started to climb inside, but Girard had pulled her back before she got her foot onto the fold-down step.

"Don't be getting any of your high and mighty ideas, missy. This carriage ain't for the likes of a wench like you."

"My pa was a gennelman. Someday, I'll be a fine lady, but my carriage'll have springs."

"A gentleman's daughter, you say? Some fine tale you made up. Everyone knows your ma was a 'good-time-girl' who got herself in the family way—never sure which of her men friends fathered you."

"You don't know nuthin, you totterin' old fool. Afore she died, my ma was the most beautiful opera dancer in all Paris," Giselle had said, sticking her tongue out at Girard.

"You're just lucky your aunt took you in off the streets and got you this steady job, where she could keep her eye on you. But one of these days, missy, that tongue of yours will get you in a heap of trouble."

~~~

After completing the hasty *toilette* in her boudoir, Clare hastened back through the bedchamber carrying her birthing bag. She set it down on a small table close to the hearth. Struggled to pull on her kid gloves.

Jacques could tell his wife was annoyed by the way she yanked at the fingers. He turned sideways in bed and raised his upper torso onto his right elbow. After all these years, he still felt his breath catch with desire. She was so beautiful.

"That wench is incredibly clumsy and stupid," Clare said. "I ought to replace her with a respectable girl from our church. If it weren't for Claudette, I would dismiss that useless niece of hers tomorrow."

"If you stayed home where you belonged, you wouldn't need Claudette either."

Clare ignored his pointed barb. "Claudette is an excellent nursemaid. We were lucky to find her."

"I don't trust her," said Jacques. "How do we know she's not filling our impressionable children's ears with her Papist beliefs?"

"When I hired her, I made it quite clear that we were not Papists and she was to keep her religious beliefs to herself."

"I still don't trust her. My children should be memorizing verses from the scriptures, not learning to make the sign of the cross."

"Then you should spend more time with them yourself, instead of sketching all day."
~~~

"That's unfair. You know I sketch new flower designs for the silk weavers. It's important for my business."

Clare picked up the large birthing bag and backed toward the door. "I must go. Kiss the children for me."

Jacques waited for her to kiss him goodbye, but she was already heading for the door. *Clare used to be generous with her caresses, especially when we were still living above the shop. Oh, I knew she was trying to persuade me to renovate this godforsaken maison, but I craved her attentions and wanted her to be happy—to forget about my brother. But things have changed since she was befriended by Lady Louise. And now she's back to birthing, even though she knows of my displeasure.*

"How long do you expect to be gone this time?" called Jacques, stretching his arms and lying back on the pillow.

"This is Lady Louise's fourth confinement. I imagine the babe will come quickly, assuming no complications arise."

Giselle stood by the door and watched her mistress rush down the stone steps to the courtyard. Once the carriage rumbled away, Giselle bolted the door. Then she ascended the stairs and climbed into Jacques's bed.

Fully awake, he smiled and reached for the brazen wench.

Chapter 18

Birth of a Noble Heir

NESTLED WITHIN THE close, dark confines of her carriage on her way to Rouen, Clare heard only the creak of the wooden wheels and the clippity-clop of horses' hooves as they rumbled across arched stone bridges. Usually she dozed during her rides to birthings, anticipating she might not soon have another opportunity for sleep.

But sleep did not come this morning. She was upset about the problems she faced at home. Being stuck with Giselle was annoying, but Jacques was starting to get on her nerves.

It's always the same, she thought bitterly. *Every time I get called out to a confinement, my husband resists and we get into an argument. Why can't he simply accept the fact that I enjoy the professional reputation I've worked hard to achieve? He knew when we were betrothed that I intended to continue midwifery after our marriage. It's not as if I abandoned his bed...well, not completely.*

Before long, Clare's driver was directing the horses up the winding driveway to Chateau Montjardin. Dawn had chased away the gloom of the night sky. It promised to be a gloriously brisk fall day, warmer than usual for this time of year.

The housekeeper met her at the door with a worried frown. "Oh dear, oh dear. Thank heavens you made it. I'm terribly concerned. The Marquis is away and Lady Louise insisted you be sent for. She did not want Madame Larque, the midwife who attended her last time."

"I promised Lady Louise I would assist her, and here I am. But what is your concern?"

"The household was awakened shortly after midnight by screams from milady's bedchamber, but the noise abruptly stopped fifteen minutes ago."

"I'll see to her at once," Clare said, handing over her cloak. However, she encountered an unexpected impediment—Father Benedict blocked the entry to the bedchamber. He was snoring on a chair, having been summoned by the housekeeper earlier. His presence there mystified her.

"*Bonjour*, Father Benedict," Clare said, causing him to jump up from his seat. "Sorry to wake you. I didn't expect to see you here so early in the morning. They don't serve breakfast until ten."

"Ah, the Huguenot midwife. I was not asleep, as you might think. No, I was, umm…in prayer for the soul struggling to be born in there," he said, pointing at the door behind him. "And for the soul of my cousin, the gracious Lady Louise."

"Right. Carry on with your prayers, but kindly move aside."

"Madame Dupres," the officious priest suggested, rubbing his hands together, "perhaps when you complete your duties, you will spend a few moments conversing with me."

"Of what have we to converse? I suppose you wish to try again to convince me to accept the King's preferred faith. I recall you approached my husband and me just before the harvest ball, and we made it abundantly clear—"

"Madame, please believe me, I am only trying to save your soul. You need only repeat a few words after me and start attending Mass at the Cathedral."

Lately, Clare had heard that French priests acted as spies, receiving monetary rewards from King Louis's confessor, Père Lachase, for every successful conversion. It troubled Clare that so many of her fellow Huguenots had abjured, mainly to stop the constant harassment by greedy local priests. "I appreciate your concern for my soul," she said, "but my husband would be vexed if I joined your church. Now please move out of my way. I am in a hurry."

He bowed his head. "Madame, you must call for me immediately if you find Lady Louise in imminent danger of dying. I am terribly concerned by the silence in there."

"So concerned that you fell asleep on the chair?"

"I knocked and called to Lady Louise through the heavy door. Indeed I did, but she told me not to come in—that she was *deshabille*."

"So you have never seen a naked lady?" Sometimes, Clare enjoyed baiting this bandy-legged priest. He always seemed to be loitering about the chateau, especially at mealtimes, when he should have been attending to his duties at the Sisters of Sorrow convent. Clare supposed the food was better at the chateau. The priest certainly did not appear underfed.

Father Benedict's pasty face turned red. "Certainly not! I am a man of the cloth," he sputtered. Sliding past the priest, Clare entered the room and closed the door before he could say another word.

Clare almost choked at the stifling-hot atmosphere. Lady Louise's room had been transformed by the servants into a traditional confinement chamber. The fire was blazing, the shutters closed, and heavy drapery covered all doors and windows. Even the keyholes were plugged, to keep evil spirits from stealing the breath of the newborn, along with other superstitions that made no sense to Clare.

She folded back the shutters and cracked open the window, letting in fresh air and natural light. Just as Maman had taught her.

Lady Louise was calmly sitting up in bed, dressed in a soft linen shift edged with lace. Around her shoulders was a brightly patterned shawl woven of fine English wool, which Clare recognized as one of Jacques's imports. Louise was busy buttering a roll.

"Why, look at you!" Clare scolded. "I thought you sent for me at this ungodly hour because you were in travail."

"The pains stopped and I grew hungry."

"Put down that roll and let me examine you. Can you still feel the child kicking?"

"Yes, very strongly," she said. Clare removed her gloves and put her hands on Louise's swollen abdomen. She was reassured to feel movement. Next, she pulled a horn-shaped implement from her birthing bag, pressing one end on the stretched skin and the other end to her ear. To her relief, there were no evident sounds of distress.

"Does it sound like a male child? I do so long for a boy!"

Clare laughed. "I know of no sounds that indicate the sex of the unborn child. I listen for other reasons."

"Monsieur le Marquis would be delighted if it were a son, after the disappointment of the three daughters I have given him. You would receive a generous reward for a boy," she said enticingly. Then a shadow crossed her face. "I'm aware my husband has fathered several male children by his mistresses, but he needs a *legitimate* son to inherit his title."

"Dear friend," Clare responded, "if I had the power to determine the sex of a child, I would only deliver baby boys. Then indeed I should become famous and exceptionally wealthy. But alas, an equal share of baby girls is necessary to ensure future wives for the baby boys."

Lady Louise looked perplexed for a moment. Then she nodded. "Oh, I see. How clever of you, Clare, to figure that out. Now if only you could find a way to tell the sex of this child kicking my insides."

"Well, we will have to wait." Clare spread a clean cloth on the table next to the bed and began to set out her birthing tools. *This might be a false alarm, but best to be prepared.* Seeing the growing concern on Louise's face, she pulled over a chair and tried to distract her until the pains resumed.

Leaning toward her friend's left ear, Clare whispered, "I think Father Benedict is listening at the door. Did you send for him?"

"No. I didn't realize he was here. He often invites himself for dinner, but rarely bestirs himself for breakfast. I wish he would leave. There is no need for him to be standing outside my bedchamber."

"Let's confound him by speaking *en anglais*," Clare suggested quietly, wanting a chance to chat with her friend without being overheard.

"Yes, let's! He can be meddlesome at times."

Clare remembered her English from Pierre's books. As a young girl, Louise had the benefit of an English governess. The two friends began conversing in the foreign tongue. Had they been able to see the priest's consternation as he held his ear to the door, they would both have been amused.

"Perhaps your cousin thinks I will try to convince *you* to become a Huguenot," said Clare.

"How shocking that would be! But highly unlikely, my dear friend. I would be banned from Court. You and I both know how King Louis feels about his heretic subjects."

Clare frowned, remembering the royal edict that had prevented Pierre from studying law, forcing him to leave the country. But then again if Pierre had stayed, she might never have met Lady Louise. *Strange how things sometimes work out.*

"You don't think of me as a heretic, do you?" Clare asked.

Louise hesitated for a second, then said, "Of course not. I know you are a Christian. But wouldn't life in France be easier for you if you agreed to convert to the Church of Rome?"

"It might, but Jacques would get rid of me and keep me from ever seeing my children again."

"I understand. To lose one's children would be a terrible loss for any mother." It was a troublesome thought, but true. Both women knew that in France, fathers legally owned their offspring—mothers had no right to them.

"Speaking of children," said Clare, "how are your three daughters doing?"

"Praise the Lord, they are all in good health. My husband is already arranging suitable marriages for them."

"Already? Surely, the eldest cannot be yet eight years of age?"

She shrugged. "They are twelve, eight and two. It is not too early for their betrothals. And what of your son and daughter, Clare?"

"They thrive on the country air. Jean-Pierre resembles his father, physically and mentally. Slow, patient and deliberate. He wants to be a soldier someday—sometimes he sits for hours, playing with his tin soldiers. Lately, though, he has developed a stutter and fear of the dark, claiming there is a ghost who roams the nursery at night."

"You are fortunate to have a son," said Louise. "What of your daughter?"

"She has an innate curiosity of the world around her, constantly asking questions. She can outrun her older brother and learned to read before he could master his letters. Lucina is destined to become a midwife one day—already wraps her baby dolls in swaddling cloths, as my mother taught her." Clare choked back a sob. Maman had died last year, and the memory of the loss was still fresh in her mind.

"Lucina, such an unusual name," remarked Louise. Her three daughters had common French names: Daphne, Marie-Thérèse, and Hélène. Although Louise was a friend, Clare felt it best not to tell her that little Lucina was named after a pagan goddess, so she simply said her mother had chosen the name.

~~~
~~~

After conversing in English for several hours, Clare began pushing up her sleeves. "Louise, it is possible that you became alarmed by false, early pangs. Since I traveled all this way, I will examine you to see if you are in true travail. But first I must wash my hands."

"You there," Clare called to the wet nurse—the wife of a farmer, who had recently given birth to her own child, but had been hired to suckle the Montjardin child. "Ask the servants to fetch Madame Dupres a basin of hot water and a bar of soap."

When the wet nurse left to do the lady's bidding, Louise asked Clare why she engaged in such unusual practice. "My other midwives never washed their hands."

Despite the extreme heat in the room, Clare felt a chill. She bit her lower lip and considered how to respond to this question. Her impulse was to laugh and say, "To keep the demons at bay." But this was not the time to jest. She thought back to Maman's admonitions. *Never voice superstitious ideas to a woman in travail. What if something were to go wrong in the birthing process? You could be blamed and branded a witch. You could be brought to trial and those carelessly uttered words used against you. Do not forget the memory of your great-great-grandmother—may she rest in peace—who was burned at the stake because the woman she attended was brought to bed of a deformed infant.*

Clare knew there were still ignorant, uninformed people who believed midwives were witches due to their skills in an area of life that was a mystery to many people—especially men, since midwifery was a profession dominated exclusively by women. So Clare was careful with her words.

"Is handwashing really such a strange practice, my friend? Do you not wash your own hands before meals?"

"Yes, I suppose I do."

"Washing my hands when attending a birthing is simply a habit taught me by Maman. I do not know if cleanliness helps, but I do it anyway. What harm can it do?"

"Oh, I see," said Louise. Clare thought her patient looked like a fragile porcelain doll, sitting in the sumptuous bed.

The servant carried in a steaming basin, along with a fragranced bar of luxurious milled soap. As Clare scrubbed her palms, fingers, and arms, she heard a loud moan.

"Ohhhhh. The pains have started again and I feel like I'm sitting in a puddle of rainwater." Clare moved quickly to the bed and checked—clear fluid, no blood—all good signs.

"Louise, your water has broken. Your child is ready to greet the world."

A shadow passed over Lady Louise's face. She reached for Clare's hand. "I am suddenly very, very afraid. *Mon Dieu.* Will I die?"

"There's always a slight possibility. It's in God's hands. But with His help, I will do my utmost to save you and the child—with as little discomfort as can be managed." She poured a small, carefully measured dose of elixir, because Louise was petite, and pressed the potion to Louise's lips, urging her to swallow.

Louise grimaced and turned her head away. "Ugh, it smells rotten."

"Yes, and it tastes worse than it smells. I know from my own experience at Lucina's birth. But I promise, it *will* help you bear the pain."

~~~

Four hours later, Clare finished delivering the child. *Why*, she thought with deep satisfaction, *I believe I could do this in my sleep.* As she wrapped the leavings and the pink ribbons in her birthing bag, she heard angry voices out in the corridor. She recognized the Marquis's loud voice demanding to know why Madame Dupres was with his wife. Had he not given explicit instructions to call Madame Larque, the Catholic midwife, if his wife went into travail during his absence?

Clare was puzzled by his anger. Why had he not wanted her to attend his wife? The Papist midwife with long dirty fingernails had the reputation of losing many of her patients in travail. She was no better than a butcher! *No wonder Louise begged me to come, remembering the horrors she had experienced when little Hélène was born. At least the Marquis did not barge into the confinement chamber. Seeing the pink ribbons holding his wife in place would really have engendered his fury.*

Mercifully, the child appeared healthy. Lady Louise gradually regained consciousness, and her husband was then welcomed into the bedchamber. Father Benedict followed at his heels like a faithful hound. The Marquis's anger evaporated when he was told he had a son. He leaned over and kissed his wife, beaming like a glowing taper.

"She did very well for you this time, milord," Clare said, wiping off her knife and stuffing the empty elixir bottle into her birthing bag.
~~~

"Did you suffer much, my poor dear?" he asked, patting the top of his wife's head. "I flinched every time I heard your screams through the door."

Father Benedict said, "I tried to comfort him during the ordeal. I explained the Church deems it unnatural for a laboring mother not to bear pain. It is the curse of Eve."

"Oh no!" said Lady Louise. "I have no recollection of any pain or screams. Clare's magic elixir put me into a sweet dream. I felt like I was floating down the river, hearing birdsong from the trees."

A smile of relief crept over her husband's countenance. He held the infant in his arms as Father Benedict baptized the newborn Louis-Armand. The future Marquis let out a wail, proving his lungs were strong. Lady Louise was able to hold the child for a minute before giving him over to the wet nurse to be suckled.

Clare heaved a sigh as she closed the latch on her bag. She was too exhilarated by this beautiful birthing experience to feel tired. Anxious to return home to her own family, she promised to return on the morrow to check on Lady Louise. *And collect my reward.* Perhaps the Marquis would explain why he had been so angry to find her there.

Chapter 19

The Shocking New Edict

Exhausted when I returned home last evening, I was grateful for the light repast Marie prepared for me in the kitchen. Everyone else was asleep. Marie shook her head and told me Giselle had not come downstairs until noon, which didn't surprise me. I spent the night in Maman's old room, not wishing my body to touch the sheets where my husband had lain with that slattern.

Giselle came into my boudoir early this morning to help me dress. She was smirking. I said nothing to her. It is time for my early-morning return to Chateau Montjardin—to check on Lady Louise and collect my reward. I have a strange foreboding. Perhaps it is simply because the weather is unusually warm for this time of year.

Journal of Clare Dupres, 11 novembre 1682

THE MARQUIS WALKED down the grand staircase as Clare was shown into the front entrance. He was informally dressed in a royal blue robe. Apparently, it was too early to anticipate visitors. Nonplussed, he politely greeted her. "*Bonjour, madame.* Please step into my study. Yesterday was a long day for you, was it not?"

"I am used to long days." Clare followed him into a long, high-ceilinged room. She looked with admiration at the tall mahogany bookshelves lining the walls, filled with leather-covered books. She wondered if the Marquis ever read them, or if they were just family heirlooms collecting dust. *Still, this is a dreary dark room. No wonder Louise wishes she could redecorate this ancestral mausoleum.*

"Might I have some refreshment, milord? I missed breakfasting this morning because I was anxious to check on Lady Louise."

"But of course!" He rang for the footman, who soon carried in a tray with a steaming pitcher of hot chocolate and a plate of freshly baked rolls with butter. Clare sipped the hot beverage slowly, savoring the sweetness of the drink.

"So, congratulations are in order," said Clare as she drained her first demitasse. "A male heir at last."

"Yes. I am ecstatic. The wet nurse says the boy feeds well and appears to be healthy, for which I praise the Almighty."

Naturally, he gives me, the midwife, no credit for my part in bringing the child into the world; but then men don't think much about the process of birthing their children or the skill involved. To them, it is like planting a seed and waiting for the fruit to ripen and fall off the tree.

Clare noticed the Marquis was not smiling as he usually did when she came to visit his wife. He stood and paced back and forth, running his fingers through his long curly wig, searching for the right words.

"I acted in an ungentlemanly manner yesterday. I should not have been shouting outside the bedchamber. And in a minute, I will explain the reason for my agitation. But first… be honest with me, Madame. Will my wife be able to bear more sons?"

Clare tried not to frown. *Why are men always in such a rush to have more children? Have they no pity for the women who must bear the risks of childbirth?*

"Your wife is still young and in good health. Give her time to rest. In a month, she will be churched. After that, in a year or two…"

He looked down at his feet. "Try to understand—I require more sons to ensure the continuation of my line. One legitimate son is not enough."

Clare suddenly felt terribly sorry for Lady Louise. Despite her beauty, sweet temper and high social standing, she was still expected to be a broodmare, to churn out child after child without complaint. *Poor Louise.*

He walked over to the window and stood silently, staring out at the drive. "Ah, Madame," he said with a slight look of annoyance, "I see Father Benedict approaching once again. I understand he was trying to bend your ear yesterday."

"Yes, he occasionally tries to convert me to your religion. I am not offended."

"These are dangerous times for you, Madame. Were you aware that Protestants are barred from leaving France without royal permission?"

"I thought that restriction applied to *all* French subjects. It seems unfair to single out the Huguenots. Especially preventing qualified men of my faith from reading for the law here. But, milord, *I* have no plans to leave France. I intend to continue my vocation as a midwife here in Normandy. So why do you say these are dangerous times for me?"

He turned and faced Clare. "Then you are unaware of the latest royal edict? The reason why I was so distressed when I came home yesterday to find you in the confinement chamber with my wife?"

The blood started to drain from Clare's face. She gripped the delicate china cup so hard that the handle almost broke off. "What royal edict? I have been isolated at home with my own small children these past two years. I came here yesterday because your wife summoned me. She is my dearest friend."

"King Louis has issued a proclamation specifically prohibiting Huguenots from practicing midwifery."

Clare sat back in shock. Her body tensed, and for what seemed like a split second, her breathing was suspended. The cup rattled in the saucer and she set it down on the table as she tried to comprehend the Marquis's words.

The Marquis looked at her with sympathetic eyes. "I see now you did not know of the recent proclamation—it was wrong to blame you. Please accept my deepest apologies for my behavior yesterday. I was not home in time to stop my wife from calling you. But you must understand my situation. I feel the King's agents may be having you watched. Even at this moment, I am uneasy having you here in my home. Your friendship with the Marquise endangers us."

As her shock slowly turned to anger, Clare drew in a long, steady breath. "Milord, help me understand why the King would prevent me from utilizing my skills to help the women of France."

"His rationale is that you might not call for a priest in time, to baptize a new infant or to say last rites for the mother."

Which explains why the servants called for Father Benedict yesterday before I got here. Why he tried to convert me. What am I to do, if I can no longer be a midwife? Clare's mind raced in a panic.

"It's not that I don't value your skills," said the Marquis, "especially now that you have birthed a healthy male heir for the house of Montjardin."

"You have other sons, too. I helped deliver your mistresses' boys."

"Yes, yes, of course. Fine boys they are. But—as to the future." He mumbled something about finding a physician to deliver his future children.

"Surely the presence of Father Benedict outside the confinement chamber…would that not have been enough to satisfy the King's concerns?"

"I'm afraid our King can be somewhat irrational," answered the Marquis.

Clare thought if she had called King Louis irrational, she would have been arrested for treason. "I am very sorry to hear our King feels that way. To deny his loyal subjects the benefit of an experienced midwife, simply because she is a Protestant. It makes no sense and exasperates me."

"What can I say, Madame? I am a loyal French subject."

"As am I." Wiping crumbs from her mouth, Clare tried to control her voice from expressing the intense fury she felt. God had given her the knowledge to help women and the gift of the elixir. Were God's gifts not more important than an irrational royal whim, a proclamation that made no sense?

"Milord, I can see you are trying to tell me that you will no longer allow me to assist your wife. Next time, for the right amount of gold, you will fetch an esteemed physician who will not know the first thing about childbirth to attend Lady Louise.

"Without a doubt, he will place leeches on her arms with his unclean hands. Bleed her when she is at a woman's most precarious time. Subject her to crude practices which will endanger her health and that of your unborn child. To say nothing of the pain she will endure—that is, if she survives."

He put his hands over his ears. "Stop! I do not wish my dear wife to die or suffer unnecessary pain. I am not a monster, despite what Father Benedict says about the curse of Eve."

"What more can I say?" said Clare. "Please call for my carriage."

The anguished man twisted his hands and turned to her with pleading eyes. "Madame, Wait a minute. Will you sell me a bottle of that magic elixir you gave to my wife? For her subsequent confinements?"

Clare was taken aback by this blunt request. "That I cannot do," she said. "The elixir is simply the correct combination of natural ingredients, which can only be freshly mixed at the time of confinement by a properly trained midwife. I am sorry, but the answer is no."

"Well then, the formula. I would pay handsomely for it."

"*Non, monsieur. C'est impossible.* I have sworn a solemn oath never to reveal the secret formula. It will cease to work if it is revealed to anyone but a Dupres midwife of my ancestral line."

"I thought you might say that," he said, his voice turning cool. "I suppose you are anxious to return to your family now. Your carriage awaits."

Clare nodded but made no move to leave. The Marquis reached into his desk drawer and pulled out a small velvet purse. He stood silently for a few minutes, looking at the object in his hands.

"I filled this last evening when I was in thrall over having a male heir at last. I must confess the thought just crossed my mind to reduce the value of this gift because of your refusal to share the elixir formula. However, I have changed my mind. You are right to feel resentful about the new edict. This royal madness is not your fault."

He handed it to her. "A small token of my appreciation. I shall always be grateful for your efforts. You are truly the finest midwife in Normandy, and I am sorry it has come to this. For all our sakes."

"*Merci*, milord. But may I go upstairs for a few minutes to say farewell to Lady Louise?"

"Of course." He ushered her out of his study. As she climbed the stairs with a heavy heart, Clare surreptitiously fingered the shape and assessed the weight of the purse contents before tucking it in her pocket. A brief smile tempered her vexation.

Seeing all was as well as could be expected with mother and babe, she whispered, "Goodbye, Louise," planting a small kiss on her forehead. "I shall always value our friendship."

"And I too," mumbled Louise in a soft, dreamy voice.

~~~
~~~

As her carriage wended its way through the narrow streets of Rouen, Clare reached into her pocket to examine the contents of the pouch. A delicate diamond brooch as well as ninety gold *louis d'or*. She drew in her breath. *The largest gift—ever. And the last*, she thought with some regret.

When Clare reached home, she placed the Marquis's generous reward in her jewel casket. She ran her fingers through the voluminous gold coins and strands of jewels piled inside. Having already amassed enough of a fortune for a lifetime of ease, the regret she felt was not at the loss of additional rewards, but at the loss of her ability to continue practicing her profession. All due to the whim of King Louis. Her shock and regret turned to rage at the absolute ruler. *How dare he ruin my life again!*

That November morning, Clare came to the realization that the King would stop at nothing to achieve his goal of converting all Huguenots to Popery. But for now, the sound of childish laughter breezing through her open boudoir window lifted her spirits. Gazing out, she spied her husband sitting in the garden, sketching the noxious yellow blooms on the bulbous buttercups. Lucina was chasing Jean-Pierre around the grassy lawn, unattended. The sky was a brilliant shade of blue with no hint of rain clouds.

"Jacques," she called out from the window, "where is Claudette?"

"She said she was ill and went up to bed. I asked Giselle to keep an eye on the children."

"Well, then, where is Giselle?"

"I sent her in to fetch me a drink. It's really quite warm in the sun," he answered absentmindedly. He was leaning over, concentrating on the flower.

Clare was irked. "The children are too young to be left unattended. They don't understand the poisonous nature of the plants in my herb border."

"They're just having a runabout," he said.

Clare could tell by the tone of his voice he was still upset that she had been away at a birthing. *Jacques will be overjoyed when he hears the news that I will be forced to stay home, to give up midwifery. He will be thrilled with the King's new edict.*

Just then, Giselle sashayed out to the garden carrying two pewter mugs of ale. Surprised at the unexpected early return of her mistress, she grinned and brazenly sat down on the stone bench, her knees spread wide and her dress pulled up. Then she took a swig of ale and called the little ones to her side.

"I *will* toss that saucy wench out tomorrow," sighed Clare. She collapsed on the daybed and was soon fast asleep.

Chapter 20

The Tightening Noose

ONE DAY, CLARE opened her journal to the last written entry—the birth of Louis-Armand, heir to Montjardin—and was shocked to realize that eighteen months had passed. How she missed practicing her profession and longed to return to birthing!

Since the fateful day when the Marquis had informed Clare that King Louis had explicitly forbidden Huguenots from practicing midwifery, she had settled in at home with her own children, bringing a false degree of domestic harmony to Maison Dupres. Jacques had been delighted—had insisted his family was safe from persecution in France, so long as Clare turned down all requests for her services and remained behind the iron gates fronting their property.

And so Clare began corresponding with Pierre. At first, she wrote to inquire about Celia's health, since Celia had stopped sending letters. When he reported by return post that his wife was sinking into melancholy over the death of their only son, Clare advised him to find a qualified midwife to treat Celia with herbs, instead of the fashionable London male physicians who were not helping her with their leeches. "If only I could get to England, I believe I could help Celia," she wrote in her letter.

Clare also told Pierre of the worsening conditions in France, news which she overheard on Sundays when the male congregants gossiped under the trees after church services. One of the men had called King Louis's growing restrictions barbaric. "As a child," he had whispered, "our tyrant King was taught to hate Huguenots, and now that he possesses unrestrained power, he flatters himself with the idea of compelling every French citizen to embrace the Church of Rome. I fear we are doomed."

"Nonsense," argued Jacques, "we are still allowed to worship in our churches."

"True for now, but lately the King has forbidden the singing of psalms in our homes. It's only a matter of time until he takes away all our religious freedoms."

"Oh, that will never happen!" answered Jacques. "We have the Edict of Nantes. Let's all just pray to soften King Louis's heart. Our faith in God will save us."

Clare was deeply concerned. Jacques frequently sang hymns in the garden while sketching flower designs. Maison Dupres was situated so close to the road that his loud voice could be heard by anyone passing by. *If spies are watching our home to see if I am working as a midwife, will they not also report his prohibited singing?*

One night she dreamt she was a prisoner on a platform with a tightening noose around her neck, as King Louis and Father Benedict stood together laughing hysterically. She woke up shaking, unable to breathe. Clare urged Jacques to take their family to safety out of France, but he said it was only a bad dream. They were safe.

In one of his letters to Clare, Pierre predicted that the vast number of Protestant artisans who were escaping to England would hurt the French economy. He urged them to leave France. Clare read portions of the letter aloud to her husband:

"Sell everything—Maison Dupres, the surrounding farms, the business. Come to London. So many French weavers have already set up their looms in the Spitalfields area of the city that several French Reformed churches have sprung up. I am sure they would welcome a talented designer like Jacques."

Jacques pulled the letter from Clare's hands and crumpled it. He waved his hand around the room where they sat. "Could you really give up this maison which you insisted on restoring?" Clare looked around the beautifully appointed room and admitted it gave her a pang.

Clare suspected what Pierre predicted had already begun to affect Jacques's business. For years, Dupres & Sons, Purveyors of Fine Fabrics, had purchased and exported excess fabric from the workrooms King Louis had established at Versailles. But supplies had dried up this spring, when the new royal palace was completed.

The Huguenot silk weavers who worked from Jacques's designs were disappearing from France at a rapid pace. At a time when the demand for luxurious French fabrics at the royal palaces of England was increasing, it was exceedingly difficult for Jacques to obtain these premium goods for export and for his elite customers at the shop in Rouen.

"Jacques," said Clare one morning over breakfast. "I notice you take fewer and fewer business trips—I think trade must be falling off."

"Don't worry your pretty head about that." *He sounds just like his father*, thought Clare. *Uncle used to say the same thing to me.*

"But, Jacques, if we left France as Pierre suggests, I could resume my midwifery in England—help out financially."

"Expect me to live off your ill-gotten gains? Never! I still own this land, and the rents from my tenant farmers are sufficient to support our family. Even if my business has slowed a bit, I'm sure it will pick up in time."

A few weeks later, she said, "Jacques, how shall I be able to train Lucina in midwifery if we stay in France?"

"The only training my daughter needs is in the arts of sewing a fine seam, painting a fancy table and becoming a dutiful wife. In my opinion, you are wasting your time teaching the children to speak English. Don't deny that you are."

"Knowledge of the English language is valuable. Look how it enabled your brother to become successful in London."

"Clare," he said, "Huguenot artisans are forbidden to leave France. You know I am an artisan. That in itself puts an end to your grandiose ideas."

But she was not so easily put off. "I hear many artisans are leaving. Bribe the authorities to allow our family to emigrate, to reunite with your brother."

"Do you seriously think they would grant such a request? They have threatened to confiscate all the worldly possessions of any Huguenot who tries to leave. We must stay in France and make the best of it. I will continue praying for King Louis to soften his heart." With that, he left the room.

Strong-willed her entire life, Clare decided to take matters in her own hands. That very afternoon, she took pen in hand and wrote to Pierre, asking for his help in saving their family and revealing details of a secret plan she had hatched.

~~~

Clare had rarely ventured into Rouen since her profession had been closed to her, except to attend church. The day after the letter came from Pierre, agreeing to her secret plan, she dressed in her finest clothing and took the carriage into the city. She told Jacques she needed to do some shopping, but didn't tell him her true intent. *If he knew, he might forbid it.*

Her first stop was Dupres & Sons, Purveyors of Fine Fabrics. The shop now catered primarily to middling-class customers. Plain muslins, nothing fancy. Sadly, the elite salon behind the shop was closed down. Dustsheets covered the upholstered chairs, and the lack of fire in the hearth or candles in the chandelier had turned the former private boutique into a sorry damp room.

Monsieur Leclerc greeted her politely but looked troubled. She asked for several lengths of fine burgundy and brown velvet. He said to take whatever she pleased—the expensive fabrics were gathering dust in the storeroom, as most of the elite customers no longer frequented the shop with their trade. The exception was Lady Louise, who still came in from time to time and always asked how Madame Dupres was doing.

"In fact," he said, "the Marquise was just here before you arrived. She ...um...appears to be in the family way again."

Clare felt a sudden emptiness in hearing this news. She knew she would be unable to help her friend in confinement but wanted to wish her well. Gazing out the window, she spotted the Montjardin carriage parked in front of the clockmaker's. "Monsieur Leclerc, I have a few more stops. When you wrap my parcels, add a dozen of the cloisonné smuggler buttons and some gold braid, *s'il vous plaît.* Place them inside my carriage with Girard." She dashed out toward the clockmaker's on the pretense of needing her watch oiled.

Breathless from rushing, Clare arrived at the shop under the large clock just as Lady Louise was stepping out the door, followed by her lady's maid carrying purchases.

"Clare!" she exclaimed, kissing her on both cheeks. "What a surprise to find you here. I'm delighted to see you."
~~~

"And you…you look blooming."

For a moment, Lady Louise was puzzled. Then she said, "Oh, you mean *this*," pointing to her belly in embarrassment. "It seems I am *enceinte* once again. The Marquis is so anxious for another son."

Poor woman, Clare thought. *How can she honestly be breeding again? If I dared speak my mind, I would recommend the simple regimen of separate rooms.* But keeping her thoughts to herself, she asked how young Louis-Armand was doing.

"He is rambunctious and his sisters treat him like a little prince. I think they spoil him."

"But he is healthy? That is the main thing, isn't it?"

"Of course. I do miss seeing you, Clare. We must get together soon. After I finish preparations for the harvest ball…oh, dear me." Louise turned red as a ripe strawberry and covered her mouth with her gloved hand. "It was wretched of me to mention that."

She apologized again—desperately sorry the Dupres could not be invited to the ball this year. Her husband was still nervous that the King was having Chateau Montjardin watched, especially as everyone at Court knew her time of confinement was approaching. "But then, we might have to cancel the ball again this year. Our timing is not very good, is it?" she said, pointing to her belly and shrugging.

Clare felt uncomfortable and made an excuse about needing to meet somebody. After saying farewell to Lady Louise, she walked aimlessly until she found herself in front of the Huguenot church. Several men were tacking an official notice on the door. When they left, she moved closer and read the sign:

BY ROYAL PROCLAMATION OF HIS MAJESTY, KING LOUIS XIV, HUGUENOT CHILDREN ARE NOW ELIGIBLE TO CONVERT TO THE TRUE RELIGION, THE HOLY CHURCH OF ROME, UPON REACHING THE AGE OF SEVEN. NO PARENTAL CONSENT IS NECESSARY.

Clare clutched her pearl necklace so hard it almost broke. She rushed back to Rue du Gros-Horloge. Crossing the street, she was almost run over by a horse-driven waggon. Gasping for breath, she found herself standing in front of the jeweler's shop. After composing herself, she entered.

Ten minutes later, she came out of the shop, climbed into her carriage, and directed Girard to return home at once.

~~~
~~~

Giselle was lazily swishing a rag back and forth across the dusty windowsill in Jacques's study. He was busy reading.

Master's ignorin' me agin. No longer visits my room at night. S'pose he's tired of me, she thought angrily. *Used to enjoy my attentions. Prefers his cold bitch wife.* Giselle saw the carriage pull up to the steps and noticed Clare coming out, clutching packages. Her eyes were tear-stained.

"Mistress is back," the wench announced. "She don't look so good."

Jacques met his wife at the door. "Clare!" he exclaimed. "What's wrong, dearest? You look terribly distressed."

Giselle took the heavy parcels and set them on the hall table, wondering what was inside. She heard Clare telling Jacques about some poster she had seen on their church door.

"Think what this means for our children, Jacques! They will be kidnapped and baptized as Catholics." He put his arm around his wife's shoulders and led her into his study.

Somethin's goin' on. Think I better finish dustin' in there, thought Giselle, picking up her rag and slipping into the room.

"Leave us," ordered Jacques to Giselle, who walked slowly out of the study and decided to polish the doorknobs—something she rarely did.

Jacques poured Clare a glass of sherry. Then he said, "Do not give way to useless alarm, Clare. Thought it is right to be prepared for the worst, there is no occasion to look on it as certain."

"But Jacques," Clare sputtered.

"Our children are still babies," he said. "We will bide our time. I will keep praying for King Louis to soften his heart."

"And I will pray that you overcome your stubbornness before it is too late to get out of France," she muttered.

"Clare," he pleaded, "how can you think of leaving all we have?"

"Pierre has offered us a place to stay. He has a flat in London as well as a country home in Kent. You are a talented designer—your floral sketches are unique. Pierre will support us until you find a design job with the weavers in Spitalfields."

"Live off my brother's charity? Have you lost your senses?"

"Send him some of the pictures in your portfolio. He can start showing them around."

"Enough! I am going out into the garden."

"Go into the woods, Jacques, if you must. You know the King has forbidden the singing of psalms outside church. There are spies all around."

Jacques stalked out.

Giselle smiled and stood aside as the master dashed by. Her thoughts were so absorbed that when she helped Clare dress for dinner that evening, she failed to notice the pearls missing from around her mistress's neck.

Chapter 21

Sewing for Pierre

My recent letters from Delphine are filled with distressing news. The church where Papa used to preach was closed by the royal authorities because the minister was accused of admitting relapsed "convertis" to Sunday services—then they razed the building to the ground. Huguenot residents of Dieppe were forced to billet marauding French soldiers in their homes. Border patrols along the Normandy coast intercepted some of Delphine's neighbors who attempted to flee without permission and fined them heavily. Others were arrested when they gathered to sing psalms in the woods.

Poor Delphine is terrified. Never as pious as Jacques, she quickly submitted to conversion. Abjured her religion to save her boarding house from destruction. She is frequently visited by missionary priests to "investigate her spiritual state of mind." I burn these disturbing letters—Jacques would disown his sister if he knew what she had done. Luckily, things are still quiet in Rouen.

Perhaps we should take Delphine with us to England. I am determined we shall soon be going there. When I finally reveal my secret plan to Jacques, he won't believe how clever I've been.

Journal of Clare Dupres, 20 juin 1685

IN JULY, JACQUES decided to close the shop in Rouen due to lack of sufficient local business. He began to talk of selling the carriage. To his amazement, Clare raised no objection. She readily agreed it was no longer needed except to transport them to church—the farm waggon would suffice.

He also used the farm waggon to transport the remaining stock of fine silk fabric from the defunct business premises to the storeroom behind Maison Dupres. "A temporary measure," he said, "to avoid vandalism and save warehousing expenses."

When Dupres & Sons, Purveyors of Fine Fabrics received a large new order from Windsor Castle for a batch of flowered silk, he fortunately had what they required in his depleted stockpile. He planned to drive this order to Dieppe himself, to ensure that the precious cargo would be placed safely on the outgoing merchant ship. *This order will generate a sum of gold, to tide us over until I can rebuild my business*, he thought.

Although prospects were not looking promising, Jacques wanted to keep up his image. Nonetheless, reality had forced the Dupres to reduce the staff at home. It now consisted mainly of Marie, Claudette and Giselle. Girard would be departing as soon as a buyer could be procured for the carriage—he was looking for a new position.

However, Clare begged Jacques not to fire Claudette. He agreed. Claudette stayed on, and so did Giselle. The latter complained bitterly about having to serve as housemaid, dairymaid and scullery maid.

Whenever Claudette brought the children down for their evening visit with their papa, she always told him how thankful she was that she and Giselle could continue working in the same household, and wasn't her hard-working niece doing a fine job?

Clare grimaced. Jacques knew she had finally given up efforts to train Giselle to be a proper lady's maid. Besides, Clare had told him she preferred not to have the snarky girl upstairs, except to light the fire and bring up her breakfast tray.

He still trusted if he prayed more fervently, King Louis would change his attitude and loosen restrictions against the Huguenots. Stubbornly refusing to face the truth about their perilous situation, Jacques was relieved that Clare had suddenly stopped nagging him to bribe the officials. He didn't understand why, but she seemed more serene these days—preoccupied with some new sewing project. Jacques relished the new peaceful atmosphere at home—he adored his wife and children.

~~~

Hearing of his brother's difficulties finding weavers to turn his designs into fabric, Pierre wrote to Clare, suggesting Jacques diversify his export products. "Tell him to consider switching to brandy or
~~~

wine. Good French wine is always in demand here among my neighbors in Kent." Clare passed on Pierre's suggestion to her husband.

"Hmmph. What does my upstart brother know about business? He had been preparing to study law when his plans were interrupted. The foolish boy sold his portion of the house in Dieppe to me before he left France. Of course, I signed the entire house over to Delphine after we married."

"Well, Jacques, perhaps he wasn't so foolish after all. He needed the money from the sale to support himself during his early days in England."

Jacques just grunted and returned to his ledgers. He hadn't written to his brother in years. *Pierre has probably forgotten how to speak French by now*, he thought. *Pierre always writes to Clare in English.* All news traveled back and forth through their correspondence, letters that Jacques couldn't read or understand. He supposed they spoke mostly about Celia's female problems—he had little interest in the health or welfare of a foreigner he had never met.

In addition to writing letters to Pierre, Clare had been busy sewing waistcoats for him since bringing home the parcels from the shop in Rouen. The bolts of velvet she had selected had been meticulously cut to size, based on measurements sent by Celia. One evening, as Clare sat embroidering a heavy brown velvet waistcoat, she remarked, "Pierre is doing very well for himself these days."

"Pierre, Pierre, Pierre. I am sick of hearing about Pierre!" Sometimes Jacques asked himself why Clare continually talked about Pierre—corresponded with him. Did she still harbor romantic feelings? Jacques knew of the affection between them when they were teens. *No*, he reassured himself, *she must be over that by now.*

"Do you object to my sewing for Pierre? Sewing calms my jumpy nerves."

Jacques looked at his wife suspiciously, but she just continued stitching. "Besides," she added, "it keeps me busy since I am forced by King Louis's edict to stay at home. Is that not what *you* always wished for? To keep me from going out birthing?"

Jacques ignored Clare's insinuation and grumbled, "Why cannot Pierre's own wife sew his waistcoats?"

"Celia is frail. She has difficulty threading a needle. Besides, now that Pierre owns a country home in Tunbridge, he enjoys parading up High Street in the latest French fashions."

"So," said Jacques, "my baby brother is rising in the world and wants to impress his new family and friends. He always was a coxcomb."

"Pierre and Celia frequently dine with some of the finest families in Kent—the Bartons, the Wellers, and the Austens. Families whose Kentish ancestors made their fortunes as clothiers and have risen into the rank of landed English gentry."

"Well, la-dee-da. If my spoiled brother needs fancy clothes for his busy social life in a provincial country village, far be it from me to complain that you sew for him."

Sometimes Jacques suspected his wife enjoyed tormenting him by boasting of his younger brother's success in England. Since Pierre had married into the Smithfield family and become a partner in Smithfield-Barton Ltd., he had apparently become incredibly wealthy.

Jacques's jealousy of Pierre dated back to their childhood. *I was the well-mannered, dutiful child, but Pierre was always my sister's favorite. Delphine doted on our dark-haired baby brother; her winsome cherub, her naughty child. She frequently blamed me for Pierre's mischief, like the time he poured clean pebbles in her stew pot.*

When Pierre had accepted Cap'n Silas's offer and left France ten years ago, Jacques had been secretly relieved. Oh, how he had gloated when Clare finally accepted his marriage proposal. For once, he had triumphed over his younger brother. Even if he *had* been forced to put up with Clare's midwifery nonsense for a few years, Jacques had won the fair lady. And now they had two beautiful healthy children in their nursery. Poor Pierre had none.

Who am I, thought Jacques, *to begrudge my brother a few velvet waistcoats, sewn by my wife?* And so when Clare asked him to package and ship the heavy brown-and-burgundy garments to Pierre, he willingly complied.

Had he known what she had sewn into the seams and hidden in the cloisonné smuggler buttons, he might not have been so complacent.

Chapter 22

Miscarriage

My rewards pouch is now empty except for the fake string of pearls, which I have worn every day for the past year—the jeweler in Rouen did an excellent job of making a paste replica. I have taken the precaution of filling my locked jewel casket with small rocks as I suspect Giselle shakes it every so often. Pierre's last letter said all had arrived safely. Celia may not be able to sew, but she was able to remove the contents from the seams and buttons, now invested safely with a London goldsmith.

Why do I still hesitate to tell Jacques about my plan? I fear he will become angry, especially since I asked Pierre for this favor without my husband's permission. Jacques will get over it in time. When we reach England, we will not be penniless. All that remains is to receive the documentation from Pierre granting us safe passage. Our fate is in Pierre's hands.

Journal of Clare Dupres, 1 septembre 1685

JACQUES RECEIVED AN inquiry from a weaver living in Lyons who expressed interest in working from his flowered silk patterns. The weaver was one of a handful of Huguenot workers remaining in that former hive of busy artisans. Most had left the country. Desperate for new suppliers, Jacques decided to travel to Lyons by horseback. As he stowed his sketches and samples safely in his saddlebags, he cautioned Clare that he might be gone several weeks and warned her to stay home with the children, safely behind the iron gates. Clare hadn't told him about Delphine—didn't want him to brood about it during his travels.

The morning after he left, Clare was arranging flowers in a vase and happened to gaze out the window at a once-familiar sight—Lady Louise traveling down the road from Rouen toward Paris with her entire family crowded in the carriage. Clare observed the Marquis, the three daughters, and the little heir Louis-Armand on his maman's lap. She wondered whether the babe Lady Louise had been ripe with last year had survived. Since the Dupres were no longer on the invitation list for the harvest ball and Clare had discontinued her midwifery services, she had been out of touch with her old friend. *How I miss our visits, our conversations....*

As the carriage approached the gates to Maison Dupres, the driver slowed and unexpectedly turned into the drive. Surprised, Clare went out to greet them, wondering why they were pulling up to her door. *Are they here to bring us an invitation to the ball?*

She was shocked to see how Lady Louise had changed since their chance encounter in town a year earlier. Her normally pink complexion was white as a sheet. She had become abnormally thin. As she alighted, she held on to her husband to keep from falling over.

During the ride, she told Clare, she felt a trickle of blood flowing down her leg and insisted on stopping. Clare helped her up to Maman's old bedchamber, deeply concerned about her friend's condition. The Marquis stood helpless on the polished black-and-white entry hall floor, twisting the brim of his hat. Clare came downstairs long enough to tell him his wife was unable to travel any further.

"But we are on our way to Versailles, to visit my parents. They are hosting a party for the children of the royal courtiers."

"Milord," Clare said, "I am quite certain your wife is suffering a miscarriage. She is feverish and has lost a great deal of blood. Leave her here under my care."

"Another miscarriage? How devastating. Two years ago, there was a premature baby girl, who died on the third day. My wife almost died of childbirth fever, but the accoucher who attended her—well, he assured me we could still try again for another son. We had that other son—stillborn, last September." He looked down, still grieving.

Clare tried to conceal her anger. *What kind of man puts his wife at such risk? Brings in a male physician to birth his child?* Clare thought of berating him for continuing to approach his wife in bed, but she understood he was simply doing what most men of his rank would do. If

Louise died trying to give him another son, he would mourn for the prescribed period and then remarry.

"I'm sorry to hear of your losses. What you decide to do today is your decision, milord. All I can say is Lady Louise is in no condition to travel. Leave her with me and I will care for her."

The impatient girls sitting in the carriage called to their father. Their baby brother was crying. Clare could see that the Marquis was torn. He obviously understood the importance of his girls' attendance at the royal party, but little Louis-Armand was too young to be traveling without his mother. Clare suggested leaving the little boy with her own two children in the Dupres nursery. Claudette would look after him.

"Thank you for offering this," he said in worried relief. "I promise I will drop the girls off with their grandparents and head straight back. Please do what you can for my dear wife."

Clare stayed at Lady Louise's side for seven days and nights, wiping her brow with cool cloths and dosing her with special herbs. At times, the Marquise was close to death, and Clare wondered if she would be able save her friend.

~~~

Monsieur le Marquis did not return as promised. He sent a message—he was delayed at Fontainebleau. King Louis's advisors were meeting there to draft a new edict for the King's signature and they had insisted on his attendance. Insulting the King's advisors was not an option.

By the time he returned to Maison Dupres, his wife had barely rallied from her miscarriage. The color was slowly returning to her cheeks. She was weak, but expected to survive.

"Madame Dupres," said the Marquis, grasping her hands, tears rolling down his cheeks. "What can I say? How can I ever thank you for saving my dearest Louise? If ever there is *anything* I can do for you—"

"There is. Tell me the news from the palace. Rumors are all we hear. You were there with the King's advisors. Are there to be yet more restrictions placed on his Huguenot subjects?"

The Marquis looked around. "Is Monsieur Dupres at home? Perhaps I should speak directly with him."
~~~

"He is away on business, but you can tell me." He paled. Clare could tell he was hesitant to share information he had learned in high-level private meetings with a lady.

Clare would not allow him to leave, even if she had to shame him into telling her the news. She supposed from his pale expression it was not going to be good news.

"I just saved your wife's life, milord. Do you not owe me a return obligation? To give me advance warning if there is danger to my family?"

The Marquis looked uneasily down at his feet.

"Milord, your telling it will be the greatest act of friendship, and my gratitude will be ensured immediately by any information tending to that end. Pray, let me hear it."

Finally he spoke. "You are right. But if you repeat what I am about to tell you, I will deny you heard it from me. Within a few weeks, it will be made public anyway. Your husband should make plans to take your family out of the country as soon as possible."

Clare felt sick to her stomach. She led the Marquis into the parlor and they sat down. He reached into his pocket and took out some notes. Put on his spectacles and cleared his throat. Clare clenched the arms of the chair, anticipating the worst.

"King Louis is about to sign a new edict. He has been advised that many Huguenots have successfully been converted, due to the practice of quartering troops in their homes."

Clare flinched, thinking of Delphine. "King Louis's infamous soldiers, the ones called *Dragonnades*, threatened to destroy my sister's home in Dieppe when she was forced to billet them. She was coerced to abjure her Protestant faith."

"It pains me to hear that your sister suffered mistreatment. But our King views his methods as the only way to save recalcitrant souls. He rejoices in all the new conversions. Therefore, he sees no need to keep the Edict of Nantes in place any longer."

Clare was thunderstruck. Jacques had long relied on the rights granted in that edict. Why did her husband not comprehend how King Louis had been systematically cutting away those rights piece by piece, like limbs from an old tree? How these growing limitations had affected his own family? Recent royal proclamations restricting Protestant prayers, lowering the age of consent for baptism. Chip,

chip, chip, little by little. *Now with a stroke of Louis's quill pen, our religious rights in France will be entirely obliterated.*

"Oh, dear God," Clare said, holding her hand to her forehead.

The Marquis put down his notes, expressing concern that she might faint. "Please believe me, Madame, I opposed the new restrictions, but I'm sorry to report that all of the King's advisors approved them. King Louis is surrounded by sycophants."

Clare grabbed her throat, promised not to faint, and asked him to continue.

He began recounting the eleven articles of the forthcoming Revocation. "All Reformed Protestant churches are to be destroyed; your ministers must convert or leave the country within two weeks. All Protestant children are to be baptized and educated as Catholics. Protestant schools will be forbidden—"

"Enough!" cried Clare. "We are being told we cannot leave France, but also that we no longer have any religious freedom. Is that fair?"

He shrugged. "Protestants will be allowed to stay without disadvantages, as long as they refrain from holding public services. I know that may not seem fair, but you know King Louis's favorite words: *L'état, c'est moi.*"

"The state, it is me. Our King is invincible and merciless," said Clare. "He dares to call himself the greatest of men, the most Christian king. He has no parliament to stop him from revoking a former law if he chooses to do so." She paced back and forth across the carpet, her face drawn.

The Marquis gazed at her sympathetically, but it was beyond his power to do more than reveal the royal intention. "It won't be signed until early November."

Clare was grateful for the early warning, but desperately thought, *What if Pierre's paperwork does not arrive in time?*

"Milord, I appreciate your frankness and I will tell no one of your confidences. But I must beg one more favor of you."

"And what is that?"

"Help my family obtain written permission to leave France, before the Revocation is signed. Please."

"Ah, I wish I could, but that is beyond my authority. Only the Intendant can issue such a permit. If I am caught contributing in any way to your escape, I will suffer huge fines."

"There must be *something* you can do," she implored.

The Marquis stood up from his chair and reached for his walking stick. "The Intendant is coming to a dinner party at the chateau, shortly before our harvest ball. I will see what I can accomplish on your behalf, but I cannot make any promises."

Just then, little Louis-Armand, Jean-Pierre and Lucina came bounding down the stairs, led by Claudette. "Papa, I had thutch fun with my new fwends. May I come again?"

The Marquis lifted the smiling boy. "We'll see. But now it is time to gather up your maman and take her home to rest. Say *au revoir et merci*, Louis-Armand." The boy dutifully responded.

As the Marquis escorted his wife and son to the carriage, he said in parting, "I am very sorry to bring such unfortunate news after all you have done for my dear Louise and my son. Believe me when I say I am eternally grateful."

"Use everything in your power to convince the Intendant to issue us a permit," she pleaded. As she watched them drive away, Clare dreaded Jacques's reaction to the Marquis's grim news when he returned from Lyons.

PART III

THE DRAGONNADES

Chapter 23

Two Soldiers in a Portside Tavern
Saturday Evening, 20 octobre 1685

A SMALL DIRT road ran behind a row of buildings on the wharf in Dieppe. A run-down building housed a tavern, frequented by sailors when they were in port, as well as the local men. Here they were able to fill their bellies with alcohol and consort with the "good-time girls."

Tonight, the *pêcheurs*, still smelling of the day's catch, noticed several strangers in their midst—two well-dressed French army soldiers, members of the cavalry unit known as Dragonnades. The hefty, burly man with the blustery voice sported a droopy black handlebar mustache and wore a curled ebony wig, which hung down to his broad shoulders. He was the high commander of a cavalry unit and had obviously just come from the public bathhouse, cleansed and thirsty.

This robust officer was Robert Souchard, but his men usually referred to him by his high-ranking title, Capitaine. The red jacket of his uniform was decorated with a number of ribbons, earned during his twenty years of loyal military service to King Louis XIV.

The short, slender soldier sitting next to him was Lieutenant Leonard Pechard, second in command. Pechard had joined the army fifteen years earlier. A second son, he had been forced to find a profession to support himself. Before his sickly father died, he had purchased the commission for Leonard, urging him to send money home to help feed his mother and younger brothers.

Pechard had fought valiantly for the King in the war against the Dutch enemies. However, for the past few years, he had found his domestic assignments distasteful. Five years before, his platoon had been sent to the French province of Poitou—not to fight against foreign enemies, but to oppress innocent men, women, and children whose only crime was worshipping as Protestants. Under King Louis's grand experiment, the Huguenots of Poitou had been forced to quarter troops in their homes until the "heretics" agreed to convert to Catholicism.

Capitaine, under direct orders from his superiors, had made it clear that his Dragonnades were to inflict serious damage on the homes where they billeted and to harass the residents until they abjured their heathen beliefs. Their efforts had succeeded in forcing most Huguenots of Poitou to convert. King Louis had been pleased that so many souls were saved, but for some reason the dragooning had stopped for four years.

Lieutenant Pechard had been relieved. *Probably because our King is preoccupied, glorying at the magnificence of his new palace at Versailles.*

But things changed. Earlier this year, Intendant Marillac had convinced King Louis to reinstate the use of the Dragonnades' "persuasive conversion" tactics in Normandy, where there was still a large population of Huguenots along the north coast. Capitaine and his unit had been sent to Dieppe, where they had claimed hundreds of new *convertis* within a few months.

One of these was Delphine Dupres, who lived in a dilapidated half-timbered house and took in boarders to support herself. A faded flowered sign on the ground floor showed evidence of a former fabric shop, now boarded up.

The poor spinster had shivered in fright when Capitaine banged on her door and burst in with his soldiers, dragging their muddy boots across her fading turkey carpets, pulling framed sketches off her walls and stomping on them. After several sleepless nights listening to the soldiers causing havoc, she reluctantly abjured and started attending Mass at L'Église.

Lieutenant Pechard had carried out his orders to the letter, but something in his Catholic conscience bothered him during the nights when the sounds of Mademoiselle Dupres's tears seeped through the walls. When Pechard had written to his mother, she had advised him to act dutifully, but to temper his actions with mercy. His mother did not approve of the Dragonnades' war against her fellow French citizens nor his commander's methods. Neither did Leonard. He was sick of being a soldier.

"Cheer up, Pechard," urged Capitaine as they sat in the smoky tavern. "The Intendant sent a message congratulating us on our amazing success in Dieppe." He punched Pechard on the arm. "You should be thrilled, soldier."

Lieutenant Pechard found it difficult to be convivial. He derived no satisfaction from harassing poor women like Delphine Dupres, and sat silently nursing his drink.

"In fact," said the boisterous Capitaine, "Intendant Marillac is so pleased that he has ordered our unit on a special mission to Rouen. A certain Huguenot family thereabouts needs to be taught a lesson for disobeying the King's proclamations. I am *personally* to see to the traitors' punishment," he boasted. "With your able assistance, of course, we will make an example of these heretics."

"A family," said Pechard cheerlessly as he emptied his tankard. "With children, I suppose."

"It is a great honor to be chosen for this mission, Pechard. Stop worrying about the children. King Louis will ensure a proper Catholic baptism and education for them."

"Do we leave at dawn on Monday, Capitaine?"

"Yes, you will lead the troops ahead and quarter them at the home. Let my men rampage to their hearts' content, but keep the family members from leaving. I have some…umm… business to finish here in Dieppe, and then I need to fetch the official signed order from the Intendant. I'll meet you at the home in a few days."

Pechard suspected Capitaine's unfinished business had something to do with a female assignation. *One of the convertis, no doubt.* The Lieutenant secretly wished this war against the Huguenots would stop soon, but he had a strong sense of duty and an obligation to support his widowed mother and brothers. He knew he would carry out this distasteful order.

"Where is this home we are to occupy?"

"Maison Dupres on the Paris road, south of Rouen. I'm willing to wager that Monsieur Jacques Dupres has a fine wine cellar. Enjoy yourselves until I arrive. Just don't let the family get away."

Lieutenant Pechard knew Dupres was a common French name, but wondered if the family was related to Mademoiselle Delphine.

Perhaps he would see her at Mass tomorrow and make inquiries. But then he thought it best not to disclose any secret military intelligence—nothing that might arouse suspicion.

Chapter 24

The Note from Lady Louise

Sunday, 21 octobre 1685

A LIGHT RAIN mizzled on Sunday morning as Jacques and Clare traveled to Rouen to attend church services. Jacques was in a cheerful frame of mind this morning. Things had gone well in Lyons and he now had at least one new weaver. "Perhaps I won't have to sell this carriage after all," he said.

Despite the closure of the shop, he was busy preparing the massive order for King James II, who had recently ascended the English throne. Like King Charles, the brother he had succeeded, King James was a pompous royal with extravagant taste in his personal dress. He and his fastidious courtiers valued and insisted upon the finest French fabric.

This past week, Jacques had personally packaged the valuable order and stacked it on the farm waggon, carefully covering it with canvas to protect it from dust and rain. "Tomorrow," he said to Clare, "I intend to drive this special shipment to the port in Dieppe, where I will personally ensure that it isn't damaged when loaded on the *Celia*."

Jacques's faith in the future appeared bright this morning, despite the dismal weather. "I hope the rain clears by tomorrow," he said, patting his wife on her knee. "The ship is due to arrive in port at the end of this week and I want to leave early, in case I am delayed on the road. It has been a while since I have visited Delphine. I'll store the loaded waggon in the stable behind her house and stay with her until the ship arrives."

Uh-oh, thought Clare. She wished she felt less apprehensive and jittery. Jacques did not yet know of Delphine's defection to Popery. Nor had Clare shared the Marquis's disclosure about the forthcoming Revocation, afraid it would distract Jacques from filling this all-important order.

"What is Marie preparing for our dinner this afternoon? We should open a bottle of my best wine and toast the new English courtiers who will soon be dressing in my distinctive floral-patterned garments."

"She is roasting *poulet avec pommes de terre*, chicken with potatoes."

"My favorite," he replied. "Have her pack some up for me to take tomorrow on my journey to Dieppe."

Clare had still not told Jacques of her covert plan—that the documents from Pierre, granting the four of them safe passage to England, were expected to arrive on the *Celia.* The long-awaited tickets to freedom. *This afternoon after dinner, I will tell him everything. How I transferred my valuable jewels and coins, securing our financial future in England.*

During the past few weeks, she had awoken each morning with the best of intentions—to tell Jacques everything. Then, sensing his happy mood as he went into the woods behind the garden with his sketchbook or fiddled with the packing up of the shipment, she asked herself, *What harm could come of one more day?* One more day turned into another, and yet another. She was worried about how Jacques would react to her scheming behind his back with Pierre. Fear caused her to procrastinate, but time was running short. She knew the Revocation was looming.

"How long before the *Celia* will depart for England, after it is loaded?" Clare asked as their carriage rumbled toward their church in Rouen.

He stared curiously at her eyes. "Since when have you taken such an interest in the shipping schedule?"

"Oh"—she fluttered her hands—"I just wish to know how long you will be away in Dieppe."

"You really missed me when I was in Lyons, didn't you?" he said with a broad grin. "Don't worry your pretty little head. It usually takes less than a week to unload the incoming crates and reload with our bundles. Sometimes even less, depending on the weather. Before you know it, I will be back in bed with you."

Just then Clare heard a disturbing sound coming through the carriage window. She rolled up the shade and peered out. A few uniformed French soldiers, perhaps five or six, were walking in a group toward *le cathédrale de Rouen*. Young maidens lined the road, excitedly waving at them. Clare became uneasy.

Could these be the dreaded Dragonnades, who trampled through Delphine's house? Here in Rouen? Although she had no idea whether the "booted missionaries" had been ordered south to Rouen, the unexpected sight of soldiers on the street today made Clare uncomfortable.

"Jacques," she said, "please turn around and take me home."

"Are you unwell?" he asked. He noticed her gripping her stomach.

"No, but I am unnerved by the sight of the soldiers."

"These soldiers look harmless enough," said Jacques. "Look, they are waving to us." He waved back.

"They think we are headed for the cathedral," Clare whispered. "Close the shade."

"You worry too much, Clare. Besides, you know how I look forward to our minister's sermons," he said, ignoring her request to pull down the shade or to turn back.

When they reached their destination, they noticed the minister and a group of fellow Protestants gathered outside. These men and their wives stood in the rain, reading an official notice posted on the padlocked door of the church. Clare's heart sank, remembering the afternoon she had walked up to that very door and read about the King lowering the age of consent for Huguenot children. This time, the crowd stood weeping, tears mingling with the rain showers streaming down their anguished faces.

"Wait here," Jacques ordered the driver. "I'll go see what is happening."

In her heart, Clare already knew the bad news without actually seeing the words on the posted notice. She trembled in the carriage, dreading Jacques's reaction.

"Oh, why have I waited so long to reveal everything to him?" she moaned. "I knew it was inevitable, but I had so hoped… The Marquis promised to help us—to talk to the Intendant on our behalf."

A few minutes later, Jacques staggered back to the carriage, his eyes misting over. Clare pulled him into the carriage and lowered the shade, tapping her umbrella on the roof to signal Girard to return home. Jacques sobbed all the way back to Maison Dupres.

"My dear, what has happened to upset you so?" Clare asked, as if she had no clue as to the reason for his distress.

"Our church has been closed by royal decree. Our minister has been ordered to leave the country within the week," he cried in disbelief. "Can you believe our sacred temple is to be torn down? Why?" Jacques was devastated.

Clare blamed herself—the fault was as much hers for delaying their departure as it was Jacques's for sticking his stubborn head in the sand when restrictions had first begun to appear. She was certain the Marquis had assured her it wouldn't be signed until November. Once again, she thought about the Marquis's promise to talk to the Intendant. *Wasn't it just last evening that the Intendant was to have dined at Chateau Montjardin?* Perhaps there would be a message when they returned to Maison Dupres—an official signed order granting the Dupres family leave to depart France.

During the ride, Clare sat with a solemn countenance, anxious to get home. She knew she had to remain calm, to keep her wits about her, just as she always had when facing unexpected difficulties at birthings. To plan a hasty departure.

Being Sunday, Claudette and Giselle will be leaving for afternoon Mass, their normal weekly half day off. As soon as they leave, I will pack up the children, along with some food and warm clothing. We will travel to Dieppe in the waggon with Jacques. But we must leave this afternoon, before the servants return. Unless, of course, the Intendant has granted us permission to leave....

After what seemed like an interminably long ride home, Clare grabbed Jacques's arm and led him into the house, clutching his Bible. Giselle stared at his red, swollen eyes as he staggered past her into his study.

"We returned early because Monsieur is unwell," explained Clare. "Go at once and tell Marie to fetch him some tea."

Dressed in her Sunday muslin and a clean apron Giselle looked wary, which didn't surprise Clare. Jacques *did* appear old and defeated.

"This here letter came fer you," said Giselle, lifting a folded parchment note from the hall table. Clare turned it over in her hands, noticing the familiar red wax seal. Trying to appear unconcerned, Clare put it in her pocket as if it were of trifling importance, while what she really longed to do was tear it open at once. *It's from Lady Louise! She must have gleaned some information from the Intendant during dinner.* Clare's hands were trembling, but she was a model of restraint.

"Don't stand there gaping, girl," she commanded. "Hurry into the kitchen and tell Marie to prepare some chamomile tea to calm Monsieur's stomach."

I think Giselle suspects something. She knows her master never misses a Sunday service, even that time he was burning with fever. And written messages never come on Sundays, unless a woman is ready to give birth. But Giselle knows I gave up birthing ages ago.

The servant girl stared rudely, then curtsied and said, "*Oui, madame.*"

As Clare walked quickly toward the parlor, she was detained by Claudette, descending the stairs in her Sunday dress and carrying a small satchel.

"Ah, Mistress, you are home early. I just put the children down for their nap. I was coming down to remind Giselle about Mass, when I heard you tell her Monsieur was unwell."

"Oh, it's only a stomach grippe."

Claudette looked concerned. "Mistress, you look unusually pale. Are you also unwell?" Clare did not answer, but stood staring at Claudette's satchel.

"Mistress, you *do* remember that you gave me and Giselle leave to stay with my friend in town this week, for settin' up the market stand at the harvest fair?"

Clare *had* forgotten. But now that she was planning to leave France, Claudette's services would no longer be needed. It was not safe to tell anyone of her plan, not even loyal Claudette. So Clare pretended all was normal. "Of course I remember. I hope you have an enjoyable week at the fair. Don't worry, we will manage fine here. In fact, you and your niece may leave right away if you like. No need to wait around till after we dine."

"*Merci*, Mistress. Mighty nice of you. Giselle, she's lookin' forward to the gipsy fortune-teller and the jugglers. We'll be comin' back next Sunday."

"Of course. See you then."

Clare anxiously watched from the parlor window. A few minutes later, she sighed as Claudette pulled a reluctant Giselle down the drive and through the gate. Giselle looked back over her shoulder suspiciously. *Well, no matter*, thought Clare, *good riddance to that trollop.*

The warm scent of chicken, roasting over the spit in the kitchen, wafted into the parlor. Clare gripped the sealed note and sank onto the edge of a chair. She tore open the seal and scanned the writing.

Dearest friend,

I know you are anxious for the news. Last evening, my husband and I dined with the Intendant. During dinner, he mentioned that King Louis plans to send the Dragonnades to Rouen next month. Huguenot families will be required to quarter the cavalry soldiers in their homes.

Clare stopped reading for a moment, clutching the note to her breast. Today was the second-to-last Sunday in October. There was still time!

She looked around her beautifully furnished parlor, trying not to envision marauding Dragonnades trampling her expensive carpets. She pictured officious Father Benedict rushing over with a crucifix in his hands, cajoling them to accept the King's faith in order to stop the destruction. Well, if the soldiers came before they left for England, she would do her best to treat them as houseguests and hopefully they would treat her with respect—not do too much damage.

Clare felt her heart thumping in her throat as she continued reading:

But for you, dear Clare, I am afraid the news is even graver. Some person in your household has apparently reported your husband singing psalms in the woods behind your maison. Accused him of preaching the gospel. Pointed the finger at you for birthing babies after it was forbidden.

Clare's face turned red. An outright lie. She *had* stopped birthing babies after she had learned of the prohibition. Unless one counted Lady Louise's recent unfortunate miscarriage at Maison Dupres. That was no birthing! She stood and paced back and forth as she read the rest of the note:

The Intendant is sending a special cadre of men to seize your husband and take him to the galleys. To take your children to be raised in a convent. And you, dearest friend, are to be sent to prison. I was horrified and asked the Intendant when this was to happen. He told me it was none of my concern.

I would beg you to renounce your faith, but fear it is too late. The Intendant is settled on punishing the Dupres family as an example to all Huguenots that the penalties for disobeying King Louis are extremely harsh.

I know you were hoping for better news. I write this at my own great peril. My husband does not know I am sending you this warning. Please burn this note at once.

L.

Carrying the note to the study, Clare observed Jacques rocking back and forth on a chair, holding his head between his hands. She decided to give him a few minutes to compose himself. Rushing into the kitchen, she confided the grim news to her Huguenot cook. Instructed her to take Clare's mare immediately and ride it home to her parents' farm at Torcy-le-Grand. Clare knew Marie's family would provide them shelter on their way to Dieppe.

Marie seemed to have difficulty understanding the urgency. "What about yer chicken, Madame? It's finished roastin'. Yer dinner…"

"Pack it in a picnic basket for us with some bread and apples. Leave it on the kitchen table. Do not tarry." Clare emptied the coins from a small jar on the shelf and pressed them into Marie's hands. "God willing, we will safely reach your family farm in the waggon by nightfall."

"Poor Madame," cried Marie, handing Clare the tea for Jacques. "I'll do 'zactly as you say."

Chapter 25

Clare's Escape Plan

Sunday afternoon, 21 octobre 1685

CLARE TURNED OUT of the kitchen and ran upstairs to the nursery. The children were sleeping peacefully, Lucina with her thumb in her mouth. Jean-Pierre clutching his favorite tin soldier. *My poor innocent children. Let them rest a few minutes longer while I talk to Jacques.*

She stumbled downstairs to her boudoir, where she grabbed her birthing bag, tucking the herb book in the bottom. Then she dashed down to the study. Jacques had stopped weeping but sat like a ghost, staring into the fire. He looked up and saw her standing there, bag in hand, and started to laugh hysterically.

"Going birthing again, are you? I saw the sealed note Giselle handed you. Well, go then. Go to Lady Louise. You think I don't know what you are about, what you do behind my back? You continue to disregard my orders."

"Jacques, you must listen—"

"Just go. Leave me. Get out of here." He pointed to the door.

"Calm yourself, Jacques. I have dreadful news."

"Dreadful news, you say? Dreadful news? What can possibly be worse than our church being closed? Than our religious privileges being torn from us?"

"Read this note before I burn it," Clare said, reaching into her pocket and holding out the folded square of parchment.

"I don't wish to read it," he said, turning away.

Clare raised her voice. "Read this!" she demanded, grabbing his arm.

He was not used to hearing her shout in this manner. Placing his spectacles on his nose, he snatched the note and shook his arm loose. She stood and watched his shoulders sag and the blood drain from his face as he read the note in disbelief.

"Who in our household would have reported us to the royal authorities?"

"Probably your Papist whore, Giselle."

"But why?"

"Because she is a spy. Because she will receive a reward. Because you tired of her and rebuffed her amorous advances. How many more reasons need I give you?" she yelled at him.

He took a moment to absorb what she was saying. "Then I will dismiss her first thing tomorrow morning."

"No, we will be gone by tomorrow."

"Gone?" Terror-struck, Jacques clutched the note and read it again. "What will become of me? Am I to be dragged away like a common criminal? Chained to the galleys of a French warship? I am to suffer because you and this lady friend of yours—"

Clare grabbed the letter from his clutches and threw it into the fire. As she watched the flames consume the note, she breathed deeply to calm herself. *So Jacques was aware of banishments to galleys, a punishment meted out to Huguenots who defy the King's laws. Somehow, he never expected it for himself. He preferred to live in denial, never believing his private psalm singing could lead to this.*

"And me, Jacques. Think what they will do to me."

"My children will be taken by the Jesuits," he said softly. "They will be baptized and raised as Papists." He said nothing about her fate. Showed no concern for his wife being thrown in prison, left to die in a dark, dank dungeon. Realization crept over Clare like a cold, wet blanket. *My husband doesn't care what will happen to me. It has always been about himself first, his religious fervor above all else*, she thought sadly.

Jacques began to weep again.

Clare saw she must take charge. She stood directly in front of him and poked his chest with her finger. "Stop sniveling, Jacques. Lady Louise has been a true friend to warn us before the soldiers came for us. I will go wake the children and tell them we are going on a picnic. We must be gone within the hour."

"Gone? A picnic? Clare, you must be mad."

"The picnic is a pretense to prevent Jean-Pierre and Lucina from becoming frightened. We will all leave for Dieppe within the hour, taking the waggon by the back roads."

She continued to unfold her hasty plan. "There is no time to unload the shipping crates. We will need them as a decoy in case we get stopped."

He looked at her in amazement, his mouth falling open.

"I have already sent Marie ahead on my mare to her parents' farm near Torcy-le-Grand. They are good Protestants and will give us shelter and a place to rest along the way. By the following day, we should reach Delphine's house in Dieppe, where we will hide until the ship arrives."

"Ship? I don't understand."

"There will be papers from Pierre arriving on the ship, providing you and our family safe passage to England on the *Celia*. There is no time to explain. We must leave the maison as soon as possible."

Clare started to head for the door, to rouse the children. Jacques grabbed her by the arm, preventing her from leaving. "Even if I agree to your crazy plan, surely this can wait a few days. We need time to settle our affairs. Sell the carriage, the horses. Arrange to have our furniture shipped to England."

"Forget about our belongings. We cannot risk waiting another day. The soldiers may come for us at any time. Just over an hour ago, you saw the foot soldiers heading for Mass in Rouen."

Clare saw a wave of reality begin to seep into her husband's stubborn brain. He looked at her and said, "But if we are stopped—"

"Our cart is loaded with goods from your company, addressed to the royal palace of Windsor. Even if we are stopped, no soldier would dare interfere with royal commerce. The bolts of silk will support our story."

"You have planned this," he said in a quiet voice.

"Yes, I have planned to get us out of France for months, years. To protect our children from being taken from us. I thought we would have more time."

"You never told me."

"I tried. I begged you to leave before it was too late. Many times."

"I understand now," he said as the pieces began to come together in his mind. "All those letters to and from England. The heavy velvet waistcoats you sewed. Were they some sort of bribe?"

"The seams. They contained my jewels and several thousand gold coins from my pouch. My pearls were hidden in the cloisonné smuggler buttons from your shop. Pierre sold them and invested the proceeds for us, so that we would have funds to live on if we made it to England."

Jacques looked at his wife in amazement as she briefly continued unfolding the details of her plan. It seemed too much for him to comprehend. His face suddenly became distorted with anger.

"You want to go to England so you can be with Pierre. You still have romantic feelings for him."

"That is ridiculous! Pierre is my brother and he has a wife." After a brief moment, she added, "I thought there would be more time, but I miscalculated. Now we must sneak away in haste."

"Sneak off like a common criminal. Leave my home, my business…" He began to sob again. Clare grabbed his shoulders and shook him. "Pull yourself together, Jacques. If all goes well, we will be out of France in a few days."

Clare realized Jacques was in shock. She pushed him toward the kitchen. "The rain is slowing. Take the picnic basket from the table. Go out and hitch the two carriage horses to the waggon. I will wake the children."

She rushed up the stairs to the nursery, leaving her birthing bag at the bottom of the stairs. She did not want to forget it in haste.

The children were awake. Jean-Pierre was standing at the window. Clare was catching her breath to tell them of the picnic, when he jumped up and down in excitement.

"Look, Maman! There are two s-s-soldiers walking up the road with Giselle. Real live s-s-soldiers!"

Clare peered out and realized with a lump in her throat that it was too late for her hastily planned departure. *This is not the first time Giselle has decided to skip Sunday afternoon Mass, but why is she coming back now? What of the gipsy fortune-teller? The jugglers?*

"The soldiers must be Giselle's friends. Tell me, son, can you tell their rank by their uniforms?" Nobody was a better authority than Jean-Pierre when it came to soldiers. He frequently pored over his soldier books. He was positively obsessed.

"Oh, they are of a low rank. Merely foot s-s-soldiers," he proudly announced. "May I go down and s-s-speak with them?" Clare quickly tried to think of an excuse. Her heart beat rapidly.

"Not now, Jean-Pierre. It is very muddy outside. Perhaps tomorrow."

"Will they s-s-still be here?"

"They surely will," she said with a sinking heart. "Now you and Lucina get dressed. I will bring your dinner upstairs. We will spread the blanket on the floor and have an indoor picnic. Marie made your favorite, chicken with roast potatoes."

"Yes, Maman," he said in resignation. He had been raised to be obedient.

As she ran downstairs, Clare desperately tried to think of a new escape plan.

Chapter 26

The Fire-Breathing Dragon

Sunday afternoon, 21 octobre 1685

CLARE HEARD JACQUES running in her direction. His face was very pale. On his way back from hitching the horses to the waggon, he had seen the soldiers turn into their courtyard through the iron gates. Startled, he had dropped the picnic basket by the stable door and dashed in through the kitchen.

Clare saw his hands shaking and pulled him into the study. "They've come for me, haven't they?" he sobbed. "The Dragonnades will march me in shackles to the coast, to the galleys. Oh dear God, how can this be happening?" His voice was reaching a hysterical pitch.

"Giselle has returned unexpectedly," she said. "These two soldiers appear to be a pair of young ragtag recruits she picked up on the road. Stay calm and sit here reading your Bible. Whatever you do, say nothing. Let me do the talking. Do you understand?"

"*Oui*," he responded in a quavering voice. Clare assumed he envisioned whips tearing his back into shreds as he sat on a wooden bench, trying to pull the oars on a French warship to the steady beat of a drum. He was absolutely terrified.

Giselle and the two foot soldiers climbed the stone steps to the front door and boldly knocked. When Clare cracked open the door, the surly girl stood there, smirking. The soldiers removed their caps and the tall one said, "*Bonjour*, Madame."

In Clare's most commanding voice, she demanded, "What is the meaning of this, Giselle? Who are these men? And girl, you should know better than to approach the main entrance. Will you never learn to use the kitchen door?"

"Hey," said the shorter foot soldier.

"*Pardon*, Madame," said the tall one, shoving his rude companion with his elbow. "We met up with Giselle on our way from town. She informed us she worked at Maison Dupres. The commanding officer of the cavalry is expected to arrive in a few days, with orders for our troops to be quartered and fed here."

"Giselle told us you wouldn't mind if the two of us came early," added the rude one.

"I invited 'em to stay in them rooms above the stable," said the saucy Giselle, moving between the soldiers. "Next to my room," she added, winking at her new friends. "I din't think you'd mind providin' these gallant men with your hospitality, Mistress."

The urge to slap her was intense, but Clare remained coldly polite. No doubt, these foot soldiers were not part of the regulars, but local Rouen youths who had joined up. She could have turned them away—they appeared to be unarmed—but decided it would only lead to trouble if they camped in her courtyard, keeping watch. She decided a better alternative was to let them stay in the stable.

"Very well, Giselle. You may take them to the rooms above the stable now."

"Oh no, they wanna come in first and see the maison. I tol' them how very grand it is inside."

"We will wait until their commanding officer brings the official order," said Clare firmly. The foot soldiers made no move to leave, standing and staring uneasily at each other, trying to decide what to do. Should they push the lady aside? They had decided on their own to come early, believing only that they were to be billeted here—ignorant of the special mission.

Clare stood her ground. Hands on her hips, she stared icily. Finally, as an enticement to keep them out, she said, "Giselle, there is a basket of roast chicken over by the stable doors. We were planning to take the children on a picnic, but the weather is too wet. Take it into the stable and share it with these men."

The thought of roast chicken made the hungry soldiers' mouths water. Giselle sighed, "I s'pose they can wait to explore the maison.

Girard won't be mindin' if we drink some bottles of his wine with our meal. Bet you didn't know, Mistress. Your fancy-pants driver sometimes brings 'em from the cellar and hides 'em in the loft when the master is busy."

Our carriage driver stole the wine? This surprised Clare. Jacques had complained about missing wine bottles, but when they had questioned Marie, she'd had no idea who could have taken them. Hearing this now, Clare suspected it had been Giselle who had stolen the wine so she could get drunk in her stable room.

Anyhow, she doubted Girard would be returning. Seeing soldiers headed into their courtyard and smelling trouble, he would have fled. *Well*, she thought, *no time to worry about stolen wine now. Let them all get drunk.*

"Ma'am, Giselle here has promised us a real good time," said the tall soldier.

"No doubt she has. Good afternoon, messieurs," Clare said, firmly closing and bolting the door and returning to the study.

Jacques was hovering over his Bible. But Clare could see his hands still shaking. He said he had overheard the conversation.

"Our plan must be changed," she said. "Go upstairs and keep the children occupied, Jacques. I have another idea."

Clare waited a few minutes, then sneaked out the double glass doors into the back garden with a kitchen knife, checking to see if she was being watched. The sound of raucous laughter emanated from the stable. "Apparently Giselle and her soldier friends are enjoying our roast chicken dinner and drink," she muttered. The very thought infuriated her.

The wind whipped the autumn leaves off the trees, a strong storm brewing. Clare searched her cultivated borders, but her mission at this time was not to replenish her supply of medicinal herbs. No, she was searching for that particular weed which persisted in invading her carefully tended garden. The one Jacques loved to sketch, with its deceptive inviting blossoms—the bulbous buttercup, *cuckow-buds of yellow hue.*

It was late fall, and not much was still blooming. She looked through the lavender, the rosemary, the spreading mint. No luck. Then she trod over to a tree, which was busy shedding its leaves. She spied something familiar growing close to the trunk, poking through the pile of fallen leaves. There it was!

Returning to the house with a few fresh stalks wrapped in her handkerchief to protect her hands, Clare bolted all the doors and closed the shutters. Her mind was racing with her daring new plan. Donning an old pair of garden gloves, she cut up the stalks and pulverized them until she had squeezed out a fair amount of sap. The noxious weeds were the key to her new escape plan.

The evening hours were nerve-wracking. The children were cranky because they hadn't gotten their promised roast chicken and had to settle for bread and cheese. Jean-Pierre was still upset that he hadn't been able to talk to the soldiers, and on top of that, he could no longer watch them from the window because they had gone into the stable *forever.*

Ominous thunder boomed and bolts of lightning flashed through the closed parlor shutters, which clattered in the ferocious windstorm. The candles flickered. Clare tried to remain calm for the sake of the children. She read them stories and promised to take them on a picnic the next day, knowing that would not happen.

Jacques played chess with Jean-Pierre but kept dropping the pieces each time his little partner talked excitedly about the soldiers and how he would get to meet them tomorrow. The boy pretended the ivory knights on horseback were real soldiers, as he slid the pieces across the board.

"Keep your eyes on the king, Papa," he said. "Or I will capture it."

"Must we always talk about soldiers and kings? Can you think of nothing better to occupy your mind?" Jacques said in an irritated voice. Jean-Pierre looked crestfallen. Having soldiers in his courtyard was the most adventurous thing that had ever, ever happened here.

Lucina sat on the carpet sketching a castle. "Tell us more stories, Maman. I absolutely love fairy tales. Stories of beautiful princesses and handsome young knights rescuing them from fire-breathing dragons. Maybe we need a few of those dragons to rescue us from the soldiers in our stable."

Jacques heard her say dragons, but he *thought* she said *dragoons.* "Stop chattering, Lucina!"

She started to put her thumb in her mouth. "Papa is being unkind tonight," she whispered to her mother.

"Come with me," Clare said, taking her by the hand to her boudoir, sure that her daughter sensed something bad was happening.

Sometimes Clare wondered if Lucina had the ability to see into the future, as Maman had predicted on the night she had birthed her and held her up to the moon.

"How would you like to play dress-up?" Clare asked her little moon goddess.

"Tonight?" she said incredulously. "You want to play dress-up tonight? Why are those soldiers in our stable?"

"You can wear my pink silk party dress."

"Maman, something's wrong. Why do you want to play dress-up games with me?"

Clare wasn't sure how to respond and remained silent for a minute. She couldn't help admiring this beautiful golden-haired child of hers. Tenderly, she pushed Lucina's long curls behind her ears.

"Maman?"

"I don't want you to worry. And if I tell you a secret, you must promise not to tell Jean-Pierre."

"I can keep a secret, I really can."

"We are going to play a very important game. Are you good at pretending?"

"Yessss... this has something to do with those bad soldiers, doesn't it?"

"Lucina, can you pretend you are a very sick princess?"

"Sick? But why?"

"Because a dragon breathed fire in your face, just like your favorite story."

"But fire would burn my face."

"This is just pretend fire, Lucina. I will rub some lotion on your face so we can pretend the dragon spat fire on it."

Lucina looked doubtful. "It will hurt, won't it?"

"You can sleep in my pink party gown tonight, like a real princess. But tomorrow morning, you must act very sick."

Lucina winced when Clare dabbed the sap from the bulbous buttercup stalks on her face. As expected, angry red pustules began to erupt. Clare knew they would last three days and then fade away.

"Tomorrow, you will go with Papa in the waggon. The soldiers may try to stop him. Remember to pretend you are very sick. Above all, you must promise to be very, very brave."

"I'm frightened, Maman. Where will you and Jean-Pierre be?"

"Your brother and I will join you the next day. We are all going to meet in …in Paris." Clare thought it best not to tell Lucina their true destination, but sensed her daughter did not believe they were going to Paris. Just as she did not believe there would be a picnic the next day.

"I will do as you say, Maman."

"Good girl. You know I love you." Lucina let her mother dress her in the much-too-big pink gown and tie a sash around her delicate waist. She quietly climbed into bed with her doll. She did not complain about her stinging face.

Jean-Pierre stomped into the nursery, his head full of soldiers. "I beat Papa at chess. S-s-six times," he bragged. "I can't wait till tomorrow. Perhaps, the s-s-soldiers will come with us on our picnic. I get hungry thinking about it."

"Don't be silly," said Lucina. "They'll be too busy."

"I expect they'll be drilling in our courtyard… and I will be able to m-m-march with them," he said with anticipation in his voice.

"Time to stop talking," said Clare. She left one candle burning on the table, because Jean-Pierre was *abso-lootly* sure a ghost roamed the nursery most nights and Lucina never contradicted him.

After Clare tucked the children into bed, she and her nervous husband retreated to their locked bedchamber. Clare went over the details of her new plan and explained about applying the sap to Lucina's face. She decided not to tell Jacques about Delphine's defection from the church—he had enough to deal with in his emotional state. His primary task was to concentrate on getting Lucina safely to Marie's farm.

Finally, Clare tore a blank sheet from his small sketchpad and drew a rough map of the directions to Torcy-le-Grand. "You and Lucina will leave at dawn, Jacques. Try to get some sleep. Tomorrow will be a long day."

She blew out the candle.

Chapter 27

The Pox

Monday, 22 octobre 1685

CLARE TOSSED AND turned all night, going over the plan in her mind. Once, she tiptoed barefoot down the dark stairs to retrieve her birthing bag from where she had left it on the bottom step. She could still hear laughing from the stable. An hour later, she sat up in bed, realizing a serious flaw in her plan—she had sent Marie home on her mare, and the other two horses were needed to pull the waggon. She would have to find another way to get Jean-Pierre to Torcy-le-Grand. It was too risky for them all to leave at the same time. Besides, the foot soldiers would not allow it.

Jacques slept fitfully, moaning. At four in the morning, Clare woke him and told him to dress quickly. Giselle did not come to light their fire. No surprise, since she was with the two soldiers in the stable.

Lighting a candle, Clare crept quietly up the stairs. As expected, Lucina's face was covered with large red blisters. There were also a few on her little hands, where she must have rubbed her face during her sleep. Clare dressed her drowsy child in a warm dark dress and cloak for traveling in the late October chill. Being careful not to wake Jean-Pierre, she carried Lucina down to the kitchen and gave her bread and butter for breakfast.

Kissing her precious baby gently on the forehead, she whispered, "Be good for Papa. Remember, today you are a princess in distress from dragon flames."

"Yes, Maman. I remember and I will try not to chatter, although you know that is very hard for me. And I think something is very wrong, but I won't say anything to the soldiers."

For a moment, Clare couldn't help but smile.

~~~

The sun was barely beginning to rise as Clare accompanied her husband and daughter out to the loaded waggon. The two soldiers staggered out of the stable toward the privy.

"Halt!" the taller one ordered. "Where do you think you are going?" Jacques froze with Lucina in his arms, unable to speak.

"Ooooh, my face hurts sooo bad," Lucina moaned. The soldiers' eyes opened wide with fear as they looked intently at her mottled face. Instinct told them to step back.

"What is wrong with this child?"

"The pox," said Clare. "Or perhaps the black plague. Do not come any closer to her!" The soldiers backed further away, staring uneasily at each other, not sure what to do.

"My husband must get her to the physician in Paris at once. Let them pass."

"Can't this wait until our officer arrives? He is expected soon, within days."

Clare stepped toward them and said in her most demanding voice, "This cannot wait even one more hour. Which one of you will accept responsibility for a dead child? Eh?"

"Oooh." Once again, Lucina groaned in their direction. "I am burning up, Papa. Help me!"

"Have you no compassion for a poor, sick child?" Clare asked. After conferring with his partner, the tall soldier pointed at Jacques. "Very well, *he* may take the girl for help."

"But you, Madame," added the other in an uncertain squeaky voice, "will stay here." Clare sensed fear pouring through his veins as he related a memory from his childhood to his compatriot. He described the devastation of the plague, watching his mother and sister perish.

Pointing at the door, the tall soldier ordered Madame Dupres to go back into the house and stay inside. Clare breathed a sigh of relief, as the men gave a wide berth to Jacques. From the top step, she watched her husband tuck the little actress into the cart, climb onto the seat next to her, and drive off. She was so proud of Lucina's per-
~~~

formance. *I do believe one day Lucina might have become a successful actress, if she hadn't been destined to be a* sage femme.

The tall soldier saw her waiting. "You there, I thought I told you to get in the house. Now go at once. *Allez, allez!*" She gathered her skirts and started to open the door. Giselle, who had been watching with the soldiers, whispered something into the tall one's ear.

"Halt!" he commanded before Clare could get inside. "I am told by Mademoiselle Giselle that there is another child, a boy. What of him?"

"The boy is feverish. I must go up to care for him. He was touching his sister's face. You know what that means." She watched new alarm spread across the soldiers' faces. Giselle appeared dubious.

"We will stay in the stable with Giselle," they said, grabbing the serving girl by the elbow and pulling her with them. "Keep the boy confined to the nursery, Madame. We will keep an eye out from the stable window, to make sure you don't leave."

"As you wish," Clare breathed with relief.

Entering the kitchen, she noticed Jacques had forgotten to take the map she had drawn. He had carelessly left it on the work table. What if the soldiers had found it? Discovered his true destination was not Paris? She tucked it in her pocket, quickly prepared a cold breakfast and carried the tray up to the nursery for Jean-Pierre.

~~~

Jean-Pierre had woken and found himself alone. Lucina's bed was empty. He raced to the nursery window and watched the entire scene unfold. At first, he thought Maman was going off with Papa and Lucina, leaving him alone. He tried to open the nursery door, but it was locked. He sniffed, trying hard not to bawl. Brave soldiers never cried. Today he would meet the two soldiers out there, even if he had to climb out the window. He didn't want them to see him with red eyes.

Soon, Maman came up with his breakfast. He noticed she locked the nursery door from the inside with her key. He began to whine, "Lucina got to meet the s-s-soldiers before me. Why can't I go out? Where is my hot porridge?"

~~~

It was only seven in the morning, but Clare already missed Lucina. And that led her to think how much she missed her own mother. *If*

Maman were alive, she would tell me what to do, how to sneak my son past those two scraggly soldiers. Oh, she would have scolded me for forgetting about the mare. Like the time she scolded when I forgot to bring back that bucket of pebbles from the beach. But Clare had no time for reminiscing this morning. She needed to think this through herself.

"Where did Papa take Lucina?"

"To Paris. To a physician. She is sick."

"I thought you didn't trust doctors, Maman. You always s-s-say—"

"Eat your breakfast. Now!"

Jean-Pierre started to bawl. Clare yawned, put her arms around the confused little boy to comfort him and apologized—said she was just tired. Reached into her pocket and pulled out the map to Torcy-le-Grand. "Here, why don't you draw a nice picture on the back? Maybe a tree—or a carriage with two horses."

She wondered how she would keep him busy, locked in the nursery as they would be until they could get away. The foot soldiers would be afraid to enter the "sickroom" so long as they believed the boy was becoming ill like his sister. She was too exhausted to think.

Feeling safe for the moment behind the locked door, Clare said, "Maman needs to get some sleep. Do not go downstairs."

"Maman is cross this morning," he muttered as he walked over to his little table.

Clare curled into Lucina's empty bed, absorbing the faint odor of her daughter's sweet scent in the sheets. The key was safely hidden in the folds of her gown; the birthing bag and journal tucked beneath her legs, under the pink quilt.

She fell into a deep sleep, filled with ominous dreams of the Dragonnades invading Maison Dupres.

Chapter 28

Arrival of the Dragonnades

More soldiers arrived early this morning, this time on horseback. Mon Dieu, I counted ten in all. Jean-Pierre was thrilled—a lieutenant and nine horse cavalry. We stood at the window and watched the foot soldiers stagger out of the stable with Giselle. They pointed up at the nursery window, madly waving their hands about, and pointing at their faces. I can only imagine how they must have exaggerated the description of Lucina's appearance in order to escape a flogging. I pulled my son back and closed the shutters, to his disappointment.

Journal of Clare Dupres, Tuesday 23 octobre 1685

CLARE STUFFED HER journal back under Lucina's mattress as she heard a set of boots pounding up the stairs. She held Jean-Pierre protectively behind her, expecting the approaching soldier to kick down the nursery door and drag them both away. Then she decided to face the beast head-on.

~~~

Lieutenant Pechard had been informed by the foot soldiers there was a lady and a small, sick boy in the nursery. He was miffed at the men for allowing Monsieur Dupres and his daughter to leave. Their sole duty, before arrival of the cavalry, should have been to secure the residence. At this simple task they had failed. But then, they were ignorant, untrained recruits from the peasantry. How were they to know? He had no reason to doubt they had feared the plague. He himself
~~~

remembered the horrors of the Black Death killing a large portion of the population some years back.

Marching upstairs, he reached out to knock on the nursery door and was surprised when Madame Dupres opened the door, slid out, and closed it behind her. She was younger and handsomer than expected. A trim figure, obviously a *femme de qualité*, wearing a dress with a lace collar. Wisps of auburn hair peeked out from her coif.

"I am Lieutenant Pechard of King Louis XIV's twenty-third cavalry regiment, under orders to detain your family until my commanding officer arrives," he said, bowing politely. "My men shall be quartered here in your home until *le Capitaine* arrives with the official written order from the Intendant."

Clare stared at him defiantly, her feisty blue-gray eyes flashing with anger. "You have no right to bring soldiers into my home. We are law-abiding Christians."

"I am unaware of the details of your criminal activities. I am just following orders until my commanding officer gets here. You may take up your complaint with him when he arrives."

"Don't worry, I shall."

She is a spirited one, thought Pechard. *A match for Capitaine, that's for sure. He has a thirst for subduing outspoken women.*

"Where is Monsieur Dupres?"

"Gone to Paris, to seek medical attention for my ailing daughter."

"Those two idiot foot soldiers will have hell to pay for allowing him to leave the compound," he muttered.

"At least they showed compassion for my dying daughter."

"How does the boy? I was told he had contact with his sister."

"Rages with fever. Poor thing is so weak, he can barely climb out of bed to use the chamber pot," said Clare. Lieutenant Pechard believed she was exaggerating—he had seen the boy standing at the window. But he let it pass.

~~~

As they stood there talking, Clare could hear the cavalry soldiers rampaging on the floors below. Apparently they did not share the foot soldiers' fears regarding the pox. She winced at the sound of glass breaking. Furniture cracking. Her porcelain ornaments being tossed out the windows.
~~~

Lieutenant Pechard watched the brave woman flinch. He was about to say something he knew would upset Capitaine. Still, he was in command until his superior arrived. Pechard made a humane decision.

"Madame, my men will have the run of the house when they are not drilling in the courtyard, but I *will* order them to stay away from the nursery floor. I know not whether the boy in there is as dangerously ill as you say, but it is my opinion that you should have a private space to care for your child until his health improves. You are both to stay up here. Understood?"

"I am grateful Lieutenant. However, my sick boy needs nourishment. Will you at least allow me to make one trip down to the larder to acquire him some food?"

The officer stood and considered her request. Huguenot children were generally taken to convents. It was not the mission of the army to starve innocent boys and girls, especially sick ones.

"Very well. Lock him in the nursery and I will accompany you downstairs one time to fetch him a bit of food. But just this once."

Clare took a basket from the larder and filled it to the brim with bread, cheese, ham, onions, milk, and a dozen eggs from their chickens. On the way out, she grabbed some butter, salt, and on a whim, some wild garlic. The kitchen had already been ransacked by the marauders, but they hadn't yet discovered the larder. Glancing out the kitchen window, she saw the men had hastily assembled an outdoor cooking pit, from which Marie's prize iron kettle hung over an open fire. Several men were in the livestock pen, slaughtering chickens.

Lieutenant Pechard knew his superior officer would not have been so generous as to allow a prisoner under house arrest to hoard this much food. The hard man would not have permitted her more than a crust of mouldy bread. Nonetheless, who knew exactly how long Capitaine would take to arrive? Madame might be locked in the nursery for several days, and Pechard simply would not let the child go hungry. He would rather risk a reprimand.

"That's enough," he said before she emptied the entire larder. He accompanied Clare up the back stairs, but denied her request to stop in her boudoir for some clean linen. Never could tell—she might have a weapon hidden in her armoire. Climbing behind her, he watched her lift her skirts to avoid dragging them on the stairs caked with mud. *Nice ankles*, he thought to himself. He was certain Capitaine would enjoy seducing her.

She turned to him and said, "*Merci*, Lieutenant. You may be an enemy of my people, but at least you have the manners of a true gentleman. Thank you for allowing me to gather this food for my ailing son." She even gave him a brief smile.

~~~

When Clare stepped inside and locked the nursery door, she breathed a sigh of relief and stashed the food in the cool cabinet under the window seat to prevent spoilage. It would have to last until she could find a chance to steal away with Jean-Pierre. She envisioned slipping out unnoticed with him at night to one of the nearby tenant farms. There, they would acquire a horse—even if she had to steal one.

She would stop at nothing to save her child. Well… perhaps there were limits. After all, she was a midwife who had sworn an oath to be a healer. *Would I be capable of committing murder if necessary? Yes, I think I would.*

She shuddered at the thought.
~~~

Chapter 29

Capitaine Appears

For the past five days, I have remained shut up in the nursery with Jean-Pierre. Keeping him busy has proven to be exhausting. We play with his tin soldiers, draw pictures of soldiers and practice speaking English. I cut up a blanket to sew him a small army uniform, which he adores. Mostly, he stands at the window, intently watching the soldiers drill in formation. I am sick to death of soldiers! He asks to go downstairs every few hours. I touch his forehead and tell him he has a fever, although he is cool. Sometimes, when my son is busy with his toys and books, I reread old letters from Pierre and Delphine, to keep myself from despair. I keep the precious packet of letters tucked under Lucina's mattress, next to this journal.

Giselle has been parading across the courtyard, flaunting the silk gowns she obviously stole from my armoire. Around her neck, my pearl necklace dangles against her hollow flat chest. It is almost laughable—that stupid girl doesn't realize it is a fake replica. I know she means to anger me, but I will not waste my energy worrying about some silly gowns. Once I escape to England, I will have new dresses made, finer than the ones I leave behind.

All day and night, the soldiers beat their drums. Rum-tum-tum. Rum-tum-tum. To keep us awake. Jean-Pierre amazingly manages to sleep through the racket, but the drumming keeps me up most nights. I am completely exhausted.

Journal of Clare Dupres, Saturday morning, 27 octobre 1685

CLARE DARED NOT venture downstairs, but she could tell that the household food stores were rapidly dwindling by observing the hungry soldiers in the courtyard, gorging themselves at mealtimes. The wheels of cheese, bread, butchered poultry, even the apples stripped from their trees, were being consumed in huge quantities.

My plan to sneak away unnoticed was unrealistic—sentries are posted round the clock at all outer doors to keep us from escaping, thought Clare gloomily. She had been rationing the food in the nursery cabinet and doubted that there was any more to be had.

She had discovered a small, long-unused iron grate in the nursery hearth, where Claudette had once warmed gruel for the babies in a small copper pan. She cooked simple dishes for Jean-Pierre, eating little herself. Saved the diminishing food supplies for her hungry little boy. There were but four eggs remaining.

~~~

Shortly after noon on Saturday, Capitaine finally arrived. Clare peered down from the nursery window and watched him being briefed by Lieutenant Pechard. Giselle sashayed out the stable door, swiveling her hips, trying to attract the attention of the senior officer. He glanced at her briefly, apparently not impressed by her attire or her manner. *He sees her for what she is, a lowly servant trying to look glamorous in ill-fitting clothing. Stupid girl is not even wearing a corset!*

The two officers conferred, pointing up at the window. Clare jumped back out of sight and closed the curtains, wishing she could hear their conversation. A few minutes passed. She felt tension tightening her chest when she heard footsteps on the stairs. It was Giselle, ordered to fetch her at once.

Giselle tried to peek inside, curious to see whether Jean-Pierre appeared poxy, but was told he was napping. Clare wanted to lock the nursery door, but Giselle said the officer had ordered her to bring her mistress down immediately. Hesitating for a second, Clare felt for the key in her pocket, then decided not to raise suspicion. She would leave the door unlocked, greet the officer and then make a hasty retreat back to the nursery before her sweet angel awoke. Holding her head high, she boldly walked down the grand staircase.

When Clare reached the entry hall, he bowed and "apologized" for his delay. *As if his arrival were an event to be anticipated, even celebrated*, she thought. Controlling her anxiety, Clare managed to curtsy, conveying a proper sign of respect. She prayed he would act toward her in a civil manner, as Lieutenant Pechard had.

Capitaine removed his cape and plumed cap, throwing them carelessly over the banister, as if he were the master of Maison
~~~

Dupres. Stepping into the parlor, he looked around expressionless at the wreckage, which a week earlier had been a beautifully appointed room. Then he crossed the hall to Jacques's study, where all the books had been torn from the shelves and her husband's prized mantel clock was missing its glass cover. Clare tried not to grimace at the unmistakable odor of urine wafting from the stained carpets.

Twirling his black handlebar mustache, the cocky officer told Clare he was pleased to see his troops had settled comfortably into their new quarters. He did not apologize for the broken crockery, nor did he hand her the dreaded written order that she could see rolled and tucked in his belt.

His muddy boots left black footprints on the carpets. Clare bid him make himself comfortable as she headed for the stairs. But her uninvited guest was no gentleman. He unceremoniously pushed her aside, climbed to the next floor, and dumped his bags into the master bedchamber.

Clare had not been in this room since Monday. She was mildly surprised to see that her bedchamber had not been wrecked, nor were there any signs it had been used. She supposed it had been saved for the personal comfort of the senior officer.

His eyes surveyed the large, pleasant room, stopping briefly at the armchairs near the marble hearth. Clare choked back a sob. *The chairs where Jacques and I used to sit together over our morning coffee, after our lovemaking. Where I set down my birthing bag and pulled on my warm gloves before leaving for a confinement…*

"Ah, this will be most satisfactory," the commander said, interrupting her reverie. He patted the silk sheets on her bed and fluffed up the pillows. "Perhaps you would care to join me here this evening?"

So this is how it is to be, Clare thought with dread. She crossed her arms across her chest, lowered her eyes, and said in a soft voice, "My responsibility is to care for my little boy in the nursery."

"Ah, the boy. I was informed he is unwell."

"Unwell? He is dangerously ill. His fever burns and I expect the pustules to erupt at any time." Clare briefly asked herself whether she would dare to apply the bulbous buttercup sap to her son's face. No, it had worked once, frightening the ignorant foot soldiers, but this man would not be so easily fooled.

"Why have you not summoned a surgeon?"

Clare's impulse was to go on a tirade about their useless leeches and bloodletting. To boast that as a midwife, she could provide better care. But then she remembered the ruse of sending Lucina to a Parisian physician. To protect her earlier lie, she simply said, "Your soldiers did not permit me to leave the house."

He nodded in satisfaction. Clare supposed Capitaine had been incensed to learn that the foot soldiers had permitted her husband and "sick" daughter to leave the maison before his arrival, but his wrath had been assuaged upon learning Lieutenant Pechard acted appropriately in securing Madame and the boy in the nursery under twenty-four-hour guard.

"You must be tired, taking care of the child," he said. "Here, have a seat," he said pointing to the armchair in front of the hearth. "You will join me in a glass of sherry."

Clare hesitated for a second, then realized it was an order, not an invitation she was free to decline. She poured two glasses of Jacques's best sherry and sat stiffly on the edge of her chair, back erect, still trying to act the part of genteel hostess.

Capitaine pulled off his boots, removed his jacket, and loosened the stock about his neck before sitting next to her. The stench of his sweaty body was nauseating. He reeked of recent sex.

"When do you expect your husband to return from Paris?"

"I anticipate his return home shortly," she said, fussing with the folds of her skirt.

"With or without the child, he should have returned by now. I give him one more day, and then my soldiers will be sent to capture him on the road."

Clare remained silent. What could she say? This man believed Jacques would return. He had no idea that Lady Louise had given them advance warning of his true mission. That Jacques had fled. How long would the officer keep her imprisoned here at his mercy, waiting for Monsieur Dupres to return? She felt his eyes looking her over from head to foot with manly admiration. His unsavory motives were obvious.

She was desperate to escape his clutches and get Jean-Pierre to Dieppe. But how? Time was running out. The ship would be leaving in two or three days. Perhaps if she could convince the officer to send his troops away, even for an hour. She eyed the fireplace poker, wondering if she could overpower this strong soldier.

"Tomorrow is Sunday, Capitaine. Won't your men wish to attend Mass?"

He leaned back in his chair and yawned. "They are good men. I shall allow them to go into Rouen for Mass. Perhaps you wish to go with them?"

What kind of game is he playing with me? Clare clasped her hands in her lap and toyed with her wedding band.

The man shook his head in dismay when she did not respond to his suggestion. "I fail to understand why you obstinate people persist in defying King Louis. You must know the reason he sends us into your homes."

Again, Clare remained silent while her mind raced with possibilities.

The huge officer stood and began to pace back and forth, waving his arms about. "Our armies will continue to be quartered in Huguenots homes until they all commit to abjure their faith. Why, do you realize how many of your fellow heathens have already been excused from quartering soldiers by reciting the Lord's Prayer in Latin and attending Mass?"

Clare thought about poor Delphine, how she had given in to the pressure.

Capitaine stood looming in front of Clare. "That is all it takes. It would be so easy for your husband and you to do the same," he urged.

Has he forgotten what he has been specifically ordered to do here? I already know what is in the written order rolled in his belt. He is here on a special mission, not an ordinary dragooned conversion. No matter what I say, I am doomed to be imprisoned for life. Unless .... perhaps there is a way to convince him to ignore the order, until....

Clare took a deep breath and leaned forward, looking up into his eyes. "Oh, Capitaine, my husband is an insufferable fool. I hate him for forcing me to adhere to his religious views."

The officer was astonished. "Then you admit he violates the King's law? That he sings psalms in the woods?"

"I have no knowledge of such things. But it wouldn't surprise me."

Capitaine unrolled the order and pretended to be reading it for the first time. His eyes slowly scanned the document, occasionally glancing up at her face. Then he rolled it back and pronounced the verdict.

"My order is to bring Monsieur Jacques Dupres to the galleys. To take you, Madame Clare Dupres, to prison. To send your two children to the Sisters of Sorrow convent, to be baptized and raised as proper Catholics. This order," he said, proudly waving the impressive document in her face, "was *personally* signed by Intendant Marillac."

Clare gasped involuntarily. Although she had tried to steel herself to the unjust verdict during the last few days, actually hearing the official words read aloud from the document caused her eyes to fill with tears.

"I am innocent of any crimes against the King, as are my children," she entreated. "My husband is weak, and he brought this upon us. Take him if you must, but spare me. Spare my son and daughter."

"You would willingly have us take your husband?" he asked.

"My husband? He disgusts me. Feh!"

This statement flabbergasted Capitaine. It was totally unexpected. Once again, he looked this handsome female over with interest, his eyes stopping on her breasts. He was clearly aroused.

"Is that so? Such a man is lucky to have a lovely, charming wife to warm that bed over there."

"Such a man, you say? Monsieur Dupres is no man. He does not satisfy me in bed. Prefers the serving wench to me. Oh, what is a desperate woman like me to do?"

"Madame, your words astonish and delight me. How utterly startling. But at the moment, I am tired and hungry from my long journey. My first order of business is to have a bath. I commanded your wench Grizelle to bring up some steaming water and a few bars of soap. I'm sure you will enjoy scrubbing my back and toweling me off after a nice soak. But first, your cook will prepare me a meal."

Clare tried not to avert her eyes, as he pulled his shirt over his head. *This is a man who expects flattery. He mustn't suspect my repugnance.* It took all her effort to smile.

"Until your husband's return, I intend to enjoy your…um…gracious hospitality," he added, with a leer in his eye. He refilled Clare's glass, from which hardly a sip had been taken. His own glass was empty—he refilled it to the brim.

"Sadly, our cook left shortly before your soldiers arrived," she said.

"Really? Imagine that," he said suspiciously. "I was wondering at the absence of any servants in this great house, except for the ill-clad Grizelle—where did your cook and the rest of the servants go?"

"I have no idea. They gave no notice. You know how unappreciative servants can be. After all we do for them, what do they do but leave us in the lurch?"

While continuing to appraise her body, Capitaine rolled down his filthy stockings. Clare was reminded of her midwifery days, when she had grown accustomed to lecherous looks from some of the noble fathers. Knowing their wives and mistresses would be unavailable to satisfy their lust while healing from their confinements, many had propositioned her to give up her vocation and become their mistress. Clare had always politely declined.

This time, however, she played along, pretending to blush and doing her best to smile enticingly at Capitaine. Licking her lips, Clare leaned forward, placing her hand on his arm. He was wearing only his breeches, pulled tightly around his broad belly, and she saw the obvious bulge of his manhood rise to the occasion. It sickened her.

"Capitaine," Clare purred, "I look forward to satisfying your, umm—hunger. But first, you must have a good wash, as you requested. I love the scent of a clean man." Such words coming from her lips disgusted her. *Perhaps Lucina gets her acting talent from me*, she thought. But sacrificing herself to the officer, until his watchdogs went to Mass tomorrow and she could slip a sleeping potion into his coffee, would be her only chance to escape with Jean-Pierre. There was no other choice.

"You must excuse me for a few minutes, while I check on my boy. Get his supper."

At this, Capitaine responded suspiciously, "You just told me your cook is gone. How have you managed to have meals prepared?"

"Oh, sir," Clare cooed seductively, "I am a woman of many talents, among them the ability to whip up a fine omelette."

The burly, partially naked man sauntered over to the window and looked down into the courtyard, where the smells of an unappetizing turnip stew caused his nose to wrinkle. He nodded his head at somebody below. Then, turning back to Clare, he said, "Beauty and the ability to cook. How admirable in a fine lady such as yourself.

How rare these days. The child can wait for his meal. You will join me in another drink."

Clare refilled his glass, hoping he would pass out from the massive quantity of liquor he was consuming. After he gulped it down, he said, "I admit the thought of a fine omelette makes my stomach rumble. You will prepare one for me. For this evening only, I will forego your attendance at my bath. There will be other opportunities for you to have the pleasure of washing my skin. But stay a few moments more. Finish your drink. Tell me how you learned to cook. I am most interested in hearing all about it."

He wants to hear about my cooking lessons? What is going on here? Feeling anxious about Jean-Pierre alone upstairs, Clare began to rise.

"Really, it is quite difficult to have a conversation with the drumming going on, Capitaine. I will need but a half hour to feed my child. Then he will be put to bed, where he will not bother us." She started drifting toward the door.

Capitaine laughed wickedly. "Madame, your boy won't be requiring his supper after all."

"What do you mean?" she asked in alarm.

"Look out the window, Madame," he coolly answered. Clare rushed to the window, pulled aside the curtain and gasped in disbelief.

Chapter 30
Private J.P.

CLARE STOOD AT the open window and screamed. Jean-Pierre was standing in the courtyard, surrounded by soldiers. She called out the window to him hysterically. "Jean-Pierre! Come back inside this minute."

"Maman!" he screeched as the soldiers grabbed him by the arms. The little boy struggled in vain to get back to the house. The laughing brutes pushed him around.

The drumming got louder and louder, or perhaps it was the blood rushing to Clare's ears. Jean-Pierre cried out again. Two soldiers—one on each side—dragged him toward the road, where Lieutenant Pechard was mounted on his horse, reaching for the boy. Clare was horrified.

Just then, Giselle bumped backward into the bedchamber, toting a bucket of hot water for Capitaine's bath, splashing large puddles on the floor. She gave him a knowing smile as she poured the remaining water in the copper tub.

"Good work," he told her, obviously not referring to the steaming water or the purple robe, which she fetched from the hook on the wall and handed to him.

Giselle shrugged. "It din't take much. The boy is crazy about soldiers. And he seemed pretty healthy to me. No sign of any poxes."

Clare turned on her heels and ordered Giselle to bring Jean-Pierre back. The sound of his cries was still ringing in her ears. Giselle spat at Clare, said she no longer took orders from her.

Ignoring the servant's sneering face and defiance, Clare turned back to the painful sight of Jean-Pierre being lifted onto Lieutenant's horse. Grown man and little boy together, riding off through the very same iron gates that Jacques had assured her would keep their family safe. Her heart sank as they disappeared from sight. In shock, Clare slowly turned and listened incredulously to Giselle's conversation with the officer.

"I done what you ast," she bragged. "I went to the nursery and coaxed the boy down, promisin' he could march with the soldiers. I taught him to say *je suis réuni* and make the sign of the cross. He insisted on bein' dressed in a silly little blanket uniform and came quietly down the stairs. Lieutenant Pechard is takin' the boy away."

Capitaine nodded. "As he should," he said, then added, "Grizelle, go feed my horse and unsaddle him. Make certain you brush him well. It appears I won't be leaving tonight after all."

"What? You promised the soldiers and me we could have the evenin' free if'n I done what you ast. It were really hard, but I tricked the boy out. Led him down the servants' steps."

"I don't know…" he said in a weary voice, weaving toward the window, clearly beginning to exhibit the effects of the alcohol. He hesitated and looked out at the soldiers, who had resumed marching and pounding their drums. *Rum-tum-tum.*

Giselle pouted. "The soldiers and me, we made plans to go to the tavern together. You promised."

She has gone too far, Clare thought. *Her insolence will be her undoing.* But she held her breath, hoping the officer would heed the servant's plea. For him to leave the house unguarded for a few hours might enable her to escape. Time seemed to stand still.

"Very well," he finally sighed, handing Giselle a few coins. "Madame Dupres has offered to cook me an omelette and entertain me this evening. Your mistress and I will be occupied until dawn… and perhaps even longer." He gave Clare a drunken, lecherous grin. She forced a slight smile, realizing Giselle was unknowingly offering her a chance at freedom.

"You may go at once, and take all my men with you. That constant drumming is giving me a headache." As she headed for the door, he added, "Grizelle, do not wake us in the morning. Do you understand? We do not wish to be disturbed. By anyone. Tell my men that it is a direct order from their commanding officer."

"Yessir." Giselle saluted, whirled around and left in a hurry.

"Capitaine," Clare pleaded, "please bring my son back. He is an anxious, easily frightened child. Where are you sending him?"

"Where he will be looked after."

"Will he be killed?"

The officer looked dazed, almost insulted by her question. "Why would you think that, Madame? The King's soldiers are not monsters. Most of us have families back home. We do not murder innocent children."

"But Jean-Pierre is only six. He is too young to be a soldier."

"*Six*? I was told he was seven. Oh well, so be it." He shrugged. "It's too late to worry about the legality of the boy's baptism. The Sisters will take proper care of him at the convent. Until he reaches the age for soldiering, a priest will oversee his education in the Holy Roman Church."

Clare immediately thought of Father Benedict, the officious cousin of Lady Louise. Had he won his quest for a Dupres convert at last? She could imagine his glee at "saving the soul" of the stubborn midwife's son—and no doubt being rewarded by the King for his noble effort.

She begged for one last chance to say goodbye to her son.

"Treat me well tonight, Madame," he yawned, as he started to unbutton his breeches for his bath, "and we shall see."

~~~

Lieutenant Pechard held the sobbing child in front of him on the saddle. The officer burned with resentment but knew a military order was to be obeyed.

Capitaine is in charge of our regiment, but why does he always assign me to take these Huguenot brats to the convents? I'm second in command. Surely, any of his men are capable of taking a small kid and dumping him with the Sisters of Sorrow. Why must it always be me?

During the past several months, he had transported several dozens of these squalling children to various convents, wrenched from their parents by royal command to be converted and educated by nuns and priests. For a split second, he wondered how King Louis would feel if his own royal children were abducted from the great palace of Versailles against his will. He shuddered. Of course that would never happen. Even to think such thoughts was treasonous. Pechard had sworn an oath of loyalty to the King when he joined the
~~~

army. It was his duty to carry out all direct orders without question. Any signs of softheartedness would be his downfall.

But there was something different about this little boy. Pechard searched his brain to figure out the reason as they rode up the road. Was it because he resembled the six-year-old brother he had left behind at home, all those years ago? The one who had since died of typhus?

"Hey, boy," he said. "What's your name?"

Jean-Pierre sniffled. "Waaa. I wanna go b-b-back to Maman."

"Listen. I asked your name. Are you such a baby you can't remember?"

"Am not a b-b-baby."

"I think maybe you are, or else you would tell me your name."

"I'm Jean-Pierre Dumond Dupres. And I'm s-s-six. But I can count to one th-th-thousand."

"Is that so?" said the Lieutenant.

Jean-Pierre started gulping again. "Take me home. I wanna go home. Maman promised me a boiled egg for my s-s-supper."

"Where did you get that uniform, Jean-Pierre Dumond Dupres?" *That name is a mouthful.*

"Maman made it for me. Out of a blanket. I wanted to pretend I was a s-s-soldier. To march with the real s-s-soldiers in the courtyard."

"And now you look like a real soldier. Just like me."

Jean-Pierre stopped sniffling and turned his head toward Pechard's chest. "Not j-j-just like you. You're a loo-tenant."

Pechard was surprised. Had the boy overheard one of his men call him by his title when they'd dragged him down the drive? He had been screaming so loudly, he probably couldn't hear anything they said.

"How do you know my rank?"

"I know all about s-s-soldiers. I read about them in my books. I can tell by the s-s-stripes on your jacket that you are a loo-tenant of the cavalry and your soo-sooperior is called a *Capitaine*."

"And what is your rank, little soldier boy?"

"Well, I have no s-s-stripes on my uniform. And I'm just learning to ride a horse, except I couldn't ride this week because Marie took the mare and Maman would not let me go out to talk to the real s-s-soldiers even though I wanted to s-s-so badly but she said I was too s-s-sick even tho' I wasn't and—"

"Whoa. Hold on there for a minute, kid. I'm gonna draft you into the cavalry right now. You will be called…umm… Private J.P."

"I like that. Private J.P. Can I be a real s-s-soldier, honest and truly?"

"Certainly. Now listen, Private J.P., I am in command here, so you must salute me and call me sir. Do you understand?"

Jean-Pierre sat up straighter in the saddle and smiled. "Maman wanted to keep me forever locked away in the nursery. I'm not a baby anymore. I'm s-s-six and I know all about army officers." He sat forward stiffly and saluted with his chubby fingers.

"I asked you whether you understood my order."

"Yes, s-s-sir," the boy responded in a soft voice.

"I can't *hear* you, Private J.P."

In his loudest soldier voice, Jean-Pierre belted out, "Yes s-s-sir, Loo-tenant."

"That's more like it. And no more sniveling. Soldiers have no time for crying."

"Yessir."

They rode in silence for a while. Then the boy started wiggling around on the saddle. "May I s-s-speak, s-s-sir?"

"Permission granted, Private."

"I need to pass my water, s-s-sir."

Lieutenant shook his head. *What's up with these rich folks, living in large maisons, talking all fancy-like? Pass water! This kid wants to be a soldier, needs to learn some army talk.*

"Private J.P.… are you needing to take a piss?"

"Uh, yes. I think s-s-so."

Pechard pulled his horse off the road and led his young charge into the woods, pointing to a bush. "There's the latrine."

A few minutes later, the boy proudly strutted back with a grin on his face. "I always wanted to try that, but Maman s-s-says I need to use the chamber pot. Now I know I'm a real s-s-soldier."

"What about your father? Hasn't he ever taught you to piss in the woods?"

"Oh, no. Papa never takes me into the woods. He goes by hisself. But sometimes he plays chess with me, when he isn't busy drawing pictures of flowers."

Lieutenant Pechard remembered his own father—an army officer, hardly the type to draw pictures. His father had taught him to be tough, beaten him regularly and shown him how to use a gun. Piss in the woods. Important things like that.

Suddenly he felt sorry for this kid. He reached into his saddlebag and found the remnants of a chocolate bar—decided to share it with little Private J.P during the rest of the ride to the convent.

Night was falling and he was anxious to drop the boy off so he could join his men at the tavern. *I deserve a night off*, he concluded with a sigh as he listened to little Private J.P. proudly counting to a thousand.

Chapter 31

The Omelette

BY SEVEN IN the evening, most people are afraid to be out of their homes. Respectable householders remain inside their individual stone cottages, shutters closed, doors bolted against intruders. Winter is coming and darkness has descended early. To save candles, poor folk go early to bed.

Nobles can afford expensive wax candles. Their servants hang the slender tapers in crystal chandeliers, to keep out the dark of night. Rush torches light their courtyards, for guests arriving in carriages for evenings of lavish entertainment.

Shivering in the nursery by the glow of a single taper, Clare gathered together the ingredients for Capitaine's omelette. A quick glance through the open shutters at the moon beginning to rise reminded her—tonight must be the night of the Marquis's harvest ball.

To think, I might have been kissing my two darlings goodnight in this very room, before leaving them in the care of Claudette. We always dressed in our finest clothes to dance and dine at the balls. Tonight, I would have chosen to wear my favorite pink flowered silk. The one my little princess Lucina slept in last Sunday, preparing for her pox performance.

Instead, the famed midwife of Normandy was imprisoned alone in the nursery at Maison Dupres, poking a few sticks into the glowing embers of the brick hearth, preheating the copper pan.

Clare's first impulse upon reaching the nursery had been to climb out the window onto the gabled slate roof and jump. But she realized it was far too high. *I must stay alive to save my children*, she repeated over and over to herself, filled with dread about the evening facing her.

She tried not to picture poor Jean-Pierre being dragged away by the soldiers. Such morose thoughts would only lead to weeping.

I have to keep tears from staining my face. Leave no trace of my grief in red eyes. Keep my mind alert for a chance to escape. The man is a fiend. He will show me no mercy. Yet it is vital that I appear to welcome his disgusting advances, if I am to survive. I will wear an alluring smile when I bring his dinner. My task, at this hour, is to cook him a dish he will never forget.

Clare opened the nursery cabinet and stared with dismay at the scarcity of ingredients. An omelette with a chunk of stale bread couldn't compare with the feasts she had enjoyed in the past. Her stomach rumbled with hunger as she imagined the roast partridge, lobster, liver pâté, buttery rolls and frosted *petit fours* now being prepared by the bevy of chefs and kitchen maids in the steamy kitchen below stairs at the chateau.

Concentrate, she chastised herself. *Grate the cheese, chop the dried garlic, and crack the eggs carefully. Don't spill anything. There is little enough to work with up here. Only four eggs, a bit of butter. One shriveled onion. Stoke up the fire to heat the pan.*

At the officer's command, the copper bathing tub had been strategically placed, facing the doorway. When Clare had left the bedchamber, he'd ordered her to leave the door open so he could watch the staircase as he bathed. He refused her request to cook his supper in the kitchen or to go down to fetch the good china plates—not that she expected any had been left intact by his marauding Dragonnades.

"No," he had insisted, "You are forbidden to descend the stairs. I assure you the nursery crockery will be satisfactory for my meal."

Capitaine might be tired and hungry, but he is not stupid enough to let me escape. Nor could I outrun him, thought Clare.

Her ears were attuned to the sounds of her eerily quiet, dark house. The drums had stopped, which meant the soldiers had already left with Giselle for the tavern. Clare asked herself, *Is that snoring coming from the bedchamber, where a few minutes earlier I heard water splashing? Could he have fallen asleep in the tub? He had been yawning. How easy would it be to tiptoe down, push his head underwater, drown him?*

Suddenly, her mother's voice filled her head. "You have never killed before, Clare. Think of the oath you took when I trained you to be a midwife—to save life, not to destroy it. You are not a murderer."

"But he kidnapped my son, and his intentions toward me are wicked—he means to have his way with me, then take me to prison. Is not that justification for killing him?"

"You cannot take the officer's life. Your first priority is to escape and save Lucina. Take her to England. She must live to carry on our family tradition—to learn about the magic elixir."

"What about Jean-Pierre, Maman? What about my son?"

"He will be safe enough for now in the convent. Besides, the nuns would prevent you from taking him."

"Maman, stay with me. I am frightened. Tell me what to do."

"I am always with you, but you don't always listen. You have inner strength, my daughter. Use that strength to find your way." With that, Maman's voice faded away.

The butter sizzled in the copper pan. Clare added garlic and onions. The enticing smell brought Capitaine to the landing below, wrapped in a towel. He called up to her.

"Madame. I have finished my bath and am impatient for that omelette you promised me. It smells delicious."

"Have patience sir, it is almost ready. A few more minutes."

"I am most hungry," he complained. "I have not eaten all day."

"This will be worth the wait," she promised. "Open the bottle of champagne."

She heard him grumble and then the sound of the cork popping. Hopefully, with more alcohol in his empty stomach—he had already consumed an entire bottle of sherry—he would pass out.

To distract herself from feeling despair, Clare briskly whisked the eggs and tried to imagine what Lady Louise was doing at the moment. Clare envisioned her friend standing in her boudoir, holding on to the back of a chair, her lady's maid pulling the strings of her corset tight. The satin gown with the plunging neckline she had chosen to wear this evening was laid out on the counterpane. Soon, she would top her freshly powdered wig, shaped like a bird's nest, with a diamond tiara. Paste a small dark mouche, a beauty spot, on her left cheek. Then, after admiring the new diamond necklace around her neck, she would pull on her gloves.

Clare closed her eyes and watched her friend sweep down the circular staircase, beneath portraits of her husband's ancestors, frowning in their ornate frames. Lady Louise, wife of the Marquis, greeted her guests in the ballroom as the butler formally announced their arrival:

"Lord and Lady Varenne."

"The Dowager Baronesse and Lord La Croix."

"Monsieur and Madame Dupres."

Wait, something was wrong with this reverie. Ah, yes. The Dupres were not invited this year. Monsieur le Marquis was afraid to entertain Huguenots at his home. Sadly, they were no longer welcome guests.

How I always looked forward to dancing at the Marquis's yearly balls. One year I wore my yellow floral silk gown, the newest attention-getting pattern designed by Jacques. The Duke's favorite mistress, whose confinement I had attended, admired the design, embroidered in gold thread. Little did she suspect that it had been inspired by the delicate golden blooms of the bulbous buttercup.

As the garlic and onions slowly browned, Clare reached into the nursery cabinet for a plate. Something on the top shelf caught her eye and her thoughts traveled back to the prior Saturday, the evening before the foot soldiers had arrived at Maison Dupres.

Jacques had asked for a special bottle of claret in the cellar that he wanted to drink with the soufflé Marie was busy baking for their dinner. As usual, Giselle was nowhere to be found, so Clare had climbed down the dark stairs with a lantern to fetch it. There, proliferating on the moist dirt floor in the corner, she'd sighted a patch of spotted mushrooms.

Her mind began to turn when she first saw them. "Why, they look just like truffles, except—"

"Clare, I'm waiting," Jacques had called, impatient for his claret. On impulse, she had hurriedly wrapped a few of the squishy caps in her kerchief and taken them up to the nursery, where she had hid them in the cupboard. At the time, her idea had been to use them to teach the children how to distinguish edible from poisonous wild mushrooms.

Now, she heard the voices of the mushrooms calling out to her from the top shelf. "Use us, use us," they chanted in unison.

Clare shook her head. *I must be losing my mind. I often hear Maman's voice in my head, but talking mushrooms?* She took down the folded kerchief and found the mushroom caps had dried out and turned black. She began to lift a piece toward her nose, forgetting her mother's warning years earlier about sniffing strange substances. Too late!

One whiff and suddenly her head was spinning. She was transported to the ballroom at Chateau Montjardin, where Lady Louise's musicians began to play. Clare stood hypnotized by the wigged gentlemen swirling their bejeweled dance partners around the floor in circular patterns. Her hands and feet started to move in perfect time to the music as she whipped up the eggs.

Mesmerized, Clare spooned the dried "truffles" into the egg mixture in a circular dance pattern. A sprinkle of cheese and her masterpiece was finished.

In the ballroom, the frenzied musicians fiddled faster and faster as Clare danced down the stairs with the dinner—to a table where a man with a drooping handlebar mustache sat in a royal purple robe, sipping champagne.

Chapter 32

The False Coquette

BY THE TIME Clare reached the door to the bedchamber with the tray, the bottle of champagne was half-emptied. *Good sign, Capitaine's empty stomach filled with yet more alcohol.*

She had located a large domed bowl in the nursery cabinet and used it as an improvised platter cover, not only to keep the omelette hot but to prevent her nose from accidentally getting too close again. The dizziness she had experienced from sniffing the pungent odor of the "truffles" had fortunately cleared. *If my plan is to succeed, I must keep my mind as sharp as the tip of his sword standing in the corner, a constant reminder of the looming danger.*

Clare set the covered tray on the table, close to the chair where Capitaine sat barefoot, loosely wrapped in Jacques's short purple robe—the one he used to wear on summer evenings when it was too stifling for wool. She forced herself to look directly at her unwelcome guest. The wide satin lapels of the robe fell open to reveal his black, hairy chest and muscular abdomen. This came as somewhat of a shock to Clare's eyes. Other than her husband, she had never before seen an undressed adult male. Not even her father.

"Oh!" she blurted out, blushing unconsciously. Her reaction pleased Capitaine. He grinned and stroked his handlebar mustache.

"Sit down and relax, lovely lady. So you like what you see, do you?" When he leaned back to drain the rest of his champagne, the loose sash on the too-small robe came undone, revealing a pair of strong, muscular legs. He made no move to cover them.

Clare felt the gall rising in her gut but managed to paste a seductive smile on her face. She momentarily compared his fit appearance to her squat, slender Jacques. The officer's broad shoulders were closer to what she imagined Pierre's shoulders now looked like, although she had not actually seen him in ten years.

Yet while this soldier might possess a brawny physique, and was now rid of the rank odor of sweat, sex and horseflesh, Clare found his demeanor detestable. She hated this man with a fervor she had never thought possible.

I must not let my disgust show. I will fight the urge to avert my eyes, she thought, straining to keep an evocative smile. Batting her long eyelashes in his direction, she refilled his glass while pretending to sip her champagne.

"Ah. Madame. I am grateful for your gracious hospitality, short as it may be. In a few days, I will be taking you to new accommodations. I fear you may not find your prison cell as sumptuous as this luxurious bedchamber," he said, expansively waving his hand around the room. "Nor the pile of straw you will be sleeping on as comfortable as that soft down mattress over there. Pity."

He gulped more champagne, watching for her reaction.

Clare leaned forward and caressed his shoulder. "No doubt I shall miss my bedchamber… but not my odious husband." This elicited a lusty laugh from *le Capitaine*, who was undoubtedly more than a little drunk by now. His words were slurred. "A few days 'n' nights with me, m'dear, and you'll not even remember your husband's name."

"Husband? What husband?" she snickered. Clare's words stung as she uttered them. *How can I be saying such hateful things about my husband to this stranger? If I escape, I will never tell Jacques. He could not possibly understand why I was compelled to say such terrible things, even considering my dire circumstances. Jacques is too proud to ever forgive me.*

"Officer," the false coquette said, "would you refill my glass?"

"Gladly, Madame." He was momentarily occupied, trying not to spill champagne. The bottle wavered in his shaky hands.

Clare took this opportunity to survey the room with her eyes, as if it were a place she had never seen before. Charted her escape route. She glanced at the copper tub containing murky cold water, the melting bar of her lavender soap floating on the surface. The wet towel lying in a heap on the floor, a disturbing sight to her inner sense of neatness and organization. She resisted the urge to reach over and fold it.

Then her eyes landed on an unexpected sight. She was surprised to see the officer's uniform, neatly folded on a small wooden chair in the corner. His tall leather boots stood at attention in perfect alignment on the floor, in readiness to march away at a moment's notice. *Habits of neatness and order from years of military training, no doubt. He probably wasn't even aware he was doing it.* Only his shirt, which he had forgotten to fold, lay crumpled on the floor next to the tub.

Clare perched close to the edge of her seat. Unlike Capitaine in his state of undress, she was still ensconced in her customary gentrified layers of restrictive attire. She had been unable to vary her outfits during the past week, the bulk of her wardrobe having been removed to the stable by Giselle. Under her long-sleeved jacket and skirt, Clare wore a shift, a petticoat, and the front-lacing corset she had worn during the last months before Lucina's birth. Lacking a servant to assist her this past week, she had been unable to wear her normal back-lacing stays. Giselle had been far too busy entertaining her new soldier friends, and besides, Clare had preferred as little contact with that disloyal wench as possible.

Her jacket had a plunging neckline, but she had tucked in a lace fichu for modesty sake. On her head, she still wore her lace-edged coif over her plaited hair.

"Madame," said the officer, "you appear hot and uncomfortable in those clothes. Now that you have finished preparing my meal, it is time for you to disrobe."

"This omelette will soon be cold," she pouted. "Do you wish to insult me by ignoring the dish I worked so hard to prepare especially for you?"

"No, no. Course not. You'll entertain me by removing those restraining layers as I eat."

She handed him a silver-plated three-pronged *fourchette* and shook a large linen napkin in his direction. Thankfully, he used the cloth to cover his exposed lap. For a brief moment, she regretted not stabbing him with the fork, but it would not have caused sufficient harm to assist her escape.

"*Commence*!" He waved the fork in her direction, indicating that she should begin disrobing. Clare stood and swiveled her hips as seductively as she imagined a prostitute might. Pulling the lid off the tray, she backed away, keeping her head far from the food. She ripped off her head covering and unplaited the braid, shaking her long, unpinned tresses down around her shoulders. Slowly flicking her hair behind her back, she removed the fichu, exposing the swell of her breasts.

The officer's eyes grew large as he stared at his hostess. He was so intent on watching her undress that Clare worried that he might forget to eat.

"I hope you are enjoying the food, as well as the entertainment," she reminded him. While he ogled her, Capitaine began forking large bites of the omelette into his mouth. She knew she had to keep his attention on her at all costs, and kept licking her lips.

Clare kicked her satin shoes off her feet, one at a time, and they flew in an arc, landing just inches from the burning logs. She placed her left foot on the chair, leaned over, and slowly lifted her petticoat up to her knee. Her performance was sensuous and measured. She untied the satin ribbon, peeled off the silk stocking.

Relieved to see that Capitaine was swallowing his food, she proceeded to remove her right stocking in a similar manner.

"Delicious," he murmured. Clare hoped he was referring to the omelette, not her bare legs. Loosening the fastenings, she stepped out of her skirt, delaying her disrobing as long as possible by folding it carefully over the back of the chair. This gave her another chance to observe Capitaine's progress with his meal. He seemed not to mind the taste of the food, probably because he was too inebriated to notice.

He ravenously shoveled each bite into his mouth, yet nothing was happening. She began to worry that the heat from the pan had somehow destroyed the desired effects of the "truffles." Wondering how much longer it would take, she deliberately unbuttoned the jacket slowly, one small pearl button at a time. She hoped that if he noticed her trembling hands, he would believe it indicated anticipation and desire on her part.

The man swallowed the last bite of the omelette, washing it down with Clare's full glass of champagne—his own had been drained. He wiped his mouth and tried to keep his drooping eyes open as she stepped out of her petticoat.

She bravely smiled, silently praying, *Soon, dear God, let it begin soon.*

By the time she unlaced her stays, again loosening each string with deliberate slowness and care, she stood in the glow of the hearth in nothing but her shift. Holding the corset in her right hand, she flung it in an air of abandon. It landed in the slimy tub water. She backed away, pretending to retrieve the soggy corset from the water, where it floated like a dead ghost.

Capitaine stood up. He was wobbling and no longer staring at her. Clare watched as he staggered toward the bed. His face turned green and he moaned, vomiting in all directions before he fell facedown onto the mattress.

Clare's first reaction was inexplicable anger. This monster was ruining her expensive silk sheets, her down pillows. Her anger rapidly dissolved into relief.

The officer's contorted body began to convulse. He was racked with nausea and loosening of the bowels. Clare practically reveled in the gruesome stench of his bodily emissions because it meant the "truffles" had finally done their job. Now, she was in control and must act quickly. He did not have the strength to lift his arms or legs. They were temporarily paralyzed.

He lifted his head and gagged out two words: "You witch!"

"Why, Capitaine, do you still believe those old rumors about midwives?" she said, but he was beyond sparring with her. He began screaming about spiders crawling over his body, slithering snakes squeezing his stomach.

Standing barefoot, clad in nothing but her shift, Clare acted quickly. She reached for the long sash of Jacques's purple robe. Cutting it into four pieces with the sword, she used them to bind the helpless officer's wrists and ankles to the bedposts, making sure they were tightly secured. Backing away from the bed, she gingerly picked up his crumpled shirt from the floor with two fingers and dropped it into the tub.

For the first time since the Dragonnades had arrived at Maison Dupres, a brief feeling of ease flooded Clare's body. There was nobody within miles to hear his screams. After tying the helpless man to the bed, Clare forced him to drink a harmless potion designed to put him to sleep for at least twelve hours. It was the magic elixir, but concentrated. Triple the normal strength. She acted not out of compassion for the fiend, but out of concern that despite his weakened condition he might be able to loosen the bindings.

Spooning the extra strong dose down his throat was not an easy task. He was lying facedown—but she managed to push his head up and to the side. Clare believed it would take a few minutes for the elixir to take effect, although she was unsure as she had never before administered it to a man.

She rechecked to be sure the bindings were tight. As she did, he retched green bile onto her chemise. The slimy substance dripped off onto her cherished flowered carpet.

Writhing around in his filth, he continued to spew epithets at her, calling her a bloody she-devil whore. It was this final insult that provoked her to taunt him. "Why, Capitaine, did you not enjoy your delicious omelette?"

He spat at her. This angered her to the point where she began to laugh maliciously. "Are the snakes still slithering between your legs? Do you picture them as *my* legs, dripping with your male fluids?" Clare was shocked to hear such terrible, unladylike words coming from her mouth and tried to think of something less provocative to say until he fell asleep.

"Don't worry, Capitaine, the potion I just forced down your throat will relieve your suffering in a few minutes. The magic elixir will provide you with a peaceful night's sleep you really don't deserve. You may still feel unwell from the truffles when you wake, but you won't die."

The hog-tied officer groaned, staring daggers at her, struggling fruitlessly with the bindings. Sleep did not come to him yet, so she gave him another spoonful of the triple-dose elixir. This time, he did not vomit.

Clare began to worry that Giselle and the soldiers would return from the tavern before her escape, but she could hardly leave wearing nothing but a green-stained undergarment.

What shall I do?

INTERLUDE

Chapter 33

Le Cheval Noir de la Morte

THE CLOCK TOWER in Rouen strikes eleven bells. The sound carries through the cobbled streets, over the stone bridge spanning the Seine, where it can faintly be heard along the highway leading to the north. A lone rider gallops up the road on a black steed.

Nobody is around to see the uniformed soldier speed by the tavern as fast as the horse can go. Who would question a fighter on a dark horse, riding into the night? Or dare to stop him? The stripes on the sleeves, the colors of the jacket, and the feather-trimmed tricorn indicate a soldier of high rank. Perhaps he rushes home to his wife, after enjoying a quiet tryst with his mistress.

Luckily, the soldiers do not see the horse rush by the tavern, where they have been drinking and whoring for the past two hours. Loud shouts and snatches of song can be heard through the windows of the filthy, dark chambers in the loft above the bar.

The rider is not spotted as the black horse thunders by in a cloud of dust, or so the rider thinks with relief. Except—there is one witness who goes unnoticed.

The tall foot soldier, the first Dragonnade to arrive at the maison last Sunday, is standing outside the tavern in the shadows, pissing against the rock wall. He looks up briefly. For a moment, his foggy alcohol-soaked brain thinks it is Le Cheval Noir de la Morte thundering by. The image of a dead soldier in uniform on horseback, which often appears on the battlefield, frightens him. The black horse of death is a bad omen.

The superstitious soldier makes the sign of the Cross. He shakes off the last few drops of piss and buttons his pants. Tells himself it has been his imagination and staggers back inside, swearing to go to confession the next day.

His companions notice his shaking hands, his blanched face. He relates his vision of death riding by. There is a silent buzz.

Two hours earlier, the Lieutenant had joined his men upon return from his distasteful assignment at the convent. He becomes uneasy when the rumor reaches his ears. He tries to peer through the soot-covered window. Wipes his sleeve against the glass, attempting to get a better view of the road. "I'll have a look outside," he says with authority, standing up from the rough bench.

By the time he pushes his way through the raucous crowd to step out the door, there is no evidence of a passing rider. He listens for the sound of hooves, but there is too much noise from the room behind him. When he walks closer to the road, he looks both ways, sees nothing.

"Just as I thought. It was the idiot's drunken imagination." He returns to his seat inside.

Giselle, who led the soldiers to the tavern this evening, has never before heard the ghostly legend of Le Cheval Noir de la Morte. The size and ferocity of the horse increases as the uneasy rumor spreads through the crowd.

She sidles over to the tall foot soldier. "Did the horse resemble Capitaine's steed?" she asks. "Could that have been him you saw, riding away from the maison?"

The men sober up for a moment at this possibility and look to the Lieutenant.

"Impossible," Pechard declares, trying to reassure himself as well as his men. "Don't you remember? Capitaine is holed up in the bedchamber, entertaining Madame Dupres."

Giselle echoes his reminder, saying, "When we left the maison, he gave us orders not to disturb them, did he not? Strict orders."

The soldiers laugh. "He is busy entertaining her, all right." They envision the fine lady being stripped and violated by their lusty leader.

"No doubt, the Protestant heathen is crying for mercy when she sees the size of his large weapon, pointed in her direction."

"I'll bet he reloads his cannon fast."

"Ha-ha."

Besides, it is rare for soldiers to have a night off from duty, with coins jingling in their pockets. They do not wish to leave, so they call for a refill of their empty tankards.

"What the hell," sighs the Lieutenant, joining in the merriment. "If our commanding officer is having a good time tonight, why shouldn't we?" Giselle grabs his arm and pulls him upstairs to the loft.

PART IV

SUNDAY

28 OCTOBRE 1685

Chapter 34

Long Ride North

1:00 A.M.

RELIEVED TO BE safely past the tavern, Clare tried to keep her head clear. Although sleep-deprived, she couldn't risk falling off the horse. Fortuitously, the road was empty this evening and the full moon provided sufficient light. Her plan was to forge ahead to Dieppe without stopping.

Don't dwell on what happened, she warned herself, but the image of the final moments with the brute in the bedchamber kept flashing before her eyes during the long ride.

The fire in the hearth had begun to fade. She had shivered, more from shock than the rapidly decreasing temperature in the room. Throwing a quilt over *le Capitaine's* thrashing body on the bed so he wouldn't freeze to death, she had realized she was still clad solely in her soiled chemise. Moving away from the bed, she tore it off and tossed it into the dying embers. A sudden flash, then it quickly burned to ash.

Clare crossed her arms and looked about for something to cover herself. She rejected the idea of wearing the silk jacket and skirt she had stripped off for her "performance," thinking it important to dress warmly for her journey. Sensing a pair of heavy, sleep-droopy eyes staring at her nude body, Clare felt certain Capitaine was wondering what she planned to do next. Perhaps his deluded brain thought this was her way of seducing him. He fought to stay awake.

Wrapping her shivering body in a shawl, she rummaged through her armoire, seeking her heavy woolen cloak, but Giselle had apparently appropriated it along with all her silk gowns. Then Clare remembered Capitaine's uniform, neatly folded on the chair.

"I hope you don't mind," she had told the prostrate officer, "but I need to borrow your uniform and horse to get to… to Paris. Not that you are in any condition to ride now."

This roused him and he struggled to speak. His words were slurred. He begged to be untied. Promised to free her.

"As if I were stupid enough to believe such a lie," she said, smiling through gritted teeth. When pleading did not work, he threatened (in between bouts of retching) that she would be caught and her fate would be far worse than imprisonment. Vowed that he would order his men to search for her and drag her back, and that he personally would see to her punishment.

"Capitaine," Clare reminded him, "do you not remember your strict instructions to Giselle and your men before they left for their evening at the tavern? Not to bother us in the morning because you would be busy entertaining me?"

Fighting off the effects of the sleeping potion, he croaked, "They *will* come find me, and the entire cavalry will be after you before you reach Paris. You will regret this, Madame, believe me."

Dangling a key over his head, Clare said, "Take a good look at this. The heavy door to the bedchamber will be well secured when I leave. The key will be placed where your men will never think to look."

She could barely make out his gravelly threats. "Grizelle will hear my shouting—my men will come and kick the damn door down."

"Now, now," Clare retorted. "We cannot let that happen, can we?" She tied his black scarf around his mouth to inhibit his ability to scream for help when the sleeping draught wore off. He tried to bite her hand.

Clare stepped back and considered the possibility that Giselle might come upstairs in the morning. The soldiers would undoubtedly obey his command to leave them alone, but what of nosy Giselle, who rarely carried out orders? What would she hear if she came to light the fire? At best, Clare hoped, the Capitaine's muffled groans through the gag.

Giselle would probably interpret such sounds as cries of morning passion, something she was obviously experienced with. Clare could practically picture the servant girl trying to peek through the keyhole, even turning the knob. Finding the door locked, she would laugh and return to her friends in the stable with an entertaining report of their commander's sexual prowess.

When Capitaine finally drifted off to sleep, snoring loudly, Clare turned her attention to disguising herself as a soldier. The officer's filthy, sodden shirt still floated in the murky bathwater. Besides, the thought of wearing something on her body that had clung to the officer's sweaty skin was not something she relished, even if it had been dry.

In the corner, she found an unwashed shirt Jacques had worn a few days earlier, before he had hurriedly left with Lucina. Pulling the soft linen garment over her head gave her a momentary feeling of comfort, as if her husband were there in the room protecting her.

The burly officer's breeches were far too large for Clare, but she managed to tighten the strings around her waist to hold them up. Even with two pair of her husband's wool stockings on her feet, Capitaine's oversized leather boots promised to rub sores on her ankles.

Next, she had pulled on his wig, recoiling momentarily in revulsion but realizing it was essential to hide her telltale auburn hair.

Finally, the uniform jacket—Clare was shocked by the sheer size and weight of it. It hung loosely on her exhausted shoulders. She needed something to fill it out to complete her disguise. Her soft-sided birthing bag! She fetched it from the nursery, placed her journal inside, and stuffed it under the jacket. When she glimpsed her lumpy profile in the mirror, the midwife was convinced she could pass for a well-fed French soldier.

Within ten minutes, she was camouflaged and ready to flee her beloved Maison Dupres, which had become a house of horrors. Upon exiting the bedchamber, she locked the heavy oak door and ran, as best as she could in her cumbersome outfit, down the stairs. Grabbed the feathered tricorn and cloak off the newel post, where he had carelessly flung it upon arrival.

Cautiously crossing the courtyard toward the barn, Clare pushed back the side curls of the officer's wig to uncover her ears, listening for possible voices. All she heard was the sound of her heart in her throat. When she passed the well, she dropped the key into the icy, deep water, hearing a satisfying *plink* as it sank to the bottom. Luckily, Giselle had not unsaddled Capitaine's horse. *For once, I'm relieved the wench disobeyed orders.* Clare mounted the large black steed and took off without as much as a backward glance. She knew she would never see Maison Dupres again.

~~~

Clare's heart thumped wildly as she kicked her feet in the stirrups, urging the horse quickly past the tavern. It felt as if she had been holding her breath for hours. At least she hadn't been stopped. Hearing no sound of horses chasing her, she assumed none of the soldiers were on her trail.

About an hour later, the disguised "officer" stopped briefly by a stream to rest and splash water on her face. Pulling the uniform sash tighter, she felt the comforting presence of the birthing bag pressed against her breasts. The pressure reminded her of cuddling Jean-Pierre against her bosom as an infant. Thoughts of her little boy being dragged away in tears caused her eyes to mist over. She had no idea where the Sisters of Sorrow convent was located. Clare fought the impulse to break down and cry—she had to concentrate on her escape.

Until Jean-Pierre is safely back in my arms, all I can do is pray he is safe and warm, being treated kindly. She began to reminisce about the past week—the hours, minutes and days she had spent locked together with him in the nursery.

During the ride north, she began talking softly to the horse, to prevent herself from falling asleep. "Why come to think of it, I never really spent that much concentrated time alone with my son before. It was always Lucina who demanded my attention when the children were with me. But this past week, I really got to know my mild, sweet-tempered son."

The horse whinnied in reply, so she continued talking. "Jean-Pierre is smarter than I thought. How proud he was to tell me all he had learned from his books on soldiers. It was his idea to use the wool blanket to sew him a uniform. He showed me he could stand on his head.

"Then there was the time he bragged that he could count to one thousand. Did I want to hear? I had stopped him at two hundred and eighty-five, telling him how impressed I was. He smiled at my approval, something he was unused to receiving.
~~~

"What a terrible mother I have been to my dear little son. In the past, I mostly scolded him and tried to correct his stuttering. I was too stern—should have encouraged him more."

Clare thought about the map of the world tacked to the nursery wall. She had been astonished that Jean-Pierre could identify the capital cities in Europe. *Jacques must have taught him.* When her son ran his finger across the north coast of Normandy, he asked his maman to show him Dieppe, where Tante Delphine lived. She was the auntie who sent him seashells.

At this moment, riding toward Dieppe on the officer's black steed, Clare felt a strong surge of love for Jean-Pierre. "When we get to England, I will buy him a new map. He will like that." She smiled at her idea, until the cold realization gripped her—she did not know how or when she would get him back.

Clare chastised herself for failing to lock the nursery door when Giselle had come to summon her downstairs. As the horse passed a road marker pointing to Dieppe, she could still hear a small stuttering voice, counting out one thousand pangs of guilt in her conscience—"two hundred s-s-seventy s-s-six, two hundred s-s-seventy s-s-seven…" Why had she stopped him from counting all the way to one thousand? Why had she not locked the nursery door? Would she ever see her son again? Despite her efforts to be brave, tears began to roll down her face.

Chapter 35

Baptism at the Convent
Rouen, 7:00 A.M.

FATHER BENEDICT YAWNED on his way to the convent to celebrate Mass for the Sisters of Sorrow. He came unusually early this Sunday because he had received notice that another Huguenot child had been brought in to be baptized. The priest was surprised to see the Montjardin coach parked outside the walls. Had his cousin Louise dropped by to bring excess food from her harvest ball last night?

His mouth watered at the thought of the candied fruits she sometimes brought to the orphanage. But at this hour of the morning? Following a lavish affair, he expected she would still be asleep. *Strange.*

Sister Mary-Augustus, the prioress, greeted him at the door. "Bonjour, Père Benedict. Last evening, Lieutenant Pechard brought us a young boy dressed in a very strange outfit. It appears to have been hastily cut and sewn out of an English woolen blanket—much finer than the rough blankets the residents of this convent sleep with."

"Did the child tell you his name?" asked the priest.

"He insisted his name was Private J.P., that he was a soldier, and that he was six years old. His little voice trembled and he clung to the Lieutenant's hand."

"Are you certain he said six?"

"Yes, and he appeared quite small for his age."

"You don't think he was a street urchin?"

"I did not get that impression. Despite the strange outfit he wore, he appeared to be clean and well-fed. He cried and said his papa was in Paris and his maman was back home at the maison preparing his egg for dinner."

Father Benedict was annoyed. The Church considered seven as the minimum age for a child to consent to baptism without parental consent. This child was apparently too young to be forcibly baptized.

"You say the Lieutenant brought him. Did he obtain approval from the boy's parents?"

Sister Mary-Augustus wrung her age-wrinkled hands. "Oh, Father, I doubt it. This poor child was forcibly taken from his home by order of the Intendant. His parents are Huguenots accused of defying the King's proclamations. Lieutenant Pechard was instructed to bring him here, after his commanding officer contrived to have the innocent child abducted from his nursery."

"If the order is valid, I have no choice but to baptize the boy," said Father Benedict with a solemn expression on his face. "Did Lieutenant Pechard tell you anything else?"

Before she could answer, the Marquis walked into the vestibule from the refectory. "Good morning, Father Benedict. I see you wasted no time in getting here."

"Not I, although my aging mule is slow in making his way up this steep hill."

The priest knew the Marquis was a generous benefactor of the convent, but was puzzled to see him at this early hour on a Sunday morning. "What brings you out so early, milord?"

"Word travels fast in Rouen," said the Marquis. "My wife and I were called away from our guests momentarily last night with the urgent message from Sister Mary-Augustus. We know the boy, you see."

"Père Benedict and I were just talking about the child," explained the nun. "When he arrived last evening, he was exhausted and frightened. The Sisters fed him some porridge and bread. They tried to persuade him to take off his strange outfit and put on a clean nightshirt, but he refused, insisting he was a soldier and needed to wear his 'uniform.'"

"I know his parents and the reason he was brought here," sighed the Marquis. "The boy's name is Jean-Pierre Dupres. The Intendant has ordered his father to the galleys for singing psalms in the woods, the wife to prison for violating King Louis's prohibition against Huguenot midwives."

At hearing this, Sister Mary-Augustus gasped. "Such harsh punishments," she said, "merely for the act of praying in private, or for assisting women in need. The poor, poor parents. What is this world coming to?"

"Dupres," said Father Benedict, "is this by any chance the child of the midwife, Madame Clare Dupres?"

"*Former* midwife," the Marquis corrected him. "I believe you remember her from the day she assisted Lady Louise in birthing my son Louis-Armand."

The priest shook his head. "Such a shame I wasn't able to convince Madame Dupres to convert. I tried, you know."

"So she informed me. My wife has still not forgiven me for interfering with their friendship." He turned aside and looked at the statue of the Holy Virgin in the vestibule. "Lady Louise was very upset when she heard the Intendant boast at our dinner party last week of the order against the Dupres. She was shaken to think of their children declared orphans, to be brought up in a convent."

Sister Mary-Augustus's face bristled.

Realizing to his consternation that Sister Mary-Augustus took his statement as an insult, the Marquis hastily tried to reassure her. "I didn't mean to imply the children are not well cared for here, Sister. I know you do your best under such unfortunate circumstances."

She bowed her head and rubbed her fingers against the crucifix on her chest. "With the Lord's help, we do our best. So many children come to us as 'orphans,' pulled from their parents' loving arms. How can a mother who loves her children not do everything in her power to save them?"

"I agree," said the Marquis. "I know my wife would not willingly let our children be taken."

Father Benedict disagreed. "It is our job to save their pagan souls. If the parents resist, what are we to do but bring them into the fold one way or another?" He was thinking of the reward he would receive for this baptism.

Sister Mary-Augustus sighed and asked the Marquis whether he was ready to stand as godfather to this little boy.

Father Benedict looked amazed. "Why would a man of your rank deign to take on the responsibility for a merchant's son?"

"Last evening, Lady Louise and I promised we would do so. Madame Dupres saved my wife's life a month ago, when an early miscarriage…" The Marquis choked at the fresh memory. "We are both indebted to her. Being godparents to her son is the least we can do to help. I only wish we could do more."

Father Benedict interposed. "Wait—I thought the Dupres had another child, a little girl."

"Lieutenant Pechard told me the soldiers are searching for her," said the nun. "She is apparently in hiding with her father. They are believed to be in Paris."

The priest was disappointed to hear this. His anticipated reward for the baptism of two Huguenot children was now halved. But hopefully the girl would soon be found, and he would have sufficient funds to purchase a proper horse to replace his cranky mule.

~~~

The Marquis pulled out his gold watch and checked the time. "Sister, please fetch the boy into the chapel so we can proceed with his baptism. I must get home to my wife. She was too distressed by the news to accompany me here this morning. I insisted she stay in bed all day."

When Sister Mary-Augustus left the vestibule to get Jean-Pierre, Father Benedict said, "I am sorry, milord, to hear that my dearest cousin Louise is in a state of distress. May I come by the chateau this evening to say prayers with her?"

"I suppose you wish to dine with us too?" said the Marquis, trying not to let his annoyance show. *Father Benedict is only a third cousin, yet he always refers to Lady Louise as his dearest cousin and is forever fishing for invitations to share our board. His prayers are merely an excuse.*

"Oh, I wasn't trying to wrangle a dinner invitation, merely wanted to offer solace to my cousin. But I confess, I do enjoy a fine meal from time to time. Our food at the presbytery is, well, rather bland."

"Very well, join us at six. Now let us have done with this baptism ceremony."

The sound of the Sisters' sonorous prayers echoed in the corridor as they marched in pairs toward the chapel, with Jean-Pierre wedged between them. The bewildered child had no idea what was going to happen to him.
~~~

Chapter 36

Sisters' Reunion

Dieppe 9:00 A.M.

CHURCH BELLS TOLLING in the distance, summoning the residents of Dieppe to Sunday Mass, were a welcome sound to Clare's ears after her long ride. As she galloped into town, she saw ship masts in the harbor. Relieved to find no uniformed soldiers about, she approached Delphine's house.

How many times as a child had Clare taken this house for granted? A home she had often visited, graciously welcomed by her relations. Now Delphine was the only Dupres left living in the house where Jacques and Pierre had been born.

The glass shop window at ground level was shattered and covered over with strips of wood. The old flowered sign, Dupres & Sons, Purveyors of Fine Fabrics, had been replaced with a simple black-and-white sign—Rooms to Let, Reputable Lodgers Welcome.

Never before had this half-timbered building looked so inviting, so welcoming to a weary traveler, as it did to Clare this morning. She patted the worthy beast, saying, "We made it, boy. Just behind is the stable, where you shall have some well-deserved oats for your breakfast."

Clare handed the reins to the groom and hobbled bow-legged up to the back door. The delicious smell of food drifted out. Fried fish, freshly baked bread, creamy butter. Even porridge, which she ordinarily disliked, smelled inviting.

~~~
~~~

Hearing hoofbeats on the cobblestone courtyard, Lucina peered cautiously out from behind the curtains of the room that had once been her papa's nursery. At first she was frightened, thinking the bad soldiers had come to take her away. When Clare pulled off the tricorn hat and wig and shook out her distinctive auburn hair, Lucina's expression turned to exhilaration. She waved wildly and jumped up and down.

"Maman!" she shouted in excitement. "It's Maman. She's come at last."

The voice of a servant chided, "Miss Lucina! You must let me dress you before you go downstairs. You cannot go down in your nightclothes."

"Maman won't care. I'm not listening to you." Lucina burst away and ran toward the nursery door.

"What an ill-behaved child you are," the servant called after the spirited girl, secretly relieved that the mother had arrived to take charge of her. "Always goin' on 'bout bein' an enchanted princess. Talkin' 'bout seein' pictures in your head. Such nonsense. You needs a good beatin', you do."

Lucina ran down two flights and banged on the door to the room where Jacques was quietly sitting and reading. "Papa!" she shouted. "It's Maman. Come at once."

Already dressed, Jacques placed a marker between the pages of his Bible and fell to his knees in a prayer of thanksgiving. When he had first arrived here, Jacques had told his sister about the soldiers coming to Maison Dupres. Hearing the word soldiers caused Delphine to shudder, the memory of the marauding Dragonnades still fresh in her mind—a bunch of beastly hooligans, except for the Lieutenant. Although Jacques had hardly approved when Delphine had confessed to becoming a *convertie*, he had not reproached her. These were not ordinary times.

He had also told Delphine about Clare's scheme to escape separately and meet up with him at the farm in Torcy-le-Grand. Lucina and he had waited there with Marie's family for two days, then, thinking he must have misunderstood Clare's intentions, he had driven the waggon on to Dieppe. Four more days and still no sign of Clare and Jean-Pierre. He had busied himself unloading his cargo, trying each passing day not to worry. God would surely bring his wife and son to Dieppe in safety. And now his prayers had been answered at last, a double blessing because it was the Sabbath day. He stood up from his knees and headed for the staircase to greet them.

~~~

Delphine was the first to greet Clare at the door. *My poor dear sister. How exhausted she looks.* She helped her remove the bulky boots, then watched in dismay as Clare took off the heavy wool jacket, removing the hidden birthing bag, which had left a large red rub mark on her abdomen.

"What shall I do with this?" Delphine asked, holding the jacket away from her body.

"Burn it, or bury it… wait, I have a better idea. Throw the detestable jacket off the limestone cliff, onto the beach. Let whoever finds it think the officer drowned," said Clare.

Delphine hesitated. *Brass buttons are expensive. Perhaps I might cut them off and save them for a sewing project. The gold braid alone must have cost several livres. Best hide the jacket away for now and fetch a dress for Clare.* "Be right back," she said. "But lookie here, there's a certain somebody who really missed you, flying down the stairs."

Lucina came running to Clare and wrapped her tiny arms around her mother's waist, repeating over and over, "Maman, you came. At last, you came. I missed you so much." Clare reached down and lifted her golden-haired angel into her sore, weary arms and squeezed her.

"But Maman, why are you dressed like a soldier? Are you pretending, like I pretended to have poxes? I was certain you would come, but what took you sooo long?"

Clare peeked over Lucina's shoulder and saw Jacques, who barely stopped to greet her. He walked to the kitchen door and stared out at the stable.

"I was delayed," Clare said to her precious child, setting her down. "Maman is very tired and hungry. Be a good girl and go get dressed."

"You won't leave me again, will you?"

"No. Never, ever."

"Promise?"

"Yes. I promise."

Lucina skipped to the stairs. She looked back over her shoulder several times to satisfy herself that her maman was not leaving.

Delphine came back holding up a black dress and frowned. She apologized for not having a nicer outfit to replace the uniform Clare
~~~

was gradually shedding. "This belonged to a widow who boarded here last year. She left it behind when she moved to her brother's house. I think it is too large for you, but we can alter it."

"It's perfect," Clare assured her. Delphine went into the dining parlor to set two extra places for breakfast.

Clare was anxious to remove the loathsome breeches, but Jacques was frozen at the open door, peering toward the stable. *He must be wondering why it is taking so long for Jean-Pierre to enter the house, and I am afraid to tell him…but I must…*

Before Clare could open her mouth, Jacques suddenly scrambled down the steps and across the courtyard, calling, "Jean-Pierre? Come here, son. It's Papa."

No answer.

"Where are you? Are you hiding? Don't be afraid… Jean-Pierre?" He walked to the open stable doors, letting his eyes adjust to the darkness inside. Searching for his little boy.

Clare stood immobilized, clutching Delphine's black dress in her left hand and her birthing bag in the other. Watched as her husband slowly mounted the steps back into the kitchen. She dreaded the question she knew was coming.

"Clare, where is Jean-Pierre?"

"Oh, Jacques," she sighed. "He's not here."

"Not here? You are joking, right?"

"No."

"What do you mean? Where is my son?"

"He's *my* son too," she answered defensively.

"I left him in your care. You said you would bring him with you." Jacques's normally soft voice was rising.

"I have every reason to think he is safe. It's a very long story."

"What did you do to him? Use some of your midwife trickery on him?"

"Don't be ridiculous, Jacques. Calm down."

His face turned red as he came closer. "I will not calm down until you tell me where my son is. I demand to know right now." He reached out to grab her arm.

Hearing the fracas, Delphine hurried back into the kitchen and screamed. Her boarders, filing down the stairs for breakfast, came upon the angry scene and tried to form a protective circle around Clare.

Delphine grabbed Jacques by both shoulders and shook him. "Brother! Have pity. Your wife has been riding all night. She is exhausted, hungry and half-undressed. Let her rest, dress and take some nourishment."

"No," he shouted hysterically. "Out of my way. I demand to know the whereabouts of my son. Right this minute!" He shoved Delphine away and stepped closer toward his wife, ignoring the warning protests of the boarders.

Clare felt the room spin. She was surrounded by a sea of concerned faces, a mangle of male voices. She tried to remain standing, but her knees buckled and then everything went black.

Chapter 37

Awakenings

Maison Dupres, 10:00 A.M.

THE SOLDIERS AND Giselle overslept Sunday. Infused with large quantities of alcohol, they had not staggered back to their stable retreat until two in the morning. Church bells woke Lieutenant Pechard. He arose and stretched. Feeling guilty, he looked around at his snoring compatriots. Giselle was lying on her stomach, her right arm draped over the tall foot soldier. The Lieutenant reached for a stick and started banging on an oaken barrel with iron staves.

"Get up, you lazy louts," he shouted, kicking one man in the side. "Do you know how late it is?"

"Aw, Lieutenant. Fer Christ's sake. It's Sunday…that's… I think today's Sunday. Not sure. My head feels like it's filled with rocks, rumbling around."

"An' *my* mouth tastes like the privy," said another.

"Phew, I can smell your breath from here."

"Hardly remember how we got back," said another soldier, rubbing the sleep out of his eyes.

"Think Capitaine will be angry?"

"Naw, he's probably still in that cozy bed upstairs with Madame," said the tall foot soldier, pushing Giselle's arm off. "Mebee sleeping. More likely enjoying morning entertainment." He winked.

"He'll have our hides for sure. Sleepin' in so late."

One by one the soldiers rose and put on their jackets. They groaned in unison when the Lieutenant suggested they all go into Rouen for Mass. "And when we get back, we'll start target practice."

"Aw," they said in unison as they stumbled out to the privy.

Lieutenant Pechard walked outside. The bright sunshine hurt his eyes. He put his head under the pump and pulled the handle until cold water from the well washed away the alcoholic fog. For a brief second, he thought he saw something shiny in the bottom of the well. *No, my addled brain is riddled from too much beer. Just a reflection,* he convinced himself.

Giselle was behind him, her stringy hair hanging out from the cap askew on her head. She was still wearing the tattered, ill-fitting silk gown and Madame's string of pearls about her neck. It was the same raggedy outfit she had worn to the tavern, only worse from wear.

Jesus, what did I ever see in this slattern last night? He shuddered at the memory of the tavern loft. He grabbed her and pushed her head under the flowing pump water. "Clean yourself up, put on a clean apron and take a tray with strong coffee up to Capitaine. It's getting chilly—he'll be wanting a fire in the hearth."

"Ain't no coffee left. Not much left in the way of vittles either."

"Then ale if there's nothing better," said the Lieutenant, considering the options for feeding his troops. The food stores in the barn had been consumed by the soldiers or ruined by their trampling horses.

As his head cleared, he decided he had better send the men out to forage food instead of going to Mass. There were probably Huguenot residents in the neighborhood with pigs, chickens, maybe even fresh buns. Target practice, shooting hares and doves in the woods, would yield more food for the soldiers. His stomach rumbled.

"Not supposed to bother Capitaine this morning," grumbled Giselle.

"Go up and check on them anyway. Make sure all is well."

~~~

Giselle entered the kitchen, grabbing a coalscuttle and shovel, muttering to herself. "Drat. Allus havin' to work. Make the fire. Bring coffee, 'cept there ain't none left. Get tray, fetch ale. Work, work, work. Sick of it."
~~~

She wobbled up the back stairs, balancing the tray on one hand and coal scuttle in the other. When she reached the heavy double doors fronting the master bedchamber, she hesitated. Putting her ear to the door, she heard low moaning. She jiggled the knob, but it was locked.

Should she knock? Call out? She didn't want to interrupt what sounded to her foggy brain like moans of ardor—lovemaking. Still, the Lieutenant *had* told her to check.

"Madame?" she said in a low voice. "Capitaine? Would you like me to light the fire?" The pewter cups teetered on her tray. While attempting to avoid spilling the ale, she dropped the coalscuttle. It made enough noise to wake the dead. But still no audible answers from the room—just more sounds of passion. Only this time it sounded like bodies knocking about in bed. She peeked through the keyhole, but saw nothing but darkness. Setting the tray on the floor in front of the doors, Giselle returned downstairs to the Lieutenant. *Let the busy lovers get their own ale.*

~~~

The officer was aroused from his heavy sleep by a loud banging on the other side of the door. He thought he heard a voice saying something about a fire and struggled to answer, but he was unable to do anything but groan due to the gag in his mouth. When he tried unsuccessfully to flip over onto his back, he vaguely remembered being tied facedown to the bedposts by that witch, after she tried to kill him with her nasty green draught. Or was it the food she had cooked, the omelette, that made his stomach explode in agony?

It was too dark to see anything in the room. The heavy velvet curtains kept out all but faint signs of daylight. The candle had burned out and the hearth was cold. He had no notion of the time. *Am I dead? In hell? Or just having a nightmare?*

He yanked at the cords binding him to this blasted bed, but was too weak to loosen them. *Damn! It's so cold in here.* The robe had pulled up during the night, leaving his buttocks and legs exposed. He was able to see the tip of what appeared to be a satin quilt heaped on the floor next to the bed. He vaguely remembered the she-devil tossing it over his body, after trussing him like a turkey. *Damn her!*

The doorknob rattled. Must be that Grizelle out there. The captive officer tried again to call for help, but the sound of footsteps descending the stairs meant the servant had abandoned him to this
~~~

dark, cold prison for who knew how long. He fell back into his drugged sleep.

~~~

The soldiers had left the stable in search of food from the neighboring houses, following the Lieutenant's command. He instructed them to ask first, before plundering. Soldiers always had an intimidating effect on civilians, and hungry soldiers even more so.

Giselle walked out of the maison, giggling to herself behind the hand covering her mouth.

"How is everything up there?" Lieutenant Pechard asked, pointing to the bedchamber window. The curtains remained tightly closed.

Giselle thought about her answer for a moment. She visualized a picture in her mind. It was one of those rare warm late-fall days. How pleasant it would be down by the river, sitting in the sun, watching the men shoot game. A day off from drudgery—she deserved it, didn't she?

"Fine. They're busy. I knocked and Capitaine tol' me to leave 'em alone."

"Are you sure he said that?"

"Absolutely. Fer sure."

"And he didn't ask for a fire?"

"Nope. Said they were plenty warm. Hot. I think them were his 'zact words."

Lieutenant Pechard shrugged. "Hopefully Capitaine will emerge before too much longer. Go make us breakfast."

"There ain't no more food. Even the larder's empty 'cause you let Mistress take that basketful up to the nursery."

"You *could* check anyway, to be sure."

"Naw, I already checked. It's all gone."

"Well, then, go make yourself useful."

"Yessir." She saluted, her muslin cap slipping off. She bent down to pick it up off the stones, trying to avert attention from her lying eyes. When Pechard sat down to clean his weapon, Giselle scampered back to her empty room in the stable and stretched out on her narrow cot for a short nap, savoring thoughts of the afternoon ahead.
~~~

Chapter 38

Head-Pictures

Dieppe, 2:00 PM

WHEN CLARE REGAINED consciousness, she saw an unfamiliar male face peering into her eyes.

"She is awake," he said. "Do you know who you are?"

"What?"

"Do you know your name?"

"Of course I know my name. Madame Clare Dupres. Who are you?"

The stranger replied, "I am Monsieur Renaud, apothecary of Dieppe. Your husband sent for me. He was very worried about you."

"And angry too, I suspect," said Clare.

Delphine walked over and picked up her sister's hand, a relieved look on her face. "No longer," she explained. "Jacques's anger evaporated when you fainted. He carried you up to this bed himself five hours ago. He is full of remorse." She patted Clare's hand. "How are you feeling now? Mr. Renaud was just about to bleed you."

Clare was relieved he hadn't. "I feel foolish for fainting. I am not normally subject to such fits."

"Whatever has happened to you, the shock has been great," said Monsieur Renaud, returning his unused surgical tools to his medical bag. "Perhaps your husband should have been more understanding, but as a father myself, I cannot blame him for becoming agitated. He is anxious to know the whereabouts of his missing son."

Clare turned her head to the window, trying to hold back tears. Thus far, she had not told anyone in Dieppe the details of her ordeal. All they knew was that she had appeared at the door in an army uniform, a week later than expected and without her son.

"Is my sister able to sit up and take some nourishment?" asked Delphine, not wishing to stress Clare in her weakened state.

The apothecary was rolling down his sleeves and donning his cape. "Something light," he suggested. "Perhaps some of that porridge you brought up. A small basin of thin gruel is all that I can, with thorough self-approbation, recommend."

To prove that she was better, Clare asked Delphine to help her sit up. She felt weak but managed to pull herself upright as Delphine propped several pillows behind her back. Taking the small basin of watery porridge from Delphine's hands, Clare began spooning a few honey-sweetened globs into her mouth, trying not to let her shaky hands drop any.

Monsieur Renaud said, "She should be fine. I prescribe a few days of bedrest—"

"*Non, impossible*," protested Clare, recalling the horrors of the past week and the need to leave France as soon as possible. "My only chance of survival is to be aboard the ship when it sails. Before the soldiers find me."

Monsieur Renaud frowned. He then shrugged, bid them adieu and said he would have a few words with Jacques before leaving.

Delphine took the half-empty bowl from Clare's hands and set it on the bedside table. "Soldiers searching for you, Clare? What is going on? When Jacques arrived at my doorstep with Lucina last week, he only said he had decided to take his family to England, to visit our brother. That Jean-Pierre and you would be joining them here soon. Then a few days later, he admitted several foot soldiers had come to Maison Dupres before he left. And this morning you arrived dressed in a uniform. Something terrible must have happened—and where is my little nephew?"

"Delphine," said Clare, wringing her hands, "I promise to tell you everything later. But has the *Celia* left yet?"

"No dearie. The ship arrived late due to wind shifts and will be loaded tomorrow. If the winds prevail, it will sail Tuesday."

"Lucina?" she asked.

"Your daughter is fine. Disappointed that you were sleeping all morning. She had so much to tell you. In the meantime, she has kept my boarders entertained with stories."

"Oh dear. I hope she hasn't said…I mean, about our plans…"

"No, just tales of talking flowers and frogs and fire-breathing dragons. She has quite the imagination for a child of five. Strange that she does not ask questions about her missing brother. This whole morning, she has been trying to reassure her father that Jean-Pierre is going to be all right."

"Yes, Lucina has always been strangely intuitive. I pray she is right. I long to see her, but first I must see my husband. Alone… to explain…"

"Are you sure you feel strong enough? I hear him coming up the stairs now. Perhaps you should wait."

"Dearest Delphine. I appreciate your concern, but there is so little time."

~~~

Jacques looked uneasily into the room.

"I will leave you two alone," said Delphine, carrying the tray toward the door. Clare heard her whisper a warning as she passed by Jacques and closed the door.

"Please, Clare," pleaded Jacques as he came to the bedside and picked up his wife's cold hands. "Forgive me, dearest. I didn't mean to raise my voice. It's just that I must know the truth. Is Jean-Pierre… dead?"

"I hope and pray that he is alive and well."

Jacques looked disappointed. Clare could tell by his expression he wanted assurances, not hopes.

"Will you please tell me now where he is?"

"The thing is…" Her head dropped to her chest.

Jacques pulled over a chair and sat close to the bed. Held both her hands. The horrific events of the past week then spilled out of Clare as if a river had broken through a dam. In a sobbing voice, she related the arrival of the Lieutenant and cavalry. How they had prevented her from leaving the house to join him as planned—forced her to remain with Jean-Pierre in the nursery.

"I did my best to keep our boy fed and entertained. The Lieutenant accompanied me down the servants' stairs on the first day to get food from the larder. The soldiers' constant drumming day and
~~~

night kept me awake…" Clare started to sob again, then continued relating her story. The terrible carnage of Maison Dupres and their belongings. Giselle's treachery—raiding her wardrobe and parading around in her gowns and pearls. And then…the hussy luring their son out of the nursery and handing him over to the soldiers.

Jacques gasped. "*Giselle* lured him away to the soldiers? How could you have allowed that to happen, Clare, when you were constantly with him in the same room?" He stood, dropped her hands, and stared at her in disbelief.

"I was forced to leave him unattended for a short time. Ordered to come downstairs by Capitaine upon his arrival. He…he detained me."

"Did you not instruct Jean-Pierre to stay upstairs? He has always been such a dutiful child."

"All week he had been begging to go down and meet the soldiers. Stood at the window for hours watching them drill. Of course I made excuses. Told him it was too wet, too cold out. That he had a fever. He was tired of being confined. I should have locked the nursery door, but Giselle was blocking it. Told me she would stay with him. I only expected to be away for a few minutes. I never thought…"

Jacques deduced the rest. "Giselle. She probably offered to take him down to meet the soldiers, something you had not allowed him to do."

"Yes," said Clare softly. "After the Lieutenant rode away with Jean-Pierre on his horse, Giselle came back into the house and boasted to the commander how easy it had been. She tricked our little boy. Told him the soldiers wanted to teach him to march."

"He loved his little tin soldiers." Jacques nodded thoughtfully. "Always enamored of soldiers. I thought he would outgrow it. I never should've painted those toys on the nursery walls." He sank back in the chair and sat quietly for a few moments, trying to absorb everything she was telling him. "But, Clare, where exactly *were* you when our boy was abducted?"

Clare hesitated, then finally admitted, "I was in our bedchamber, where Capitaine… the commanding officer of the Dragonnades had taken his bags. He told me to sit down. It was more of a demand than an invitation. What choice did I have? I stupidly thought I could convince him to ignore the Intendant's order. I could see the parchment rolled up in his belt."

As she stopped to catch her breath, Jacques stared daggers at his wife. He couldn't believe what he was hearing. "In our bedchamber!" he said, clenching his fists.

"I asked to see the order, Jacques, to determine if Lady Louise had been mistaken. He read it aloud, then handed it to me. It said exactly what she warned us of."

Jacques winced. He remembered the wording of her note. "Go on," he said.

"Capitaine asked for a drink and I tried to be polite. He detained me awhile for questioning about your whereabouts, and I told him you would be back from Paris in a few days' time."

Jacques leaned back on the chair and sat with his hands covering his eyes, trying to imagine the terror in his home. He blamed himself for leaving his wife and son to the mercy of the soldiers. Poor Jean-Pierre was the one to suffer most. Afraid to hear the worst, Jacques worked up the courage to ask, "Clare, did you see the soldiers take our boy away? Was he upset?"

"Capitaine let me look out the window. Jean-Pierre… seemed happy enough to go for a ride on the Lieutenant's horse. That's the last I saw of him. I don't even know in which direction they went."

"You didn't see him harmed, did you?"

"No, Jacques. I want to believe he is safe with the Sisters of Sorrow, that Papists do not murder innocent children."

A deep silence, as Jacques tried to absorb her faith that their son was alive, despite the painful thought that Jean-Pierre would be baptized as a Catholic. *All those prayers I offered to God for King Louis to soften his heart have been of no effect. The King has won.*

As he sat hunched over, his hands on his head, Clare dabbed at her teary eyes. Jacques looked up and, with a hint of blame in his voice, said, "You got away, but didn't try to find Jean-Pierre. Just came straight to Dieppe without him."

"I wanted to, but I didn't know where the convent was—I wasn't thinking straight."

Jacques walked over to the hearth and picked up a seashell from the mantel. He squeezed it so hard it cracked into pieces and he flung them into the fire. *Clare blames herself more than I do. While I have been busy in Dieppe, arranging and rearranging the parcels for the ship, she has had to deal with the soldiers. But they let her go free, didn't they? He thought bitterly of her abandoning their child.*

~~~

Changing the subject, he told her Pierre had sent travel clearances, hand-delivered by Cap'n Silas to Delphine the previous day. The *Celia* would depart at dawn, day after next, with the silks for Windsor Castle.

Clare threw aside the quilt. "That is welcome news. Don't worry, Jacques. I shall be strong enough to travel by Tuesday. Look, I am climbing out of bed now. I already feel much better."

He stared at her as if she had gone crazy. "What are you saying, Clare? We cannot leave France without Jean-Pierre. There will be another ship in three weeks."

Clare could not believe her ears. Up to this point, Jacques had been so consumed with the fate of Jean-Pierre that he had not thought to question the manner of his wife's escape or her appearance in a military uniform this morning. Jacques was unaware that the authorities would soon be on her trail. *Poisoning an army officer is an offense far worse than singing psalms in the woods. Does he not care that I am in greater danger than he? Is he willing to risk our capture by staying in France another three weeks?*

"Send a note to Lady Louise," Clare said in a panic. "She has high connections in their church. She can make inquiries—perhaps convince them to let our son come to her for a while. We can send for him when we get to England."

Jacques paced back and forth, wringing his hands. "That is sheer madness, Clare. We cannot leave France without our son."

Clare had already begun grieving the loss of Jean-Pierre. She did not believe they would ever see him again. He was lost to them. Their only chance of saving Lucina from the same fate was to get out of France as fast as possible.

Her heart ached. Crazy thoughts began to permeate her sleep-deprived brain. Perhaps Jacques and she could try for another child once they got settled in England. She was still young enough to bear more children. She would not use sponges anymore. In fact, she would give up seeking wealthy patients—her services as a midwife and the magic elixir would be available to the poorest among women. She would stay home more.
~~~

But Clare did not share these thoughts with Jacques. First, her husband and she would have to reconnect with each other, grieve the loss of their son together.

"Luckily, the soldiers think we are in Paris," said Jacques. "We have time. You can stay here in Dieppe with Lucina. I will ride back to Rouen and search for our son. I know where the Sisters of Sorrow convent is located, on the northern outskirts of town. I will find him."

"Jacques, your plan is madness. They will capture you and send you to the galleys. For all we know, the soldiers may be on their way to Dieppe as we speak."

"Dieppe? Why would they come here if they think we went to Paris?"

Clare ran her hands up and down her arms and looked down at her knees. "I hoped that I would never have to tell you, but you must know. It is *me* the soldiers are after now."

"You?"

"The commanding officer tried to rape me. I poisoned him with a mushroom omelette, drugged him and tied him up. Did you not wonder why I arrived here wearing the uniform of an army capitaine, riding a strange horse?"

"Poisoned him? Drugged him?" Jacques was enraged. "Of course, I keep forgetting that you are a midwife-witch. You and your magic elixirs and your…your…insistence on renovating and moving to Maison Dupres. I never wanted to live in that cursed house—"

"Stop! Enough! I forgive you for saying such hateful things because I know you are upset. When you say your prayers tonight, ask for forgiveness. Also ask God to keep the soldiers from finding the three of us before we are safely at sea on Tuesday."

Lucina was standing outside the room when Jacques stormed out. She tiptoed over to the bed, where Clare was attempting to stand up on shaky legs.

"Maman, were you and Papa fighting? I came when I heard shouting."

"No, dearest one. We were not fighting. Papa wants to stay in France for a few more weeks, but you and I want to leave for England in two days, don't we?"

"What about Jean-Pierre?"

Clare sat back on the edge of the bed, too weak to stand. She placed her hands on the girl's shoulders. "Lucina, you know your brother wanted to be a soldier. Right? How he always played with his tin army toys?"

"Yesss…but—"

"After you and Papa left, he went downstairs to meet the soldiers. He was so excited. They promised to take him to a special place where soldiers train."

"Ohhh." Lucina tipped her chin down. Clare knew she did not believe her.

"Papa is sad because he will miss Jean-Pierre," said Clare. "We all will, but we can write him letters and you can draw him pictures."

Lucina sat beside her mother, closed her eyes, and started to speak in a soft, dreamy voice. "Maman, I already know my brother is in a convent. I saw it in a head-picture."

"You saw that in a head-picture…a vision?"

"I get these pictures in my head sometimes. Like dreams, only I know I'm awake when they come. These head-pictures are different from dreams. I can hear voices talking to me. At first I got scared when they came, but not so much anymore."

Clare sat in disbelief. *Maman predicted this on the night Lucina was born, that she would have the second sight. I am afraid to ask her what she sees in her vision of Jean-Pierre.*

Lucina kept her eyes shut. "I am seeing Jean-Pierre in the convent with a man he admires, who has taught him new things. He brags to me about these new things…aaaand…"

Clare clenched her eyes shut and tuned out the rest of Lucina's recitation. *A man in a convent he admires. That must be a monk. New things? He will stay with the Jesuits and be raised as a Papist. If Lucina's vision is correct, Jean-Pierre is destined to become a monk. I can see him in a black cowl.* Clare felt sadness and peacefulness mixed together.

"Maman, you stopped listening. I didn't tell this to Papa. He doesn't like to hear about my head-pictures, either."

"I do want to hear them, but not now. You were right not to tell Papa; he would be very upset."

Lucina climbed into bed next to Clare. "Maman, may I sleep with you tonight?"

"Yes, my pet. It's getting dark and I'm tired. Let's say our prayers and then cuddle together in bed."

~~~

Jacques walked into the kitchen, where Delphine was putting clean platters on a shelf.

"What did you do with that wretched uniform?" he asked.

"I threw it down the cellar steps. I didn't want to distress Clare."

Without saying another word, Jacques headed for the cellar door.
~~~

Chapter 39

Riverside Picnic

Maison Dupres, 4:30 P.M.

THE HUNGRY SOLDIERS were grouped by the river. In addition to shooting some hares, they had managed to spear a few fish. The foot soldiers had "borrowed" a dozen freshly baked baguettes, a chunk of salted pork, and several bottles of wine from a frightened cook several houses down the road. Two of the cavalrymen were busy lighting a small fire over which to cook dinner. They were all in fine spirits at this unexpected riverside picnic.

It had been a sunny afternoon, rare for late October. Perched on a horse blanket, Giselle had lazed close to the bank—shamelessly allowing the sun to burn her face. Hadn't Aunt Claudette warned her about ruining her skin? She did not care enough to fetch a bonnet. She watched the soldiers play cards and dangled her feet in the chilly water. One of the men sneaked up behind her and shoved her into the river. She screamed and spluttered, grabbed for an overhanging branch, and managed to pull her dripping body onto the shore.

The soldiers guffawed, joking about how the stink had vanished from her body. She shrieked a string of curses in their direction, pushing her wet hair behind her ears. This only served to make them laugh harder.

~~~

Lieutenant Pechard did not join in their jollity. After skinning a rabbit, he walked nervously back to the house, looking for signs of Capi-
~~~

taine. The curtains on the bedchamber window were still closed. His uneasiness turned to grave concern. Surely Capitaine and Madame Dupres should have risen by now and opened the window coverings. Raising his eyes to the roof, he noted that there was no smoke coming from the chimney. He went into the barn to check on Capitaine's horse.

The black steed was gone! Had his commander left without telling his men? Perhaps he thought his soldiers had gone to attend afternoon Mass at the Cathedral in Rouen, to strut among the young ladies like red-and-blue-feathered peacocks. His leader always bragged that there was nothing like a brightly colored uniform to attract the attention of churchgoing women on Sundays.

But what of the prisoner? Surely he wouldn't have left Madame Dupres unguarded. Something felt wrong. Hadn't one of the soldiers reported he had seen *Le Cheval Noir de la Morte* pass by the tavern last night?

Lieutenant Pechard jogged back to the gathering. Giselle's teeth were chattering and she sat close to the fire wrapped in the horse blanket, stuffing a baguette in her mouth. Some of the men were passing a wine bottle back and forth, wiping their mouths on their sleeves. A few were roasting fish on sticks over the campfire.

"Has anyone seen Capitaine today?" he inquired of the soldiers who had been out foraging food from the neighbors. The men looked at each other and shook their heads. "Anyone notice him riding away this afternoon? Heard his horse?" No, they were busy at target practice.

"Giselle," Pechard said sharply. "I fear something is amiss with our commander. Come with me. We'll go back to the house and check."

"I'm still wet," she grumbled.

"Tough," he said, grabbing her sharply by the elbow and pulling her up. "Let's go." The blanket slipped off her shoulders. He lugged her back to the house, ignoring her complaints and pleas to change into dry clothes. She dragged her muddy bare feet, trying to slow him down.

As they entered the kitchen, there was a certain foreboding about the silence within. They stopped to listen for signs of life. Nothing. It wasn't until they reached the second landing that they heard a weak squawk from the bedchamber: "Help!"

"Capitaine?" said Pechard, his ear pressed to the door. He wrinkled his nose at the malodor seeping through the narrow opening. Normally his commanding officer was unusually fastidious about cleanliness. The Lieutenant remembered his visit to the public bathhouse in Dieppe a week ago. And yesterday he had insisted that Giselle bring buckets of steaming water to this very room. "Is all well in there, sir?"

"No, you damn fool. I've been screeching for help since late this morning. My voice is hoarse. Where the hell have you all been?"

Giselle looked down at her wrinkled, river-soaked silk gown and tried to wring the excess moisture out. It clung to her body. She wanted to get away. Back to the campfire—anywhere but here. She sensed trouble brewing.

The Lieutenant twisted the handles—tried to push open the locked double doors. He glared at Giselle and hissed, "I thought you told me everything was under control this morning. Go get the key."

"There ain't but one. Mistress keeps it."

Pechard leaned closer to the opening and shouted, "Madame Dupres, are you in there? Unlock this door at once," He waited for an answer. "Madame, do you hear me? I order you to open the door."

A weak male voice hoarsely answered, "She's not here. Break down the door. I can't…can't reach it from here."

Pechard was a short, slightly built man, but in reasonably good physical shape. He shoved his shoulder and elbow against the door as hard as he could. Once, twice, thrice. It was solid as a granite boulder and did not budge.

"I could go down, git some soldiers from the riverbank to help," offered Giselle.

"No, you're not going anywhere. Get me the heaviest chair you can find," he demanded.

Giselle went into Monsieur Dupres's studio across the hall and pushed out a heavy mahogany chair. Using the chair as a battering ram, the Lieutenant finally heard the wood splinter. He continued to thump until the double doors flew open and the chair tumbled inside. He grabbed Giselle's elbow, to prevent her from leaving.

Gagging on the stench, they stepped forward into the room. Giselle staggered through the darkness to pull aside the curtains. Sunlight streamed in, blinding them for a moment. Her eyes grew wide at the sight on the bed. The nude officer was lying facedown, his wrists and ankles tied to the bedposts, the remnants of a chewed-through gag around his mouth, his buttocks heaving in a pool of excrement and vomit.

"*Mon Dieu*!" choked Pechard, looking around for signs of Madame Dupres.

"Untie me, Grizelle," said Capitaine to the serving girl, who stood frozen in place, unable to move.

The Lieutenant reached for his rapier and cut the cords, freeing the frazzled commander, who rolled over onto his back and lifted his legs off the bed. Pechard helped the massive man sit up. Looking around for something clean, Pechard spied a damp towel on the floor, crumpled next to the copper tub, and handed it to his commanding officer, who tried unsuccessfully to wipe the dried muck from his body.

Unsteadily, Capitaine stepped over to the tub and, despite his shivering, quickly lowered himself in the icy, murky water. Using his wet shirt still floating on top as a sponge, he beckoned for Pechard to help lift him out. Still sick to his stomach, it took all the commander's will power to keep from vomiting again.

"That bloody witch put a spell on me. Tried to kill me."

"Where is she now?"

"How should I know? She locked me in here. Look at my wrists—they are raw from trying to loosen that she-devil's ropes."

Giselle started backing toward the door, hoping they wouldn't notice. She wondered how she was going to get out of this scrape.

"You, girl. Stop right there. Don't pretend you didn't hear me this morning when you knocked. I heard you. Why didn't you go get help?"

"Me, sir? I didn't hear nuthin'. I came up to light the fire and the doors was locked and I heared some … I means, I didn't hear nuthin'. No, not me."

"Sit down on that chair," Capitaine barked, pointing to the heavy battering-ram chair lying on its side. "I'll deal with you in a minute. And stop staring at me. I'm sure you've seen a naked man before."

"Oh, no, sir. Not me."

Remembering the previous night in the tavern loft, Pechard felt a pang of guilt, which quickly turned to anger. He righted the chair and used the ropes in his hand to tie Giselle to it. "This girl lied to me this morning. She said you were fine and wished not to be disturbed."

Capitaine looked at the Lieutenant and sputtered, "I suppose you trusted her word." He did not expect an answer. Rubbing his sore wrists, he looked around for something to wear. Nothing but the wretched, soiled purple robe and the soggy shirt in his hand. Pieces of Madame Dupres's outfit, the ones she had peeled off last evening, were lying water-logged in puddles around the floor. Reminding him…

Lieutenant Pechard said, "You did give us orders…"

"Well, things did not exactly work out as I expected. These Huguenot women, you know. Most of them don't willingly submit to my—well, never mind that. This one got away and when I find her, I will deal with her. I've had hours to dwell on her punishment. She'll be burnt at the stake, if I have to light the fire myself. May she burn in hell."

Then he looked around the room. "Where the fuck is my uniform? It's freezing in this hellhole." His brain was still foggy from the alcohol, the omelette, the bitter sleeping potion Madame had forced down his throat.

Slowly he began to remember. She had stolen his jacket…his boots… his expensive new wig. Everything except his sodden shirt. Frustrated, he balled up the wet shirt and flung it across the room.

"Lieutenant, I am in need of another uniform." He gazed momentarily at his junior officer's uniform, but the man was shorter and leaner than he. It would not come close to fitting him. Nor, to his dismay, would any of his other soldiers' uniforms fit his husky physique. His soldiers were all much thinner.

"Grizelle, I assume you are familiar with your master's wardrobe. Would his clothing fit me?"

Her answer did not surprise him. That blasted robe he had worn last night was far too small.

"Are there any large male servants who keep clothing around here?"

"We only gots one—Girard, the carriage driver. He's sorta bulky like you, but he's gone like all the other servants, 'cept me. His rooms is over the stable, next to mine."

The shivering commander instructed his Lieutenant to search the driver's room for something suitable to wear until he could procure another uniform. And some boots.

"I'll go look," offered Giselle, "if'n you untie me."

"Oh no," Capitaine laughed menacingly. "Not a chance. You will stay here and answer my questions." With that, he motioned Pechard toward the door. The naked Capitaine circled Giselle on the chair. He grabbed her stringy wet hair, pulling back her head until her chin faced the ceiling.

"Well now, wench, tell me when your mistress left. You servants always know what's going on."

"Really, honestly and truly sir, I got no idea. I never seen her leave."

"Is that so? Where have you been?"

"Went to Mass."

"A likely story. And how did you get wet on this sunny day? Did the priest spill holy water on you, or did you fall in the baptismal font?"

Giselle tried out a few different excuses, none of which he believed: Lieutenant had sent her to the river to wash his shirt. She had skinned rabbits to make stew for his hungry soldiers. Just doin' her job, that's all.

"Why did you lie to the Lieutenant after you knew I was locked in here?"

"Thought you was busy screwing Mistress."

He paused for a second. That *had* been on his mind last evening. "Is your mistress hiding? Is there a secret chamber in this maison?" He seemed to remember these old mansions frequently contained hidden rooms to protect inhabitants in times of war or persecution. He ran his hands along the silk-covered walls, pressing to feel for a button that would unlatch a hidden doorway. Put his ear to the wall, listened for sounds of the fugitive. Finally, he kicked the wall in frustration, knowing his hopes of finding the woman lurking in a strange closet were hopeless. She had left the maison, no doubt of that. And now, in addition to all his other indignities, he had bruised his toe.

"Please sir. Untie my hands. They hurt."

"Ha. I understand *that*," he said, rubbing his wrists again. "Now answer my questions before I gag you too. Where is your mistress?"

"I tol' you. I haven't seen her. Last time were… she were here with you in this room, when I brung buckets fer yer bath."

"And where did you spend the evening?" He was still trying to understand why he hadn't been discovered earlier. "Don't you usually bring food to the nursery?"

"Nobody up there anymore. You tol' me to take the boy downstairs, so Lieutenant could take him away. Then we all went to the tavern 'cause you din't like the drummin' noises."

Capitaine winced as Giselle reminded him he *had* given them leave. She continued her story: They got home late 'cause the music was so good, then they slept in the stable. They all assumed Mistress was locked in here with him. Reminded him again that he had ordered them not to bother him in the morning.

He became infuriated by her insolent smile. He slapped her across the face, and continued to circle and interrogate her.

Where did she *think* Madame had gone? She didn't know—maybe Paris to find Monsieur, because that's where he took the girl with the pox. Did Madame have any friends that she knew of? She didn't know of any.

"You stupid, stupid girl," he said as he shook her by the shoulders. He lifted her head by the chin. "Think! Surely your Mistress had some friends, visitors, neighbors who visited her at the maison."

"I ain't stupid. Madame stayed home most days since she stopped goin' birthin'. Sewed a lot and worked in her garden. Was allus mean to me."

"Do you expect me to believe that the woman had no visitors? Cloistered like a goddamned nun?" He raised his hand to slap her again, which sparked Giselle's memory.

"Wait. She does got one friend, stayed here for a few days last month. A real fancy lady, excepting her gown was ruined by blood and I had to scrub it real hard—"

"What was her name, Grizelle?"

"Lady Louise, wife of the Marquis from Chateau Montjardin," she answered proudly. *See, I ain't stupid. I knows what goes on round here. I even told on the master, about his psalm-sing-songing in the woods. But I ain't volunteering any more stuff to you, mean man. You shouldn't have slapped me. I ain't stupid. Yer the stupid one. Can't even say my name right.*

Capitaine knew of the Marquis, an aristocrat whose parents were among King Louis's courtiers, but he had never met him or his wife. Why had the Marquise been here?

Despite her determination not to volunteer more information, Giselle continued to blather, to keep the Capitaine from hitting her again, or worse. "Last Sunday, Madame got a note from Lady Louise. I recognized the red seal, from before. Her servant telled me it was urgent."

"You didn't happen to open it, did you?" he said sarcastically.

"Oh me, never. Not me."

"Ha. Another one of your lies."

Giselle hung her head—whispered, "Didn't bother openin' the note 'cause…'cause I never learned how to read."

Probably the first truth she had uttered. "Where is that note now?"

"Madame proberly throwed it in the fire."

Frustrated, the naked man squeezed his hands around Giselle's neck, wanting to kill somebody. Lieutenant Pechard saved the serving girl's life by entering the room at that moment.

"I searched the driver's room. He must have taken his clothes when he fled. This livery uniform is all he left behind. It might fit you." He handed the commander a stiff pair of black breeches, a large bright green jacket, and a shirt. The boots he set on the floor were caked with mud. The jacket bore the Dupres family coat of arms on the left breast, a sign of their wealth. The wig was dirty white, with two short ear curls. The uniform of a servant. Capitaine groaned at the sight.

A few minutes later the senior officer descended the stairs with as much dignity as he could muster. The soldiers returning from their relaxing riverside retreat tried not to snicker when they saw their leader, a man who usually treated *them* with contempt, dressed in this outlandish livery.

They stood at attention, saluted, and listened to the man with the sickly green face which nearly matched the jacket. He commanded them to search for Madame Dupres along the road to Paris. She might have gone to join her missing husband and daughter. He was sure they were hiding somewhere. Search every house in that direction. Question everyone along the way. Madame could not have gotten far. They were to keep their eyes out for his familiar black horse, which she had stolen.

He turned to Lieutenant Pechard. "You will accompany me to Chateau Montjardin. The rest of these soldiers are to meet us there by noon tomorrow. They are to bring the prisoners back in chains, all three of them. Understood? Leave no stone unturned. Monsieur and Madame Dupres are dangerous criminals, blasphemers, horse thieves, murderers—an affront to his royal majesty, King Louis."

"Yessir," they all chanted in unison. Private Laurent, one of the cavalrymen, offered his horse to Capitaine. Realizing the commander was not only missing his uniform but his mount, the soldier wanted to make a favorable impression. But mainly he wanted to stick around Maison Dupres for more good times with Giselle. Capitaine accepted the reins and ordered Laurent and the two foot soldiers to stand watch in case the wretched criminals tried to return home.

"As for the wench upstairs, leave her tied to the chair."

~~~

After the troops galloped off, the two officers trotted side by side toward Chateau Montjardin. Very slowly, because Capitaine's stomach was still roiling from the she-devil's brew. The senior officer swore a stream of invectives against the wrongdoers. Complained to his companion that he had done nothing to deserve this treatment by that woman, had he? He was just a loyal subject, trying to carry out the Intendant's order.

"I am an innocent man, doomed by that witch," he complained. His predictions became increasingly foreboding as they crept up the road. If he was unable to capture the Dupres, he would be blamed for incompetence. Demoted. Dishonorably discharged from the army. Stripped of his medals and whipped. He shuddered when he told the Lieutenant he feared he might even be imprisoned. The Intendant would blame *him*, he had no doubt of that. He was ruined. A wronged man. A true victim, to be sure.

Lieutenant Pechard listened quietly to his commander's rant. He knew the big man had fought bravely in the French army for many years. Had risen steadily in the ranks, on a path to a promotion to general someday. *It was his singular pride and weakness for a pretty woman that led to this disaster. Why couldn't he have satisfied his lust with a servant as the others, including me, had done?*
~~~

He almost felt sorry for his superior, except he felt sorrier for the innocent boy who had been abducted from the maison. He hated to admit it but he had developed fond feelings for little Private J.P and wondered how the kid was faring at the convent.

Chapter 40

Dinner with the Marquis

Rouen, 5:00 P.M.

FATHER BENEDICT AROSE from his nap around five o'clock and set off from the presbytery to sup with Marquis and his wife. Since it was still early, he decided to stop by the convent and check on the Dupres child.

He set off on his old mule as the sun was sinking through the clouds, causing the crimson sky to glow. This brought to mind *tartes aux cerises*, his favorite fruit baked in a crisp crust. Cherries were out of season, but the priest knew that the Marquis would have spared no expense to obtain some for his guests last evening.

Rushing out of the refectory to answer the door, Sister Mary-Augustus looked surprised to see Father Benedict. She wiped jam from her mouth and stuffed the worn cloth napkin beneath her apron.

"Forgive me for interrupting your meal, Sister."

"The orphans finished a few minutes ago. When you rang, I was just eating Jean-Pierre's untouched trencher. I hate to see food wasted—especially on Sunday, when we allow them a smear of apple butter as a treat."

"May I visit with the boy for a minute?"

Sister Mary-Augustus seemed hesitant. "The time is not propitious for a visit, *Père*. He's finally settled down after weeping all afternoon, and one of the Sisters is sitting with him on his cot, trying to teach him a proper bedtime prayer. It would be unsettling. I'm sorry…"

"Then he is doing better? Has he eaten today?"

"Not much. He seems unhappy with our food. I suppose he was coddled at home with fancy meats and bonbons, served on decorated china plates. He kept talking about eggs—how his cook Marie prepared him an omelette whenever he wanted."

Father Benedict thought a nice fresh omelette would be a tasty meal indeed. But the child was now living in a convent, where he would have to learn to eat the simple porridges and rough rye-bread-and-cheese diet which sustained the Sisters of Sorrow. No more sweetmeats, chocolates, or other treats, except on rare occasions when leftover candied fruit was donated to the convent by his dear cousin.

The priest's mouth practically watered with thoughts of such delicacies. He anticipated partaking of such treats at Lady Louise's table in a short time. His stomach rumbled in anticipation of a lavish meal—perhaps their chef would be dressing a quail. Surely there must be ample birds hanging in their larder. The Marquis had taken his male guests hunting yesterday, while the ladies rested before the ball. But by now, the guests had returned home and it would be just the three of them sitting down for dinner, an intimate gathering *en famille.*

"Well, Sister Mary-Augustus, it is good for the boy to learn to live simply. Better for his health, I think," said the priest, patting his own paunchy belly. "I will expect periodic reports on the boy's progress. I shall personally monitor the situation daily and report every detail directly to the Marquis."

"I understand, Father," said the nun, bowing her head. *If it were not for the boy's illustrious godfather, Père Benedict would not have a care for any of the Huguenot orphans flooding our convent. However, this child receives special attention. I suspect our confessor is trying to curry favor with the Marquis. Humph, personal monitoring indeed!*

They were heading toward the door when the Sister remembered a detail about the boy to share with the priest. "Oh, there is one matter on which I seek your advice. Jean-Pierre is for the most part well-behaved, but he refuses to take off that bizarre outfit he was wearing when he arrived yesterday. It really needs to go into the rag bag, or at least be washed."

A look of annoyance crossed the priest's countenance. *Our confessor is obviously in a rush to get to his dinner. Let me see how concerned he really is about the Dupres boy's welfare.*

"On second thought, *Père*, I've changed my mind. I think it would be beneficial for you to go to his bedside and sit with him awhile, pray with him and convince him to change his clothing."

Father Benedict was irritated to be detained with such a trifle when his tartes aux cerises were waiting. "Let him keep the soldier suit on. I will come by tomorrow and persuade him to change," He was not about to trouble the Marquis with the insignificant matter of the boy's resistance to undressing.

Thirty minutes later, he tied his mule to a post in the castle courtyard, momentarily admiring the handsome steeds being brushed down by the grooms. Lord and Lady Louise were just sitting down for their meal when the butler announced his arrival.

"Bonjour, *Père Benedict*," said the lady coolly. Although he was distantly related to her family, she always addressed him by his clerical title to maintain proper decorum. "Please, join us."

She winced when he said, "Ah, my dearest cousin. So gracious of you to invite me to share in your repast." He sat down and eagerly tied the linen serviette around his clerical collar.

The Marquis glanced at his unsmiling wife. He could tell she felt unwell, but thought it was due to the early stages of a new pregnancy. Barely two weeks after her miscarriage, she had surprised him by inviting him back into her bed. He had already made alternate arrangements with his latest mistress. Ah, well…women. One could never be sure.

The priest gave an extremely brief blessing, anxious to eat. The food smelled heavenly. Before the Marquis could finish unfolding his napkin, the prayer had ended. The first course was served swiftly.

"It's always such a pleasure to visit the chateau. Everything runs so efficiently in your household," said the priest with a touch of envy in his voice.

The Marquis watched Lady Louise toy with her spoon, moving the soup around in her bowl, whereas their "guest" had already slurped most of the delicious vichyssoise from the small soup tureen down his gullet.

"Did I thank you for granting me the high honor of sharing your supper?"

"You did," said the Marquis. "No need to repeat."

An uneasy silence filled the air in the room. The footmen removed the soup bowls and replaced them with sparkling china dishes, embellished with the family coat of arms. Several platters heaped with fish, gammon, partridge and potatoes were carried around. Father Benedict began ladling hearty portions onto his plate and noticed Lady Louise taking very small amounts off the same platters.

Father Benedict was never long at a loss for words. "Such fine weather. Unusually sunny and warm for October, don't you agree? There is nothing I enjoy more than a balmy breeze on the Sabbath day. Our Lord's special blessing."

"Yes," murmured the lady, looking at the untouched food on her plate. She took a small bite of potato.

"Oh, by the way," announced the priest. "I almost forgot to tell you. I stopped by the convent on my way over to check on your boy…I mean your new godson, Jean-Pierre Dupres. He is settling in nicely. Eating well. Learning Catholic prayers. Within a few months, he will have forgotten all about his family."

Lady Louise turned pale, arose abruptly. "If you will excuse me, I am feeling unwell." She swished her long satin gown behind her as she rushed from the dining room, leaving the two men watching. They remained on their feet until the door closed behind her.

After hesitating a moment, the host said, "Be seated, Father."

Father Benedict looked alarmed. "Should we go to her?"

"Finish your food. My wife may be…um…breeding again. The early weeks are always a difficulty."

A look of relief washed over Father Benedict's face. "For a moment, I thought I might have upset her with news of the orphan. Ah, congratulations, I suppose, and just think, another fine baby on the way."

"It is far too early for congratulations. Please, continue eating before your food cools." The Marquis was not surprised to see the priest help himself to another serving of fish from the platter. He hoped to finish the meal as quickly as possible without arousing any suspicion in his dinner guest. Picking up his silver *fourchette*, he politely listened to Father Benedict complain about his mule and hint that he could visit his parishioners more frequently if he had a horse, but of course such an idea was beyond his humble means.

The host resisted the urge to run upstairs to his wife. During the ball last evening, she had become disconcerted when informed that Jean-Pierre had been brought to the convent. She had insisted to her husband that they become his godparents. Earlier this morning, too exhausted to leave her bed, she had waited for more news. Her husband had attended the hasty baptism and thought she would be relieved to hear that the child appeared well.

Still, her sudden bout of illness during tonight's dinner was not the result of a "delicate" condition. No, he sensed something else was going on. Something about the boy's mother, her friend Madame Clare. *The Intendant told us last week that the midwife was destined for prison. If the boy was already in the convent, his mother must now be…how horrible. No wonder my wife is upset.*

Lady Louise had expressed displeasure that her husband had invited Father Benedict to join them to dine. "That man is such a busybody," she had said. "Always intruding on our privacy. I know it is wrong to harbor such ill thoughts about him…still…"

Her husband had apologized to her and hinted the priest had virtually invited himself. How could he refuse when Father Benedict wanted to congratulate Lady Louise in person, on the baptism of her new godson? The Marquis regretted the invitation. *I should have made some excuse—not imposed this priest on my anguished wife tonight of all nights. Unfortunate decision on my part.*

The clock struck seven as the gluttonous Father Benedict began to dig into his third helping off the dessert platter, oblivious to any further concerns about his dear, dear cousin Louise.

This is going to be a long evening. The Marquis sighed, wondering how much more food the priest could possibly stuff down his throat. But this evening would soon prove to be more than inconveniently long. Two unexpected intruders were on their way to the chateau.

Chapter 41

Claudette Returns
Rouen, 7:00 P.M.

IN THE ROOM with bare stone walls, Jean-Pierre turned from side to side on his hard cot. He fingered the buttons on his little soldier uniform, remembering how Maman had cut them off his old velvet pants and sewed each one onto his jacket. Sister Mary-Augustus had tried to make him take off his uniform, but he was afraid he wouldn't get it back. He insisted on wearing it all night, even if it was itchy.

The women who lived in this cold place wore long black dresses with funny white brims and instructed him to call them "Sister." Why was that? They weren't his real sisters like Lucina. He missed her, even if she did beat him at games.

Sister Mary-Augustus fed him a small wooden bowl of icky porridge for supper, with pieces of dried turnips and a hard trencher. No soft buns, no fruit. He had only choked down a few spoonfuls between bouts of tears, and now his tummy rumbled. He reached into his pocket and found the last bit of the Loo-tenant's chocolate, which he licked off the wrapping.

Jean-Pierre thought longingly of the fresh eggs in the nursery. Maman had promised him an egg for dinner if he behaved, stayed in the nursery until she returned from welcoming the Capitaine.

I suppose I was terribly naughty to go downstairs with Giselle. But I did s-s-so want to march with the s-s-soldiers. Just for a few minutes, that's all.

Jean-Pierre reached into his left breast pocket and pulled out the folded picture on the back of the hand-drawn map, but it was too dark in this cold cell, lit only by the thin ray of moonlight, to see it. The mean sisters-who-really-weren't-sisters refused to leave a candle burning. Told him candles cost too much.

The little boy tucked the picture under the hard pillow. Stared at the wooden cross hanging over his cot. He was frightened and missed Maman.

Tomorrow Loo-tenant will come take me home and I'll give him the picture I drew. I'll be soooo glad to see him, and Madame Claudette too. But not that ghost in the nursery.

~~~

Claudette was coming up the road from Rouen, returning to her nursemaid duties for the two sweet Dupres children. Her weeklong holiday had ended, and she was totally unaware of what had been happening at the maison during her absence.

She had an uneasy feeling as she stepped aside to allow a group of soldiers to thunder by on horses. A few minutes later, trotting in the opposite direction were two other riders. One was wearing an army uniform and the other…well, strangely enough, he was dressed in the green livery usually worn by the Dupres' carriage driver. But this man looked sickly and had a droopy mustache. She wondered whether Madame had hired a different driver in her absence.

Darkness was descending quickly, so she hurried her step. Her feet hurt from walking, but it was time to prepare the children for bedtime. Although she had enjoyed her week off in Rouen, she missed the little ones.

As she entered the kitchen, she noticed the absence of a fire in the hearth. *How odd, Marie should be cooking the evening meal.* Claudette lit a candle and gazed about. The abandoned kitchen was disheveled. Unwashed crockery in the scullery. Broken dishes everywhere. The larder was empty, except for a mouse nibbling crumbs off the stone floor. The animal became alarmed and scurried away when he saw her.

She crept up the backstairs to the nursery, expecting to hear the chatter of its little occupants. Throwing open the door, Claudette was appalled by the mess. Broken eggshells, scorched copper pan on the little grate.

Had the Dupres left the maison and taken the children visiting? Perhaps in her anticipation to leave last Sunday, she had not paid attention. Madame *had* seemed a bit distracted, and Claudette remem-
~~~

bered they had returned early from church, something about Monsieur feeling unwell.

Claudette found a broom and swept up the eggshells. She took a rag and washed the dried food from the pan—tidied up the nursery. Walking out onto the landing, she heard the faint sound of drunken laughter floating up from the master's bedchamber. What in heaven's name was going on?

She crept silently down the main staircase. The double doors were battered, stood open, and the sight inside shocked her. Her niece Giselle was lying undressed on the flowered carpet, surrounded by three strange young men. Claudette was overpowered by the sight and stench from the room. She held her kerchief over her nose and stepped inside.

"Giselle," she said sharply. "What's going on here? I don't understand. Where is everybody?"

"These are my new friends," Giselle hiccuped. "Lessee, this here is Charles and that there is Laurent and him…I forget his name."

The three soldiers stood up and quickly pulled up their breeches. Embarrassed to be seen in such disarray, they attempted to straighten their attire.

Pulling the sheet around her chest to conceal her nakedness, Giselle said, "Aunt Claudette—what are you doing here?"

"Out!" Claudette ordered the disheveled soldiers, who appeared relieved to leave the room and the scene that was certain to follow. Giselle had cajoled them into untying her after the officers had left, promising them more fun and games and hidden bottles of ale.

Claudette stepped gingerly around puddles on the floor toward the window, which she pushed open. Cold air flooded the room.

"What is happening here, Giselle? Where are Master and Mistress? And where are Jean-Pierre and Lucina? This place is a mess and the family is gone. Has some plague descended while I was away?"

Giselle was defiant. "Me and my soldier friends were just havin' some fun. The family are gone and left."

"Where to?"

"Don't know. Why do I allus get blamed for everything?"

Claudette stood by the window and shook her head. "Get up and put on some decent clothing." Seeing Madame's yellow silk gown on the floor, she looked around suspiciously for Giselle's uniform. "Have you been wearing Madame's clothes?"

"She gived them to me."

"You're lying. Why would she give you her dresses?"

"Afore she left, she said to me I could have my pick. She gave me her pearls. Tol' me I could keep everything, even her warm cloak."

"More lies. What is going on with the soldiers? Mercy, have they been here long?"

"They are the Dragonnades, Auntie. Came last week to arrest the whole family. They deserved it. Breaking the King's laws."

"Where are the children? Were they placed in your care?"

"No. I tol' you. They're all gone. Never comin' back. The girl got sick with poxes and Monsieur took her to Paris. Madame…well, she disappeared in the night, after Lieutenant took off with Jean-Pierre. Ain't my fault."

"Nothing's ever your fault, is it?" said Claudette in disgust. "You are just like your mother. I tried to bring you up rightly, but I guess I failed. I even got you this job here, to keep you out of trouble. I covered for you when you was flirting with the master. Think I didn't know what was going on? Well, I did. All along, I did."

"He forced me, the master. Against my will. I tried to tell him no, but he was allus grabbin' at me when I came to light the fire or dust or whatever—"

"Stop. No more lies. I'll go upstairs and find you one of my old dresses. Then we will leave at once, take nothing."

"I'm not leavin' with you."

Claudette grabbed her niece by the shoulders and shook her. "Not leaving? You have disgraced your name and my reputation. We will be dismissed without a reference. Everything is ruined. I can't face Madame when she returns. Now wait right here."

With that, Claudette went upstairs to her room. She had to get Giselle out of here. She poked around in her bureau drawers until she found a simple black gown and stockings. As she took a last look around the windowless room she had slept in for the past six years, she heard a ghostly voice singing: *Take heed, all ye maidens, be wary, take car-ee.* Claudette shook her head. Maybe the ghost wasn't a figment of Jean-Pierre's imagination after all.

By the time she returned with proper clothing for her niece, Giselle was gone. Looking out the window, Claudette saw the girl running barefoot across the courtyard to the stable, carrying the yellow silk over her arm. Giselle ignored her aunt's pleas. Her threats.

Claudette slammed the window shut. *I'm done with her. I did my best, but she is just like her mother. A lying, stealing good-time girl.* Claudette took her few belongings and walked out through the iron gates. She heard the sound of drunken songs from the stable as she headed back toward her friend's house in Rouen. Angry tears poured down her cheeks.

Chapter 42

Unwelcome Visitors

Chateau Montjardin, 8:00 P.M.

FATHER BENEDICT WAS relishing his after-dinner brandy, praising the smoothness, the fine flavor. Holding the glass up to the glow from the silver candelabra, he commented on the clarity. His host was attempting to hide his impatience. Would this meddlesome priest never leave?

In silence, the butler entered and whispered in the Marquis's ear. "Milord, there are two men at the door to see Lady Louise."

"Excuse me, Father, but I must see to some business. Please stay, refill your glass. I'll be back shortly," he said, rising to his feet.

Overhearing the butler's message, the inquisitive priest decided to follow. Gulping the remaining brandy, he pulled his heavy body from the chair and trotted behind his host, muttering about the urgency of returning to the presbytery.

Recognizing one of the two men standing in the entryway as the soldier who had brought the Dupres child to the convent, Father Benedict stopped in his tracks and stepped out from behind the Marquis.

"Why, Lieutenant Pechard, what a surprise to see you here. I didn't know you were acquainted with the Marquis. I came for dinner and was just leaving." Seeing the puzzled look on his host's face, he realized the soldier was unknown to him. "Lieutenant, please allow me to introduce his Lordship the Marquis de Montjardin, husband to my dear cousin Lady Louise."

The Marquis nodded to the officer but frowned at the unkempt appearance of his companion. *His servant, perhaps?*

Pulling the Lieutenant aside, Father Benedict whispered, "Who is this man wearing green livery that presumes to approach the Marquis? Has he no sense of his proper place? For shame!"

"Let me introduce my superior, Capitaine Robert Souchard, commanding officer of the King's dragoons. We are here on official business," said Lieutenant Pechard.

The Marquis and the priest were confused. This man was being introduced as a high-level army commander, yet his appearance belied his supposed status. Not only was this intruder dressed in an unseemly manner, he fairly reeked, and the ill-fitting chartreuse livery was stained with remnants of an apparent digestive disturbance. His face was tinged green.

Not bothering to apologize for his lack of proper uniform, Capitaine removed the white wig and explained that he had encountered some mishaps during the past few hours. His military attire had been ruined. He assured them his soldiers had been sent to fetch him a clean uniform, but certain matters of the utmost seriousness could not be delayed. Pechard confirmed Capitaine's explanation for his unkempt appearance.

"I am here to question Lady Louise," said Capitaine in a hoarse voice of authority, puffing out his chest. "A matter of supreme urgency, you understand."

"The Marquise?" said the Marquis in surprise. "No offense, but I do not understand the urgency. My wife has taken to her bed already. She is ill and cannot be disturbed."

"I am sorry to hear of her indisposition. I myself have been feeling…rather unwell myself, but duty presses. I must speak to her."

The presence of the cleric in his black robe unsettled the Lieutenant. "Surely she is not near death, is she?" said Pechard.

"No," said the Marquis, "it is but a female complaint. Still, cannot your questions await the morrow, after she has had the benefit of a night's rest? Let me have my servant bring you both some refreshments before you leave." He tried to direct them to the door.

Lieutenant Pechard would have welcomed a meal, even a hunk of bread, a cup of warm ale. As for Capitaine, the very thought of food raised bile in his throat—he declined the offer on behalf of his companion and himself, but made no move to leave the chateau.

"My interrogation of your wife cannot wait. I must insist. Time is of the essence. Order of the Intendant and all, you see. A matter of military importance. A dangerous fugitive on the loose… a hardened criminal…" He stopped ranting when the longcase clock in the corner struck eight with enough force to prevent any further threats from being heard.

Lieutenant Pechard thought his superior officer had exaggerated. *I hardly consider an unarmed woman who escaped my commander's unwelcomed sexual advances to be a dangerous fugitive.* Embarrassed by Capitaine's rude insistence on invading the peace of this aristocrat's home at such a late hour, he longed to leave. But the dutiful officer remained silently respectful, gazing at the ancestral portraits on the walls.

The Marquis tried not to let his annoyance show. "The Intendant is a close acquaintance of my family. I am certain he would not wish to have my wife disturbed when she is feeling poorly. Do you accuse her of harboring a fugitive criminal here? If so, I can assure you—"

Pushing his way past the Marquis, Capitaine said, "I *will* see Lady Louise immediately. The Intendant acts under direct orders from our sovereign King Louis."

Father Benedict, ever curious, announced his return to the presbytery was not quite as urgent as he had moments earlier declared. He bounded up the stairs, knowing exactly the location of Lady Louise's bedchamber, unwittingly leading the way for the officers.

The Marquis was furious. *How dare these intruders push their way into my home, official order or not. The nerve of this man, who lacks a proper sense of decorum or dress, accusing my wife of harboring a fugitive. Still, if he is acting under the orders of the King…*

He reluctantly followed the unwelcome visitors toward his wife's room, but warned them that their stay had better not extend more than a few minutes.

~~~

Lady Louise could hear the ruckus of men's boots marching toward her chamber. Edgy all day, she wrapped her shawl tightly around her shoulders and propped herself up higher on the pillows of her chaise lounge. Her lady's maid handed her a small vial of aromatic vinegar in case she felt faint.

Her husband entered the room first, asking the others to remain outside until he determined whether she was *deshabille.* "My dear,
~~~

there are two officers waiting at the door who demand to speak with you. One is dressed suspiciously and is incredibly rude. Father Benedict is with them. I tried to delay them but they are insistent. Some ridiculous notion that you have information regarding a dangerous fugitive."

"Fugitive?" Louise paled. The officers had taken Jean-Pierre to the convent. Had they discovered her note at Maison Dupres? She was certain she had warned Clare to burn it. "I feel too unwell," she moaned, pulling the smelling salts to her nostrils. "Send them away."

"I tried to, but they claim to be acting under orders of King Louis. Bear with them for a few minutes, my sweet. Then I will insist they leave and you can be sure I will visit the Intendant tomorrow to get to the bottom of this outrage."

The doors opened and the ill-clad Capitaine, followed by Lieutenant Pechard and Father Benedict, walked in and bowed to Lady Louise. She could not believe how disheveled this big man with the mustache appeared. Looking carefully at his clothing, she recognized the Dupres coat of arms displayed on the green livery. Her heart sank.

Lady Louise mustered her courage. "Yes?"

"My apologies for disturbing you. We are searching for a dangerous fugitive from the King's law. Calls herself Madame Clare Dupres." Capitaine watched for a reaction, but Lady Louise's expression remained impassive. Trying to mask her shock, she reached for her fan.

"Why do you come here?" she asked. "It is late, and as you can see, I am quite indisposed this evening."

"The Dupres' serving girl informed us you were Madame's friend. I thought we might find her hiding here."

"Madame Dupres has helped me as a midwife. I would hardly qualify that as a friendship. She is not here."

Capitaine started to approach her. The Marquis grabbed his arm to stop him. The beefy officer yanked loose but stopped moving forward. Even in his desperation, he knew that he was out of order, barging into a sick noblewoman's bedchamber. He backed away and looked about the room, to see if there was any incriminating evidence. In the corner was a small, elegant writing desk. He walked over and lifted a stick of red wax—rolled it back and forth between his fingers. He was aware that many people used red wax to seal their correspondence. Still…

He turned abruptly toward Lady Louise. "When did you last see Madame Dupres?"

"Let me think. My family and I were traveling to Versailles, taking the children to visit my husband's parents. We were forced to stop at Maison Dupres when I began to bleed. It was an emergency…" She wiped imaginary tears from her cheeks with her sleeve.

"Madame Dupres saved my wife's life," added the Marquis, as he moved toward his wife and touched her shoulder protectively.

"The serving wench Grizelle told me her mistress received a note from you about a week ago," said Capitaine. "She recognized your red wax seal."

The Marquis looked at his wife with questioning eyes. Father Benedict's mouth dropped open.

"I frequently write notes, Capitaine. I don't specifically recall sending any notes to her last week. I did write a belated note of appreciation for helping me with my medical emergency, but I have no clear memory of when it was sent. Did you actually see a note written in my hand?"

Capitaine watched her warily. *Should I pretend I saw a note? Better not, she would ask me to produce it.*

"No. Unfortunately the girl believes Madame Dupres burned it. Of course the wench is untrustworthy—lies a great deal. But she did seem quite certain of seeing a note from you, recognized your seal before handing the letter to her mistress."

Lady Louise struggled to find the right words. Her mouth was dry. "Did the girl tell you what was contained in the supposed note?"

"The girl is totally illiterate. Can't read. But remembered you spent a few days and nights as a guest at Maison Dupres."

"Guest? Better described as a patient than a guest, although I was treated with great kindness until I was strong enough to return home."

"And you haven't seen her since then?"

"I have not."

"Do you know where Madame Dupres may be hiding?"

"Hiding? Why on earth should she be hiding?"

"Capitaine, this has gone on long enough," said the Marquis, clenching his jaw. "My wife has given her word that she has not seen this woman in the recent past. I must insist you leave. Now!"

"I regret this inconvenience, but I have one more question. Monsieur Dupres and his daughter are also missing. We were told that he took the girl to a Parisian physician, to be treated for the pox. Have they any family or friends that you know of in Paris?"

"I know of none," said Lady Louise, fanning her face. She was alarmed to hear Lucina was ill. The dear little girl and her brother had entertained young Louis-Armand so charmingly during his stay in the Dupres nursery, while she recovered from her miscarriage.

"Very well," said Capitaine. "I bid you good evening and take my leave. If the fugitive comes around here, you will notify the authorities."

Lady Louise winced behind her fan at hearing her friend described as a fugitive. She prayed that Clare had somehow escaped to safety, along with her husband and Lucina. *I'm not sorry I sent that warning note, even though my husband will now demand the truth from me—berate me for putting our own family in danger for doing so. At least the note was burned. Of course if they capture Clare and torture her, the truth might still come out. Oh dear!*

The men turned and left the room. Capitaine asked leave of the Marquis to bunk down in his stable until his soldiers returned from Paris the next morning. For a brief second, the Marquis considered offering them the use of a comfortable guest room, of which there were many in the chateau. Then, considering how the senior officer had treated his wife, he politely told them where horse blankets were stored in the stable.

PART V MONDAY

29 OCTOBRE 1685

Chapter 43

Search for the Fugitives

Rouen, 8:00 a.m.

FATHER BENEDICT RODE back to the chateau early Monday morning, anticipating that the soldiers would be bringing back the fugitive parents and daughter in chains. He gleefully planned to claim the girl and take her directly to the convent to be baptized. The reward money would finally enable him to buy the horse he so dearly desired. However, he swore his sole intent was to save the child's soul—that is, if she had survived the pox.

With a cheerful smile, he waved to Capitaine and the Lieutenant as they walked out of the stable, brushing straw off their heads. Pechard nodded at him, wondering why this cleric seemed to have such an abundance of idle time.

His stomach still queasy, Capitaine was not inclined to waste time in idle banter. The agitated commander was certain he would never sleep well again until the fugitives were apprehended. His eyes were focused on the road.

Around ten, the troops finally straggled back empty-handed. They claimed they had searched every farmhouse along the deserted road toward Paris, questioned every man, woman and child. No sign of the Dupres anywhere. It might have been called a "fruitless" search, except that their saddlebags were now stuffed with pilfered Normandy apples, as well as bread and large chunks of cheese.

Capitaine's eyes turned cold and hard as flint. He refrained from swearing, however, due to the presence of the annoying priest, who persisted in nagging him for advice about the horse he planned to purchase.

Hearing the sound of voices from the courtyard, Lady Louise peered out the window of her bedchamber and saw that none of the Dupres family members were in the soldiers' custody. She breathed a sigh of relief, hoping they were safely on their way out of France. As for Jean-Pierre, her new godson, she had conceived a plan during the wee hours of the morning. Young Louis-Armand would soon be needing a boy to attend him as a valet. Perhaps in a few weeks' time she would ask her husband to take the Dupres child into their home. She remembered Jean-Pierre as a well-bred boy, exactly the right age to become a companion to their son.

Lady Louise saw this as a way of thanking her friend for saving her life. She had already anticipated the letter she would send to Clare, words to gladden any mother's heart: "Your son is safe. We will tenderly care for him." But where had Clare disappeared to? She would ask Father Benedict. He always appeared to be well informed about local gossip.

The priest was privately disappointed that the little girl had not been found. He wanted to be of assistance to the soldiers so that perhaps Capitaine would help him acquire a horse. He stood next to the commander, munching an apple.

"Tell me, Father Benedict, where do *you* suppose Madame Dupres might be hiding?" asked Capitaine. "You seem to get about."

"I have prayed on the matter all morning and the good Lord has graciously given me the answer. The road to a mother is through her child."

"What kind of nonsensical babble is that?"

"Her son is at the convent as we speak," said the priest smugly. "Have you not thought to question the boy directly?"

Capitaine slapped himself on the forehead. "Of course, why didn't I think of that earlier? My brain is as addled as my poor stomach."

Father Benedict beamed. He was excited to be the first to put the soldiers on the right trail. Jean-Pierre would surely provide some clues to his mother's whereabouts.

The commander called for a horse and announced to his weary soldiers they would leave at once for the convent of the Sisters of Sorrow. The tired men groaned in unison. He was merciless in his quest to find thc prisoners.

"Step lively and stop complaining," he ordered. "What a bunch of weaklings. I should replace you with girls."

When the troops arrived at the convent gate, Capitaine banged on the heavy door. "Open up in the name of the law," he shouted. "By order of our great sovereign, King Louis XIV."

Sister Mary-Augustus tipped open the door and saw a filthy, green-liveried servant. She might have mistaken him for another beggar seeking alms—so many frequently came to these doors—except that this ill-clad man appeared to be in charge of a troop of properly uniformed men on horseback.

"Kindly lower your voice," she said quietly. "This is a house of silence."

When Lieutenant Pechard stepped forward, she recognized him as the soldier who had brought the little Dupres boy to the convent Saturday evening.

"Please forgive the intrusion, Sister," he said in a quiet voice. "This is my commander, Capitaine Souchard. His uniform met with—umm, an unfortunate accident."

The commander pushed the Lieutenant aside. "I demand that you allow my men in to search the sleeping quarters of your convent."

"*Impossible*! No man enters there—not even our priest." She attempted to close the door, but he placed his foot in the gap.

"Don't be difficult, Sister. We are looking for Madame Clare Dupres, a convicted felon. I have reason to believe she came here to see her son."

"Jean-Pierre has been with the Sisters of our order since your Lieutenant brought him. But if you are suggesting we are harboring his mother, you are mistaken."

"I doubt it." Turning to his men, he waved his soldiers forward and ordered Pechard to lead them on a search of the premises.

Sister Mary-Augustus stood tall and tried to block the passage, but she was no match for Capitaine, who pushed her roughly to the side. Heads down, the soldiers walked past her, obeying their leader's command. Embarrassed, Lieutenant Pechard uttered words of apology and shrugged as he went by.

"I am appalled," she said to the ill-bred Capitaine, "that you refuse to believe me when I tell you Jean-Pierre's mother is not within these sanctified walls."

Capitaine waved his arms in the air. "She is a dangerous witch, agent of the devil himself. A terrible threat to your nuns. To the children under your care. She must be found."

"Is there something awry with your hearing, Capitaine? Let me repeat. Madame Dupres is not here."

"We'll see for ourselves. Now, where is the boy? I wish to interrogate him."

"Interrogate a frightened six-year old with your rough talk? All you'll accomplish is to upset him. He is in a fragile condition at the moment."

"Shall you bring him to me, or must I burst into the orphans' quarters and grab him myself?"

"This is highly irregular," said the nun, but as he started to stride in the direction of the children's voices, she consented to bring Jean-Pierre to the visiting room.

"Wait here," she said, pointing to a chair. "And compose yourself. This is a house of worship, not a barracks."

~~~

The anxious commander, hands clasped behind his back, paced like a rabid wolf about to pounce on a rabbit. When Sister brought Jean-Pierre into the room, he said, "Sit down!" to the child.

Jean-Pierre stared with wide eyes. He remembered standing at the nursery window, watching this man with a droopy mustache ride up to his house two days ago. But then he had been properly uniformed as a high-ranking army officer, a capitaine. Now, he looked like…like Maman's driver!

"Were you d-d-demoted?"

"None of your insolence, young man. I said sit down!" he snarled, pointing at a wooden bench.

Shaking from fright, Jean-Pierre obeyed the bully-man. He clung to Sister's hand.

"Where is your mother, boy?"

"Really, Capitaine," Sister Mary-Augustus intervened. "Can you not see he is scared? Must you bark at him as you do your soldiers?"
~~~

"Leave us," he told her.

"No, the child has been entrusted to our care. I shall remain here by his side." It was clear she would not leave.

"Where is your mother?" the officer bellowed again.

"Maman is at our m-m-maison. She promised to cook me an egg for my s-s-supper." Memory of that egg brought tears of homesickness to the boy's eyes, and his little body trembled.

Jean-Pierre's mention of the egg caused bile to rise in Capitaine's throat. Reminded him that egg had been used instead for the she-devil's omelette. He reached for the boy, lifted him by the shoulders and tried to shake information from his body, which only caused loud howls from the boy and protests from the nun.

Just then, Lieutenant Pechard walked in to announce that the soldiers' search of the convent had been unsuccessful. He saw what was happening.

"This child is most uncooperative," said the frustrated interrogator, pushing Jean-Pierre back down on the bench with a thump.

"Wait a second," said Pechard. "Allow me, Capitaine." He bent forward so Jean-Pierre could see him.

Almost at once, the little boy's tears stopped flowing. "Loo-tenant Pechard, is it r-r-really you?"

"I see you are still in uniform, Private J.P. Have you forgotten how to salute me properly?"

"No sir." Jean-Pierre was overjoyed to see his friend. He stood at attention and raised his chubby fingers in salutation.

"Sister, is there an outdoor garden where my little soldier friend and I can visit alone?"

"The cloister is through that door," she said, pointing her finger.

Capitaine stood, dumbfounded. Stunned, he made no effort to stop Pechard or the boy from walking out into the late morning air.

Fifteen minutes later, Pechard returned and handed the smiling boy to Sister Mary-Augustus, just in time for lunch. As she led Jean-Pierre out of the visiting room, he strained for a last look. The little soldier didn't know whether to be happy to get away from the wicked man in green or to worry about Loo-tenant leaving him again.

"Did you find out anything from the uncooperative brat?" inquired Capitaine.

"Actually, I did. We talked about his mother and what they were doing up in his nursery during the week the soldiers were—umm, carrying out your orders before your arrival. Apparently, while he was busy counting to one thousand—something he is very good at, by the way—she was reading from a packet of letters."

"And?"

"He is a smart lad. Knew some were from an Uncle Pierre, who lived across the sea in England. And some from an aunt, but he couldn't remember where she lived, only that she had once brought him seashells."

"Did his mother keep the letters?"

"Oh, yes. She apparently kept them hidden under his sister's mattress in the nursery while we were busy ransacking the home."

"Then the letters may still be there. A possible clue to her whereabouts. Hmm, seashells…Paris is not on the coast. She may be headed in the other direction, toward the north coast. Perhaps the port of Le Havre? Round up the men and let's go search the nursery at Maison Dupres for those letters," said Capitaine. "Hopefully, she didn't burn them. Ladies have a habit of saving family letters and re-reading them many times."

Mildly disappointed that their search of the sleeping quarters hadn't revealed any nuns in a state of undress, the soldiers prepared for another long ride. Whether or not nuns really did shave their heads would remain an unsolved mystery. Departing in a hurry, the soldiers failed to notice a man hiding in a grove of apple trees, patiently waiting for them to leave.

Chapter 44

Jacques's Note

Dieppe, 11:00 A.M.

AFTER DRESSING ON Monday morning, Clare and Lucina headed down for a late breakfast. They tiptoed past the room where Jacques slept. Clare placed her ear against his door, hearing silence within. Lucina told her mother that since arriving in Dieppe, her papa had been taking long morning walks up the cliff, watching for the ship.

Clare knocked on his door and softly called his name. There was no answer. She turned the knob and peeked in. The bed was made, his portmanteau was on the floor, and his Bible was on the small bedside table.

Jacques's sketchbook was open on the desk. He had drawn a picture of a young girl in a pale blue bonnet, face hidden by the brim, sitting alone on the ground and gazing out to sea. For some reason, he had not signed his name to the bottom corner, as he usually did. *Maybe it is incomplete because he is waiting to sketch Jean-Pierre sitting next to his sister.* Clare choked back a sob.

Looking out the window, she saw the *Celia* bobbing in the harbor. *Jacques may have left early this morning to talk to the crew, to oversee the loading of his valuable cargo. I see bundles with the Dupres & Sons, Purveyors of Fine Fabrics label piled on the pier.*

Lucina scampered down the stairs, anxious for breakfast—she was hungry. Clare felt her stomach growling, and the smell of bacon was inviting.

In the dining parlor, Delphine smiled and gave them each a big hug. "Good morning, lazybones," she chirped. "The weather is perfect today and Cap'n Silas says we should keep our fingers crossed. His men will finish loading today and set sail at dawn tomorrow."

Lucina crossed her fingers on both hands and then tried to lift her spoon, looking perplexed. The boarders were unused to having a child at the table, and the little storyteller with the golden hair was a source of great delight to them. They laughingly assured her that crossing her legs was just as lucky as crossing her fingers.

Delphine handed Clare a small cup of hot chocolate. When Clare protested, Delphine assured her that Cap'n Silas kept her well supplied with this delicacy when his ship returned from foreign ports. Clare warmed her cold hands, wrapping them around the cup.

"You look much better this morning, Clare. Your color has improved. I think a good night's sleep was just what your maman would have ordered, bless her soul." Clare set her empty cup on the saucer. Legs crossed, Lucina was busy spooning porridge with bits of dried blackberries into her mouth.

After helping Delphine clear the breakfast dishes, they went into Delphine's private parlor, the room Clare remembered as Uncle's book-lined study. She could still smell traces of his pipe tobacco clinging to the old velvet drapes. Nothing had changed in this room since she had visited as a child, except a new clock now occupied the mantel.

"That's a gift from Cap'n Silas," Delphine explained. "He's always bringing me souvenirs from his journeys."

"Really! He must be a very *special* friend," Clare remarked. "Lucky you finally learned to speak English."

"Oh, don't be getting silly notions in your head about me, Clare. He's a married man. Lives in weaver-town, a neighborhood called Spitalfields in London. Sometimes he brings his wife along—she runs a lodging house there, like me. They always stay here in one of my guest rooms when the *Celia* is in port. Missus says she tires of eating dried salt pork onboard and a bowl of my fresh hot mutton stew is the very thing to boost her spirits after a week of sailor food."

Lucina piped up, "I won't mind eating sailor food."

"Ah," Clare said, nodding, wondering how she knew what sailors ate. But then again, she was a quick learner and had been here for almost a week.

"Cap'n Silas sometimes brings news of Pierre. He still laughs at the recollection of Pierre's first nightmare of a voyage, him being so sick at sea. But just before they docked, Pierre pestered him with questions about the owners of the ship—where they lived, were they married, how much were they worth? Cap'n Silas said he was about ready to throw our brother overboard for being such a pest."

"Sounds like Pierre, all right."

"Now that Pierre is one of the partners in Smithfield-Barton, he is Cap'n Silas's boss. Pays him well, Silas tells me. He's mighty glad he didn't chuck him over the rail after all."

So am I, thought Clare with a smile. Her thoughts drifted back to an earlier time. Shortly after Uncle Dupres had died, Delphine had announced she would stay in Dieppe, refusing Jacques's invitation to move into Maison Dupres with them. Clare had been disappointed. It had seemed a natural thing for their sister to join their household, as she was by that time destined for eternal spinsterhood. *Frankly it would have been a help to have her living in our home, especially when I was out birthing. I think after wasting her youth looking after two younger brothers, she didn't wish to raise another brood of babies.*

Turning the half-timbered house into a respectable lodging place, Delphine lived a comfortable life of independence off the rents. Unlike many of her single friends, who were forced to become nursemaids to their brother's children, Delphine was head of her own establishment. Once the terrible Dragonnades had left and she put things back in order, her life had gone on as before. She had many, many friends in Dieppe and was well-respected. Greeted with smiles, whenever she stepped out. *In retrospect, I see that she made the right decision*, thought Clare.

Clare walked through the rooms, recollecting how luxurious this half-timbered house had seemed to her during her childhood. Now, she realized it had grown a bit shabby, especially in comparison to Maison Dupres. Nonetheless, it provided her with a comforting sanctuary during her final anxious hours until Jacques, Lucina and she would board the ship.

In Delphine's parlor during the afternoon, Clare sat altering the black dress her sister had found for her. The seams needed taking in—the prior owner had obviously been a person of large proportions. Earlier that day, when Lucina had busied herself playing with a cat in the stable, Clare had briefly explained to her sister what had happened to her at the maison. Delphine had clucked in sympathy and advised her to try not to dwell on it, wondering what she would have done in the same circumstances. She thought Clare was the bravest, most courageous woman she ever knew.

Delphine handed Lucina a ball of wool and two wooden needles. Showed her how to cast on forty stitches, the beginnings of a scarf.

"Did your maman teach you how to sew?" asked Lucina.

"I was very young when she died, but she taught me to knit, which has been a great amusement."

"My mother taught me how to concoct elixirs," Clare said. They all laughed. It felt good to be lighthearted, if only for a few hours.

"Pierre writes that his wife Celia has trouble with a needle. I think she wears spectacles," said Delphine as she began trimming a black bonnet with a heavy veil.

"You're not trimming that hat for Celia, are you?"

"No, Clare. This hat is for you to wear when you board the ship tomorrow. To keep your head warm."

What she means is that I need that veiled hat to conceal my face and telltale auburn hair. Coupled with the black dress, Clare realized she would appear to be a widow. She shuddered at the image and pulled her chair closer to the fire. Despite the rays of sunshine that poured through the glass windowpanes and the roaring fire in the grate, she could not seem to get warm.

Every so often she strolled over and peeked out the window, fearing the arrival of soldiers. *By now, they will have broken through the locked bedchamber doors, found and unbound Capitaine. Of course, he does not have his boots or uniform, but that would not have stopped him from sending his men on a frantic search for me.*

The hours passed like molasses. Clare could almost hear the hoofbeats of horses pounding up the road, following the tracks she had left. The sun was dropping in the sky. She watched the seamen heave the last of the heavy barrels from the dock onto the *Celia. Where is Jacques? He should have returned to the house by now. He must still be very angry with me.*

~~~

Jacques did not return that afternoon. "Delphine," said Clare, trying to hide her growing anxiety. "Did Jacques say anything to you before he left this morning? I mean about skipping supper?"
~~~

Delphine was busy ladling stew onto pewter plates and Lucina was helping by placing a biscuit on each one. "No, I didn't see my brother this morning. I figured he left before I came down."

"When *did* you last see him?"

Delphine stopped and wiped her hands on a cloth as Lucina carefully carried the tray into the dining room.

"Last evening, after you and Lucina went to bed. I was finishing the cleaning up when he came into the kitchen."

"Was he upset?" Clare whispered so Lucina could not hear.

"I don't think so. Well, I suppose he *was* distressed, what with Jean-Pierre missing and you fainting and all that. But Jacques always appears calm, even when he is angry. Yesterday when you got here—well, I never remember him being *that* mad."

"What did he say?"

"Let me think. Oh, he asked me what I did with that red army jacket and I told him it was in the cellar—good gracious! I better go see if he fell down the stairs." Delphine rushed to the cellar door, calling, "Jacques? Jacques?" No answer.

At that moment Clare knew he was gone. Without searching, she knew Capitaine's uniform and his black steed would be missing. She ran up to Jacques's room, hoping to find some clue. Nothing had changed from the morning. Everything shipshape. Neat and tidy. The open sketchbook, the portmanteau, the Bible. All in the same place.

Then Clare took a closer look at his Bible. What she had thought was the bookmark he customarily used to mark his place was a folded letter—addressed to her, in his unmistakable handwriting. Clare's hands shook as she unfolded the note.

10:30 p.m., Sunday

My dearest wife, Clare:

I have gone to fetch Jean-Pierre. It is utterly impossible for me to leave my son in France. The nuns will mistake me for a high-ranking army officer and will not dare stop me. Have faith and try not to worry. I will find our boy and bring him back to Dieppe in time to sail on Tuesday. But if I see the miserable bastard who dishonored my wife, I swear I shall be tempted to kill him with my own two hands.

Please board the ship early with Lucina. If we miss the Tuesday sailing, Jean-Pierre and I will hide at Delphine's until the next ship arrives. I realize now how foolish I have been to doubt your advice these past few years. I promise things will be better when we get to England. I do not blame you for anything.

I love you. J.

Clare sank down on her knees. This was the first time Jacques had ever said he loved her. He was bravely risking his own life to save their son. She realized that she had grown to love her husband and didn't want to lose him. *Oh dear God, please bring them both back to me. Keep them safe.*

Chapter 45

The Hand-Drawn Map
Rouen, 12:00 NOON

RIDING ALL NIGHT, Jacques had arrived at the convent Monday midmorning, but seeing soldiers' horses outside the walls had given him pause. He was impatient to snatch his son, but understood the danger to himself if spotted. Hidden among the apple trees in the orchard, he waited until the troops rode away, relieved to see that they had no child with them.

Jacques suspected the blustery green-clad villain at the head of the troops was the monster who had dishonored his wife. He was sorely tempted to leap out from the trees, grab him off his horse and pound his head on the ground until he was dead. He knew these violent thoughts were unchristian, but in times such as these… *No, I must not lose patience. Must concentrate on freeing my son from the clutches of the Papists. Get him to Dieppe before the ship leaves.*

He held his breath as the army men thundered by with not so much as a glance in his direction. *Dear Lord, thank you for removing this obstacle from my path. Forgive me for having evil thoughts.* While standing stock-still, he whispered the words to his favorite psalm to hush his pounding heart.

~~~

Fifteen minutes later, as the children chattered over their fish chowder at the long-worn refectory table, Sister Mary-Augustus sat and watched Jean-Pierre slumped on the bench seat. The poor child's
~~~

momentary hope had vanished when the Lieutenant left him for the second time. He looked so forlorn.

After lunch she would firmly but gently insist he remove his dirty soldier suit and put on a proper smock like the other orphans. He must learn proper obedience. Passing the dormitory this morning, she had noticed his bed was disordered. At home, the nursemaid had apparently tidied up after him. *Well, he needs to understand that there are no nursemaids to care for him here.*

Before she could take him to the dormitory, she heard the bell sound at the convent door again. *Really! Must these interruptions continue?* But she could not ignore them. It might be delivery of another Huguenot orphan. The question of where she would put another child troubled her. Already the orphan wing was overfilled, many youngsters forced to sleep two to a cot. If it weren't for generous benefactors like the Marquis, there would not be nearly enough food to feed so many empty bellies.

With a sigh, she walked toward the door and opened it to find yet another army man, bearing the ribbons of a high-ranking officer on an ill-fitting red coat. She became suspicious—after all, Lieutenant Pechard had told her Capitaine Souchard's uniform "met with misfortune." Perhaps this thin man was an imposter, the thief who had stolen it.

"I'm sorry. Your men left already," she said, starting to close the door in his face.

But before she could, she heard a voice say, "*Attendez, s'il vous plaît.* Sister, please read this." He handed her an official-looking letter, "authorizing removal of one Jean-Pierre Dupres from the Sisters of Sorrow convent into the custody of Capitaine Dumond." She read it carefully, trying to decide whether it was a forgery.

This had never happened before. She began to wonder why there was such interest in this particular boy. The Marquis rushing over to be godfather. Père Benedict insisting on daily updates. The intrusive bully in soiled green livery, supposedly high commander of the guard, interrogating the frightened child. And Lieutenant Pechard walking alone with him in the garden. Was this a child of royal blood, entrusted to this convent? Had they hidden him here for a reason?

Her breath caught in her throat. *I think Jean-Pierre may well be one of the King's bastards.*

Sister Mary-Augustus shivered, uncertain what to do. If she released the royal child to this so-called Capitaine Dumond, she might anger the Marquis, get in trouble with the authorities. Her initial impulse was to deny his request.

"The boy you seek cannot be removed from our care. Please leave us in peace." But deep down, Sister Mary-Augustus sensed something different about this man. She saw in his gentle eyes a haunting, pleading look. "Who are you?" she demanded. "I am perplexed. Why are you wearing that uniform? It is far too large for you. Did you steal it?"

Jacques decided to tell her the truth, to drop the pretext of being an army officer. "I am Monsieur Jacques Dupres, Jean-Pierre's father. I did not steal this uniform. Shall we just say I borrowed it temporarily, to enable me to safely travel the roads to Rouen." He was careful not to reveal where he had come from. "I have come to get my son back. He was wrongfully taken from our home. According to the King's law, he is too young to be baptized without our consent."

"We were told he was seven, although I thought he was rather small for his age. But I'm afraid it is too late. Jean-Pierre belongs to our church now—he has already been baptized."

Jacques winced at the word *baptized*. He slowly inched his way into the entry. "Please, Sister, just for a minute. Would you prevent a father from seeing his son? I have traveled all night. Please…."

By this time the children had finished eating and were walking in orderly pairs out of the refectory. Recognizing his father's familiar voice, Jean-Pierre came running toward him. Reaching down and lifting the boy into his arms, the father covered the boy with joyful kisses.

"Papa! Oh, Papa, I am so glad to see you. But have you j-j-joined the army? Just look at your medals. I should s-s-stand and salute you but, oh, I want more kisses."

Sister Mary-Augustus shook off the thought that she was harboring a royal bastard. This was clearly Monsieur Dupres's son. Despite her harsh demeanor, the nun had a soft spot in her heart. She remembered the day long ago when her own father had brought her to this convent to be raised. Her mother had died of the plague and he had been forced to leave her with the Sisters of Sorrow. How she had cried for days on end, knowing she would never see her family again.

"You may only have a few minutes," she warned as she led them into the visiting room. "Please understand my position. I cannot allow the child to leave the convent." She tucked the "official" letter inside the sleeve of her habit and patted the black fabric to reassure herself it could not fall out. If questioned about her action later, she would have a written alibi.

"Jean-Pierre," she said, "I am going to lay out some clean clothes for you on your cot. I will come back for you in a few minutes."

Straightening the blankets on the boy's bed, Sister Mary-Augustus noticed a paper under the pillow. Unfolding it, she saw a childish sketch of a soldier standing in front of a horse. This morning during lessons, Jean-Pierre had been observed using his pencil to print something inside his copybook. It was this separate piece of drawing paper. Smudged black letters on the bottom edge proclaimed: "MON AMI, LE LOO-TENANT."

This must be his picture of Lieutenant Pechard. It had been sticking out of the pocket of the blanket soldier outfit when Jean-Pierre had arrived. She turned it over and saw a hand-drawn map with directions to a farm near Torcy-le-Grand. Puzzled, she turned back to the portrait. This was obviously an important little possession, hidden as it was under his pillow.

She returned to the visiting room to give Jean-Pierre the picture, but Monsieur Dupres and his child had fled. This came as no surprise. Oh, she knew she would get in trouble for allowing him to be whisked away, but in her heart she felt she had done the right thing. The boy belonged with his father. She had not sinned, but to be on the safe side, she would ask for forgiveness in her prayers this evening.

Sister Mary-Augustus, kindhearted nun, refolded the picture and slipped it back under Jean-Pierre's pillow. In case he returned.

Chapter 46

The Packet of Letters

Maison Dupres, 1:00 P.M.

ALONG THE WAY back to Maison Dupres from the convent, the Dragonnades stopped at a copse of beech trees. Lieutenant Pechard convinced Capitaine that the men absolutely needed to halt for a few hours—to rest and eat. They had searched the Paris road all night. Despite his irritation at the delay, the leader reluctantly agreed, worrying that the soldiers might mutiny. As the men quickly dropped into a deep slumber, he paced back and forth, unable to sleep or face food. His stomach still felt like a volcano about to erupt at any moment.

Pechard sat with his back against a tree, munching on bread and cheese the soldiers had appropriated during their search. He dreaded returning to the maison, recalling how disgustingly filthy and smelly it had been when they found the Capitaine tied to the bedposts. Almost twenty-four hours had passed and he felt certain no servants had returned to clean the mess. As for Giselle, she was as useless as Father Benedict's old mule. He wondered whether she was still tethered to the chair. Somehow, he doubted it.

Today was Monday. Hadn't Giselle told him at the tavern that her aunt, the children's nursemaid, was due back last evening? If so, she'd probably released Giselle and taken her away. Lieutenant secretly hoped she was gone. Capitaine's anger at the wily servant for not discovering him earlier had increased with each passing hour. Yesterday, he had left her tied up. Never could tell what he would do this time—maybe Capitaine would kill Giselle.

"Sir, you appear tired," suggested the Lieutenant. "Why don't I ride by myself the remainder of the way to Maison Dupres so you and the men can rest. I will fetch the packet of letters and bring them back here."

"No, I will go too. However, you are probably right about letting the men rest. I predict a long night of riding ahead."

Lieutenant Pechard nodded. He was glad that he himself had been able to sleep well last night in the Marquis's stable and now his stomach was full.

Capitaine shook one of the privates awake and instructed the drowsy man to take charge until they returned. The young man saluted. After watching the senior officers leave, the tired soldier returned to his makeshift bed of leaves under the tree canopy. Soon he was snoozing again.

When the two officers rode up to Maison Dupres, Capitaine excitedly pointed up at the window of the bedchamber. "Look, Lieutenant. Someone has opened the curtain. Madame has returned!" He eagerly rubbed his hands together.

Lieutenant Pechard doubted she would be in there, especially since the uniform and horse were missing, but he chose not to contradict his superior who was obviously not thinking clearly.

Capitaine was practically drooling in anticipation of meeting with his torturess, forgetting that he left Giselle fastened to a chair in the bedchamber. "The letters! I'll bet she remembered leaving them and came back to destroy those important clues to her destination. She is inside, I'd swear to it." At that, he reached for the pistol tucked in the belt of the green livery. Vowing to blow Madame's head off, he clambered up the stone steps to the front door followed by the Lieutenant.

But the overpowering stench that assailed them when they opened the door reminded Capitaine of his ordeal two days earlier, and he simply lacked the stomach to go upstairs and revisit the scene of his shame. He backed down to the courtyard.

"Lieutenant, we cannot let her escape again. You go up to the nursery and search for the letters. I will stand guard in the courtyard in case the witch tries to escape. When you catch Madame inside, bring her to me at gunpoint."

Pechard shook his head when he walked through the ruins of this once-sumptuous maison. He knew Capitaine was a man who had fought in the trenches, had shot foreign enemies and left them wounded, lying in filth. He had waded through puddles of rotting corpses with great bravery. Yet he was a coward when it came to facing the location of his own downfall.

The Lieutenant clutched his kerchief over his nostrils and quickly ascended the stairs, two at a time, to the third-floor nursery. He watched for signs of Madame Dupres or Giselle, but the maison was deserted. It took him less than five minutes to locate the thick packet of letters under a nursery mattress, still covered with a pink satin comforter. The letters were there, just as Jean-Pierre had said they would be. *Smart little guy, very observant for his age.* Looking up for a minute, he spotted the boy's little tin soldiers in disarray. One had fallen off the windowsill. Without thinking, Lieutenant Pechard picked up the tiny toy soldier and dropped it in his pocket.

Turning his attention back to the packet of letters, he untied the ribbon and delved into them. A few were beginning to fray, indicating they had been reread many times. They dated back ten years. He felt uneasy, almost guilty, reading a lady's personal correspondence. But he was carrying out a military order. *God, it stinks in here!*

When he opened the letters from England, there appeared to be two correspondents. A few were from a lady who delicately signed her name Celia Smithfield Dupres. The majority, however, were written in a strong, manly hand. These were signed Pierre Dupres, probably Jean-Pierre's uncle.

Other than the Dupres' signatures, Pechard was dismayed to realize he was unable to decipher the contents of the letters from London. They were written in English with only a few recognizable French terms interspersed. He was quite sure that neither Capitaine nor any of the troops could translate these letters.

He continued flicking through the letters. Another one from England, and another, and another. Finally, he got lucky—one single letter written entirely in French. He scanned the wordy letter, mostly news about friends and neighbors and domestic matters, the type of letter one sister might write to another.

My dearest sister Clare,

Where shall I begin? Which of all my important nothings shall I tell you? First, I find my straw bonnet looking very much like other people's and quite as smart…Mrs. A. sat darning a pair of stockings the whole of my visit…The evil intentions of the guards are certain…

Nothing of great interest, thought Pechard, except perhaps the note about the guards—probably his Dragonnades. Yet this letter did contain one valuable clue, the signature line—*Yrs affect'ly, Delphine*. He remembered the tearful spinster who owned the boarding house above the shuttered shop near the beach—Delphine Dupres, the sister from Dieppe.

He flew down the stairs with the letters. Breathless, he looked about for Capitaine and spotted him standing directly in front of the stable door, pointing his pistol at a person blocked from view by the officer's bulky green body. All Pechard could see was the edge of a yellow silk gown, trailing on the gravel.

His first thought was that his leader had found Madame and was preparing to kill her. Then, as he stood frozen on the top step, he saw that it was Giselle. *Of course. Giselle has been wearing Madame's clothing since our arrival—but what is she still doing here? Did her aunt not take her away last evening?* Noting the downcast gazes on the faces of the partially dressed foot soldiers standing around her, Pechard didn't take long to assess the situation. Left to guard her, the stupid fellows had fallen for her promises of more drunken fun in the stable. They were in immense trouble, and they knew it.

"Capitaine!" shouted Pechard at the top of his lungs. "Madame is not inside, but I found the letters."

Perhaps for the second time, his shouts saved Giselle's life. Turning around and dropping his pistol, Capitaine ran to the stone steps where Pechard was standing with the letters and grabbed for the pile with such force that he nearly fell backward off the step.

"Where has that she-witch gone? Tell me what you learned from these letters!"

"The sister, Delphine Dupres. Remember the spinster whose boarding house we occupied in Dieppe? There is also a brother in England. If I were to hazard a guess, I would say the Dupres are already at the port, waiting to escape by sea."

Neither the Lieutenant nor Capitaine noticed as Giselle reached down for the pistol. She waved the loaded gun in the direction of the shocked foot soldiers, silently warning them to get back in the stable. They were too frightened to tip off the officers. They slinked silently inside, unobserved.

Capitaine was enraged. "Outsmarted by a woman, a midwife! She purposely sent the King's army on a wild goose chase down the road to Paris when she and her husband and daughter were headed in the opposite direction. How often do ships leave from Dieppe?" he asked, strewing the letters on the ground like a pile of litter.

"Not too often, I suppose. Most ships use the port of Le Havre."

"Then perhaps it's not too late. They are probably hiding in this sister's house. We will tear her door down, the traitor. One of our *convertis*, no less, aiding and abetting our enemies."

"The Dupres are too clever to hide in their sister's house," said Pechard. "They know we would look for them there." *Poor Delphine has suffered enough damage to her home.* But his plan to discourage his officer from tearing down Delphine's door took an unexpected turn for the worse.

Capitaine let out an evil laugh. "You're right," he said. "There's only one sure way to smoke out the fugitives. We'll take the boy as bait. Ride through the streets with him. Can you not hear his pathetic little voice crying out, 'Maman, my egg. Maman, I want my egg.'"

Lieutenant tried to dissuade him from this plan—the poor little lad dragged from the convent, given false promises that he would be reunited with his family. "Capitaine, surely we should leave the boy with the Sisters of Sorrow. He would…slow us down. Believe me, when I took him to the convent, we had to stop every ten minutes so he could piss in the woods."

"No, I am determined. It's not far out of our way to Dieppe to stop at the convent. Since you are so friendly with the boy, go get him. He will be delighted to ride on your horse with you."

Lieutenant Pechard knew Capitaine was right about Private J.P being pleased to see him. But his heart ached for the child.

The senior officer saw his hesitation. "That is an order, Lieutenant. I will stop and collect our lazy troops from their snooze, while you proceed to the Sisters of Sorrow and bring me the brat. Meet us on the main road to the north."

Lieutenant mounted his horse. Before he rode off, his commander added, "And be quick about it. No strolling about the cloisters making nicey-nicey with the kid, understand?" Pechard rode away without answering. He tried to be philosophical about the situation. *There will be little rubs and disappointments everywhere and we are all apt to expect too much.*

Chapter 47

Giselle in the Ruins

Maison Dupres, late afternoon

CAPITAINE STOOD BY the gate watching Lieutenant Pechard leave to pick up Jean-Pierre from the convent. Suddenly he remembered dropping his pistol out by the stable. His head was groggy from lack of sleep. Rubbing his eyes, he walked toward the stable doors. *Now, where did I drop that weapon?*

When he opened his eyes, Giselle was coming out of the stable, pointing the pistol directly at him. He started to rush at her, aiming to wrestle the gun from her hands.

"Stop or I'll shoot. I means it," she said calmly. "I din't appreciate what you done to me yesterday. Leavin' me up in the bedchamber, trussed like a turkey."

The officer was larger and stronger than this insolent, stringy-haired wench, but even in his unbalanced mind, he sensed she knew how to handle a loaded firearm. *Where in the devil are my useless foot soldiers when I need them?*

"Lie yerself down on the ground. Flat on yer back," she ordered. Capitaine complied, lowering himself and stretching out on the sharp gravel.

"Now you need to do some 'pologizing fer what you done. Say yer sorry fer tying me up. Fer callin' me stupid and slappin' me," said the girl, slowly approaching him.

"Please put the gun down," said the man warily, lifting his head off the ground.

"Not 'til you 'pologize, proper-like."

"Very well, Grizelle. I'm sorry for the things I did and said."

Hearing the officer mispronounce her name again only served to agitate her further. "My name ain't Grizelle." She walked closer, holding the pistol in two hands and aiming it at Capitaine's head.

"It's *Giselle*."

"Sorry—Giselle. A lovely name for a pretty young thing."

"That's not good 'nough. Call me *Mademoiselle* Giselle. I tol' you, I is the daughter of a gennelman." Walking up to the prostrate officer, she kicked him in the arm. He grabbed her by the ankle, pulling her off balance. The gun went off, shattering the glass in the upstairs stable room.

The two foot soldiers ran out from the stable and seized her wrists, forcing her to drop the pistol. Private Laurent helped Capitaine up and brushed him off.

"I've had my fill of this accursed place and all its inhabitants. Lock the wench in the stable and bolt the doors from the outside. Then burn everything down!"

"Everything, sir?"

"Everything. That's an order. Burn the maison, the barn, the dairy, the storerooms, the stable."

"The stable, sir? What about Giselle bolted in there?"

"Who cares? She deserves to burn in hell, along with that mistress of hers when I catch her. When you're done, march back to the barracks. No more fun and games, hear?"

"Yessir." They saluted and watched him limp over to his horse and ride away.

~~~

An hour passed. The soldiers were busy spreading gunpowder around the house. Of the four people remaining at Maison Dupres, only Giselle stood motionless in the courtyard, watching in disbelief as the flames consumed the maison.

As soon as she had realized she was locked in the stable, she had rushed up to her room and grabbed mistress's silk gowns, now badly soiled and torn in spots, and the fake pearls. Looking around the bare room, she pulled the thin blanket off her pallet and bundled her treasures inside, tying the heap to a bent broomstick handle.

An ear-splitting roar assaulted her as the windows of the maison exploded. She tossed her bundle through the stable window that had
~~~

been shattered by the bullet, climbed out onto the sloping roof, and slid down to the ground. Laurent was standing in front of the stable, holding a torch close to the bolted wooden doors. He was relieved to see she had escaped.

Filled with hay, the last structure to be burnt caught quickly. Black smoke billowed from the inferno that was once a stable.

The three soldiers finished carrying out Capitaine's final order, ensuring that nothing remained of the formerly grand estate, except for the few treasures they managed to remove before the maison was burned. Silver candlesticks now safely stowed in their rucksacks, they set their heavy packs on the ground by the gate and straightened their uniforms.

"Are you leaving now?" asked Giselle, coughing from the thickening smoke.

It was getting dark and they had a long march back to the barracks. But the sight of the burning buildings was awesome enough to hold their attention for a few minutes.

"Shame we never got to see the grand insides, 'cause of the poxes in there," said the tall foot soldier. He was the first to have arrived last week.

"We better get going. Goodbye, Giselle," they said.

"Wait for me. I'll go with you to your barracks. We can still have a good time there…"

They laughed. "Sorry. We're tired of your good times. Look what trouble you caused us."

"'S'not my fault. You can't jus' leave me here. What'll I do? I've no place to go." Tears streamed down her cheeks.

"That's your problem, not ours."

Laurent laughed. "Try Paris. Wear one of them fancy dresses and you'll find business in the streets."

"Business in the streets?" she said indignantly. "I'm not that type a girl."

"Ha-ha. Farewell and good luck." The soldiers grabbed their gear and took off. "Don't try to follow us," they warned.

Giselle sank down on the stones and watched the walls of the stable collapse. She rubbed the tears off her face with her grimy hands, leaving muddy streaks. Her hair hung in tangles; it had not been combed in days, and in the turmoil, she had forgotten to pack her comb. She was all alone in the world now.

"Never liked this place anyhow. Everyone allus mean to me." She stood, grabbed her bundle on the stick, and headed down the road toward Paris.

Chapter 48

The Chase Commences

Rouen, late afternoon

"WAKE UP, YOU sleepy louts," shouted Capitaine as he roused his snoring soldiers, sleeping among the trees. His arm ached where Giselle had kicked him. "I am fairly sure I know where the fugitives are headed. Did any of you remember to bring chains and shackles?"

"Yessir," said one of the drowsy soldiers, standing and brushing dirt from his uniform. "I still have them from our search on the Paris road yesterday."

"Lucky for you, Private. That saves your butt for ignoring my order to take charge of your fellow men. Sleeping on watch is a serious infraction, but since we are on an urgent mission, I will overlook your dereliction of duty this time."

The soldier stifled a yawn and stood silently at attention, having no ready response to this reprimand. He smelled smoke coming from the direction of Maison Dupres and wondered what had happened there.

"Well, how excellent to see my men, all so nicely rested now," said the senior officer, his voice dripping with sarcasm. "What a motley assembly. Ready for the long ride ahead of us?"

"Where are we headed, sir, might I ask?" said the yawning private. Capitaine kicked a pile of stones, letting out a string of curses in frustration. His toes were still sore from kicking the bedchamber wall.

"We have reason to believe the fugitives are in Dieppe."

The soldiers looked at each other in dismay. *Dieppe! On the north coast of Normandy? Last night we were sent on a search to the south. Capitaine seems mighty confused since he was discovered tied up in the bedchamber.*

One man ventured to ask, "Can we not wait till morning, sir? It's getting dark out."

The commander could not believe his ears. "No, you imbecile. Time is of the essence. Now look sharp, all of you. I sent Lieutenant Pechard ahead to fetch the boy from the convent. I was….um, delayed at Maison Dupres, so they are probably already at our meeting point."

The weary men stood and saddled their horses, mumbling under their breath.

~~~

Pechard reluctantly trotted up toward the gates of the convent. He saw Father Benedict standing in front of a bony, uncooperative nag. *So*, thought the Lieutenant, *the officious priest traded his mule for a real horse. He must have baptized a few more innocents since this morning, collected rewards for bringing in more Huguenot orphans to the convent.*

The priest was holding his chest and gasping for breath as he lumbered over. "Lieutenant, oh dear, oh dear. Something terrible has happened. The boy is gone missing."

Pechard perceived he was talking about Jean-Pierre. "What do you mean, gone missing? I am under orders to pick him up and bring him to Dieppe."

"I tell you he is gone! My poor cousin Louise will be distraught. This very afternoon she sent me a note asking my opinion about taking Jean-Pierre into her home as a companion to her son. I prayed on the matter and the good Lord told me, not as an equal—that could never be. But a valet-in-training might be more appropriate—"

"Get on with it, man."

"In any case, I stopped by to discuss the matter with Sister Mary-Augustus. That's when I learned the boy was gone."

"This must be a joke," said Pechard. "Perhaps the boy is hiding in the garden. I'll call to him. He trusts me."

"Oh dear, oh dear. I'm afraid you are too late." The priest rubbed his hand back and forth over his tonsured skull.

"Too late?" Pechard sensed a sinking knot in his stomach. He felt responsible for the little boy. "Did he drown in the well? Fall and hit his head? Is he—dead?"
~~~

Father Benedict continued rubbing his head, eyes flitting side to side. "Sister Mary-Augustus said an officer in uniform came to pick him up. He handed her an official letter of authorization. Sneaked off with the child when she left the visiting room for a moment."

"I need to talk to her at once, examine that letter of authorization."

"She is at prayer now, but here—she gave me the letter. She was reluctant to part with it, but I insisted. I told her the boy's godfather, the Marquis, would want to see it for himself." He showed the letter to the Lieutenant, who examined it and handed it back in disgust.

"This is a forgery. Can't you see it is written on a sheet of drawing paper? Did Sister describe the officer who abducted the child?"

"Only that he wore a uniform with lots of awards on the jacket and identified himself as Capitaine Dumond."

Lieutenant Pechard was confused. He was unaware of any cavalry officer named Dumond. Could the Intendant have already heard what happened and sent another high-ranking officer to ensure the safety of the Dupres child? He pressed the priest for further information.

"Oh, my heart. My poor nerves. This is terrible. What will dear Lady Louise think of me now?"

"I had better speak with Sister Mary-Augustus myself," said Pechard. *The bumbling fool probably failed to ask her for a physical description of the imposter.*

"Wait, I remember now. Sister said the officer was short, thin, and the uniform was ill-fitting, as if the officer had lost a lot of weight."

Pechard began assembling clues in his mind. Short and thin—how Giselle had described Monsieur Dupres, when asked whether her master's clothing would fit the Capitaine. The note written on drawing paper—Jacques was an artist. The name Dumond matched the kid's fancy middle name. Was it possible that Monsieur Dupres had gotten hold of Capitaine's jacket, the one appropriated by Madame after their unfortunate tryst? Disguised himself as an officer in order to reclaim his son from the convent?

Lieutenant Pechard convinced Father Benedict to hand over the letter. He knew it could be important evidence. Forging army papers and impersonating an officer were capital offenses. If they succeeded in capturing Monsieur Dupres, he would undoubtedly be broken on the wheel, a dreaded form of punishment—worse than being sent to the galleys.

A wave of pity washed over Lieutenant Pechard. He had never really wanted to be this kind of soldier. Tearing families apart? Treating fellow Frenchmen as mortal enemies? This bothered his conscience.

"I will carry the news to Capitaine," said Pechard with a heavy heart as he mounted his horse. *What choice do I have? There is no doubt in my mind that Madame Dupres is already with her sister Delphine in Dieppe. The imposter the priest described must have been Monsieur Dupres come to take his son.*

"You see I have a horse now," said Father Benedict proudly. "I will accompany you."

Pechard examined the sorry-looking animal and tried to convince the priest that his horse would not be able to keep up with the swift-moving cavalry. It was a bag of bones. He suggested riding to Chateau Montjardin instead, to console his cousin, Lady Louise.

Before Pechard left the convent, he heard Sister Mary-Augustus calling to him. "Wait, Lieutenant. I have something Jean-Pierre made for you." The aging nun waddled out through the gate like a black-and-white penguin and handed Lieutenant the folded picture she had found under the pillow. He stuffed it in his shirt pocket and planned to examine it later. He had already wasted too much time here.

Off he rode, leaving the priest and nun in the dust. As he galloped toward the appointed meeting spot, he dreaded Capitaine's reaction to his arrival without the child. Lieutenant Pechard privately hoped the Dupres would succeed in escaping to England. He knew such thoughts were treasonous, but such was the future he wished for his little Private J.P. The boy belonged with his family.

Night was falling when he reached the main road. The soldiers had not yet arrived at the meeting spot. He wondered what could be taking them so long. Lifting the folded picture from his pocket, he smiled at the words scrawled on the bottom edge. Then he noticed writing on the back. Turning it over, he saw a roughly sketched map with directions to a farm near Torcy-le-Grand. This must be the carefully planned rendezvous spot for the Dupres. Jean-Pierre had unknowingly provided an important clue.

Pechard grappled with his conscience. Should he show the map to Capitaine? If the Dupres were hiding in Torcy-le-Grand, they surely would be discovered and captured. If, on the other hand, they were already in Dieppe, a detour to the farm might delay the troops from reaching the coast before the ship sailed.

He heard the sound of horses approaching from the south and decided to show the map to Capitaine and let him make the decision.

~~~

Father Benedict fretted. He worried that unless Jean-Pierre was returned to the convent, he would be asked to repay the reward money. He might have to sell his new horse. Instead of going to console his dearest cousin Louise, he decided to ride his nag to Dieppe. Maybe he could be a hero and bring the Dupres boy back himself.
~~~

Chapter 49

Papa and J.P. on the Road

North road, evening

"PAPA, I THINK YOU took a wrong t-t-turn. This is not the way Loo-tenant brought me from our maison to the convent."

"We are not returning to our maison in Rouen. We are going to pick up Maman and Lucina at your Tante Delphine's house."

"Oh, I s-s-see. Then we are all going home together."

"Yes, but to a new home across the sea."

Jean-Pierre worried about his prized possessions back at the maison, his precious tin French army men. *Papa promised to buy me a new set in England. But they will be English soldiers, not French soldiers.* The boy was confused and wondered if he would like his new toys as well as the familiar old ones.

"How will we get across the s-s-sea? Papa, you know I can't s-s-swim."

"On your Uncle Pierre's sailing ship."

"An adventure. I have to th-th-think about that."

Jacques told him he had plenty of time to think. It was a long way yet to Dieppe. Jean-Pierre fell asleep, and Jacques held his son around the waist so he wouldn't fall off the horse.

A few hours passed as they rode north. When Jean-Pierre awakened, they stopped at a coaching inn for a quick meal and a fresh horse. The innkeeper looked with suspicion at their attire and was taken aback when the boy asked for an omelette.

Jacques grimaced and said no, bread and cheese would suffice. He looked at the clock on the wall. It was just after six. They were making good time and should reach Dieppe before midnight.

Back on the road, Jean-Pierre began talking again. "Papa, what did the surgeon in Paris do to Lucina? Did he cut open her arm and drain her blood? Did he put leeches on the poxes on her face?"

"No. Her poxes went away by themselves."

"Maman was afraid I would catch those poxes. She kept telling me I couldn't go down and march with the s-s-soldiers because my head felt hot."

"I know. Jean-Pierre, tell me what happened when the soldier took you away."

"At first I cried because I was very scared. But the Loo-tenant made me a real soldier. I got an army name, Private J.P., and he gave me chocolate and taught me to piss in the bushes and I thought he was my friend except he took me to the convent and left me there and—"

"Whoa, slow down. I have to concentrate on the road signs to Dieppe."

"Papa, may I ask you a question? The nuns told me to call them Sisters, but they are not my real sisters like Lucina, are they?"

"No."

"I noticed they all had gold rings on their fingers, like the one you have." The boy stopped talking for a minute and rubbed his finger on Jacques's gold band. "So I asked Sister Mary-Augustus, isn't that a strange name? I asked her who was her husband and she said all the nuns were married to Jesus."

"Is that so?" Jacques was glad to let the boy prattle on, as it helped keep him alert. It had been a trying day and the heavy food at the inn caused him to feel extremely fatigued. The danger of falling asleep on horseback was in the forefront of his mind.

"I thought maybe she was m-m-married to Father Benedict because he s-s-spends a lot of time coming to the convent. He is the priest who back-sized me."

"Back-sized? Oh, you mean baptized."

"He touched my head with some water and made me repeat some words and then s-s-said something about the Holy Ghost and that I was now a Roman Catholic boy."

Hearing this from Jean-Pierre made Jacques wince. "You are *not* a Catholic boy. You were not of a proper age to consent."

"Does that mean the back-sizing—I mean the baptizing—didn't count?"

"That's correct," said Jacques, convincing himself he was right.

"This is a very warm cloak, isn't it, Papa? Where did you get it? It's much like the one the mean Capitaine wore when he first came to the maison."

Jacques decided his son need not know that it was one and the same. He wrapped it around Jean-Pierre to keep the light drizzle from chilling the boy. "Why do you call the Capitaine mean?"

"Because when he came to the convent, he intragated me and pushed me hard onto the chair. I was going to kick him, but then the Loo-tenant came and took me into the garden for a chat."

"What did you and the Lieutenant chat about?"

"He asked me if Maman had any brothers or sisters—real sisters, not like the nun-sisters. And where they lived. Papa, would you like to hear me count to a thousand?"

Jacques was more interested in hearing about the chat. He told Jean-Pierre to think really hard about what he told the army officer.

"I told him Maman had a brother Pierre, who was once a cousin but now a brother by marriage. Isn't that weird, Papa? One day he was a cousin and the next day he changed into a brother. That is hard for me to understand."

"What else did you tell him?"

"I said Maman had a s-s-sister Delphine who also was once a cousin except—"

"Never mind about that. Did you tell him where Maman's brother and sister lived?"

"He asked me that. Papa, you must be a mind reader. Were you listening in on our chat? Madame Claudette always says it is wrong to listen in on people's conversations."

Jacques was becoming vexed. He needed to know if the soldiers had learned that Delphine lived in Dieppe. If so, they might be close on their trail. He tried to be patient.

"Son, it is important for you to answer my questions. Did you tell the Lieutenant that your Tante Delphine lived in Dieppe?"

"No. I couldn't remember where she lived."

Jacques breathed a sigh of relief. He was about ready to let Jean-Pierre begin his count to a thousand, when suddenly the boy remembered another part of the chat.

"Did you know Maman keeps all her letters? The ones from Uncle Pierre in England and Tante Delphine?"

"I did not know that."

"When the soldiers came, after you left with Lucina, Maman sneaked down to her bood-war and brought up a packet tied in a red ribbon. When I was busy playing with my tin soldiers or drawing pictures, she untied the ribbon and read the letters over and over again. She must have had trouble reading the words or why would she keep reading them? But then she stuffed them under Lucina's mattress."

Jacques dreaded the answer to his next inquiry. "Did you tell anyone about the letters?"

"Not the horrible mean Capitaine. I didn't tell him anything." The boy paused for a minute to think. "But, yes, I did tell the nice Loo-tenant where she hid the letters. Then he left in a real hurry and didn't say goodbye to me. I didn't have time to give him the picture I drew on the back of the map. OH NO! I left it under my pillow at the convent. Can we go back for it?"

Jacques's shoulders drooped. Undoubtedly, the soldiers had searched the nursery and were on their trail. They were doomed. Jacques made a fateful decision. Instead of riding directly to Dieppe, they would hide out at Marie's farm in Torcy-le-Grand for a few weeks. The soldiers wouldn't think to look for them there. Another ship was due to arrive in several weeks. They would travel on that one.

Because he was so tired, Jacques failed to make a connection between the picture his son was prattling on about and the map his wife had drawn for him. When they reached the fork in the road, he turned and headed for Torcy-le-Grand.

Jean-Pierre started to count to one thousand. "*Un, deux, trois, quatre, cinq, six*…wait—if we are going to England, I must begin to count *en anglais*." He began anew, very slowly: "One, two, three, four, five, six…" By the time they reached Marie's farm, Jean-Pierre was up to one hundred sixty-six.

PART VI

THE FINAL HOURS; TUESDAY MORNING

Chapter 50

Capture at the Farm
Torcy-le-Grand, 4:00 a.m.

CAPITAINE HAD SCOFFED when Pechard showed him the map. "Just another of the she-devil's tricks, trying to put us off her trail."

"It's your decision," said the Lieutenant, shrugging his shoulders.

His superior officer took another look at the map and decided there was sufficient time to sniff around the farm at Torcy-le-Grand and still reach Dieppe before the ship sailed. The map had apparently been drawn before the omelette incident, because the boy had had it in his possession when he was rightfully taken from the nursery. The longer the commander thought about it, the more he convinced himself the Dupres family had planned all along to hide at their cook's farm.

~~~

Jean-Pierre was sleeping next to Papa in Marie's barn. He awoke and reached for a candlestick perched on a wooden stool in the corner. An owl hooted. Bats flew over his head. It was very scary outside, but he needed to use the privy. Suddenly he heard a horse trotting toward the farmhouse. He peeked through the opening in the barn door and saw a familiar face.

Before Jacques awoke from his deep sleep and realized what his son was doing, Jean-Pierre burst out the door calling, "Loo-tenant! It's me, Private J.P." Lieutenant Pechard scooped the boy up onto his saddle and turned the horse back.
~~~

"Wait," the boy cried out, pointing to the barn. "We can't leave Papa alone in there."

"Shhh. You're coming with me."

"B-b-But…" Suddenly ten soldiers came running from behind the trees toward the barn, carrying heavy chains, yelling, "Capitaine, we got 'em!"

"Is the she-wolf in there too?" the man in the green jacket shouted back, exulted with excitement. They were closing in on the kill. "I told you the bait would work, Pechard."

Entrenched in the officer's tight grip, Jean-Pierre did not see or hear anything more. Pechard galloped back toward the Dieppe road before the boy could witness the gruesome capture of his father. *At least I was able to spare him from that horror.*

Jean-Pierre started to weep. This was all wrong. The Loo-tenant was supposed to be his friend, but he was separating him from Papa. "Why?" he asked over and over. "Why was the mean man shouting about bait? Are they taking Papa fishing in the middle of the night? Everyone knows you can't catch fish with those big heavy chains." He gulped.

Pechard listened to the child's sobbing questions, which caused a rent in his heart. At least Capitaine had agreed to let him take his young charge ahead to Dieppe. They were to meet at the dock.

When they reached the crossroads, he slowed and studied the arrow pointing south to Rouen, the opposite arrow pointing north to Dieppe. He was torn, longed to turn south and take Jean-Pierre away. Back to the convent, or to Chateau Montjardin, to be with his godparents. Anywhere but Dieppe.

With a pang, he turned northward—he had no choice. It was his duty to obey his commander.

"Know what, Private J.P.? War is hell." Then Pechard reached into his pocket and handed the boy his little tin soldier, hoping to offer him some comfort.

~~~

"Where is your wife? Is she hiding in the barn?" demanded Capitaine after his men had stripped Jacques of the red jacket and boots and handed them to their leader.

"How did you know we were here?"

"I'll ask the questions. Now tell me, where is your wife hiding?"
~~~

"Around here somewhere," Jacques said, waving his arm at the fields and orchards. "She went for a walk in the moonlight." His heart was beating fast. He needed to detain them at the farm as long as possible.

Two soldiers gripped him tightly by the arms, while the others began to search for Madame. They woke Marie's family and interrogated them, but they hadn't seen the lady. Marie insisted the last time she had seen Mistress was in the kitchen at Maison Dupres, a week earlier. She feigned ignorance, denying any knowledge of their escape plans. When shown the map, she swore she had never seen it. Didn't know Monsieur and the boy were in their barn—they must have sneaked in there after her family had bedded down for the night. The poor cook was frightened out of her mind.

The soldiers' search of the barn and farmhouse failed to turn up any evidence of Madame Dupres or her daughter. They kept looking, calling out her name as they fanned out into the open fields.

~~~

"This is *my* uniform you were wearing," demanded Capitaine. "How did you get it? Oh, wait, your wife brought it here to the farm, didn't she? Where she planned to meet you. We have the map, you know."

Jacques remained silent. The map! He began praying for the sun to rise, the ship to leave.

"You used my uniform to abduct your kid from the convent under false pretenses, didn't you? Impersonated an officer with a forged document. We'll stretch the truth out of you on the rack."

Jacques held his ground.

Capitaine restrained himself from choking this skinny nobody, this shriveled silk merchant. What did Madame ever see in him? She told me her husband disgusted her. No wonder!

"Where did you take my son?" the captive asked.

"Ha! If you want to save your kid, tell me where to find your evil wife. She poisoned me, can you believe that?" He paced back and forth. The nervous twitch in his jaw made him appear antsy. Finally, in desperation, he tried a different tactic. Torturing Monsieur Jacques was not going to lead them to his wife. She was the one he wanted to capture, more than anything in the world.

"You know something, Monsieur Jacques? I'm a reasonable person, but I'm running out of patience. Let's barter."
~~~

Barter? This lunatic tried to rape my wife, kidnapped my son, and now he wants to barter with me?

"You're a businessman, Monsieur Dupres, right? You understand trade. I can offer to keep you from the rack, the galleys, give you back your son. Set you both free. What do you say, Monsieur Jacques?"

"What do you want from me? I thought you were acting under an official order from King Louis? You showed my wife the Intendant's parchment. She told me everything when she came to join me…to join me here at the farm."

"Oh, *that* order," he said, brushing the thought away with a wave of his arm. "Easily fixed—a mere misunderstanding. Based on a tip from your serving girl Grizelle, that she heard you singing psalms in the woods. Turns out she is a liar. Good riddance to that untrustworthy wench."

"I have no money," said Jacques. "You want to bargain? Let us *all* go free—my entire family—and you can keep Maison Dupres for yourself."

Capitaine laughed like a hyena. "I have no use for your opulent house. It's just a pile of ashes by now. Oh no—*I* want the midwife, Madame Clare Dupres. Lead me to her hiding place and you will be a free man. I'll even convince the Intendant to allow you to leave France with your children."

"Somehow I don't trust your word," said Jacques, with as much dignity as a barefooted prisoner stripped to his breeches could muster. The soldiers were still searching for Clare in the surrounding fields. Jacques hoped they would not give up.

Capitaine examined his red jacket and noticed the buttons were missing. "What did you do to my uniform, you wretched man?"

"I traded the buttons at the coaching inn for food. Jean-Pierre was hungry for one of his maman's delicious omelettes. They *are* delicious, are they not, Capitaine?"

This infuriated the officer. *So the story of my shame is known. When Madame handed her husband the jacket, they must have laughed together at her trickery. But where is she now?* He ordered his men to put shackles on the shivering husband and throw him over a horse. The sun was just beginning to rise and their search of the farm had failed to uncover Madame's whereabouts. *She must be in Dieppe! We shall use the boy as bait to entice the she-devil out of hiding. Pechard has probably hooked her by now.*

The commander put on the buttonless jacket and smiled at the brilliance of his plan.

Chapter 51

Aboard the Celia

Dieppe, 5:00 a.m.

"WAKE UP, LUCINA. It's time to go."

The little girl rubbed her sleepy eyes and asked whether her papa had returned during the night.

"Not yet, but there are still two hours until the ship sails." Surely he must be on his way by now, thought Clare, desperately holding on to a thin thread of hope. "Cap'n Silas warned us that we need to board well before seven. He runs a tight ship—always on time."

They dressed by candlelight, as the sun had not yet risen. Delphine brought them each a cup of warm milk. She looked around for their satchels, as she planned to accompany them to the wharf. Clare had only her birthing bag to take, the journal tucked inside.

In the corner of the dark room sat Jacques's bag, his sketchbook poking through the top and his Bible weighing down his few personal possessions. Delphine had packed it for him, but wondered if he would be back in time to catch the ship.

Crossing the windy street, they looked both ways, searching for the sight of a man with a small boy in tow. Sadly, all they saw were a group of fishermen preparing their nets for the day's work. The pêcheurs waved a friendly greeting at Delphine.

A small crowd began to gather at the shore to watch the ship leave. Clare remembered being with Pierre, doing the very same thing when they were young. *Pierre. I wonder if he will recognize me when the ship arrives. No time to think about him now—I must continue praying for Jacques and Jean-Pierre to get here soon.*

"There's still time," said Delphine doubtfully as they reached the edge of the pier. "But you two need to get settled in your cabin." Tears ran down her cheeks. She said farewell, hugged them and watched as they climbed the ramp. Turned and walked back across the beach—but she wasn't headed for home quite yet. Delphine strode over to her fishermen friends.

"You all remember Clare Dupres, don't you, boys?"

"Yup, the old preacher's girl. She wedded your brother, Jacques, didn't she?"

"That were some long while ago, warn't it?"

Delphine told the men the wedding had been ten years ago. Much had happened since that day.

"That her, the redhead up there?" they asked, pointing up at the deck. Delphine was dismayed to see that Clare had already ripped off the black veiled hat, her telltale auburn hair blowing in the wind.

"Clare has a serious problem and needs your help," said Delphine. They gathered around, listening to her whispered request.

"Glad to oblige," they said and ran to their fishing boats.

~~~

After Clare placed their few possessions on the bunk in their assigned cabin, Lucina begged to go back on deck. Clare was sitting with the quill pen in hand, attempting to write in her journal, an impossible task. She dabbed at the inkblots, trying to rub them out. *Jacques is too late. In a few minutes, this ship will be leaving without him.* Her hands were shaking.

She would have preferred to stay inside the small, dark compartment. It would be too painful to watch the alabaster cliffs of her childhood recede from view, knowing she would never return. But fear, anger, and frustration knotted up inside her until she was about to burst. Clutching the journal to her chest, she took Lucina by the hand and went to face the rising sun with fading hopes.

Standing at the ship rail, Clare started to fling the journal into the deep harbor, as if that could erase the nightmare. Lucina stopped her in time, touching her arm and saying calmly, "*Arrête, Maman. Ne fais pas ça.* Stop, don't do that," as she took the journal from Clare.

~~~

Cap'n Silas stood on the quarterdeck and shouted, "Let go." The clock tower in the marketplace rang out the hour: *Bong-bong-bong-bong-bong-bong-bong.* Clare thought about Jean-Pierre, remembered how he loved to count to seven and beyond. Someone on board rang the ship bell, and the sailors began pulling the lines.

But something was amiss. The boatswain shouted to Cap'n Silas, "We can't leave yet, sir. The fishing skiffs are blocking our way. They're arranged in a giant shell formation around the bow."

Clare looked over and saw Delphine's *pêcheur* friends smiling and waving at her from their bobbing skiffs in the harbor. The *Celia* had drifted no further than twenty yards from the pier. Far enough to preclude anyone from storming onto the ship but close enough to hear voices on shore.

Dressed in black, the Huguenot refugees who had emerged from their hiding places in the hold looked at each other in alarm. Why had this ship stopped moving forward? They swarmed around Clare, who handed Lucina to a kindly refugee matron. She sensed trouble brewing.

"Take my daughter below and hide her, quickly." The woman in black obliged.

"What the hell?" Cap'n Silas roared. "Tell those pêcheurs to move out, or by gum the *Celia* will run them down."

Delphine stood and watched the ship rock in place in the deep harbor, struggling against the winds trying to push it out to sea. She wondered how long her friends could delay the *Celia's* departure. Perhaps there was still time for Jacques and Jean-Pierre. She anxiously watched for their arrival, never anticipating what was soon to happen.

A flock of hungry white gulls glided over two fishermen, who had purposely tethered their skiffs at the very end of the pier, several yards apart. They batted their oars in the air, pretending to protect their live bait from the birds while keeping a careful eye on Delphine.

Suddenly, a loud commotion broke out on the shore. The detestable Dragonnades were back in Dieppe, thundering onto the pebble beach! The crowd of townsfolk gasped and divided in half like the Red Sea to avoid being trampled. Their mouths agape, they stood in shock as Capitaine stormed through the open lane to the shoreline on his black steed.

When Delphine spotted them, she whistled loudly—a prearranged signal to her fisherman troops, who quickly rowed their skiffs out of the path blocking the *Celia*. The appearance of the soldiers was a bitter disappointment to her.

"It's too late," she said sadly to a neighbor standing next to her. "The ship must leave now, without my brother…"

Capitaine was screeching and laughing hysterically like a madman, as waves washed over his boots at the shoreline. Next to him, Lieutenant Pechard stood silently, holding a frightened boy in a little blue-blanket uniform.

Even Father Benedict stood among the crowd, believing he had reached Dieppe in time to recapture Jean-Pierre as well as his sister Lucina. Seeing all the refugee "blackbirds" on deck, he gleefully anticipated collecting many more "orphans" to baptize.

"I order you to return this ship to the dock at once, under the authority of his royal majesty King Louis XIV," roared Capitaine.

Cap'n Silas shouted through a megaphone, "This is an armed English merchant vessel. As sea captain of this ship, I don't take orders from the French."

"I warn you, harboring dangerous criminals will not be countenanced," bellowed Capitaine. At once, a massive moan arose from the huddled refugees on deck.

"Quiet!" cried Clare. She was trying to listen to her little son.

"Maman, Maman, come back," sobbed Jean-Pierre pitifully, holding out his hands. "*Ne me quitte pas, Maman.*"

Cap'n Silas looked through his spyglass and saw two soldiers dragging a man in shackles up to the pier. Delphine gasped when she recognized her brother and ran over to him. She tried to shield Jean-Pierre from witnessing his papa in chains, but the boy was crying too hard to notice. Then Clare looked away from her son and sighted Jacques.

The deranged commander pulled out his short sword and held it to Jacques's shackled throat. Clare screamed, "Jacques!"

"Madame, only you can save your husband's life," yelled Capitaine. "Convince Cap'n Silas to bring this ship back to shore and I'll free him and your children."

Every eye turned to the defiant midwife, her bright auburn hair waving wildly in the wind. "You monster!" she screamed. "I should have killed you when I had the chance!"

She lifted her skirts and began climbing over the ship rail. She would swim to shore and save her son. The seamen knew the undertow would pull her heavy skirts underwater and drown her. They grabbed her before she could jump and held the struggling woman by both arms. She began to sob. *My poor husband in shackles. My sad little boy calling for me.*

The soldiers aimed their rifles at the *Celia*. "Don't be stupid," the Lieutenant hollered at them. "The ship is armed with cannons. They can blow up the whole beach and everyone standing here." The guns were lowered.

Cap'n Silas rushed over to Clare. "It not too late to pull the ship back to the dock. I'll do whatever you say. Jacques has always been a good friend to me. Before he left Dieppe the other night to fetch Jean-Pierre, he explained the terrible story. Tell me what to do," he said.

Clare's mind was in turmoil. The vicious beast on the beach lied—she knew he would never let any of them go free. Her husband was already in custody, doomed no matter what she did. But her little boy—was it possible to save him by giving the word to turn the ship back? What about Lucina? Would the soldiers take her to the same convent as Jean-Pierre?

Clare faced the most difficult decision any mother could ever face. Sacrifice one child to save the other? Her daughter was the only person who could carry on the birthing tradition, the secret formula for the magic elixir—and Clare was the only one who could teach it to Lucina.

Suddenly through the silence came the sound of Jacques's unmistakably clear voice. "Don't turn back, Clare. You must keep going. Just remember, I love you." He began singing the Sixty-Eighth Psalm, battle hymn of the Huguenots:

Let God arise, let his enemies be scattered, let them also that hate him flee before him.

As smoke is driven away, so drive them away; as wax melteth before the fire, so let the wicked perish at the presence of God.

Soon the émigrés' singing voices joined him in defiance of King Louis, *le roi soleil.* Together, their voices drowned out the madman Capitaine's threats and curses as well as the sad cries from Jean-Pierre.

But let the righteous be glad: let them rejoice before God; yea, let them exceedingly rejoice….

Clare turned away from the rail with her decision. "Sail ahead, Cap'n," she said. Then, running to her cabin, she threw herself down on the bunk and buried her sorrowful tears in the soft-sided birthing bag.

"I've lost them both forever," she wailed, "my beloved husband and son."

~~~

As the sails unfurled, the defeated cavalry commander foamed at the mouth and began slashing his sword recklessly at the innocent bystanders. Pechard realized his leader had become totally deranged, no longer able to command. He decided to take over—ordered two of the soldiers to restrain the raving lunatic and return him to the barracks. Two others were assigned to take Jacques away.

Holding the sobbing child in his arms, Lieutenant Pechard felt the earth shift. Within a few minutes, the *Celia* was on course to England.
~~~

Epilogue

Le Grand Prix des Pêcheurs (The Great Prize of the Fishermen)

CAPITAINE SOUCHARD WAS demoted to foot soldier for his untoward behavior. As he had anticipated, he was stripped of his medals and flogged. Subsequently, he was committed to a lunatic asylum.

Lieutenant Pechard was promoted to the rank of capitaine, a man of valor combining proven strength with compassion. A few years later, while attending the opera in Paris with his new wife, he thought he saw Giselle (or a girl who closely resembled her) on the stage.

Jacques was never heard from again. His inner strength and faith had come through in time to save his wife, whom he had truly loved. Did he survive or perish? Nobody knew for sure, and Clare considered herself a widow, for at least a few years.

The dejected Father Benedict returned most of the way back to Rouen on foot. His sorry nag drowned in the river when stopping for a drink. The meddlesome priest continued to wrangle invitations to dine at Chateau Montjardin. The Marquis politely referred to his wife's cousin thusly: a man who has nothing to do with his own time has no conscience in his intrusion on that of others.

Nobody blamed Delphine for causing the short delay in the ship's departure. She was celebrated as a heroine in the history of Dieppe. From time to time, Cap'n Silas stayed at her boarding house, continuing to bring her chocolate and other treats, and tidings of Clare's new life in England with Pierre and Celia.

But what of Jean-Pierre? Have you, dear reader, guessed that Lieutenant Pechard took him back to the convent, where he studied to be a monk? That he went to live with the Marquis's family as companion to little Louis-Armand? Or perhaps that he grew up in Tante Delphine's house and joined the French Navy, as his Uncle Pierre had once wanted to do?

If so, heed the wisdom of Jane Austen, who famously wrote more than a century later: *Let other pens dwell on guilt and misery. I quit such odious subject as soon as I can, impatient to restore everybody, not greatly in fault themselves, to tolerable comfort, and to have done with all the rest.*

~~~

Lucina had not stayed below deck with the émigré woman. As the *Celia* began to set sail toward England, while her maman was sobbing in the cabin, Lucina calmly watched what was going on at the pier. She felt sad about her papa but was not worried about her brother. In her head-picture, she saw Jean-Pierre in England—at age sixteen.

With all the confusion on shore nobody had paid notice to Delphine. She swooped Jean-Pierre out of Pechard's arms and the surprised officer had offered no resistance. None whatsoever. Just stood and watched the spinster run.

Delphine darted to the end of the pier, holding her nephew tightly. A few of the soldiers tried to chase after her, but several burly locals blocked their way.

When she reached the end of the pier, she kissed her little nephew's soft blond hair and whispered, "Be brave and count to ten," before lifting him high above her head and flinging him out to sea.

The crowd gasped. "Has everyone gone mad?" yelled a woman. The sound of a large splash resonated with the onlookers.

Before Jean-Pierre reached three, the fishermen in the waiting skiff winked at Delphine and pulled him up in their net. "Ooh, we got us a big'un. Biggest darn fish we ever caught."

His partner laughed. "Wrap the wet *poisson* in a blanket. Got some serious rowing to do."

Lucina ran to alert the boatswain. He threw a rope ladder over the side of the *Celia* and hauled the precious bundle on board. Soon, Jean-Pierre and his sister were safely wrapped in the arms of their maman, who, had she not been stopped by two sailors, might have jumped over the rail and drowned.
~~~

"But Lucina," Clare said much later, "in your head-picture, you saw your brother in the convent with a man he admired, a man who taught him new things. I thought he was learning to be a monk."

"You stopped listening to my head-picture too soon, Maman. The man I saw was the Lieutenant."

"The Loo-tenant was my friend," said Jean-Pierre. "He taught me to piss in the woods. But I've decided. I *don't* want to be a soldier after all."

They all laughed and cried together for the rest of the sea journey.

THE END

Acknowledgments

Where do I begin? I owe thanks to many more people than I can express. First and foremost, to my wonderful husband Perry Krowne for tirelessly proofreading, suggesting changes, encouraging my early efforts and being my number one cheerleader.

Like my muse Jane Austen, who showed her novels to her family and friends in her small English village and took pleasure in their reactions, I owe my heartfelt thanks to the friends and neighbors in my very own Northern Arizona village for their encouragement; to the early readers Marie, Billie Faye, Maureen, Darla, and Pat; to the members of my writer's critique circle: Honey, Nancy, Maureen, Karen, Gisele, and Jim; to my dear friend Yolanda who, through the magic of Photoshop™ gave my author photo a more youthful appearance and formatted the photo of Clare's "birthing bag" on the Title Page.

Huge thanks to my fellow Austen enthusiasts, members of the Phoenix Region of the Jane Austen Society of North America, who began envisioning a publicity campaign even before this novel was completed.

Special thanks to my daughter-in-law Deanna for the biblical inspirations and quotes; to my grandson Preston for a teenager's critique; to Heidi Shoen for her valuable input; to my editor Eliza Dee, cover designer Victoria Cooper, and mentor Melissa Bowersock for their invaluable assistance and encouragement. And to Caleb for book formatting.

I drew from many books and internet sources while writing, including

- *The Huguenots in France* by S. Smiles (1875)
- *The Huguenots: Their Settlements, Churches and Industries in England and Ireland* by S. Smiles(1881)
- *The Huguenots: France, Exile and Diaspora* by R. McKee and R. Vigne *(2013)*

- *The King's Midwife; A History and Mystery of Madame du Coudray* by N. Gelbert (1998)
- *A Modern Herbal (bulbous buttercup)* by Mrs. M. Grieve(1931)
- *A Book of Poison or Medieval Cures?* https://bookaddictionuk.wordpress.com/2014
- *The Revival of Priestly Life in the 17th Century in France* by H. Lear (Google Books)
- *Pregnancy and Childbirth for the Historical Author,* www.elenagreene.com
- *Joseph Dandridge(silk pattern designer of Huguenot descent)* https://en.m.wikipedia.org/wiki/Joseph_Dandridge
- L*ucina-goddess;* https://en.m.wikipedia.org/wiki/Lucina
- *Virtual Museum of Protestantism, Rouen (Seine-Maritime)* *http://www.museeprotestant.org*
- *Château de Dieppe*, *https://en.m.wikipedia.org*

Most invaluable of all were the complete works of Jane Austen, from which I borrowed lines from her six published novels, surviving letters to her sister Cassandra Austen, and an unpublished manuscript (which was not yet completed at the time of Austen's untimely death in 1817). For a complete listing of these quotes, please email me at Carole.Penfield@gmail.com. You can also find me on Facebook at AustenMidwives.

Thank You for Reading

I sincerely hope you enjoyed reading *Midwife of Normandy* as much as I enjoyed writing it. If you did, I would greatly appreciate a short review on Amazon or your favorite book website. Reviews are important for any author, and even just a line or two can make a big difference.

To follow the adventures of the Dupres family as they begin their new life in England, watch for *Secrets of the Austen Midwives—Book Two,* coming soon.

53232879R00199

Made in the USA
San Bernardino, CA
11 September 2017